23 Minutes Past 1 A.M.

A Novel by Robert J Dornan

23 Minutes Past 1 A.M.

This novel is dedicated as always to my children, Jamie and Christopher but also to the survivors of Chernobyl and Fukushima.

I hope you remain healthy, safe and happy today, tomorrow and every day, forever.

23 Minutes Past 1 A.M.

Copyright 2016

Paperback ISBN: 978-0-9879511-2-0

Digital ISBN: 978-0-9879511-3-7

Contents:

You will hate me initially and believe me to be a monster without conscience or moral boundary. The sham practitioners known as psychologists will portray me as inhuman and decipher my writings as narcissistic or delusional. In actuality, I am quite sane and acknowledge my lowly beginnings as a catalyst to my behavior but certainly not as a foundation. If you wish to formulate your own opinion, study my manifesto and then read your daily newspaper for a week. If you are not intrigued by what you have learned, then I have failed you. If the opposite has occurred and you are instead enlightened, I encourage you to follow your feelings and maim as directed.

The Prince,
Valeri Markov

Prelude: April 25, 2013

"I would bring an extra round of bullets," the beautiful woman warned. "If I'm correct in my assumptions, this man is still scary dangerous."

The police officer leered wantonly as the tall dark-haired icon walked away into her cousin's lavish apartment building. After all these years, she was still stunning to admire from all directions.

Sergei Subatov was alone today, not that this was unusual. His so-called partner left early to meet a mafia kingpin in Lugansk who promised his brother-in-law a job. It angered Subatov that all good construction jobs in Ukraine went to men with mafia connections but given his current monetary situation, he seriously considered using the same association.

A diminutive five-foot five and rakishly thin, Sergei hated his job as much as he despised his boss. As a teenager he dreamed of being a secret service agent in the SBU but those aspirations were dashed when he failed the organizations' competency exam three consecutive times. The final results said that he was too small, too scrawny and worst of all, he panicked too easily.

This candidate is a bag of nerves, the report read.

Sergei argued the tests were unrealistic and was met with a cliché reply of '*every day in the SBU was a test comrade*'. With few options remaining, he took a position with the local police force thinking that even this lowly job could be romantic and thrilling. It was neither of the two and to make matters worse, the pay was a joke. If not for the few bribes he collected every month, he would be forced to live with his mother.

He stepped out of the rebuilt Lada cruiser and cursed the rain pelting down on his porous cap. The twenty-eight-year old officer had driven almost two hours from Kiev to the village of Dubovi Makharyntsi, based on the rant of an overweight man that Sergei believed was responsible for the death of two of his fellow officers. He appreciated that a national hero was also involved in this accusation but that being said, his sole reason for driving in the typhoon-like rain was entirely selfish. If what he was told was true, then he was on the verge of moving up the ranks and that was all that mattered. His sole priority was to capture one man and bring him in for questioning. No big deal.

Just give me this. I've been good, give me something.

He had been here before. The village itself had changed since his last visit twenty years ago and many of the new bungalows were actually nice to look at as opposed to the dilapidated sheds that once lined the main street. The roads were still a minefield of potholes that could eat up a car driving too fast but the land was clear of the rusted tanks and jeeps that had cluttered the landscape for decades. There seemed to be a pride in ownership that never existed many years ago. Western ideology was creeping in, he surmised.

A six-foot high cherry wood fence surrounded the suspects' white brick home, which Sergei found odd as it was the only house on this cul-de-sac. He didn't understand the words on the wood carving nailed to the black front door. When no one answered his knock he walked around the side and peeked through the rain streaked windows. He couldn't see anyone but after driving two hours there was no way in hell he was returning to Kiev without getting a glimpse inside. The police officer walked around the back, found another entrance and turned the knob of an open door that led him into the kitchen.

It was immaculate inside.

What kind of fucking mama's boy lives here?

Every inch of the kitchen was shiny. Sergei imagined the suspect spent hours every day polishing the floor, sink and appliances. It was an obsessive clean. There was no way anyone could attain such cleanliness without having some kind of compulsive disorder. His wet shoes left footprints on the waxed linoleum and he chuckled knowing the effect it would have on the homeowner. He lifted the lid of a soup pot to see carrots, leeks and barley seeping in cold water. Three identical red flashlights hung on a corner wall next to the white refrigerator and below them a large blue plastic barrel appeared as if out of nowhere. It had a large padlock sealing the lid. Sergei shook the container and heard liquid splashing against the sides.

The kitchen led to a narrow hallway with polished wooden floors that reflected the thirty or more paintings hanging in perfect symmetry on freshly painted white walls. Each of the artwork had matching frames, and each was spaced precisely one inch apart. If these were originals then he was looking into the very soul of the painter.

Some of the paintings were outright beautiful, and it was evident the artist was painstakingly meticulous. The largest painting was of a blond-haired woman walking in long grass with the sun's rays hitting her like a spotlight. He had seen this woman before but at that moment, Sergei could not place her face. He speculated on whether the artist was portraying her as a religious idol because her open hands were pointed towards the heavens.

Other paintings were not so beautiful and were instead macabre or demonic. There were several with a demon peeking through windows or watching young women from a tree perch. The strangest of all was of a man with a ponytail sitting at a dinner table. He's staring into a mirror, holding his knife and fork preparing to feast on a woman's head. Across from him sat a decapitated corpse in a red dress with charred skin. Sergei shuddered thinking this may be a self-portrait and nervously pulled his gun from its holster. He stared long and hard at the painting wondering what type of animal would think of something so gory and it dawned on him that the woman in this artwork also seemed familiar to him. The decapitated head looked eerily similar to Mila Kharmalov, the woman who sent him here.

Something was definitely not right.

He made his way to a small bedroom
and promptly noticed a photograph of Josef Stalin hanging above the bed frame.

Mama's boy is a communist.

The queen-sized bed was made with an almost military like precision. A white comforter was adorned with four fluffy white pillows. *What single man makes his bed?* A purple throw rug lay useless at the foot of the bed. He opened the clothes drawer and found nothing but order. Black or grey socks in the top drawer and white underwear in the bottom drawer. There were only men's shirts in the closet and all were plain, one color and long-sleeved. The pants that were doubled over wood hangers were grey or black. Other than the rug, it seemed to him that nothing was out of place, as if each piece of furniture was an individual entity to itself. The room was as sterile as a hospital

11

and Sergei deduced that no one other than the owner had ever slept in the queen-sized bed with the spotless white comforter.

The officer left the room, pondered for a few seconds and returned to take a closer look at the purple rug. His boss always impressed upon him that if something did not look normal then it must be investigated.

If it doesn't look right… it's not.

The circular rug was a deep purple and did not come close to matching the blandness of the white walls and black furniture. He stepped lightly on the carpet and felt a dull protrusion under his right boot. *Fuck me*, he muttered. His heart quickened to an almost throbbing pace when he kicked away the rug to find a round copper latch attached to a two foot by three feet polished floor plank.

I'm going to be famous.

Don't panic.

The cop tried desperately to control his breathing that was suddenly so rapid he was near hyper-ventilating. He twisted the latch to the right and stood to lift the large floorboard. No matter how hard he strained his eyes, he could see nothing but the top rungs of the ladder and darkness. Sergei hurried back to the kitchen and grabbed one of the flashlights he had seen earlier. He pressed a hand on his chest hoping to diminish the increasing ache but it was futile. The SBU was right. He was too jumpy to be one of them.

He descended the ladder and when certain his feet were on solid ground he turned on the flashlight. Unlike the level above him, the makeshift basement was less orderly and had an unusual smell, like when potatoes spoil in his mother's cupboards. He aimed the flashlight on the floor after bumping into a wood lathe.

A long string hung against the rim of his cap and he yanked on it. Light spread throughout the basement and Sergei's eyes were instantly treated to a grotesque horror. He suddenly wished he was not alone and was instead leaning on his car outside the apartment building that he staked out daily.

Against the farthest concrete wall, a naked teenage girl with long dark hair was slumped over on a simple wooden chair. Her feet were bound to the chairs' legs exposing her bluish thighs. Her hands were tied tightly behind the arm posts. The girl's roundish chin lay against her upper chest and from a short distance Sergei could not see her face. Sweat dribbled off his forehead and stung his eyes as his wobbly legs approached the motionless body. He wiped his wet palms on his pants before lifting her head. Nothing in his previous six years of police work had prepared him for what he was looking at. He gasped and fell backwards onto his elbows. He swore loudly as his back scraped against a sharp piece of discarded metal, ripping his shirt and tearing through his skin. Blood spout out of the fresh gash and dripped down the back of his pants.

The girl's throat had been gutted, leaving a gaping, tunnel-like hole. Nerve endings hung aimlessly like electrical wires after a windstorm.

He washed her clean after the mutilation.

Don't panic.

His body quivered with pain as he struggled to stand. Several thoughts ran through his mind but one thing was for certain: There was no way he was staying in this house by himself. He had seen enough evidence and would drive back to Kiev for reinforcements. With trembling arms, Sergei climbed the ladder into the bedroom. His increasingly dizzy head throbbed as blood continued to ooze down his back. Stumbling into the kitchen he bumped into the blue barrel and then grabbed it to hold himself straight.

Why was this in the kitchen of all places and why is it padlocked?

If it doesn't look right...it's not.

He cocked his gun and fired at the lock, missing by a good three inches. The bullet pierced the thick plastic and a foamy clear liquid spilled onto the floor by his feet. His hand shook violently but this time he pushed the gun against the padlock and pressed the trigger. The lock split in two and twirled one hundred and eighty degrees. Sergei removed the hot catch, tossed it over his shoulder and opened the lid. An acidic smell filled his nostrils and he choked back the onslaught of bile rushing to his teeth.

A head with only half its skin bobbed in the waves of the burning liquid. The white bones of a detached hand pressed against the head.

Crazy bastard is disintegrating body parts in acid.

Don't panic. For God's sake, don't panic.

This new discovery was too much for the fragile police officer. Sergei fell to his knees gasping for tiny breaths from his burning lungs. He wheezed uncontrollably. The back of his shirt and pants were now entirely soaked with blood.

Stand up and get the hell out of here.

He tried to pull himself up by grasping the barrel but when doing so the weight of his body tipped the container, causing him to slip and fall while the contents of the barrel swirled on the floor around him. He screamed as acid burned his hands and back causing him to twitch spasmodically. Detached legs, arms, feet and another head rubbed against his pants and

14

shirt. A whitish sludge pushed across his hand. Tears streamed down his face and he couldn't stop screaming. He wanted to stop but the agonizing pain shooting through his body would not allow him to close his mouth. The small man leaned over, grabbed the refrigerator handle and lifted with whatever strength remained.

Sergei waddled gingerly through a puddle of acid to the kitchen door leading to the backyard. He couldn't bear to look back at the human remains sliding slowly towards him. The driving rain had subsided leaving behind a mild wind he could hear through his own groans and whimpers. Opening the door with his seared left hand, he took one step outside and breathed the sweet smell of spring. It felt like freedom.

He did not see the sharp blade of the axe that crushed his windpipe and snapped the C1 bone of his vertebrae. Sergei flopped to the cement tiles never seeing the face of the man who ended his life. Steam from the acid burning through his shirt, rose off his crumpled body and a new flow of blood began its path towards a perfectly cropped patch of grass.

"Fucking prick," the long-haired murderer swore. "Do you know how long it's going to take to clean your mess?"

Chapter One: Welcome to Ukraine

Byrd Brain

"Oh, for the love of God… shut up!"

Okay, I didn't actually say that, but I was thinking it. Trust me, if you were in the same situation, you would be thinking the same.

My name is Byrd. It's a surname that has inherited a great amount of teasing from a young age but if there's any consolation, it's spelled with a "Y" like the Renaissance composer and not an "I" like the Boston Celtics basketball player or your common flying rodent. My friends get a kick out of it and have recently begged me to join Twitter because whenever I send a message, my followers can brag they received a tweet from a Byrd. When trends are catching up to you, you gotta know you're riding the edge of something or worse – falling off the aforementioned edge.

My tiny name insecurity has led to me ask everyone I meet to call me by my first name, which is Aaron. Yet, like everything else in this world, when you think you've got it bad, you can rest assured that someone has it worse. I have suffered the à propos amount of name calling but nothing - and I mean nothing - like my cousin, whom I adore simply because of the courage she has to wake up in the morning. Why you ask? Her first name is Robin.

Some parents don't deserve their children.

A few years ago, I had an epiphany of sorts and decided I would go into business for myself, writing biographies for average, everyday people who wished to leave some sort of legacy for their children and family. Pretty good idea eh? Not really but I guess Lady Luck shone upon me as the business took off fairly quickly. Word of mouth spread and I was soon juggling three clients a month. When I launched an Internet site half a year ago, my clientele shot up to eight a month. Do the math at fifteen hundred bucks a crack and minimum costs. Even I can't believe how fortunate I am considering any other writing adventure I have finished in the last decade has been a dismal failure.

Auto-biographies is not difficult work as long as my recorder functions properly and since I've created a template of questions, I've found I can complete a minimum one hundred page life story in five days or less if the customer doesn't call with new information, which of course was often the case. *Hey, I was taking a crap this morning, and I remembered a crazy night that involved magic mushrooms and a fat chick named Glory.* Experience has taught me that editing for future generations of grandchildren is a gentle topic.

My workload is divided between the very interesting and those who had nothing much to be proud of other than offspring who I figure will eventually turn out just as boring. Today's client fit the latter profile to perfection.

Rhonda Greenberg was pretty for a middle-aged housewife. Actually, she was drop-dead gorgeous and defining her as a housewife is a misnomer. Her hair was dyed blond to hide the grey that sprinkled her natural brunette but to be fair, the blond suit her. She jogged every day and bragged that she could do two hundred sit up's in a row. Based on what I was staring at whenever she looked elsewhere, I had few doubts of her exercise routine. In fact, before I learned more about her, I would have considered dating the woman if she wasn't married. That's the beauty of attraction, ain't it? Once we get to know someone better our hormones take a nose dive. Well, not always but if I was a betting man I would lay down my cash each and every time.

Anyway, Rhonda fit the profile of someone I would have dived into if she never said a word but once that mouth opened and she started to drop the f-bomb every second sentence, I kind of went limp. I felt like asking her where she hid the moonshine and straw hats but in the end, fifteen hundred bucks will never be something I'll say no to, so here I was sitting in the expansive dining room with the posh motif listening to Rhonda talk about her cheerleader days.

Yah... big surprise there.

Not surprising was that this gorgeous woman had found herself a sugar daddy and lived in a home that could only be illustrated as a mini palace. Chandeliers hung from the front hall, in the kitchen and oddly enough outside the first floor bathroom. Clearly, sugar daddy did not pay much attention to Rhonda's lack of vocabulary or design skills and hell, I don't blame him.

My buxomly client was about to detail how she lost her virginity to her second cousin while their families were observing a religious fast when mercifully my cell phone rang. Looking at the call display, I saw a very long phone number, which looked more like Bill Gate's paycheck than any phone number I was accustomed to reading. I was tempted to push the Ignore button but my curiosity got the best of me and I answered hello while lifting a finger, asking Rhonda to hold on.

"Aaron, it's Lena," the sexy voice began.

I nodded my head after figuring out the long string of digits was coming from Ukraine. Realizing a need for quiet and privacy, I excused myself from the mammoth dining room and headed to the equally huge front hall. I rolled my eyes when a brooding Rhonda exhaled an exaggerated long sigh.

My friend Lena mentioned last week that she had to fly to Kiev but did so in a rushed text message, which was something that has always bugged the shit out of me. I have told her a countless number of times that it is so much easier to pick up a phone and call but for some unknown reason she is more comfortable with impersonal typing on tiny buttons. Personally, I think she's conscious of her accent and preferred this mode of communication but I gotta tell ya that this is just silliness because Lena's voice is both soothing and alluring with only a hint of inflection. I've never struggled to understand what she's saying, so that being said I have to believe she persists on texting just to irk me.

I met Lena at a lackluster conference about three years ago and we immediately hit it off. I can't recall exactly how we met but we sort of bumped into each other and have remained friends since then. We tried dating but something didn't click and agreed to stop before our friendship suffered. In hindsight, I wish I knew why things were so awkward at that specific time but no matter how I try to piece together those few months, I can't find an answer as to why we couldn't make it work. One thing for sure, I've always found Lena rather guarded and not willing to share more than she has to. There were other obstacles of course and many had to do with my experiences with Eastern European women. Don't get me wrong, Lena is extremely attractive and at times hilarious but in the back of my mind I always waited or expected for the crazy temper to burst through. A temper I have witnessed all too many times from pampered Russian princesses. Aside from that, there was a weird stigma attached to these girls, like they were all con artists working for the mob or some Russian pimp.

"Hey Lena," I answered, "Good to hear your voice. Wassup? Where are you?"

"I have arrived in Kiev yesterday but had no manner in which to call you," she answered.

Okay, I'm flattered to say the least but not quite sure why she found it necessary to contact me while on vacation.

"Aaron, my aunt is very ill. The doctors insist she has only three weeks, maybe less to live."

"Oh," I said still dumbfounded and wondering what this had to do with me.

I felt a pang of despair for my friend realizing that these situations are never easy. I peeked around the corner into the dining room and saw Rhonda staring at me with blank eyes wondering when I would be done talking so that she could continue talking.

"I'm sorry to hear this but it's good that you're there with her."

Damn, that was lame. I never have any clue what to say in these circumstances.

"This is the aunt I told you about," Lena replied, fully realizing that I wasn't following her. "She lived in Pripyat before the nuclear reactor accident."

Bells whistled in my head and my attention was now focused entirely on the phone call. Lena had once mentioned that if ever I should write a biography on anyone, it should be her aunt.

"Oh yah, I remember now. Pripyat is close to the Chernobyl nuclear plant."

"Aaron, she has agreed to speak with you but you must leave immediately. Is your passport up-to-date?"

"Say what?" I replied almost too comically. "You want me to fly to Kiev? Are you kidding me?"

"No, I am not kidding you", she answered back with a hint of anger. "There is a flight leaving Pearson Airport tonight. I checked for seating and there are still some spots available so if you hurry there will be no problem. Call my friend Anna, she is a travel agent and she will book it for you. I will text you her phone number in five minutes."

I was uncertain how to reply other than, *"Another text Lena?"* I knew in my gut that this could be the story I had been waiting for since the day I began writing biographies. More than likely, every other piece of work I had written beforehand would pale in comparison.

"This is gonna max out my credit card," I blurted sheepishly.

My response did not please Lena and I could hear her grumble thousands of miles away. I coughed hoping she would quickly forget my unintentional rudeness.

"This is going to change your life, stop being so indecisive. Text your flight number and I will meet you at the airport. You will stay with my relatives. If anything Aaron, you will do this for me and our friendship."

She said goodbye without giving me a chance to defend my position and I was left shaking my head in wonderment as was often the case when dealing with Lena.

I hurried back to the dining room, apologized to an extremely displeased Rhonda, packed my laptop and then sped to my apartment. Lena had already text her friend's phone number and I called the travel agent the second I walked through my front door. The midnight flight was booked fifteen minutes later. The first thing I did following my phone call was surf the Internet for weather in Kiev and then packed accordingly. I was to expect lots of rain and temperatures between ten and fifteen centigrade, which was normal for mid-April. After throwing whatever clean clothes I could find into a suitcase, my final task was the most difficult, and that was of course, calling my mother and letting her know where I would be. She approved of Lena but not of the culture she came from. No matter how many times I explained that Lena was Ukrainian and not Russian, my mom could not let go of her antiquated beliefs. I took most of this with a grain of salt especially since the day she described Russia as the land that nurtured Stalin and John Lennon.

At six a.m. the next day I was flying over the English Channel, eight hours from Kiev.

As anticipated, Lena met me at Kiev International at 9pm Kiev time. Her blond hair was hanging free of her normal head bands and she wore a short blue skirt that accentuated her near perfect body. When she wrapped her arms around my hips the smell of her hair excited me to no end and I was suddenly wide awake. She didn't normally dress so revealing so I was surprised, albeit very happy.

"Kiev agrees with you," I complimented.

Judging from her puzzled facial expression, I could tell she was not certain what I meant but had a general idea and it pleased her. After seventeen years in Canada, Lena had still not caught on to many simple expressions.

"I am worried of gaining ten pounds a day. If the prepared food is not sweet, it is filled with mayonnaise. You'll need new pants by the time we return home."

Well, in your case it's ending up in the perfect spots, I thought to myself. "We'll have to take long walks after each meal. I'm looking forward to meeting your family."

Lena smiled at the long walk comment. "And they are excited to meet you; I said some nice things. I should warn you that they may have mistaken my words as you being my boyfriend. My Russian is not as strong as it used to be and not only that, many of my family refuses to speak Russian and will only speak Ukrainian so that makes it even more difficult for me."

"Don't worry about it. I liked being your boyfriend when I was actually your boyfriend so you won't hear me complaining."

Lena looked me in the eye and half-grinned shyly before turning away. Okay, what I am about to say will sound incredibly vain or perhaps over hopeful but I wouldn't say it if I didn't believe it. Truth be told, I believe that Lena is in love with me and has been for at least the last two years. For whatever reason, she prefers to remain friends and as I said earlier, I don't get it, as it makes no sense. From what I know from our circle of friends, she has never discussed her feelings with anyone even though many suspect that she wishes that she and I were still together. Anyone who ever saw the two of us chatting at parties or over dinner would come to the same conclusion. The comfort level, the laughter and the obvious sexual tension are as evident as the nose on your face.

I didn't sleep a wink on the flight and never do on an excursion with moving parts. I once stayed awake throughout a two-day train ride to Moncton. My girlfriend at the time said that by the end of the trip I resembled a ninety-year old Robin Williams on Quaaludes. After a quick stop at a washroom – yah, I was feeling the effects of eight coffees - we stepped outside and found a taxi almost instantly. Lena got in the smallish vehicle first and told the driver where we were heading. I found it odd, and to a certain degree annoying, that she kept looking out the back window. I decided to keep this to myself as arguing half an hour after arriving was never a good idea.

"We can't visit my aunt this evening," she said, buckling her seatbelt while advising me to do the same. "It is much too late but I have asked permission for tomorrow morning."

I didn't understand the permission remark and like the rear window scenario, my Spiderman senses told me it would be better not to inquire.

"How is she doing?"

"Considering her situation, I would like to say as fine as expected." Lena replied. "She is in good spirits and burst into tears when she realized who I was. It was very touching Aaron, a moment I will never forget."

This perplexed me a bit, so I had to ask the obvious. "She has no photos of you?"

"Yes she does but face to face is different. She has been living in the Exclusion Zone for the last fifteen years."

This piece of information confused me even further and Lena caught on swiftly.

"In time Aaron, there is much to learn. For now I will explain the Exclusion Zone as surrounding villages in and around Chernobyl. It was a very lonely life for her and for the few that choose to live there."

I wanted to ask why she had preferred such and existence but decided to wait. Even if I had asked, Lena could only have answered what she had been told by her relatives. So instead, I asked the most palpable of questions.

"How does she look?"

Lena shrugged. "She looks like someone who has lived with radiation for twenty-five years. Most of her hair is gone...she has yellowish skin and a few open sores on her arms. The nurses have wrapped the wounds with gauze but she scratches nonstop as if she is filing her nails. She looks like a dying woman, a woman who is prepared and welcome to die yet she has summoned the energy to speak with us." Lena looked out the rear passenger window for a few seconds and then glanced back at me. "What has both intrigued and disappointed me Aaron is that my relatives are not as anxious to visit her as I. It is disturbing to say the very least and when I question my cousin Boris as to why, he refuses to answer. I want to slap him...but he is a grown man and I am sure he has his reasons."

Strange, I thought. "I did some research last night, which seems like an eternity ago, but I read that the citizens of Pripyat were not very welcome when they were evacuated."

"Let my Aunt Tania tell her story," Lena said quietly. "Hearing it first hand is better than an article off the Internet."

I agreed and held Lena's hand. Thankfully, she did not push away and instead held my hand tightly.

Within half an hour, we arrived at the home of Lena's cousin, a heavy set man with one brow that seemed to begin and end at each ear. He was much darker than everyone else in the room and appeared to me as someone with a Gypsy heritage. He was introduced as Boris Kharmalov, a merchant who owned a successful cell phone store. It was obvious the man was doing well as his apartment in central Kiev was very large with every imaginable luxury. I was amazed at the size of the dwelling considering contradictory stories that clearly said most residents of this city lived in one bedroom apartments. This home had three bedrooms, a spacious chrome kitchen and a living room the size of six pool tables. Original paintings hung on most walls and a large television graced the wall in front of a leather lounger. I was graciously welcomed by several of Boris's friends including a couple of stunning women who hung on every word Boris spoke. Before I had an opportunity to shake hands with every guest, I was handed a shot glass of Vodka.

"Drink," Boris said with a heavy accent. "Welcome to my home, Aaron."

It didn't take me long to notice that Boris was near fluent in English although I didn't ask where or when he learned a second language. Three hours and several shot glasses later, I was allowed to say goodnight and sleep came very quickly. The only thing I cared to remember this morning was that Lena never left my side the previous evening and more amazingly, was lying next to me when I awoke.

Meeting Tania

I realized today why Lena met me at the airport dressed 'to the nines'. While walking the streets of downtown Kiev, I was subjected to a visual assault of stunning women in either short dresses that accentuated long legs or tight jeans that hid very little. I was in a bachelor's paradise and a married man's hell. This was truly unbelievable and it took every iota of concentration to make my gawking inconspicuous as I'm certain that Lena was waiting for me to slip.

At approximately ten a.m. we were standing outside Tania's hospital room. A nurse or an attendant - neither of us was sure - explained we may not be allowed to stay longer than an hour as the hospital was to have a surprise inspection. Lena asked how it was a surprise if the attendant knew it was going to happen, which in turn was met with silence. Perhaps this was a question she should not have asked.

Mental note: Don't ask the evident.

Lena grabbed my arm and I turned to face her. "Listen to me Aaron, my aunt has tubes in her arm and more than likely will have a bandana covering her head. She has no eyebrows and as I mentioned yesterday, her skin is rather yellow. Try not to look shocked as it will cause her to become very shy. I will show you photos of Tania this evening and you will see for yourself how beautiful she once was. She has met only one foreigner in her lifetime...you are her second and she is only meeting you because she thinks we are lovers."

This was nice to know, and I wished it was true. "Care to kiss a bit before we go in?"

"Really, you choose this moment for jokes?" she replied wide-eyed.

I shrugged sheepishly realizing perhaps my comedic timing was off. Lena had a gift of making a silly comment bounce off her and back at the person who was foolish enough to say it. I took her hand, and we walked into the cancer treatment room. There were several beds, each with light blue curtains that divided them from the other patients. Lena led me to the last bed on the west side of the huge yellow room. There was a nauseating smell of urine as if no one had bathed in weeks. Tania was upright and waiting for her niece. She smiled at me and said hello in Russian.

"Privet", I replied with the only Russian word I knew.

The two women spoke for a good two minutes before Lena told me to find a chair to sit on. I did as requested and placed a white padded chair next to the bed while Lena sat on the bed holding her aunts hand.

"My Aunt believes you to be quite handsome. I told her I would not tell you this because it would go to your head." I grinned and shook my head. "She will speak and I will translate," Lena continued. "You can ask questions at any time."

"Can you tell her first off that I am honored to be sitting with her today and honored to be your lover?"

Lena glared at me for ten seconds before saying a few words to her Aunt. "She says it is her honor," Lena responded making no reference to my inappropriate, off-the-cuff remark. I figured I had one more strike before she pounced.

"Aaron, that is a Jewish name, yes?" Tania asked.

"Maybe but I'm not Jewish. My parents are Protestant."

"There was a Jewish couple on my apartment floor...wonderful people," she began. "They had a dog that barked

29

a lot, I very much disliked this dog. I liked the couple, disliked their dog. The woman, she wore beautiful frocks that her husband ordered from a seamstress in Belarus. I was envious of how well they fit her and wondered how much these outfits cost. I realized one day that they had no children so as a couple they had more money than the rest of us. Neither had any family staying with them, which was not unusual in our city. We needed special security papers to allow family to follow us from wherever we arrived from and quite often, requests were denied. Her name was Edith; she was quite lovely with small black eyes and long silky black hair. They were newlyweds, her and her husband. He was a fireman and when he was working a night shift, she would sleep at the fire hall. We became friends and I would spend weekend afternoons at her apartment drinking tea and telling the dog to go away."

Hmm, that was an interesting beginning. "Tell me about *your* Pripyat", I asked.

"Oh yes, it was a gorgeous modern city; the jewel of nuclear cities. We were considered a secret city of sort yet we had a hotel for dignitaries from the Kremlin and around the world. Our buildings were all fairly new and our homes were large in comparison to what we came from. It was almost as if we were privileged based on our primary occupation. I can recall the first day we arrived. Papa was near tears when he saw our new apartment. Lovely curtains were hung, the paint was fresh and there were no cracks in the walls. We had two very large bedrooms, which if you are not aware, was unheard of in the sleeping zones of Moscow at the time. The bedroom I shared with my siblings was almost as large as the entire apartment we had in Moscow.

Pripyat is about one hundred miles from Kiev thus not too far from shops if ever we wished to travel but we rarely if ever did, other than to meet with relatives. We had a large shopping center and many stores that provided us with whatever necessary. Buses, trucks, trains and even boats would arrive twice a week with supplies plus some of the villages that surrounded us were collective farming towns so food, for example, was never a problem.

There was much to do on sunny days and the mayor organized many events such as Polynesian days. Men and women would dress up in straw skirts and we would set small rafts out to sea. It was a great fun. Boys would wind surf on summer afternoons and we had a small beach which served us well. There were flower beds everywhere you walked and beautiful roses bloomed two months a year. Mothers would congregate with their small children in the parks never fearing for their safety. It was an ideal life that we took for granted… a life I am certain we all miss."

I was genuinely surprised by this as it did not concur with the dreary grey Soviet life that I so often read about.

"I imagine there must have been a police presence?"

"Most definitely. We were a town full of intellectuals working at a nuclear plant. Even the police that knew us would inquire if we carried our citizenship papers yet the town itself was not a restricted military zone. No one could enter the plant without their identification. If you forgot your ID you were sent home.

Our phone calls were monitored, we knew this but only because one entire section of our apartment complex was inhabited by KGB employees. It did not bother us as we were

31

used to scrutiny and had nothing to hide. As a people, decades of this type of security taught us that there was no way we could outsmart the KGB and there was really nothing worth fighting for other than Mother Russia. Understand though that we were very happy with our life in Pripyat. I never once heard anyone complain about their time in this town."

"So, you were all good communists?" I questioned before wishing I could take back my words.

Fortunately, Tania did not bat an eye as if expecting me to inquire at one point or another.

"We were all good citizens. If you live so long under a certain regime or government structure you do not comprehend any negativity against communism because it is all you have ever known. Our lodging was paid for; our education and health care was excellent and paid for. Even as a teenager, I was aware of the movement towards democracy that some Muscovites discussed in quiet rooms but I could not grasp the reasoning simply because in our little town, we were very content. Life was good...as I said before, we were happy citizens."

Good answer and unanticipated, I thought. "Ok, so when did you arrive in Pripyat?"

"I was fifteen, so late August, 1981. We were a family of three children, which again was rather uncommon in Moscow. My sister Mila was two years older than me and my brother Roman was only seven. We would tease him and say he was an accident but in our hearts Roman was the bright spot of every day." Tania closed her eyes and her voice quivered slightly. "I wish all accidents had such a wonderful result.

Papa worked at the nuclear plant. A bus would pick him up six days a week and he would not return until after seven in the evening. Excuse me, except on Saturdays, when he would work only half a day. My sister Mila and I attended a secondary school, a beautiful building with a very advanced education program unlike the other schools close by. Our students were profiled over a period of two years and placed in specific curriculums that would benefit the nuclear plant. This was not openly discussed as professors worried it might create early class struggles but we were not stupid, we knew it existed. I secretly wished to enroll in the School of Arts but my father would not permit me and in hindsight I was not talented enough with my paints.

We had an Olympic-sized pool close to our home that turned into a blessing for me. All the children spent a lot of time there because it was not only mandatory but also because it was where we would meet to fraternize. Many relationships began within these walls including my love affair with a boy named Yuri."

"Yuri?" I questioned with a grin. "Let's talk about Yuri a bit."

Lena's eyes dropped when repeating my question. Tania was silent for a few seconds while inhaling and exhaling several difficult breaths.

"He was very handsome with wavy brown hair and blue eyes. He was tall and well-built and probably intimidating to someone who did not know him well but truth be told, he was a sensitive man. He was a man who wore his heart on his sleeve. Many of the girls dreamt of him but he was rather introverted...very shy. At the age of sixteen he was the top swimmer in all of Pripyat and there was talk of officials from Moscow planning to visit our town with the sole purpose of enrolling Yuri into the Olympic swimming program. It never happened and although he never spoke of it, I believe he was disappointed no one gave him the opportunity to showcase his talent. He accepted that his role in our system would be as an employee of the nuclear plant."

"How did you meet?" I interrupted unknowingly.

Tania half smiled before continuing. "We were not in the same classes in school but most of these classes in our particular secondary school were segregated anyway. Very few of our courses had both boys and girls in the same class. His cousin was a good friend of Mila's and we were formally introduced this way. Our parents believed it a good match as Yuri was an excellent student and being educated in engineering while I was profiled as a future doctor or nurse. The other girls were so jealous of me. It was at the time, uncomfortable but as the years passed all was accepted as a type of forced fate and these same girls became my friends."

Tania rubbed the gauze on her arm and winced before continuing.

"Our time together was simple as the town had limited facilities for young teenagers other than the recreation centers. We had many cafes and restaurants as you would call them but no bars like the ones you would find in Kiev today. Alcohol was readily available from merchants and their carts or kiosks but as I have said before, this was not Moscow or a village town. We were high security thus public drunkenness was frowned upon. You can imagine that a nuclear plant employee who was a known drunkard would face eventual dismissal or even incarceration. Anyway, we would meet at the pool and often walk through the park outside our apartment complex.

Yuri had a fascination with this ancient yet enormous oak tree on a hill not far from where the Ferris wheel would soon be built. He called it a magnificent wooden planet that offered solace and shelter to species we would never envision. It was indeed magnificent, at least sixty feet high and if we included its thick limbs, ten yards in width. From a distance the long limbs looked as if they were embracing the sky, welcoming it home. After a year of dating, he brought me to the tree to show me where he had carved our initials in a heart. This was actually dangerous as such an act was considered vandalism but it filled my entire body with warmth I shall never forget. It was at that moment that I realized I was in love with my handsome swim star and that he would someday become my husband."

I was intrigued with her story and Tania seemed extremely happy to be recounting it but today's visit would be a short one. The same *nurse* as the one Lena and I spoke to earlier walked into the room and asked us rather curtly, to leave. Her apology was less than sympathetic but given her stressful face we decided not to argue too much. I said goodbye and Lena kissed her Aunt promising to return first thing tomorrow morning. What could we do? Lena gave an unappreciative glance to the ladies at the main reception and we took an elevator down to the first floor. My friend mumbled a lot of words I couldn't understand and finally said something that sounded like, "Black holes never change; they just get bigger."

****

Kiev or Kyiv, is one of the oldest cities in Eastern Europe. From what I saw during our two hour walk, I compared a lot of the buildings to downtown Montreal and the same would apply to the fashionable women. For a city that went without churches for decades, there was one on every second street. What instantly caught my eye was that the older buildings were a rainbow of colours almost as if the designers were involved in an architectural Easter egg contest. I found it odd that I didn't see many men older than me. It was almost as if they hid from tourists to attract the swanky young elite from Russia and across Europe. Aside from that, Kiev was as modern as any Canadian city I've been too. There were lots of expensive cars, which blew my presupposed ideas out of the water. Unfortunately, some of these cars were parked on the freaking sidewalk. On just about every corner I saw road workers filling in potholes and about half a dozen cops watching from their cars or sitting on the several bus benches.

Lena told me not to be too impressed, and it was nothing but a mirage. I am seeing the gold but not the pot it is carried in. She made it very clear that seventy-five percent of Ukrainians lived in poverty. I found that hard to believe but had no evidence to dispute her claim. Lena saw my expression and promised to show me what she meant before we returned to Canada. A car braked quickly in front of us, barely missing a stray dog. The driver yelled something and drove away. The dog ran to a large fountain and drank from the circular pool before being chased by a police officer. For a second I honestly believed the cop was going to shoot the frightened mutt. I learned later that there was a serious amount of homeless dogs and cats prowling the city streets and that cops did indeed shoot them. A trio of beautiful women walked by me and one of them smiled. I forgot about the dog and almost forgot about Lena. Ok, not really but my God, it was hard not to stare.

We had lunch at a small cafe restaurant. She had wanted to eat "real" Perogies since her arrival but Boris kept ordering food from restaurants close to his apartment. *I did not fly twenty thousand miles to eat fake Chinese food,* she quipped. Her eyes lit up when our stacked plates were brought and she felt it necessary to teach me how to eat Perogies like a local. I found this endearing and told her so. After a meeting with her aunt that was cut short by bureaucrats, Lena was not in a loving mood and changed the subject quickly.

"I am going to bring you somewhere today that few tourists ever visit. Boris insisted we go."

"Oh yah…where are we going?"

"You'll see when we get there," she answered with her head staring down at her plate. "Perhaps you will learn more about Tania, and I guess me, during this tour."

"Learning more about you would be a pleasant change of pace," I said without thinking of the consequences.

Lena looked up at me briefly but didn't reply right away. It was obvious that my words struck a nerve, and she was not prepared at this moment to comment. She stuck her fork into half a Perogie and swiveled it in the bowl of creamy sauce that dripped off the side of her plate.

"Sometimes Aaron, new learning experiences are not what you hoped for."

Evgeni

If you're not looking for it, you'd probably never find the Ukrainian National Chernobyl Museum. This was Lena's choice for our tourism jaunt. Given the circumstances, I guess it was an understandable destination. We took the metro and got off at a station called Kontraktova Plosha. There were no street signs to tell us where the building was as if it was intentionally hidden but Lena later told me that the lack of signs was not uncommon in Kiev.

The museum was tiny in comparison to what I'm used to. Fortunately, there were more staff members than visitors. A tour guide met us as soon as we walked in and checked her watch to make sure she had enough time to do one last tour. Lena waved her off and explained she would translate everything to me. The guide shrugged complacently and from her expression I could see she was pleased we wouldn't ruin her departure time. Lena knew most of what was being displayed in the different rooms but I silently wished the tour guide was with us as there were images I would've liked to know more about.

Some of the photos were grotesque to look at and I imagine this was done with a strong purpose in mind. From what I had seen through the first fifteen minutes, I felt this was more a memorial to the victims as opposed to a learning experience into what really happened at the nuclear plant. I was somewhat disappointed until an average looking man in his mid-thirties with a ponytail, pointed at the tiny Canadian flag on the backpack I was carrying.

"I studied in Montreal for five years," he said approaching Lena and me.

"Oh great, we're from a town east of Toronto but we visit Montreal about once a year. It's only five hours away by car."

The man nodded and took a quick admiring look at Lena. He then stuck out his hand, which I politely shook.

"I am Evgeni Rosmov, the Director of this museum."

"Nice to meet you Evgeni, I'm Aaron and this is Lena. We're in town visiting her aunt who coincidentally lived in Pripyat. I plan to write a short book on her life."

"Oh, yes?" Evgeni questioned with a new degree of interest. "You flew in from Canada to meet with her? That's fascinating." He then turned towards Lena. "You say your aunt was from Pripyat, did she relocate to Kiev?"

"Yes, for a decade or so," Lena replied somewhat disinterested. "She returned to the Exclusion Zone for the last fifteen years."

This caught the man's attention and his eyebrows rose as if he had never met someone from this area.

"What is her name please? I may have more information for you and your friends' book."

Lena was perturbed that the man somehow realized that I was a friend and not something more.

"Aaron is more than a friend," she answered with a tight grimace. She paused before saying Tania's name as if it was some sort of secret. "My aunt's name is Tania Kharmalov."

Evgeni paid no attention to Lena's tone and seemed more intrigued to meet a family member of a select group of survivors.

"Follow me to my office. I have kept detailed accounts of every citizen from Pripyat and the surrounding towns."

39

Lena was less than impressed and somewhat hesitant, which was something I picked up on immediately. She turned up her lid, which was a sign that Lena knew the man was hiding something or lying. When we were inside the office, Evgeni requested I close the door.

"I can never be too cautious," he said hoping he could trust his guests.

We sat in front of Evgeni's desk while the Director turned on his computer. The office was itself a memorial to Chernobyl. Pictures of the nuclear plant before and after the explosion were on every wall as were blueprints and maps with circles around the names of affected towns.

"Tania Kharmalov; born 1966 in Moscow," he said popping his head over his monitor. "She moved to Pripyat in 1981 with sister Mila, a brother Roman, father Anton and mother Tatiana. She was educated at Secondary 3 with medical sciences as intent. Obviously above the norm in intelligence, she was chosen to participate in advanced education. Married to Yuri Larinov, in May 1986..."

"No, that is incorrect, they never married," Lena interrupted.

Evgeni stared at his screen and turned the laptop so that Lena could see for herself. "My records show May 3, 1986 in Moscow." Lena shook her head a few times but did not speak. "Yes, I can see she relocated to the Exclusion Zone in 1997. Only 400 or so chose this option simply because by doing so they gave up monthly pensions and any benefits. There are of course other blatantly apparent disadvantages." He turned his attention away from Lena and focused on me instead. "The citizens within the Zone are eating food from contaminated soil, housing is cold and

40

there is a minimum communication. It is a barren life at best and they are surrounded by wild, radioactive animals. I have always found this choice to be odd yet I hear of more and more survivors discussing the possibility of returning. It is truly a very sentimental subject. Your aunt's sister, Mila..."

Lena halted him quickly saying something in Russian and Evgeni stopped in mid-sentence. His face went from studious to blank in an instant and he said *very well* in English before continuing. Feeling somewhat rejected, he then turned his attention away from my friend and back to me.

"Aaron, I want you to consider the following when you are writing your final copy." I nodded and Evgeni continued. "Consider that life in the former Soviet Union was extremely secretive, and this included our nuclear facilities."

"Sure, no surprise there," I replied shrugging. *Who in the western world did not know this?*

"From this point on I want both of you to think twice about almost everything you have or will read concerning the Chernobyl disaster. Whether you are reading a report from the World Health Organization, the International Nuclear Federation, and IAEA or so called professional articles on the internet...they are all lies. Every last one of them is misleading. How do I know this?" It was a leading question, which I wasn't going to reply to thus causing an awkward pause before Evgeni continued. "For one, I have the citizenship and medical records of over fifty thousand people from in and around the Number Four reactor. I have interviewed hundreds of people but unlike you Aaron, I cannot write a book without fear of reprisal. It's all *bullshit* as you would say in the west."

"Ok, I'd like to hear this," I said crossing my legs.

Lena, meanwhile, was fidgeting uncomfortably and I would have to remember to ask her about this later tonight. Not that it would matter, Lena was not one to disclose more than she cared to and judging from her tight facial expression, I would be barking up the wrong tree.

Evgeni was enthused to have an audience that cared about what he was discussing. He gesticulated a lot with his hands, which was a distraction but at the same time, it seemed to confirm his passion for the subject. The one bothersome and rather distracting habit he had was stroking his ponytail that he placed on his shoulder like it was a pet bird. I had an urge to throw bread crumbs at it.

"Let us go back to the very day of the explosion because the sequence of events has born many inquiries and suspicious results. The tests performed that early morning on April 26th were unnecessary but seemingly harmless. Basically, all they were doing or intending to do was check the backup power supplies and possibly save energy in the long run. That is it in perfect summary… they were checking backup power generators to see if they could run the plant if there was some unforeseen power outage. The Chernobyl plant was run by the power it produced, meaning it was all cyclical generation of power. The thing to mention though – to make very clear - is that these tests should have been done three years earlier before the reactor was even open." Evgeni rolled his chair a few feet from his desk to a black metal cabinet which he then opened, pulled out a large ledger and rolled back to his computer. "First of all, a lot of people do not know this but the tests were initially to begin the morning of April 25th. They could not perform them because it required decreasing energy production to thirty percent and during the daytime that

42

was not acceptable as energy consumption in Kiev was too high. This is important to note because it meant that during the early morning of April 26th, junior technicians would be performing tasks they were unfamiliar with as all the senior technicians worked during the day."

"That's interesting," I mumbled through my hand.

"Just out of curiosity, do you know how the energy is produced in a nuclear plant?" Evgeni asked.

"No, I don't," I said. "Lena, do you?"

My pretty friend, who had remained very quiet to this point, whispered no.

"Ok good, I will explain in simple terminology," the Director responded. "The reactors are like steam engines in old trains but instead of coal they use uranium rods that heat water. The steam from the water drives the enormous turbines, and that is how the power is produced. The amount of energy produced is regulated by boron control rods. You can take some out, put some in, whatever you need to produce the energy required. More rods in the core lowers the amount of steam, less rods' means more steam thus more power. Think of it like a tea kettle. Steam comes out when the water is boiling but if you add more water to the kettle then the steam will stop."

"That's it?" I asked, surprised with the simplicity.

"More or less – yes," Evgeni answered. "Two pounds of uranium will produce the same amount of energy as thirty three hundred tons of coal. That is substantial yes?"

I raised my eyebrows and answered yes.

"Ok, so they begin at midnight and everything seems to be going well. They lower the power levels and all is fine until 20 minutes later when the power levels drop significantly.

Remember, we are dealing with junior technicians who are good but not as good as the seniors. So this tech – his name was Leonid – deals with the issue and again, everything looks fine...what do you call it... copacetic." Evgeni seemed pleased with his command of a second language. "At one a.m. the levels are as expected. New guy in the picture, his name is Alexander, and he switches on two water pumps but hey, Alexander has screwed up because too much water has been forced into the reactor and if there is too much water then not enough steam can be generated to drive the turbines – like the tea kettle...right? This is a nuclear reactor guys, everything has to be perfectly balanced. Now, Leonid comes back and decides he is going to increase the power and that in turn will make the steam that will drive the turbines. Are you following me?" Both Lena and I nodded in tandem. "Great, so what he does is decrease the amount of core fuel rods. If you recall what I said earlier, the fewer rods lowered means more heat and therefore more steam. Seems to work and once again Leonid thinks he has fixed the problem except the minimum ever allowed is twenty six rods and he has lifted all except six. Big mistake and he doesn't know it's getting really crazy hot beneath the core. So after all this drama what do you think the supervisor expects them to do?"

"Continue the test," I answered.

"Exactly, continue the test like it still mattered. They have no clue that things are heating up in the reactor. Leonid, like I said, he's freaking out of ideas at this point so he removes all but six boron core fuel rods. I repeat, from what I told you before if you have fewer rods then you produce more power. Meanwhile, Leonid and Alexander are not communicating very well because Alexander realizes he has allowed too much water to flow into the reactor so he cuts off the water not knowing that there were only six core rods. In this case, think of it like a tea kettle that has no water left but is still on. Sounds crazy but these junior techs…*somehow,* they think they everything under control so they continue with their little test and away from the control room, a different operator, shuts off the turbine – as he was told to do - and power starts to mount even quicker. Guess what time it is at this point?

'Twenty three minutes past 1 a.m.," Lena replied in a hushed voice.

"Exactly, 1:23 Saturday morning. Everyone is panicking because the monitors are showing great power surges so Leonid presses the shutdown valve, known as the AZ-5 button but it doesn't work or at least he doesn't think it does. Nothing stops and the power is skyrocketing. The technicians have no idea what is happening or what they should do next and moments later they hear a thud and a minute after that a *huge* thud. A two thousand ton roof is blown to its side and radioactivity is released into the atmosphere."

"Jesus Christ, it's a freaking comedy of errors," I understated.

Evgeni slanted his head to the left and sighed heavily as if out of breath. "Yes it is but not very funny in the end. Now, we can go ahead and point the blame at Leonid and Alexander but the truth is that the reactor was flawed and the same disaster was averted only a year earlier at a different Russian nuclear plant. Fourteen people died in a steam explosion at the Balakovsky nuclear plant and no one was aware of this because it was a Soviet secret. These technicians at Reactor Four were lowering power to do a test not knowing that there were severe flaws."

Evgeni paused for a few seconds studying our interest. He was obviously pleased and continued his story.

"Ok, this is a bit off topic but here's another item of significance that few people know of. A few years earlier a Russian nuclear reactor in Iraq was bombed by Israel's air force. Since that event, Soviet scientists demanded tests to see what would happen if they came under attack and their power supply was knocked out. The test done on Reactor Four that evening was requested by the Russian Atomic Agency. These politburo guys were war crazy," he said banging his index finger against his left temple. "It was still the Cold War so in the back of their minds they were doing the right thing but in hindsight it was this test that actually began their undoing...the unraveling of the Soviet Union.

The next little tidbit is also something few have ever heard. The test that evening was supposed to be done at a minimum of seven hundred megawatts but the egomaniac supervisor believed there was little risk at two hundred megawatts as if he had something to prove. Leonid and Alexander contested their boss's belief and were told they would be removed from their jobs if they argued any further.

I am guessing that you are starting to get a picture of cover up's and lies, yes? Here is more. Reactor Four at Chernobyl was full of flaws and the big reason for this is that it was built with great speed. The directors of the program were promised large bonuses if the job was completed quickly and indeed it was. Unfortunately, it was completed with the word safety omitted from the end result. The KGB documents that became public after the fall of the Soviet Union showed there were many warnings about the serious design flaws at Chernobyl yet they were all ignored. The roof for instance, was supposed to have fireproofed materials but instead was completed with combustible materials so yes, when the roof blew open it caught on fire.

"Wow," I exclaimed. My mind was racing from an overload of fascinating information. "That's some serious neglect. Talk about your abuse of power."

"Not done yet," Evgeni remarked. "The AZ-5 button I told you about did actually work but none of the technicians were aware that the boron rods were tipped with graphite so when so many of the rods were inserted at one time, it led to a surge in power they could not contain. Twenty-three minutes past one a.m. The first explosion shook the building and seconds later a second explosion blew the roof off.

Lena was sitting next to me so I was holding back a desire to swear loudly. "It's as if the plant was fated to explode."

Evgeni thought of my observation and was pleased. "Yes, it was a testament to the Soviet Union. Imagine how it was guys, well Lena I am certain you have heard this all before." He waited for her to acknowledge but she did not. "Everyone was terrified of reprisals while at the same time, the Kremlin wanted to be *better* than the west so they hid all their lies. The builders lied to the Kremlin, and the Kremlin lied to nuclear officials. This is what happens when you live in fear. Ok, so those were the lies about the plant and the explosion but there are many more. The aftermath of Chernobyl is a disgusting never ending string of misinformation."

"Go on," I said eager to hear more.

Lena continued with her stoic face but in all honesty I was enthralled with what I was learning and was paying little attention to her complacent and fairly rude attitude. Evgeni continued without missing a beat.

"The fire was burning for thirty-six hours before the Kremlin gave the order to evacuate. In fact, until the Swiss government reported high levels of radiation in their atmosphere, the Kremlin had not released any warning or any news at all to the world...nothing. The unbelievably absurd thing about this is that Gorbachev himself had no clue. You can imagine his rage when he learned he was receiving bullshit from the men he trusted."

"The leader of the Soviet Union had no idea of what was happening?"

I was totally shocked by this and yet again it was an example of what fear does to frightened men. No one wants to chat with the bully who waits at the end of the hallway.

"Yes man, but there is much more Aaron, I have not even touched the surface. It took seven days before citizens in the outlining areas, such as Kiev, were told not to drink any milk or eat any fresh vegetables. We were swallowing radiation and the only thing mentioned in our newspaper concerning Chernobyl was a small blurb from TASS about four sentences long. You get the picture right? Over a thousand buses of people being transported into Kiev and surrounding cities yet nothing is being reported. *Carry on folks, business as usual.*

"That's criminal," I gasped.

"Sure it is and so was the protocol after the accident. We learned everything by word of mouth but sit back as there is a ton of info to digest. After any nuclear spill of any amount, iodine is always distributed to nearby residents. In this instance, iodine was given to no one within a 100 kilometer radius. Iodine treatment is believed to put an immediate halt to thyroid problems yet shipments were refused from the West and none was handed to the victims. Does this not throw up what you call red flags? Suddenly all the medical experts have forgotten about iodine pills? There is one exception from what I have been told. A nursery school class received pills the morning after the blast. Where they came from has never been documented but I would guess some merciful and thoughtful employees from the hospital distributed whatever they had in inventory.

Moscow had been studying the effects of radiation for years in preparation for war against the west. If you choose to believe that Russia has changed their "game plan" concerning war and world relations then so be it. For me, I can tell you they have not. Protecting Mother Russia is in their blood; whether it is economically or via force they will jump at the chance for domination, to take back what Glasnost lost. Everything is still a secret, even in these days of cell cameras and the Internet we know only a small percentage of what is happening in Moscow. The Kremlin intentionally took forever to make decisions... the explosion was an accident, the aftermath and the slowness to act was intentional."

I wasn't sure where Evgeni was heading with these last comments as it sounded like a bizarre conspiracy theory. I despise conspiracy theories as they usually lack any evidence whatsoever and are used primarily to promote a book or website.

"That's a huge accusation and a troubling one," I said.

"I can see in your eyes that you're thinking I am some kind of nutcase but Ukraine's history is not hidden, it's only ignored. We have been nothing more than a colony to Russia for hundreds of years. We were once considered the breadbasket of Europe, did you know this?

I nodded no.

"In nineteen thirty-two, Stalin decided to quell our traditions and modern day thinking by starving us. He took away all our food and if by chance you looked healthy - as in still eating - you were shot. Seven million Ukrainians died in one year. This is the true definition of genocide. Artificial famine is what we now call it, or Dolomar. All is forgotten, of course. There was no war crime tribunal…the criminals continued to rule over us for decades. Our desperate politicians have recently considered signing an economic deal with Russia instead of the European Union even after we begged them not to. They still have us under their thumb. So yes, Aaron, I hate Russia. I hope you take the time to read about how they have enslaved us for centuries. Then you will take into consideration the theory I presented."

"I'll do that," I promised.

"We are still waiting for proper compensation for the nuclear accident. You have no idea of our life Aaron. There is much on YouTube about the Chernobyl disaster; many videos, some of them very good yet…yet Chernobyl is still to some extent, a secret. These videos tell you what happened and they show before and after footage of Pripyat. There is little that discusses what is happening today. Anything written in my country is dismissed as *the past* or even censored thus the news has to come from reputable sources in the west. That's not happening because when it comes to any type of energy you are censored as much as we are. I would advise you write your story as fiction and publish it anonymously."

This was disturbing, but I shrugged the comment off as the innocent rant of a frustrated man. I am almost positive I saw a book with hundreds of Chernobyl articles written by Russian scientists so maybe Evgeni thought he was preaching to the choir. I let it slide.

"Years later we are still eating food grown in contaminated soil and we are not told about it. It's as if no one cares. Did you know that Ukrainians are considered the second sickest population in the world? Our immune systems are deficient; we can't fight difficult viruses. Only six percent of Ukrainians are actually considered healthy. Our children have a high degree of thyroid problems, second highest in the world after Belarus which borders on Chernobyl. Miscarriages and abortions are also amongst the highest in the world but don't expect to read about it because those statistics are not shared outside the doctor's office. Our women won't speak of deformed fetuses because the stigma attached is too great. We are a sick nation and it is all due to Chernobyl and either no one knows or no one will admit to the correlation. It will take five generations for us to recover so imagine living with that knowledge. It explains why we choose to forget…*and we have*. Our children learn of Chernobyl through video games. It is nothing but a point of amusement now. Do you know what else is sad? What we have here in Ukraine is not near as bad as Belarus. It's a silent, ongoing disaster over there."

"So you're saying that radiation in Kiev, for instance, is still a huge issue?"

Evgeni raised his finger as if to say one moment. He opened an unlocked vault behind his chair and pulled out a map that was in a large plastic zip lock bag. He then opened a desk drawer and handed me a dosimeter or Geiger.

"The ON switch is the yellow button."

I turned it on and then waved slowly across the map. The reading on the dosimeter went to the highest level of 3.6 and stopped.

"Is 3.6 high?"

"No, it is not, but it is the highest level on this dosimeter, it won't go any further. If I had a proper Geiger you would see the reading as 81.9 or approximately fifteen times the accepted level."

Lena backed her chair away from the table immediately. Evgeni stopped speaking for a few seconds and then continued.

"This map and dosimeter are from Chernobyl. This is what they were measuring the radiation with after the explosion. Is this not a joke in itself? Over twenty-five years later Aaron, the map is still fifteen times the accepted level. What does that tell you?

"It tells me that I want you to put it back in the vault," I answered with a worried tone.

"Why would you infect us with this?" Lena shouted. "We don't wish to be contaminated!"

She stood abruptly and rushed to the office door.

Evgeni was surprised at her reaction but also nonplussed as if he had received the same admonishment before.

"Whoa, take it easy girl. You got a worse dose when you went through security at the airport."

Lena settled down quickly but refused to return to her chair and remained standing in front of the door. Evgeni threw the map into the vault and shut the door.

"My point is this. After all these years the radiation is still in our apartment buildings, shops, soil and on our clothes to some degree. It won't wash away for centuries. Did you know that nuclear authorities, to this day, still claim that only sixty-four people died in total from the accident? It's a travesty when I personally know hundreds that have passed away. Never believe the terminology, 'clean energy'. It is a silent, invisible killer. The true figure when all is said is done is in the millions. Millions of deaths will be attributed to Chernobyl. It is the third greatest genocide known to man." He stared at Lena and then looked briefly at me before lowering his head and closing his ledger. "I suspect it will affect many more people you know…even perhaps those close to you."

Seeing that Lena was extremely uncomfortable, I stood and shook Evgeni's hand.

"Thank you for your time, it has been very, very informative."

"No problem," he answered. "Do me a favor and don't mention my name in you book. I need my job."

Lena and I hurried out of the museum and the silent walk to the metro was way too brisk. I asked her to slow down, but she ignored me. Without notice, she turned abruptly and put her hand on my chest. Her angry eyes told me little about anything she was about to voice and she refused to enlighten me on why she was so enraged.

"If you keep stoking the fire Aaron, I can guarantee you'll get burned."

For someone who struggled with expressions she managed to pull a good one out of nowhere. I didn't inquire why she said this and she didn't offer. It was a long ride back to the apartment. Traffic was heavy as the Kiev work day came to an end. Frigid April winds slapped our faces several times over before the sky opened up with a driving rain. We had no umbrella.

Fucking perfect.

Kharmalov Home: April 25th 1986

Tania loves Yuri and Yuri loves her
Tomorrow they'd wed underneath the giant Fir
He kissed her lips and stroked her face
He had to go to work, had to make haste
At the Plant in town
Their beautiful town

Mama loved Alex he was her only boy
He made her so happy, he was her pride and joy
He set off to work it was his very first day
Start a new life, bring home some pay
From the Plant in town
His beautiful town

23 minutes past One A.M.

Tania opened the front door, removed her flat black loafers and put on her old wool slippers.

"Mama, I'm home."

"I'm in here baby," Mrs. Kharmalov replied.

The tall twenty-year old walked into the kitchen and kissed her mother on the forehead. She opened a drawer and took out a sharp knife to help scrape and cut carrots.

"This is your last time helping me," her mother said, wiping sweat from her eyebrow.

"Oh mama, you know as well as I do that this isn't true. I'll be ten minutes away."

Her mother shrugged a bit. "I've gone from two pots a night to just one and now I'll have to cook and wash by myself," she added before chuckling.

"Mila eats here three to four nights a week and I would bet that Yuri and I will be visiting the same amount of nights. If anything, you will need more pots." Tania rinsed the carrot she was holding and handed it to her mother who cut it into small slices. "The apartment is ready, the curtains have been installed and the electricity has been turned on. I had to open all the windows because the smell of fresh paint is still very potent."

"When do you get your own keys?"

"After the wedding ceremony," Tania replied. "The mayor will be there, which is exciting."

The mother sighed loudly. "KGB, don't be excited my dear child, be careful. Yuri's father has dangerous friends."

"We've had this discussion before. It is not the same in this town. We're closer to being elitists than communists here."

The mother eyed her daughter for a quick second and grunted. "You are young. They will wear you down eventually. Nonetheless my daughter; tomorrow is your big day and nothing or no one shall ruin it for you. Your dress is hanging in your bedroom and I ironed it one last time. Don't let Yuri see it this evening. It's bad luck.

Tania wrapped her arm around her mother. "Thank you."

"Tell me if the idiot caused you problems today."

"Vilisov?" Tania answered with a tone of revulsion. "He's a disgusting worm. What is it with these men that think we are simple sexual vessels for their sick fantasies? He stared at my breasts all day and commented that my ass was delicious. Single women have no means to protect myself and no one to report this filthy animal to. Next week I will be married and report him to the authorities."

"At least you're fighting him, I'm certain others bow to his power. Perhaps your unwillingness fuels his desire."

"I don't care, mama. I'll stick a knife in his heart if he ever forces himself on me."

"Speak to the mayor. Maybe a visit from the KGB will frighten him. Perhaps they're good for something other than spying on us."

At that moment the front door opened and the voices of Tania's sister, Mila, and her young brother, Roman, both said hello quietly being careful not to wake the baby sleeping in her carriage. Mrs. Kharmalov rushed to the front hall and picked up the sleeping child being careful not to unravel the blanket surrounding the baby's entire body. She kissed her children, admonished Mila for wearing blue jeans instead of a skirt and left for the living room to stay with the infant.

"Take off the cap," Mila told her brother, and he complied reluctantly. "Mama, stay with the baby. Tania and I will finish up," she said strolling into the kitchen.

Roman rolled the carriage into the main room, turned on the television and flopped onto the beige couch.

Mila wiped a strand of black hair from her eyes and rubbed her eyes before speaking. Like her sister, she was tall and thin with similar facial features. The difference between the two was that Mila had jet black hair while Tania was blonde like her brother. Both were well known in Pripyat as the beautiful Kharmalov girls.

"All he wants to do is go fishing," the elder sister began. "Mila, can we go to the lake; Mila can we get on our bikes and ride to Kopachi, it's only twenty minutes away. Most boys are out playing soccer, he wants to go fishing. That's papa's fault, Roman should be in organized sports."

She took out a knife and began peeling the potatoes that Tania would then cut into tiny cubes.

"He likes what he likes," Tania answered. "No use in complaining or worrying. At least he isn't up to no-good like other boys his age. He has friends that are smoking already. I saw Josef hiding in a bush with a cigarette in his mouth," she said shivering. "He'll be dead by the time he is forty. He's a stupid boy with stupid parents."

"True, Roman's a great kid. I tend to act more like his mother than his sister. I guess it's a bad habit."

She stared momentarily at the knife she was cutting with. Her mother had brought it from Moscow so long ago and it was still a kitchen staple. Mila found herself feeling nostalgic for the simpler days of teenage life.

"I never liked that Josef kid. He is kind of scary to look at, like an accident waiting to happen. His eyes are like big black empty eggs. I want to crack them open to see if there is anything inside."

"Will Simon be joining us this evening," Tania asked, changing the subject.

Her head was strategically bent over, preferring not to look into Mila's eyes. The tall, dark-haired beauty was not fooled by her younger sister's sudden shyness. Thousands of conversations had taught her that Tania was timid of anything controversial.

"My darling sister, why do you always ask the same question when you already know the answer? He is at the school working on his great masterpiece," she said sarcastically with a *pishh* to end the sentence. "If I had known he would turn into such a fanatical communist, I would have never dated him. It's as if nothing else matters. He rarely spends any time with his daughter...it's exasperating."

Tania could feel the anguish in her sister's voice and silently thought whether her own marriage would become as unhappy. It had happened so quickly, almost without warning although the rumors about Simon were nothing new.

"What exactly is this painting about? Why is he so consumed with it?"

Mila rolled her eyes and grimaced. "Oh my...it is the quintessential communist portrait. It will make him famous Tania...*famous*...so he thinks," she said, again with great sarcasm. "It is his gift to Mother Russia as he calls it. If he had the same passion for his wife and daughter I would be the happiest woman in all of Pripyat."

"Then you have regrets about marrying?"

There she said it. She had wanted to ask for a while now and she finally did.

"Most certainly I do," Mila replied with absolutely no hesitation. "I wish the exact opposite for you though. Yuri is not a dreamer; he is a strong man with principles. You will be very safe and happy with your man, this I am quite certain of."

"I'm so sorry for you Mila."

Mila waved her hand suggesting her sister's empathy was not necessary.

"No need to be sorry. I have my family and that's sufficient for the moment. Perhaps Simon will come to his senses eventually, we will see but in all honesty, I believe that time has come and gone."

Mila scraped the cubed potatoes off the cutting board and into a pot that she then filled with water.

"I'm not sure why I don't know the answer to this but is Simon an army reservist?" Tania asked.

"That is an odd question but no," Mila answered nonchalantly. "His eyes are too weak so he spent three months at an administrative camp. If ever there's an attack of paper clips, Simon is your man."

'Mila..."

The elder sister chuckled at her own joke. "Ok, that was unkind and I apologize. As you can tell, I am not pleased with the man. We haven't made love since the baby was born. Thirteen months... I'm not hormonally challenged Tania, I need release from time to time. Keep this between us and don't speak of my issues with mama and especially not papa."

"I would never mention this to anyone. I would also hazard a guess that Simon would need some form of sexual contact from time to time. Do you think he is getting it somewhere else?

"I don't believe so. I check his underwear for stains...none in the front, only skid marks in the back."

Tania snickered and put her hand to her mouth, muting her laughter. "That's the funniest thing you've ever said."

"I have my moments," Mila replied. "I found him very chatty with Yulia last time we were all together, did you not notice this?"

"Yes, I did but don't fret. She has turned into the village whore from what I'm hearing but I doubt your man has been one of her conquests. She is more interested in nuclear technicians and the prestige that life brings. I heard a rumor that she was sleeping with a married man who works in Reactor Two but rumors are rumors. Poor Alex is still in love with her, I wish he would move on. It's been three years already since they broke up. Plus, Alex is out of her league now, he stands no chance."

Mila sighed and shook her head as if amazed. "I don't understand the fascination men have with Yulia; she is really nothing special. Her face is long like a cucumber and her short hair is thin and lifeless. If she didn't have a vagina I would mistake her for a teenage choir boy."

Tania giggled thinking of the comparison. "I don't agree with your choir boy description. She is revealing and sexy, you have to admit this. I believe the expression is that she wears it well."

"She might as well not be wearing anything. Last time I saw her she was wearing tight jeans with high heels and no bra beneath her t-shirt. Every time she bent over I could see all of her tiny skinny breasts. She dresses like a slut... she *is* a slut."

"She has her good points Mila and she'll be at the ceremony tomorrow so please try to be nice."

"Never worry about me my sister, I am a rock...I will be the sweetest little bridesmaid ever and when it is all over and you and Yuri are locked in a mad passionate embrace in your apartment, I will track down Yulia and beat her to a messy pulp... joking."

Tania placed her cutting board under the tap and wiped it with her hands.

"Give her a break, Yulia has lost her mother. She is so worried of losing her apartment that she's dating married men hoping for anything to happen."

"Then I don't envy her but I won't condone her actions and neither should you. She is taking her problem and giving it to someone else, this is far from admirable. If this married man has children, she is destroying a family. Have we considered this at all?"

"We are hearing rumors Mila. Do not presume until the rumors become fact."

The older sister filled the two pots of vegetables with water and placed them on the stove. All three pots were finished, and the girls leaned against the laminate counter with their arms crossed.

"You have grown into such an intelligent and beautiful woman Tania. I don't say it often enough but I am very proud to be your sister."

"And I yours," Tania replied. "Don't make me cry, I have no desire to redo my makeup."

At that precise moment in their conversation, the front door opened and their father entered, yelling a loud hello. Mrs. Kharmalov instantly got up off the couch and told him to stay quiet as the baby was sleeping. It was no use. The infant awoke and began crying.

"Look what you've done old man," she said through a grimacing face.

The tall, broad shouldered man with thin blond hair waved her off and grinned.

"Babies cry, come here and give your husband a wet kiss."

She shook her head and embraced her husband while Mila left the kitchen to pick up her child.

"Hey boy," he grunted comically towards Roman. "Get your tiny ass off the couch and give your father a hug."

Roman did as he was told, punched his father in the stomach softly and then hugged the man for a good five seconds.

"What are you watching?"

"Alien Conquest," Roman replied.

"Again with Alien Conquest? They look like men in cosmonaut suits."

"Not in the least," Roman argued. "They don't look at all like cosmonauts."

"Russian nonsense," Mrs. Kharmalov cut in.

Roman sighed loudly. "Aliens are real, *everybody* knows this. It's an awesome program mother and scary. I like to be scared."

"If you want to be scared, spend some time with your uncle's gypsy wife later this evening."

Anton Kharmalov shook his head and sighed loudly. "She's not a gypsy, she's from Lugansk."

"She is a Lugansk gypsy" Mrs. Kharmalov returned. "Don't look her in the eyes, she'll pin a curse on you. Remind me to hide the good cutlery after dinner."

This caused Mr. Kharmalov to burst out laughing. His brother's wife was a constant source of jokes around the dinner table. In truth, she was a nice woman who put up with a less than reliable man.

"Where do you come up with this gibberish, my wife? Please avoid these situations at all costs." He then strolled into the kitchen and kissed Tania on the forehead. "How is Tania Kharmalov doing today?"

"Enjoying her last day as Tania Kharmalov, my wonderful father."

"Ah, don't get me started," he replied, tapping his daughter's behind with the back of his hand.

He walked out of the small kitchen and grabbed his wife once again.

"Your mother and I are going to our bedroom for half an hour. Please do not disturb us if you hear loud shrieking noises."

"Is it December already?" his wife retorted.

The two disappeared into their bedroom arm in arm and laughing to themselves.

Tania walked into the living room to face Mila. "Are they going to...?"

Mila shrugged and giggled. Her daughter was sitting on her lap drinking a bottle of milk.

"Are they going to what?" Roman questioned.

"Watch your silly alien invasion, fish boy," Mila ordered. "They're probably going to discuss Tania's wedding and need privacy."

"Oh okay, I thought you meant they were going to get naked together... you know... hoochie-koochie."

****

"How's it going punk?" Yuri said while plopping himself on the couch next to Roman.

The tall blond-haired man was there to eat his last dinner as Tania's boyfriend before becoming her husband.

"Hello older punk," Roman answered. "Are you here for another free meal?"

"No, I asked permission to come and torment you. Your sister was against it but your mother offered me money."

"Oh, yah?" he answered mischievously. "Let me ask her."

"Ok, stop…you win. The last thing I want the day before I become family is your mother's reprimand."

"Lesson learned older punk, you can't beat me," Roman sneered. "If you ever need advice on pranks please feel free to speak with me… but make an appointment first."

The food was ready and plates were being set at the kitchen table.

"Boys, come sit down, dinner is ready," Mrs. Kharmalov beckoned.

The two stood and Yuri rubbed Roman's head. He lowered his head and whispered into the boy's ear.

"Some day you will have a mother-in-law and then you will beg for *my* advice… but make an appointment first."

"Ok you two," Tania interrupted. "Sit and be civil. It's my last dinner at this table as Tania Kharmalov. I wish it to be special.

"Yes," Yuri piped in proudly. "Tomorrow at this time you'll be the happily married, Tania Larinov."

Anton Kharmalov was less than impressed with this discussion. "She is taking your last name by marriage Yuri," he responded all too quickly. "She will always be Tania Kharmalov. It is the foundation to her very soul. It's the Kharmalov genes and traits that you fell in love with."

"Yes sir," Yuri responded shyly

"He is playing with you Yuri," Tania chuckled. "Papa?" she questioned looking for an apology.

"What? It's true, you are my daughter, and I raised you as a Kharmalov. There is little fairness for any woman to take a man's name just because of marriage. One day this will change."

"Bravo papa," Mila said applauding for a few seconds. "You can become the spokesperson for a new Russian woman's movement. I agree one hundred percent. There is no need for us to change our names. It is a senseless practice created for male dominance and old taxation purposes. In America, they have evolved and women are moving towards equality. I read this only last week."

"America, stop speaking nonsense Mila," Mrs. Kharmalov huffed. "Their lives are decadent, filled with greed and hate."

Mila would not be deterred. "They wake in the morning and make their own choices Mama. We are profiled and told to follow the politburo's choices."

"You have no clue how lucky you are," her mother shot back.

"To be living here in Pripyat?" Mila shot back. "Of course I know how lucky I am. We're the fortunate few. Life is a vacation in this city in comparison to our earlier days. I haven't forgotten my roots in Moscow, mama, nor have I forgotten the bleakness of our everyday life and the smell of piss in the corridors of our apartment complex. The old women lining up for bread; the men passed out drunk on the sidewalks...what is not to remember?"

"Oh please," Tania said loudly. "My last dinner will not be on yet another discussion of the decadence of America or the hopelessness of Moscow."

Everyone at the table except Roman dropped their head and fiddled with their vegetables.

"Very well," Mr. Kharmalov said changing the subject. "Yuri, you may have a surprise test this evening."

Yuri lifted his head. "I heard that too. I saw Boychik at the bakery and he mentioned the same. It is not much of a surprise if so many are aware. What type of test sir?"

"I'm not certain but I think it's for the backup generators. It's normal activity so don't worry about it. Only Reactor Four though. My first thought when hearing about it was why it wasn't done before the plant opened because anything to do with backup generators is a precautionary test."

"Good, then there will be no maintenance to be done, I'll have an easy evening."

"For a couple of hours at least," Mr. Kharmalov added.

"It means two hours of no chance of seeing Dyatlov," Yuri said, referring to the supervisor of the Control Room. "I apologize if this sounds offensive but I strongly dislike this man. He is an arrogant, rough old goat. He looks right through me as if I am some kind of insect to be swiped at. Two minutes with him and I check myself for wings."

Roman laughed and Yuri smiled at him.

"I agree," the elder Kharmalov replied. "He's a very distant man and has few friends if any at all. To his credit he is very capable and knowledgeable. Don't be too hard on him, Yuri; he's had a difficult life."

"With respect sir, I am Ukrainian. Before Pripyat my family was destitute."

"And we are Russian," Mrs. Kharmalov kicked in. "Before Pripyat we were also living a difficult life as Mila reminds us every day, so no need to differentiate between our countries."

"Yes, yes we are better off now, the past is the past let's move on," Mr. Kharmalov said, tired of the constant reminder of their previous lives. "My mention of Dyatlov's earlier years is beneficial to you, Yuri, and this discussion shall remain within these four walls." Yuri nodded and laid his utensils gingerly on his dinner plate. "He was born on a farm in Siberia and from an early age he vowed not to become a farmer like his father. He studied hard and eventually found himself working with nuclear submarines. One of the subs he was working on had an explosion, and he was subjected to heavy doses of radiation as were many others onboard and those living near to the base. It's been said that he lost his son to leukemia soon after this."

Yuri listened closely and Kharmalov searched for changes in his future son-in-law's facial expression. There was a hint of sympathy and nothing more, which the older man found disturbing if not disappointing.

"You are not yet a parent Yuri but let me assure you that a loss of a child is devastating, especially if you are the cause."

"He was responsible for this mishap?" Yuri asked, hoping for a yes response.

"No, I didn't mean to insinuate that he was. The events of that day are a well-guarded secret and I guess only Dyatlov could tell us. Didn't you hear me, the man lost his son."

"I heard you well sir and if I appear cold towards his loss it is because I find it hard to feel any sadness for someone who treats me with such unwarranted disrespect."

"He is still your indirect boss so be respectful...no matter how difficult. One stupid comment and my daughter will be living in a small apartment very far from me. For that, I would never forgive you."

Yuri nodded, picked up his fork and scooped a mouthful of chicken. The message was very clear. He turned to his future wife and chewed before speaking.

"I saw Alex today."

Tania looked surprised but happy. "How is he? Where has he been? It's been at least six weeks. Will he be in attendance tomorrow?"

"Yes, he and his mother will be there. He was finishing his exams and the good news is that he begins at the plant this evening. I'm meeting him later and we'll walk in together."

"What will he be doing at the nuclear plant?" Mrs. Kharmalov asked, suspecting she knew the answer.

"Security," Yuri replied.

The mother grunted loudly and then spoke derisively. "Wonderful, he is KGB... just like his father."

"Mother, Alex and Yuri have been friends for five years, please watch what you say. They were the two best swimmers in all of Pripyat." Tania put her hand on Yuri's shoulder. "If Yuri didn't win he was beaten by Alex. Mind you, that didn't happen too many times. I often wondered if this bothered Alex but he never made indication of so."

"More reason to be careful," the older woman said.

Like he did many times over the last few years, Yuri sighed quietly and smothered his future mother-in-law's comment.

"He is not KGB, just security at the main entrance. I don't even think he'll have a gun. He's excited about tomorrow and wanted to know if Yulia would be there. He will never give up on Yulia, poor bastard."

"Language in front of the boy," Mrs. Kharmalov reprimanded.

"Yes Yuri, I'm very impressionable," Roman said seriously before grinning snidely.

"We were just discussing her," Mila blurted. "It will be interesting to see if she shows up at the wedding with anyone." She then whispered in Tania's ear. "Or wearing clothes."

"I hope not," Yuri replied. "Poor Alex will be alone with his mother. No one should be left alone with Alex's mother."

Mr. Kharmalov chuckled before taking a bite of chicken. "So very true, she's a real piece of work."

"*She* is a widow, show respect Anton," his wife said, tapping her fork on the table. "You're not teaching your son tremendous values."

"Agreed," the father answered before facing his son. "Roman, don't spend too much time with Alex's mother. That is today's lesson." He looked at his wife and winked. "My parenting skills impress even me."

Mila laughed out loud while covering her mouth. "I love my family."

One Last Walk

While Mrs. Kharmalov and Mila cleaned up, Tania and Yuri took one last walk together as an unmarried couple. Tania wore high heels and was almost as tall as Yuri. A late evening wind caused her long hair to wrap around her neck. She lifted the collar on her white sweater and held the bottom of her shifting skirt with her one free hand.

"I love you Yuri Larinov," she smiled.

"And I you, my dear. It will be the happiest moment of my life to place a ring on your finger. I will awake every morning and kiss you like there was no tomorrow. I will love you each day more than the day before."

Tania held his hand tighter. "Even when I nag you?" She said, referring to a comment made earlier in the evening.

"Ah…for that I have vodka."

"Don't you dare become one of those men Yuri, you are not so typical."

"Hmm… you've started nagging already," he joked. "Not to worry my love, I hate vodka."

"And do not become Simon either. He avoids his wife and child. Promise me you won't shun me like he does my sister."

"Hey," Yuri answered with his hands held high. "I always told you that Simon was a girl with a man's equipment. No one believed me. He shuns Mila because he is repulsed by her. Maybe his interest in Yulia is because she has tiny breasts and a skinny ass. He's working his way down towards his true desire."

"Do you honestly believe this?"

"It is a crime in Russia and he wouldn't risk his work for another man. Someday though, he'll' screw up and his world will crumble. I don't doubt my assumption but please don't tell Mila I said this."

Tania nodded. "It would explain much. I feel bad for Mila; she is so affectionate and loving."

"Damn nice looking too," Yuri replied lifting his eyebrows in an exaggerated fashion and chuckling. Tania slapped his behind. "The beautiful Kharmalov girls…how many times have I heard this? I think every boy and man in Pripyat has said it at least ten times."

"And you are marrying me because of my looks?" Tania said with her hands firm on her hips.

Having forgotten the ever increasing wind, her skirt whipped up above her hips and she quickly tugged it down.

Yuri acted as if he saw nothing. "No, but I do appreciate your long legs and butt."

Tania rolled her eyes and then pinched Yuri's arm. "Is Alex meeting you here?"

They had arrived at a small park with slides, a sandbox and a couple of wrought iron benches. There was one lamppost behind the slides that was only partially lit. A rosebush next to the benches showed signs that it was ready to bloom. Considering how beautiful a day it had been, it was very quiet on the Pripyat streets.

"Yes, and I see him in the distance."

They sat on one of the benches and Yuri took his fiancée's hand.

"Tania, tomorrow I will marry you and you will make me the happiest man in Pripyat. Every day we have spent together

71

these last three years has been magical. I can't imagine my life without your smile, without your passion… without your kiss."

"Don't make me cry Yuri. I am much too emotional today."

The tall man touched her face with the back of his fingers. "I mean every word I say. My life would have no meaning without you and my heart would ache without your eyes staring back at me. I love you more than my words can say."

"Hi guys," Alex said, interrupting the romantic discourse.

He was dressed in brown military gear. His dark brown hair was combed back and held in place by too much grease. Alex Mishkin was neither handsome nor unattractive. His features held no distinguishable character, and he was a bit shorter than the average Russian man. What anyone would remember about him was a smile that never seemed to disappear off his face.

"Good timing buddy," Yuri sneered while glaring at his friend.

Tania stood, wiped her eyes and hugged Alex. "Welcome home Sasha and congratulations on your new job."

"I get the feeling that you two were in the middle of something. I can come back in five minutes."

"No, we're fine," Tania said, grabbing Alex's arm while tugging on her skirt. "I am just very happy and excited to marry your best friend."

"I thought you were marrying Yuri?"

"Never mind asshole," Yuri said, punching Alex lightly. "Let's go and get you a paycheck. Maybe somehow we can make you respectable. I doubt it but we can certainly try."

Alex couldn't resist one last dig at his friend. "Tania, you will look lovely in your wedding dress and I'm looking forward to you coming to your senses and running away from the ZAGs building as fast as your feet can take you."

"Very funny," Yuri replied trying his best not to grin. "And I'm looking forward to watching you dance with your mother."

"Oh, that was low…" Alex said shaking his head. "It's true but still so very low."

The two young men started to walk away when Yuri stopped, turned around and walked back to his future wife. He grabbed her hips and kissed her passionately.

"The next time I kiss you, you'll be my wife. I love you, Tania Kharmalov."

He then trotted back to his best friend, and the two began the long walk to Reactor Four of the Chernobyl Nuclear Plant.

The stunning blond woman smiled briefly as she watched the two men disappear into the shadows. The moon reflected off the rippling waters of the Pripyat River. The stars in the black sky were brighter than she ever remembered. All was good with the world.

Life was beautiful in this beautiful town.

Chernobyl Nuclear Plant: April 25th, 11PM

"Hey David, look who I found," Yuri said while extending his hand to the somewhat disheveled security guard.

David Asimov was short and stocky but a popular man in the Plant even if his security position was very low on the totem pole. The men - and the few women - loved his attitude and his willingness to help in any way and at any time. Yuri had made sure that he was part of the wedding guest list. Nonetheless, and as Yuri had pointed out on several occasions, David had his quirky side. The plant security guard was not ashamed to admit he washed only once a week. He claimed that by cleaning every day, one becomes more susceptible to disease and the immune system weakens. He argued very strongly that any child who was not immersed in dirt and mud was sure to become a strong candidate for sickness. So, every Sunday morning, David had a one hour bath with salty suds and a toothbrush to scrub every inch of his body. Yuri laughed at the man's claims when they first met but after three years and never seeing David call in sick, he thought that maybe – just maybe – his friend was on to something, even if he did smell rather funky by Friday.

"Yuri, I've told you once before, you can't bring your pets to work. Bring the monkey home and I will keep this a secret between you and me. No one has to know."

"Oh, that's so funny," Alex mocked. "It's my first day, please treat me with the respect I am due."

"It is indeed your first day, silly rookie....no respect will be offered by anyone. Did you just fall off an onion cart? Yuri, bring him with you please, I can't bear to think I have to spend the next two hours with this chimp."

"Thanks David, I'll show him around."

"No problem," the security guard replied. He shook Alex's hand and gave him a locker key. "Welcome comrade, glad you're with us. I arranged a locker close to Alex and me. Keep your badge around your neck at all times and please don't fling your feces at the other employees."

"Ha...ha... ha. No problem and thank-you David. I'm glad to be here and away from my mother," Alex said, laughing at his own comment.

He stood still, staring at the front door and then at the large structure he had once only dreamed of working at. He stretched his neck backwards to glance at the long reactor tower. He likened it to one of the rocket missiles he saw on television. Other night shift employees passed by, paying him no attention. He relished the moment and closed his eyes. This was a long time coming. His father would be proud.

"Excuse me," Yuri said. "Dream time is over, time to work. You do understand the concept of work… right?"

Alex grinned at his friend and put his hand on Yuri's shoulder. "My life begins tonight."

Kharmalov Home: April 26th, One Fifteen A.M

Tania had finally fallen asleep but Mila was still awake. She should have gone home and tried to speak with her husband but having spent the entire evening with her family, she felt home was where she was right now. She had her daughter, her parents and siblings. This was her family and Simon was on the outside, refusing to look in.

Roman's bed was partitioned off by a sliding curtain for obvious reasons. Living in the same room as two mature sisters could not have been very comfortable at the best of times. Mila stepped around the curtain and stared lovingly at her little brother. He was handsome like his father and every bit as funny. The things that came out of his mouth sometimes should be written down for television. She sat down on the side of his tiny bed and softly rubbed the boy's blondish locks.

"Why are you still awake?" he said, frightening his older sister.

"Good God, you scared me," Mila said, still shocked. "Why are *you* still awake? It's almost twenty after one in the morning. You should be fast asleep."

He rubbed his eyes and yawned. "Too much vodka." His sister did not find this humorous. "I'm just kidding. I was thinking this room will be very lonely without my sisters. I wasn't ready for you to leave and now Tania will be gone too."

Mila kissed her brother on the forehead. "Yes... well, maybe I'll return. Tania and I are close by and will always come for dinner, without or without our husbands. Let's not forget that someday soon you'll have a girlfriend or many girlfriends that will join us."

"There are several that have a crush on me but the girls in my class are stupid. I like Natasha but she's stupid too."

"Natasha is very pretty, I like her. The girls will be less *stupid* in a few years but as I remember, boys tend to become very stupid as teenagers. It will be many, many years before both the boys and girls are equally stupid."

Roman shrugged but grinned. "I'll remember this Mila," he said before changing the subject. "Can I go fishing tomorrow after school?"

"Are you for real?" Mia exclaimed. "Your sister is getting married tomorrow, fish boy. There won't be any time. Mama will have a fit if you're missing and not dressed in a suit as soon as you get home from school."

"It's April; the fish are hungry and easy to catch, even in the late afternoon."

"Yes, well one more day won't kill you," Mila empathized. "Think of Tania and how proud she'll be to see her brother dressed up and standing next to her."

"I like Yuri, he's fun," Roman said without thinking.

"And Simon?"

Roman turned his head and averted eye contact with Mila. "I don't see him very often. I don't appreciate the way he treats you, Mila. Sorry."

Mila was not hurt by his words and in fact, it was gratifying to hear. Maybe her brother's words were exactly what she needed to hear to finalize the decision that she dreaded making.

"Don't be sorry" she sighed. "It says you love me, and that my dear brother means more to me than any breath Simon exhales."

"I do love you Mila, with all my heart. You're my best friend."

Roman's words touched her deep but before she could reply a loud noise shook the two from their quiet conversation.

"What the *hell* was that?" Mila exclaimed. "It sounded like an explosion."

No one else in the apartment including the visiting aunt, uncle and cousin awoke from their slumber. Mila and Roman raced to the apartment balcony to see what happened. The elder sister could not utter a word when she saw what appeared to be blood red fireworks coming from the roof of the nuclear plant. It was like slivers of volcano lava with a rainbow background shooting thousands of feet into the star. Years later, the initial sight of the multi-colored eruption would be explained as a confusing mix of joy and puzzlement.

It was beautiful.

"I thought they were doing fireworks during the May 1st celebrations," Roman said with a baffled tone. "That's next week…they can never get *anything* right."

April 26th 7 A.M.

The banging at the door was loud and persistent. Tatiana Kharmalov pulled the bedcovers off her tired body and prepared herself to give the early morning intruder a good talking to. The floor was still cold and her bare feet left a trail of quick disappearing, moist prints. She opened the door and stared at a frantic Edith Borovski. At that same moment, the telephone rang awaking everybody in the apartment except for the six-year old cousin, Boris.

"Edith, it's seven in the blasted morning."

"Mrs. Kharmalov," she begged, "Please, may I speak to Tania."

"It's her wedding day Edith, she needs her sleep." The telephone had not yet been answered. "Someone get the phone before I tear it out of the wall!"

Anton Kharmalov walked into the main room wearing only his pajama bottoms.

"Relax woman, you'll pop a vein."

Edith was in panic mode. To Tatiana Kharmalov, the thin, tiny woman crying in front of her looked like a child who just received a spanking.

"Please Mrs. Kharmalov, I must speak with Tania."

"Very well…" Tatiana replied, unhappy with her decision.

She looked at her husband who had already hung up the phone. His face was blank.

"What's wrong with you Anton, you look like you did the day we ran out of vodka." She laughed at her own joke but only for a brief second. Something was not right.

Anton didn't answer and walked to the balcony. He forced the door open and stared at the reason for his early morning awakening. Black smoke smothered the sky above Reactor Four. It hung below the morning sky like an enormous immovable head. His wife followed and stood next to him gasping.

"My foreman has instructed that I must work all day."

"You are not walking into that Anton," his wife insisted. "I forbid you."

Anton looked at the street in front of their apartment. "He said it was a minor fire. From where I'm standing, it doesn't look minor to me. The road wouldn't be flooded if it was minor."

Tatiana looked down, and her face changed from worried to frightened.

"What is that foam? It isn't water. Do not go to work Anton."

"If I don't, you will spend the next ten years visiting me in jail."

He wrapped his arm around his wife hoping to comfort her. He knew her all too well, she was scared for him. They returned to the kitchen where Edith was now sitting with Tania and her Aunt Vera. Both women were still wearing their nightgowns.

"I don't know where he is," Edith said. "We were upstairs sleeping when the alarm went off."

"At the fire hall?" Vera asked.

"Yes, the wives stay there with their husbands when they are working later shifts. Yanush came upstairs to say good-night and fell asleep with his arms wrapped around me. It happened so quickly. There was lots of yelling and in two minutes the whole crew was gone."

As soon as Edith said her last word there was another banging at the door and Alex walked in without waiting. His face was a light brown as if he had returned from a summer vacation by the sea. Tania immediately stood and rushed towards him with anxious eyes.

"Sasha, where is Yuri?"

"He's fine Tania," Alex replied assuredly. "I'm here solely to tell you this. I have to get back."

"You're not going anywhere young man," Mrs. Kharmalov ordered. "Tell us what's happening."

"Did you see Yanush?" Edith questioned immediately. "He is with the fire brigade."

"I don't know who Yanush is. If he's one of the firemen then you may want to check the hospital. They spent hours on the roof dousing the flames. My guess is that his lungs are being cleared."

"Then I will go there now," she said pushing her chair back too fast.

Her sudden burst caused the chair to fall to the floor. Vera bent over and picked it up while holding her ample breasts in place.

"I'll leave with you," Tania said. "Give me five minutes with Sasha."

Alex raised both arms with the palms of his hands opened wide. "He's still working and there is a lot to do. No one should be alarmed, everything is under control."

"Yuri's shift is over," Mrs. Kharmalov interjected. "He's getting married today so tell us why he is still at work if all is fine?"

"Guys, all Reactor Four staff have to report for work this morning, there are no exceptions. Most of the fires were extinguished two hours ago and there is a ton of clean up to do."

Mr. Kharmalov had been in his bedroom getting dressed for most of this conversation but he heard the last part.

"Bullshit," he said with authority.

"Sir?" Alex answered with a hint of fear.

"I was just on my balcony Alex. The black smoke tells me the firefighters have extinguished the less important flames… the combustible flames. Behind the smoke I can see the pretty rainbow colours. That tells me that radioactivity has escaped."

"Mr. Kharmalov, the dosimeters all show acceptable levels. None have surpassed 3.6 therefore we're safe."

The elder Kharmalov was not impressed with the new security agent at this moment but the boy's ignorance was not his fault.

"Alex, they haven't passed three point six because they are incapable of doing so. We don't have any Geiger in the Plant that functions properly. Have you looked at your face?"

"What's wrong with my face?'"

"Your foreman will tell you that you have a thermal heat bronzing. It's not thermal heat Alex. Only radiation can cause skin to turn brown in such a short period."

Alex was not sure what to reply. He had known Mr. Kharmalov for almost three years and the man had always been very straightforward with him. At the same time, he was spreading gossip that was contradictory to what a Soviet foreman had claimed to be the absolute truth.

"With respect sir, I have been working for the last six hours and my superiors have been forthcoming and courageous."

"Spoken like KGB," Mrs. Kharmalov added.

"Mother!" Tania exclaimed. "Sasha came here out of the goodness of his heart and as a friend to give us good news about Yuri. I won't stand for this talk."

"Thank-you Tania," Alex exclaimed.

Over the years he had grown increasingly frustrated with Mrs. Kharmalov's remarks about his family history.

"What is Yuri doing at the moment?" Tania begged.

"We spent the night pumping water, finding new supplies and lengthening hoses. Within thirty minutes of the explosion we had two fire stations in full force working on the roof. That's all I can tell you at the moment. Yuri volunteered to climb the ladders and bring water and vodka but Brechevski put him on a tight leash real quick. Before I came here, Yuri was attending to the firemen on the ground that needed a break. He'll be done in a couple of hours and then we will all watch you wed this evening."

"I hope so," Tania answered with a doubting tone. "Sasha, you tell my man that he is not to be a hero. I do not need a dead hero, I need my husband."

"I will say these exact words to him my friend and I'll watch him closely. Again, there's no reason to be worried, everything is under control."

"How did you get here?" Mr. Kharmalov questioned. "I will return with you."

"I got a free ride. There are a lot of buses coming in from Kiev to help out. The driver is waiting for me downstairs."

"Let's go," the older man said. Before leaving he whispered in his wife's ear. "No school for Roman. Keep everyone close to home and shut the goddamn windows." He kissed her and she held him longer than usual.

The two men departed and before stepping into the bus, Mr. Kharmalov stopped Alex and looked him directly in the eyes.

"How many are dead?"

Alex did not hesitate to reply. "There is only one that I know of, sir."

"That is not as ghastly as I expected."

"It is one comrade sir, one comrade too many." Alex was about to board the bus when he stopped and faced the man again. "Unfortunately, out of my utmost respect, it's my duty to inform you that I have been lying to you and your family."

Mr. Kharmalov raised his eyebrows and then nodded as if he knew all along.

"How bad is it?"

Alex took off his cap and held it to his chest. "A couple of the men from the control room were heroic if not totally misguided. Their faces are black sir…not brown. I watched as almost all the firemen were carted off to the hospital. That woman inside your home looking for her husband…I don't see her returning home this evening with a smile on her face. Within the reactor itself, it's chaos and no one knows what the other is doing. The constant hissing inside the building is eerie; it's like a field of one million snakes waiting to attack. Men are vomiting and collapsing. The streets are lined with puke.

I spent most of the evening carrying workers over my shoulder and onto gurneys to take them away. Most of the power is out, and it's difficult to maneuver inside without tripping over concrete and imploded windows. I just spent an hour removing slivers of glass from my soles that were cutting into my skin. It is bullshit, as you said, Mr. Kharmalov. I'm not so blind that I cannot create my own analysis and dismiss what the supervisors claim.

84

That being said and if you can excuse my language, I will share my thoughts on how bad it is." He paused and took a deep breath. "The lion is out of the cage sir and we're all dinner."

Alex boarded the bus, sat down and buried his brown face in his hands.

****

"When Grigori returned to the station at five a.m. he was vomiting," Edith said to Tania. "There was only myself and another one of the wives there. We were having tea as if the men were out on a normal run. The instant he appeared in front of us, we were terrified. His face was very brown, like a toasted marshmallow."

"Did he say anything?"

"He said that they were not told it was dangerous…he said that they were on the roof for hours like kamikazes. Like kamikazes, Tania. Grigori was so tired he could barely move. He said his hands felt like pins and needles and he couldn't open one of them. I tried to help him but he swore loudly. He yelled, *stay the fuck away from me, I'm radioactive.* I covered my mouth and backed away, not wishing to become contaminated. The other wife had already vanished, she had figured out what was going on a lot quicker than me. I put on my jacket and ran to the reactor but was stopped by a police officer. He told me to go home and wait. I begged for information but he ignored me. How can I wait for news when none is being given?"

As they turned the corner on Druzhby Narodov Street, two large army tanks drove past them. Tania did not say anything but experience had taught her that army tanks could only mean trouble. She saw a young man that she knew from secondary school and asked him if he had heard any update about the power plant. He answered that it was a beautiful day and that she shouldn't worry. Enjoy the sun and get a tan, he said with a huge smile.

"He's oblivious," Edith muttered.

The two girls approached the front door of the hospital and were immediately stopped by two army officers wearing protective clothing and gas masks. *No visitors*, each of them said brusquely while temporarily removing their masks.

"Gentlemen," Tania began, "We have reason to believe that my friend's husband was brought here earlier this morning. He's a fireman who performed a commendable job therefore out of the kindness of your heart, could you please allow her access."

"Ladies," the shorter officer presented, "Entrance into this hospital is strictly forbidden, as per the Mayor and our commanding officer."

Edith was less patient. "I have never heard of a hospital disallowing their patients a visit from family. Push aside and let me see my husband."

The army officer grabbed her by the shoulder and shoved her back.

"Madam, we will forcibly detain you if you do not leave."

"What's going on?" she insisted and then blazed on with a tirade of questions. "You're wearing gas masks and telling us what we can do? If something is wrong why aren't you telling everyone? You should be screaming it from the rooftops but instead you stop a wife from seeing her husband? This is your contribution to Pripyat?"

The other officer raised his hand and spoke softly. "Come back in the afternoon at around 4 p.m. You can see him then."

"Come Edith," Tania said while staring down the officers. "They're doing as they are told. A real man would show compassion. These *comrades* are simple order takers. It's lucky for them that Mila is not with us, she would tear them a new asshole."

"I don't understand," Edith moaned as new tears fell down her face. "I only wish to see my husband."

Tania wrapped her arm around her friend as they walked away. *I only wish to have a husband*, she selfishly thought.

****

Anton Kharmalov and Alex arrived behind several other buses filled with men from Kiev. A helicopter was circling the reactor while others were landing in any available spot, lifting and spreading dust across the two kilometer area and into the workers eyes and noses. A red, green and blue translucent smoke from the damaged Reactor Four streamed towards the clouds. On the ground, Anton watched almost mesmerized by the chaos. Russian nuclear experts stood next to military commanders examining the debris while a few selected photographers walked unprotected through the compound. One of the photographers was slapping his camera trying to make it work. As he walked closer to the man, Anton heard him say his batteries must be dead. The engineer knew better. Radioactive isotopes had seeped into the camera and rendered it useless.

"There's nothing I can do here," Anton told Alex without a hint of doubt. "We should look for Yuri."

Alex agreed. "He may be sleeping by the river."

"No," Anton whispered. "He's over there."

Amidst the yelling of supervisors; the lines of dormant hose and grey soot that flew carelessly through the air, Yuri was sitting upright against a tire of a fire truck. He was still wearing his mandatory lab coat but his head was covered with a white cloth and a gas mask hung from his neck. His face was not brown like Alex's and this was a small relief to Anton. Yuri didn't notice his future father-in-law or Alex until the latter lightly kicked the sole of his boot.

"Hey," he said, shielding his eyes to look up.

Anton sat down next to Yuri and put a hand on the young man's shoulder. "You okay, son?"

"I guess I am. This is insane sir, it's futile, and this was supposed to be my day with Tania... it's my wedding day."

Anton did not reply but Alex answered yes while crouching to sit next to his best friend.

"I should be in my bed listening to my mother prepare a large cake in the kitchen while she simultaneously butchered a Beatles tune."

"Then why don't you go home?" Anton questioned.

Yuri sneered before answering. "Breshevski asked me to stay a bit longer. We have to pump water from the river, just in case. He said it's only precautionary as the worse is over. He actually said that the reactor would be reopened in May and that it's safe enough to place in the middle of Red Square." Yuri chuckled but in a mocking manner. "Fucking idiot." He rubbed his forehead and then sighed. "I've been sitting here thinking about the people in my life and I remembered the stories my grandfather spoke often about, especially the day the Germans entered his village during World War Two. He said they stood tall, taller than anyone in the village. Even the short ones appeared tall and when he made eye contact with one of the Germans he said it felt like the man was looking through him. He knew there was no doubt that the soldier was his enemy."

"We defeated them in the end," Alex responded, not really following his friends thought process.

Anton, meanwhile, remained quiet. Yuri coughed several times before continuing.

"When the firefighters arrived after one-thirty this morning there was no time to clear a path to the roof from inside the building so they climbed ladders to the roof. These poor fools arrived at the reactor thinking there was an electrical fire; they had no clue what they were up against. I was holding the ladders and checking the hoses for any slack. One after another they climbed with hoses straddled to the shoulders. Some had masks, but they all had useless rubber boots or fake leather boots...whatever but they fucking melted within minutes. When a few climbed down, incapable of continuing, David offered to help."

"David Asimov?" Anton asked. "Our David, the security guard?"

"Yep, that David," Yuri sighed. "He's always been the one to go the extra mile... always the guy to help his comrades."

"Is he okay?" Alex asked anxiously. "What happened to him?"

"He didn't wear a mask," Yuri continued while shaking his head. "I offered him mine, but he told me not to worry, I was getting married in a few hours so I needed it more. Most of the guys stayed on the roof for a maximum of fifteen minutes. When they came down they all claimed that half the water coming from their hoses turned to steam before it hit the flames. You could tell which guys stared into the crater instead of standing further back because they had dark brown faces. There were a couple of guys who made multiple trips. They would lie against a truck like we're doing now and puke their guts out and then climb back up the ladder. David didn't bother taking a break. He stayed up on the roof for a good half hour. I was told he vomited several times and that near the end he was so weak that he was kneeling next to the crater while holding a hose."

"Where is he now?" Alex enquired.

Yuri took a deep breath and exhaled. He treated each gulp of air like a dear friend thankful that it arrived.

"The fires around the building were contained quickly, most were out by five this morning. At about three a.m. the Kiev boys showed up. A couple of them carried David through the building to one of the buses. I followed and told them that David was a friend so they let me onboard. His eyes were open but I don't think he could see me. I spoke, but he didn't answer, he couldn't answer. His lips were soldered together, liquefied into one pink blob. His eyes were blue. David had brown eyes but not then... they were blue, almost glowing. I'm ashamed to say that I truly found him horrific to look at. Such a wonderful man... always laughing and all I could see was a deformed, half dead monster. Skin had melted off his right arm and was hanging below his sleeve. I'm sure that if we had peeled off his shirt, his

90

skin would have fallen off liked a cooked chicken. His face was unrecognizable. It wasn't brown like the others, it was black. Most of his face was black... his neck, his ankles..." Yuri closed his eyes and bit his lower lips. "The enemy got to him Mr. Kharmalov and he won't be at my wedding. He won't be there and no one should be there. No one should be here either... this is a war zone. My grandfather saw his enemy but we can't see ours. There is absolutely no way we can win. *Our enemy is invisible.*"

The three men lay their heads against the radioactive firetruck. They watched soldiers running past them, obeying orders. Helicopters blocked the sun and dust fell on their heads like snow in mid-December. A photographer stopped and took a picture. Not a word was spoken for another half hour.

The Bridge of Death

The rain is pouring down this morning. From everything I have heard in the last two days I made sure I had a large umbrella. I didn't specifically mention fallout from the sky to Lena but I don't think I had to. She refused to leave the apartment without an umbrella so a very tired and hung over Boris, got up early to buy one.

We were back in the hospital at ten a.m. sharp. Before we had a chance to enter Tania's room, a nurse took Lena aside and mentioned that Tania had had a difficult night. She thought it necessary to inform Lena that their previous assessment of three weeks was hopeful and that we should expect Tania to pass within ten days or less. I found that a shitty thing to tell Lena but given she was the only one visiting; I guess it was warranted. We waited an additional ten minutes for my friend to stop crying before we visited Tania.

Lena's aunt was sitting upright but half asleep when Lena touched her arm. She smiled and then kissed her niece several times.

"The drugs they give me are very strong and make me sleep. I would rather stay awake as the dreams I am having are extremely vivid. I wonder if the other patients are experiencing the same. I like your shirt Aaron. I have always found a nice white shirt to be very appealing on a man."

I thanked her in Russian and Lena giggled or at least half giggled. Hey, I'm trying.

"Where did we leave off yesterday?" Tania questioned.

"Yuri was still working and your friend Edith was to return to the hospital at four p.m. to see her husband."

"Oh yes, poor Edith. She stayed with me the entire morning and most of the afternoon. When we left those awful guards we decided to stop at one of the outdoor cafes. The place was packed and everyone was discussing the accident at the power plant but no one seemed excessively worried. Like Edith and I, they sipped their tea or coffee on the patio. We had no idea that we were breathing isotopes that were one hundred times the acceptable levels. I overheard one lady say that her neighbor was working inside the plant all evening and that he could taste the radiation. He said it had a metallic taste but all we could taste was the cinnamon in our coffee.

Edith had calmed down when a friend of hers joined us for a few minutes. As a passing thought the woman said that several men were taken to the hospital for precautionary reasons. At the time I had no inclination or reason to disbelieve this lady as I had not heard about David yet. I wouldn't hear any horror stories until my father and Yuri returned."

"Were you not thinking about getting home to prepare for your wedding?" Lena questioned.

"Oh my, of course I was. It was all I was thinking about but Edith's problem was a bit more severe. I could wait another hour or two without panic. I will tell you though what I personally found unnerving. There were many army tanks entering Pripyat. Most of our citizens thought this was a good thing because if the army was there then they would take care of any problem. My thinking was that if the army was there it was not only a problem but a *big* problem. The radio that was playing in the background kept repeating that all was fine but no one was allowed to enter or leave Pripyat for the rest of the day. Suddenly we are learning that we were prisoners. This did not translate into a little problem for me. And to make matters worse these big water trucks would pass every two hours and spray the roads with a foamy substance that I later learned was a decontaminant. *Do not worry, all is fine and we have everything under control. By the way, you can't leave and don't step in the decontaminant."*

"So you couldn't get any valid information?"

"What's new, this was the Soviet Union. If you said anything that would spread panic or was against the party line, you went to jail for eight years. Don't forget, we were living in the jewel city. No matter how big the problem, we just wanted it fixed so that we could continue our normal lives. God forbid we would have to leave Pripyat and return to Moscow."

"That psychology stays with you Aaron no matter where you end up," Lena added. "The fear of government leaves a permanent imprint. It extends to many facets of your everyday life."

Tania nodded her head as if she understood which in hindsight was adorable. I tried to decipher Lena's comment as if it was a hidden meaning but drew blanks. Over the last three days Lena was dropping subtle hints on my lap and all I was doing was trying to piece them together. I was failing miserably. Tania stared at me wondering if I was paying attention. I smiled at her and she continued her story.

"After an hour we walked home. Mothers were out with strollers, kids were in school. It was a normal Saturday but warm, very warm for April. I saw people on the beach, sun tanning while their children swam in the water. They had no concept of what was happening around them and I imagine they have paid the ultimate price. My mother was home with Aunt Vera, Mila and the baby. Boris and his father went for a long walk disregarding Aunt Vera's pleading. I loved my uncle, but he was not an intelligent man."

Lena agreed and then shook her head several times. "Uncle Georgie was in a word, ignorant."

"The windows were shut, so it was very muggy inside the apartment yet no one complained. Father was not an authoritarian but when he asked for something we complied. At noon we spent ten minutes on our balcony. We could see the plant from there as well as the bridge that led to Reactor Four. There were some helicopters, but we were pleased that the black smoke had dissipated and replaced with a multi colored haze. It was crazy, but we thought that maybe everything was repaired. It did not strike me at the very moment that the gorgeous colours were killing us. It was beautiful and ugly at the same time like an egotistical movie star. What I could never understand is why so many people decided to hang out by the bridge to watch the plant. Surely there were several better spots to watch what was happening, but they stayed there all day."

"What is the significance of the bridge?"

"Ah, the railroad bridge… because of its proximity to the plant, the wind, and of course, the structure. It became known as the Bridge of Death."

April 26th, 2 PM:

"Where the hell is Georgie?" Mrs. Kharmalov barked. "He should have been back an hour ago."

"He'll be here Tatiana," Vera sighed. "Have faith. Boris gets hungry every three hours so not to worry."

Mila and Roman were sitting on the couch together, grinning. They had grown all too familiar with their mother's complaining when it came to Aunt Vera and Uncle Georgie.

"Tomorrow I'm going fishing and nothing is going to stop me," Roman whispered to his sister.

"And what is Boris going to do while you're gone?"

"Eat… he can eat all he wants. I like fishing, he likes eating. We're both happy."

Mila smirked and smacked her brother in the arm. "Can we please watch something else? How many times can they air Alien Conquest in one day?"

Roman scratched his chin in an exaggerated manner. "That would be no, and forty-eight."

"Smart ass," Mila snorted. "You are turning more and more into me every day."

"Ha! I actually had a teacher say that to me last week. She said your sister was a joker too, but the difference is that your sister is beautiful… what are you going to do? I just laughed."

The phone rang and everyone hoped it was Yuri. Instead it was a friend of Roman's who was talking hysterically, claiming that the amusement park was open. Mrs. Kharmalov answered that it was impossible as the park was slated to open on May 1st. The boy was adamant saying that officials opened the rides to calm everyone. Mrs. Kharmalov hung up and relayed the information to Mila and Roman. Their eyes opened as wide as possible and they jumped off the couch.

"Two hours and only two hours," their mother warned. "I want you both back here at four fifteen or there will be hell to pay. If you see your uncle and cousin tell them the same. If you see your father; hide and run back home."

"Yes mama," they answered in tandem.

"The baby will be sleeping for another two hours so we're good all around." Mila kissed her mother as did Roman. They rushed to the door and fought playfully to get out first.

"Those two," Tatiana grinned at Vera. "Born ten years apart yet inseparable, have you ever seen anything like it? Two peas in a pod, makes my heart happy."

"I've never seen anything like it," Vera said sincerely. "Never."

****

There were many children at the Amusement Park but it was not packed like it would have been a week later. Mila and Roman entered without a lineup and rode the bumper cars for a good half hour before deciding to ride the Ferris Wheel. They waited five minutes and laughed with Uncle Georgie and their cousin Bruno who had been one of the first to walk through the opened gates. Bruno would claim for years to come that he was on the first Bumper Car ride ever in Pripyat.

Dark clouds had set in, but it was still uncommonly warm for late April. Mila wished she had worn shorts like Roman instead of the tight fitting jeans that were chafing her thighs. The brother and sister tandem were the first on and were now in the air waiting for the last two seats to be occupied before the Ferris Wheel began its rapid spin. From this height they could see a good portion of the city. Roman pointed out his school and their apartment building. He noticed the army trucks blocking the main street out of Pripyat and then told Mila he would have to ride his bike through the back streets if he was to go fishing tomorrow morning. His sister was more interested in the drama that was evolving west of the amusement park. A wedding party was trying to enter the front doors of the administrative building that housed ZAGs, the official office where Tania and Yuri were to marry in a few hours. The groom and his friends were pounding on the door but to no use. The bride dressed in the traditional white gown sat down on the front steps and buried her head in her arms. Mila directed Roman to see what she was looking at.

"Oh, oh," he uttered. "This is not good. Tania will be heartbroken."

"I recognize the bride even from this distance. It's Olga Timoshenko; she was a couple of school years ahead of me. Her family has been in Pripyat since the day the first apartment buildings were constructed. This is a disaster but maybe it is only temporary," Mila hoped. "I wouldn't doubt if some dumbass went to lunch and forgot there was an appointment."

The wheel started to turn slowly and then increased in speed. Both screamed with joy albeit only temporarily. When the ride was done, and it was their turn to disembark Mila grabbed Roman by the hand and walked briskly towards the crying bride.

Their legs were shaking from the ride and from what they soon expected to hear.

Olga saw Mila from a distance and summoned her to sit. Roman remained standing at the first step and watched the men who were still banging on the door. The parents and a few guests were off by the side discussing in whispers. The women wore lovely gowns, and the men wore blue suits. Two of the men had full length beards. From afar, these hairy men looked like Bolsheviks he saw in history books.

"I had a bad feeling this would happen," Olga said before blowing her nose on a tissue. "My papa said that everyone was due to report to the Reactor by three p.m. I had hoped this did not include ZAG employees."

Mila wrapped her arms around the distressed bride to be. "If it's any consolation, Tania was also to be married today. I'm very sorry for you Olga."

"Poor Tania, she was such a cute girl from what I remember." Olga wiped her nose and continued. "Victor is a pilot. Tomorrow morning he is to begin dropping sand on the fire. I probably won't see him for a week or two, but from what my father has blurted out, the mission is more dangerous than just dropping bags of sand."

"Then you'll be married when his job is completed."

Olga did not see this as a viable solution. "I'm pregnant. We're hiding this from our parents and any delay will make it all too obvious. I needed today to happen."

"Oh shit," Mila sighed.

An army truck drove up in front of the group and parked. A man dressed in full military regalia stepped out and approached the bride and Mila. The rest of the group joined immediately.

"Stop banging on the door," the stocky man ordered.

His serious tone frightened Olga, and she stood up to stand next to the groom. The brim of the soldier's military cap hid most of his eyes and a thick black mustache hung over his lips. Olga thought of challenging his authority but the man raised his hand to stop her.

"This building is closed until further notice. You may have noticed we have a crisis at the moment that requires all government personnel to change outfits and assume new duties. I am sorry for your inconvenience and understandable distress but your special day will have to wait. I therefore ask all of you politely to disband and not return."

With that finality he walked down the stairs and back into the truck. The entire group watched him drive away hoping he would turn around and change his decision. He did not.

Olga bid Mila farewell and then sobbed on Victor's shoulder.

Roman stared at the unhappy bride to be and thought of how his sister would react. It made him tear up, and he held Mila knowing she would have to be the one to break the news.

No more marriages would be performed today in this beautiful town.

Their beautiful town.

****

At the same time that Mila and Roman were making the long walk to the family apartment to tell their sister that her big day would not happen, Yuri and Anton Kharmalov were also on their way home. Alex had remained at the Reactor for another hour to help in the cleanup. Yuri was worried for Alex as his face had turned a light brown. *One hour and you're out of there*, he warned his best friend.

"Look at these idiots," Anton pointed as the two men approached the bridge.

Yuri shrugged not understanding what his future father-in-law was alluding to.

"Do you feel the wind against the back of your head?" Anton asked.

The young man then nodded and understood. "They're breathing radioactivity. Actually, it's pretty strong in this area, as if the wind is choosing this spot to spread a hateful vengeance."

"Yah, and this guy to the right of us has two kids with binoculars sucking in millions of isotopes. Fucking idiot, what kind of father can be so ignorant?"

"He doesn't know sir. I'm sure if he did he would be in his home with the windows closed. Maybe you should speak to him."

Anton believed this to be a good idea and approached the balding red haired man. "Excuse me sir but I should warn you that this spot you have chosen to view the fire is not safe. I advise you to go home and watch on your balcony for short periods of time."

"And who are you?" the man answered defiantly. "I just spoke with a military officer who told us quite the opposite."

"What did you expect?" Anton replied raising his tone. "I am a nuclear technician and I am telling you to go home. It is not safe for your children." The man stared back at Anton wide-eyed but did nothing. "There's a reason they sprayed the streets this morning or have you not made any reasonable conclusions of your own. Go home!"

"Move away from us crazy man. You're scaring my children, I should have you arrested."

One of the young boys picked his nose not caring who was watching.

Yuri grabbed Anton by the shirt and tugged. "It's no use," he said.

Anton walked backwards for a few steps to stare at the ginger haired man a bit longer. "Even the metal railing along the bridge is contaminated," he shouted before turning around. Anton placed his mask over his mouth. "Another statistic waiting to happen."

Yuri did not respond. He had other things to worry about other than someone else's children. His boss had asked him to return later this evening. It was a request he found extremely odd since the man knew he was getting married in three hours.

"Is it wise for Tania and I to marry under these circumstances," he asked Anton, hoping for assurance.

Anton slapped Yuri lightly on the forearm. "You're asking me if it is a good idea to marry Tania Kharmalov? Ask any man in this town the same question and they'll question your sanity."

"You know what I mean sir," he whispered.

Anton exhaled a big breath and thought of his reply. "Tatiana's father despised me until the day he died. He believed me to be a smart ass with a lousy sense of humor. It didn't matter that my education could assure a good life for his daughter. To this man, I was not one of the boys. I wasn't a big drinker, and I didn't spew profanity like a prison guard. To him, I was boring and no one he wished to spend time with. He didn't show up to our wedding. He refused to be part of it or shell out for anything. I paid for the festivities with the small salary I was earning at the time. So right away there was a dark cloud over our ceremony but we didn't let it ruin our day… not a bit. We had a great time, honored her father in a short speech and sort of forgot about him for the rest of the evening. Nothing beautiful or satisfying can ever play out Yuri without great effort or great sacrifice. Except lovemaking… that's the sole exception but you'll never know about that."

"Yes sir," Yuri replied grinning.

"Why are you grinning? Seriously, touch my daughter and I'll kill you."

The two men continued their stroll home in a pleasant and somewhat jovial mood. The day's events had not escaped them but the evening ahead would be one of happiness and celebration. An army jeep drove by them. The soldiers inside did not wave or salute. Their faces were blank and forgettable.

"Thank-you," Yuri said.

"You're welcome my new *son*," Anton replied, emphasizing the word son. "Why are you still grinning?"

Present Day, April 23rd

Boris sat down on a leather burgundy lounger he called his and only his. "This chair has a heat massager function. It is almost better than sex. Sometimes I spend an hour at a time letting my rolls of fat shake in total bliss."

I looked at him with one eye closed and one eyebrow raised. "That's probably something you should keep to yourself and any of your female companions who needs a bit more than you can offer."

The large man smiled briefly before asking a very direct question. "My second cousin, she's not your girlfriend is she?"

I dropped my eyes and deeply sighed. "She used to be, I wish she still was."

He nodded several times probably pleased with his astuteness. He rubbed his thick eyebrow. "Ah, don't worry; she is very much in love with you. Give her time."

"I've given her ample time Boris; Lena is a complete enigma to me. I don't know what to do, what to say… it is an impossible relationship."

"It's a relationship that you will wait for. Lena is a difficult girl. Even as a child she was stubborn and defiant. You should stop being a pussy."

I raised my right arm in disbelief at both his comment and his knowledge of English slang. "I'm not being a pussy, I'm being a realist. Lena spurns me for no reason."

"And what makes you believe there is no reason? Why do you think only of yourself and not my cousin?"

"That's totally unfair; I do nothing but think of Lena. I can't be with any other woman because I only think of your cousin. What is it that I am not being told Boris? You seem to know much more than me."

"It's not my place to speak for Lena. When she is ready she will reveal what needs to be said."

"Are all Ukrainian women like this?"

"Why single out Ukrainian? Women are women, children are children and men are pigs. I was taught this at an early age and have yet to see any proof otherwise. I am a happy, singing, dancing pig and as long as women expect no more from me, I am free." Boris paused and rubbed his nose hard as if it was itching inside and out. "I know little of any other women other than what I see on the Internet. I'm not allowed to leave my country Aaron. If I could I would move to China and date twenty women at a time."

I disregarded his remark as it sounded strangely out of context. "Do you have a criminal record?"

"Not that I know but I'm listed as someone with mafia connections. It's true, I know many men in my businesses that are not...*reputable* but I am not a member of their group. It is a crime of association. I have inventory that did not arrive at my door in bubble wrap from the manufacturer. How else could I survive in this country without the black market? Take a look outside my window Aaron, there is always police nearby… watching me. They are watching you too… crime of association."

This piece of news caught me off guard and angered me. I am sure that Boris saw my facial expression and immediately recognized the near popping blood vessel in my forehead.

"That's just wonderful. I am a foreigner being watched by police in a country that shoots stray dogs in broad daylight... just fucking lovely. Thanks for the heads up though... any idea where the Canadian Embassy is?"

Boris glared at me with a face that could only be described as disenchanted. "They won't bother you, take a deep breath and relax. They no longer bother me either. They will sit in their car all day long but they won't dare approach me."

"Well that explains my suspicion today. Lena said there was no one following us but I sure as hell know there was. She's been checking behind her since I arrived."

"What are you talking about? There's no one following you. Why would they, you are just being neurotic. They stay parked and watch, nothing more."

"If you say so but I know what I saw. So what's the point then? Why won't they approach you?"

"Aaron, it's complex for you to grasp that your country and my country are not living in the same decade. We're still recovering from years of communism and have not yet figured out glasnost. We tell ourselves we are a democratic country but it is impossible to go from one political ideal to another without a period of quiet chaos. Kiev is a large city as is Odessa but do not mistake these cities for what really exists in my country. We have many, many villages and we are an agrarian society. Unemployment is high and alcoholism is rampant. To add, Ukraine is many years away from being totally free of Russia and because of this and a weak economy I compare us to Chicago in the nineteen-thirties."

"You mean like Al Capone and the rest of his cronies?"

"Yes, I had forgotten his name… like him. The only difference is that we have more alcohol than we need."

"Boris, you just told me that you are not part of the Mafia."

"I'm not but I survive because of them. I will explain so don't judge me quickly." The big man adjusted his body on his leather recliner before continuing. "Two years ago I was returning to my flat from a night of drinking. I had two gorgeous young ladies with me and I was a bit drunk and probably making too much noise. When we arrived at my home, two officers stopped us at the front door. They told the girls to leave and threatened to arrest them. Of course they left immediately, and I found myself alone with these two… cops… you call them cops. One of them grabbed me by my collar and pushed me towards an alley next to the bakery." Boris pointed to a window behind me. "You can see the bakery from that window. The other struck me with his fist in the back of the head and I fell to the ground. I saw their ratty torn shoes and pondered how they could even walk in them. Then they began to beat me with wood sticks... how do you call them… batons. This went on for twenty minutes. They hit me so hard and with so much energy that they grew tired. I couldn't move and could barely see because my eyes had puffed up. I swallowed three teeth and three more fell to the pavement. Mrs. Petreshko, the lady who owns the Bakery found me the following morning and had her son drive me to the hospital. The same hospital my cousin Tanya is lying in."

"Why did they do this to you?"

"Many reasons my friend but mostly for bribes. Police in this country make shit for money and when they see a guy like me making twenty times their salary - Christ - fifty times more… it pisses them off. They want their share so they insisted I pay them money to ensure my safety. I already, kind of, pay for protection to the Mafia. If you own a shop, you pay protection so why was I going to pay more. I told them many times to fuck off, but this was not an appropriate response. They decided to teach me a lesson but in the end it was they who got taught."

"Go on," I said curiously.

"You look at me now and you can see I have fully recovered. I am more handsome than I was before their attack. The *cops* did not expect this. To them, I was an example to others who refused them. It took a full month and my shop was closed but I got out of the hospital bed and returned to my own bed and my shop. Five days later, outside my home, the same two cops came rushing towards me but this time – before they could get near me – bullets pierced their bodies. My mafia connections had been waiting all week on the roof. I didn't even know they were there, it was a total surprise. The cops were dead, but the shooters were not finished with them. Aaron, this was during the day so anyone and everyone on the street could see what was happening. These Mafioso ran down from the roof to the street and dragged the dead cops to the center of the road. They then got in their cars and drove over the heads of the dead men several times. It was grotesque and I have nightmares about this. It took a sanitation crew ten hours to clean the mess and much of the time they were puking so they had to clean that too. That is my story. The cops are outside my door Aaron but they never approach me. They won't harm you."

"Does Lena know this?" I asked.

Boris sighed and lit another cigarette. "Lena knows nothing. Why would I tell her and make her worry for no reason. It is a fact of life here, she knows this much. The black market is

108

alive and prospering. It feeds and clothes us because we cannot do it ourselves. Kiev is a bustling city but often I can't tell where everyone is rushing to. We live on the dark side of life and pretend to make it sunny. Can you imagine this?"

"I can't conceive living like that so my answer is no."

"Exactly, you wouldn't know. You live in a country with too much; it's at your fingertips all day long. Blackberry, IPods, Victoria Secret and Lady Gaga; it is a consumer anarchy. We pretend to have much but it is all generic...I believe you call it cheap knock-offs. Chinese merchants sell to Russians and Russians sell to us. Even our cheap goods are more expensive. But there is always a reason to wake up in the morning. Our women are hot and if you are rich like me, it does not matter if you are ugly. I buy them good clothes and dinner, which is more than the police who watch me can do.

"Be careful, Evgeni tells me there is a lot of HIV in Ukraine because your immune systems are weak."

Boris rolled his eyes. "Sometimes I think Evgeni's hair is wrapped too tight. He blames everything on Chernobyl."

"Yah, that's basically what he was saying," I replied.

"Man, we're the Bangkok of Europe. Chernobyl has nothing to do with HIV or AIDS in this country. Prostitution and dirty syringes is more of a staple than potatoes. Odessa is one big whorehouse for mongers across the world. It's not our immune systems...it's our hopeless economy."

I had no clue about Ukraine's economy and every conversation was an education. Boris changed the subject abruptly.

"Tell me Aaron, what does Lena do in your city?"

That was a quick change of subject, I thought.

"If you mean what she does for work, she is a programmer and she is well paid too. Her apartment is beautiful. Not as big as this but very comfortable for a single woman."

"How does she spend her earnings? Does she own lots of clothing or other meaningless goods?"

I shrugged not understanding the purpose of his questions. "We worked on our budgets together. She spends money on clothes for sure but nothing outrageous. Like most of us, she saves money for a house and for retirement."

"This is interesting to me. In my city Aaron, most of the single women are not well paid and are often lucky to find work. When they receive their pay they spend small amounts on food and large amounts on clothing. You may have noticed this when walking our streets. We have so many average women who look gorgeous with thin bodies and expensive clothing. They do not think of their future because they have no future. It is and always has been a day-to-day existence for them. This will not change."

Interesting description but nonetheless confusing. I was learning rapidly that Ukrainians talked in riddles unless they were drinking. I wondered if bewildering foreigners was in their genes.

"Why are you telling me this Boris?"

"It is our nature to live frivolously; we are born with this mentality understanding that what is here today will be gone tomorrow. It is not a philosophy that disappears in a different environment. Lena saves her money and prepares for her future, which is a contradiction to us. She does this Aaron because she already has what she is looking for… she has you."

"And you know this for certain?"

"Lena and her mother lived in my family home off and on for ten years. When they were not in Moscow, they were with us. I know my cousin Aaron and we have kept in touch all these years. If she has not mentioned me I can tell you she did so to hide her past from you."

"Well there you go then. To me that is pure inconsistency. I'm sorry Boris but all this is tricky for me to grasp. Like every man on the face of this planet, I don't pretend to know anything about women. Lena has never mentioned you yet she lived in your home. It makes no sense to me. Why did she stay at your home?"

"After Chernobyl, they had nowhere to live, and we lived in downtown Kiev."

"What?" I replied with my mouth wide open. "Lena lived in Chernobyl?"

Boris coughed loudly after swallowing his own breath too quickly. "You have to be joking. Yes, we were all there the day of the explosion. Tania was to be married… how could you not know this?"

I huffed loudly. "You tell me man. I have known her for several years now and she never once mentioned Chernobyl until a few weeks ago. You would think this was a conversation requirement… no?"

"I told you before, she has her reasons and I personally don't know them. When we speak, we speak of her mother. She has mentioned you on many occasions but as always she was quite secretive."

"Ok well let's talk about her mother whom I have never met. I'm told she lives in Calgary."

"Yes some city in Canada with cowboys and oil; this is all I know about it. Lena is a fighter just like her mother was." Boris got out of the recliner and walked a few feet to an oak living room table to get another cigarette. He lit it and returned to the recliner. "Her mother's story is legendary. It was front page news in Kiev for a week and I someone wrote a song about her."

"Do you wanna share it with me? I want to learn more about the woman I am in love with and if learning about her mother helps me understand Lena, then tell me. Tell me as much as you can."

Boris took a long drag of his cigarette and then exhaled a cloud of smoke. It circled around his face impeding my desire to see his eyes when he spoke.

"Your future wife will be mad at me but she is not here for another two hours. I will tell you this story Aaron but only because it will better explain the woman that Lena has become. There is deep pain involved my friend, a pain that has never disappeared and never will."

"I need to know," I said adamantly.

"Very well," he nodded. "It begins on the afternoon of April 27th. I remember the mayor and an army of buses entering Pripyat like floats in a parade. Many police and army personnel were yelling at us to gather our belongings and get in the buses. They said that everyone must evacuate. This was a day after the same police claimed all was fine and we were not to worry. The story evidently changed, which was not uncommon in the Soviet Union. There were many citizens trying to board the buses with cats and dogs but all pets were forbidden. The cries from the owners for these animals were strange to me yet to this day I feel goose bumps throughout my body just thinking of it. It was haunting. The police would grab the animals from people's arms and throw them to the street and even kick them if they tried to return to their masters. I was six-years old at the time and I asked my mama why the pets were not allowed on the buses. She said that they were infected and that they were now dangerous. I didn't understand at all. I remember driving away and watching dogs running after the bus, barking loudly and trying to keep pace. The owners could not bear to look out their windows. I imagine the guilt was overwhelming. There is a popular legend that one dog found its owners in Kiev. It is, of course, not true.

We waited outside one of the buses paying little attention to the men ordering us to embark. Mila had not returned from the apartment and Tania was inconsolable. She had been crying for thirty minutes, wanting desperately to see Yuri before she left. It was not to be, and she left for Moscow with a neighbour once we arrived in Kiev."

Boris stopped speaking and stood suddenly. His head was hung low as he walked to the refrigerator, threw his cigarette into the kitchen sink and then brought back two beers. He sniffed a couple of times and rubbed a finger under his nose before handing me one of the cold bottles.

"I need one," he said clearing his throat before dropping into his favorite chair. "Lena was still an infant, sleeping in her grandmother's arms as if all was well. Looking at my father and my uncle I could tell that something was very wrong. Uncle Anton was almost ash in colour and when my mama whispered in my ear that Roman was missing, I knew he had snuck away to go fishing. He had asked me the evening before not to say anything and I promised I would not. I thought for sure he would change his mind.

113

I wish I had broken that promise."

23 Minutes Past 1 A.M.

Sunday April 27th 1986 – The Village

They were sent on buses to cities down south
And waited for news via word of mouth
Strangers in their own land, from Kiev to Dnieper
Locals kept their distance, called them lepers
They shouted, go back home…
To your filthy town

23 minutes past 1 A.M.

Mila had stayed overnight with Tania hoping to console her but it was difficult with a full house. Uncle Georgie and Aunt Vera were sleeping in their parent's room and their son Bruno was snoring on the living room couch.

It was still very early when Roman snuck out of the apartment with his fishing rod in hand. If he timed this perfectly he would be back by ten a.m. latest. The bike ride to Kopachi was usually no more than twenty minutes but because he had to take the back roads to avoid the soldiers, he estimated the ride would be extended by another ten minutes.

There was a buzz of activity on the main roads heading the opposite direction towards the reactor. Roman counted five army trucks filled with soldiers and another ten or more buses packed with men. He turned right at the café that Tania had visited yesterday and then made a left at the hospital. This would lead him to a back road used primarily by villagers shopping or selling their goods to Pripyat merchants. The villagers often carried their produce on horse-drawn carts, which Roman found old-fashioned

116

but he loved to see the horses. The only drawback was the horseshit he was now trying very hard to avoid and there was plenty of it.

After thirty minutes of pedaling as fast as he could, the twelve-year old had worked up a good sweat but when he spotted the creek he had fished in dozens of times before, Roman felt a rush of excitement. He leapt off his still moving bicycle and ran down the small hill to lean against a large boulder while he quickly pinned a worm to a hook. What he saw next was extremely odd but made his hands shake with anticipation. He would probably catch ten fish in the next hour and get home before anyone wakes up. The fish were poking their mouths out of the water as if trying to catch their breath. There were hundreds of them in this small area but they were not swimming in circles like they normally did. This morning they were all swimming south against the tide, away from Pripyat. He cast his line into the water and within seconds had his first bite. He reeled in the flopping fish and dropped it into his leather sack.

This was going to be too easy. Mama will be happy to see so many dinners in one sack.

By nine a.m. his satchel was full and he could carry no more. His legs would get quite the workout from such a heavy load but he did not care. The expression on his mother's face would be worth the couple of days of dull pain. Roman climbed on his bike and started pedaling but the bike was wobbling. He got off and let loose a large angry moan when he saw the back tire was punctured.

"There's always something," he muttered. Nothing was ever easy.

****

Earlier that day, notices were posted everywhere in Pripyat and the radio blasted the same message every fifteen minutes.

"Attention residents of Pripyat! The City Council informs that due to the accident at the Chernobyl Power Station in the city of Pripyat, the radioactive conditions in the vicinity are deteriorating. The Communist Party, its officials and the armed forces are taking necessary steps to combat this. Nevertheless, with the view to keep people as safe and healthy as possible, the children being top priority, we need to temporarily evacuate citizens to the nearest towns of Kiev Oblast. For these reasons, starting from April 27, 1986 2 pm each apartment block will be able to have a bus at its disposal, supervised by the police and the city officials. It is highly advisable to take your documents, some vital personal belongings and a certain amount of food, just in case, with you. The senior executives of the public and industrial facilities of the city have decided on the list of employees needed to stay in Pripyat to maintain these facilities in a good working order. All the houses will be guarded by the police during the evacuation period. Comrades, leaving your residences temporarily please make sure you have turned off the lights, electrical equipment and water and shut the windows. Please keep calm and orderly in the process of this short-term evacuation."

Anton and Tatiana Kharmalov waited for Mila outside their apartment building. Half an hour earlier, Tania and Edith boarded a bus headed directly to Kiev. Another bus would take them to Moscow proper by tomorrow evening.

Tatiana held her grandchild over her shoulder, rubbing her back every ten seconds.

Mila returned alone. "He's nowhere in the city, meaning he went fishing. I'm betting he's in Kopachi."

Anton exhaled loudly. "Ok, I'll stay here and catch a ride to the village."

"No," Mila exclaimed. "Mama needs you with her and I know where the little brat hangs out. I'm going to kick his sorry ass to Kiev. Mama, take care of Lena, her milk is in the red bag."

"I know baby," Tatiana replied. "Be careful, there are a lot of soldiers around."

Mila grimaced. "And you're talking to…? Really mama?"

Anton hugged his daughter for longer than usual. "I love you baby. Don't kick him too hard."

"But hard enough?" Mila grinned.

Anton smiled back. "But hard enough…"

"Don't worry papa, I'll probably meet him half-way there."

The parents and baby embarked the crowded bus and waved to Mila as they pulled away. She turned to leave and noticed Simon about to board a bus with Yulia. Her suspicions had been correct all along. Her husband saw her in the distance and stared back in fear of what might happen. Mila raised her middle finger and walked away. Roman was far more important.

****

Roman walked his wobbly bike with his fishing rod strung over his shoulder. Sweat beaded on his upper lip and he stopped to wipe it off. Up ahead he noticed an old woman walking towards him. He stood still preferring she approach him. Mila had warned him to be careful with whom he spoke as they might alert the soldiers. The woman was now in front of him.

"Does your bicycle have a flat tire?" she asked. A solitary gray hair hung motionless from a large mole on her chin.

"Yes, some fool broke a bottle by the pond and didn't clean it up."

The older woman looked the boy over, assessing whether he was a threat to her. He had kind eyes, much like her eldest son.

"Come with me then, I have glue and a foot pump...somewhere in the house. This used to happen to my boys often when they were your age."

To Roman she looked like the photographs of grandmothers from earlier decades. It was very warm outside yet she wore a sweater and the usual babushka headwear. Her face was weather worn with deep creases on her forehead and sagging cheeks. Her ankles were blotchy red and swollen. The boy wondered if they were painful and how she could walk at all.

"Thank you very much. If I don't get home before dinner my mother will scold me until the day I enlist in the army."

The woman asked Roman to call her Baba, and he complied. Up close her teeth looked like scraped corn. After only five minutes of walking they arrived at Baba's well-kept home. It was old and the gray wood was rotting in a few spots but the grounds themselves were immaculate. Every inch was used for either flowers or vegetables. Roman was astounded at the rows of sprouts popping out of the black soil. Hollyhocks were already blooming in several colors. Roman made sure not to mention that his father called this flower the menacing weed of Ukraine. Maybe if he saw Baba's garden he would change his mind.

"Come in boy," she motioned. "Have some water and cake; I just made it this morning."

Roman entered the home and was once again amazed at how proper and clean it was. Baba was obviously someone who worked the entire day and was proud of her belongings.

"It's very nice in here Baba," he complimented.

"Yes, it is. Thank-you for that. My husband and I made a good home for our sons… and for us too."

"Is he still with you?"

"My husband?" she asked while lifting a plate from her cupboard. "No, he passed away two years ago. The Russian plague finally caught up with him."

"What's the Russian plague?" Roman immediately questioned.

Baba placed a plate with a large portion of cinnamon walnut crescent in front of Roman. "Vodka," she replied somewhat curtly. "Stupid men think it is entertainment to drink massive amounts of this poison. My husband was a stupid man… a good man but stupid to the core." She left for a few seconds and returned with a glass of water. "I will find the glue and then fix your tire. You sit here and enjoy your dessert, I won't be long."

She disappeared outside and Roman gobbled down the crescent cake. He stared at the pictures on the wall in front of him. The common theme was a rifle. An older man he surmised was

121

Baba's husband was on one knee holding a rifle. Two young boys were posing with a rifle and in another photo a younger Baba was holding a dead rabbit in one hand and a rifle in the other. Roman refused to judge the woman and quickly analyzed that perhaps life in the village was much different than in the city. He was tired; the afternoon sun had been too much for him. He laid his heavy head on the clean kitchen table and within seconds fell into a deep sleep.

Hours later, he awoke shivering and still very tired. The sun had long disappeared, and he was now staring up into a star filled sky. Somehow Roman had fallen asleep in a patch of very tall grass at least fifty meters from Baba's house. He had no idea how he got there and at that very moment all he could think of was his mother's stern look and the screaming that would ensue the second he walked through the front door. He was also quite certain that everyone was worried about him and this filled his heart with guilt.

"Do not rise too quickly or you will stumble from dizziness," a gravelly voice said.

Roman turned quickly causing his head to spin. He watched as a man in his late twenties inched closer to him.

"My mother brought you here when the soldiers arrived." The man knelt down beside Roman and handed him a cup of water.

"What soldiers?" Roman asked before taking a sip from the cup.

His legs felt numb, and he rubbed them hoping for increased circulation. His shaking caused water to spill onto his legs.

The stranger watched Roman with fascination. The young boy's blonde hair was well groomed and his fingernails were clean.

"They loaded villagers on a bus to take them away. There was a lot of shouting and those that said no were forced onto the bus at gunpoint."

Roman was not sure if the man was telling the truth. It seemed like a very odd story and the man was very introverted, almost refusing to look the boy in the eyes. He slapped and then wiggled his legs to no avail. They felt like tree trunks.

"This makes no sense, where is Baba?"

"She would not go. We heard a neighbour scream that men were taking her away so my mother dragged you to this field and then returned to greet the soldiers with her rifle fully loaded. Not long after, a large white bus parked outside the house. It was near full with people I have never seen before. They all appeared frightened to me... or confused as if their lives had been torn away from them. I heard someone say *run away* but the soldiers also had guns. I stood still, bolted to the ground below me. Dogs were barking loud in the distance but none dared to rescue us. My mother cursed and threatened the soldiers but these men were very insistent. When a soldier grabbed her by the arm my mother panicked and she shot the bastard in the leg. Within seconds another soldier retaliated with his own firearm. People on the bus were screaming." The man paused before speaking again. "Baba is lying in her dried blood outside the front door."

123

The young boy wiped his nose and then tried to stand but his legs gave in. Baba's son offered his hand and the twelve-year old took it. The hand had three fingers missing, and this did not go unnoticed by a now tremulous Roman.

"She gave you a root called Valerian. She grows it next to the tomatoes. In certain amounts this root will put you into a deep sleep for hours."

"What? She cooked it into the cake she gave me?"

The man nodded as if ashamed. "Yes, she did the same to me quite often. I never knew when I would be sleeping but I ate what she gave me otherwise I would starve."

"Why would she do such a thing? I never did anything to harm her, she said she would fix my bicycle tire, and I believed her. I was told she did the same for you many years ago."

"I, nor my brother, have ever owned a bicycle," the man replied shaking his head. "She would have kept you here. The soldiers you did not see and perhaps will never know, saved your life. It is a poetic reflection of our world is it not?"

Roman did not understand what the man said and quickly disregarded the remark.

"Why would Baba keep me here and why should I believe anything you say? Maybe it is you that is lying to me."

The man's eyebrows rose for a second and he exhaled a short breath. "She saw the bird... the large black bird. It came to her when she slept. Others saw the same. It is said that the red-eyed monster is a harbinger of bad days to follow. My mother believed that a sacrifice would appease the bird."

"I was to be sacrificed because of a nightmare?"

The man dropped his eyes unwilling to allow the boy to see his shame. "Come walk with me to the neighbour's home,

124

there is no one there and perhaps we can find some food to eat. I don't want a young boy to view a dead body."

He started walking west and Roman hesitated but then followed, albeit slowly as his legs still felt numb. The man waited and then continued speaking.

"Eleven years ago I came home and announced that I would be marrying the girl I was madly in love with. My mother congratulated me and asked that I stay home that evening so that she could cook a festive family meal. I agreed thinking that Baba was happy with my decision."

"It must have been a good time in your life," Roman interjected. Each step brought an increased energy and his legs tingled.

"One would believe this, yes. I remember she made chicken with roasted potatoes and milky coleslaw. I devoured the meal and followed it with dessert and some vodka with my father. My brother was much younger but I believe he snuck in a cup of vodka too. Ten maybe fifteen minutes later I had passed out from fatigue."

"She fed you the root you spoke of?"

He nodded yes. "My mother was very powerful in our village; people were terrified of her. There were always whispers that she was responsible for some deeds that were never explained to me. From a young age I noticed that the other villagers always tip-toed around me as if they feared some repercussion if I spoke ill of them."

"She seemed very sweet to me," Roman added.

"That is how she drags you to her web. When I awoke the next morning I was missing three fingers. She had snipped them off while I slept. The roots affect was so powerful I did not feel

125

any pain until I opened my eyes. She was standing next to my bed, and all she said… the response to her evil treachery upon her eldest son was that she makes all decisions in our family. I was forbidden to marry or leave the home until she determined I could. My punishment for being in love was the loss of my fingers."

Roman immediately thought of Tania and the loss she felt yesterday and wished he was sitting next to her. "I am sorry for you, this is truly unthinkable. Why did your father not stop her?"

"Because my pain was more endurable than my father's fate. Life for my father was complicated, and he chose to find love in the arms of a woman that other men in our village sought out frequently. They paid for sex… I'm not sure if that is appropriate for a young boy to hear but this is what happened. My mother became aware of this arrangement and at dinner that same evening my father was also sent into a deep slumber. Unfortunately she buried him after putting a bullet in his brain. He is entombed in the field where you were sleeping."

"Oh my God, she was horrible."

The man nodded in agreement. "What is horrible is that these acts are accepted. We are all this way. It is the despair that has soaked into our skin and veins. Do you understand the word despair?"

Roman shook his head.

"Despair is when you wake up in the morning knowing that your life will never change. It is the anguish of realizing that your life is a blank canvas of nothingness. Once despair takes over your spirit you become an easy vessel for people that wish to control you. As for my mother being horrible, she was raised to be this way. You are from the city; this is obvious to me and would

126

be to anyone else in this village. Unless you understand the uniqueness of our life you can never accept our choices. This is true for any village, city or country."

"What do you mean to say?"

"There is a large population where you live and probably a great deal of police - am I right?"

"Yes, they are everywhere."

"We are not a collective farming village therefore few Kremlin officers bother with us. It has been this way for many years. The same families have resided here for decades or centuries. When you have an environment like this then the likeliness of one family or person attaining a degree of power is more probable and my mother was this person. Superstition is more relevant, daily activity is routine and marriage becomes almost incestuous as our bloodlines have become one.
We *depend* on one person to control our lives…it is our tradition. Baba was our judge and jury."

"This does not give her the right to cut off your fingers or murder your father."

"Oh but it does. The girl I wished to marry was a second cousin and this was frowned upon. Our partners must be three generations removed. My choice would have caused uproar and this was upsetting to my mother. Love was no longer an issue and my happiness was secondary. The men visiting the village whore was an accepted activity but my father was excluded from this pleasure. He brought shame upon the *controlling family* and therefore had to be punished. The same applied to the whore.

The next morning Baba hung my father's lady friend in front of the woman's daughter. She dangled from a tree just off the gravel road for two days. The others in the village were scared of cutting her down even though birds were ripping strands of the dead woman's hair for their nests. Ravens would take turns sitting on the head. They jabbed their beaks into the mesh of hair searching for bugs. I remember my mother showing off her handiwork as if it was a war prize or a trophy. I saw the daughter staring at me wondering why her mother was taken from her. For a moment I did not think of my missing fingers as they became insignificant at the time. I wanted to hold her and tell her that in time she would understand the punishment… that she would be okay. I wanted to pick her up and run away and to never come back."

Roman did not speak as the man's voice began to trail as if he was lost in time. They arrived at the neighbor's home and walked in unannounced. As expected, no one was there. A few photos hung on one wall. The only couch had two blankets covering the torn cushions. Unwashed pots rest on the wood stove.

"Sit down," the man said. "I will cook whatever I can."

He rummaged through the cupboards and found canned soup. He opened the can with a knife he found in a utensils drawer and deposited the contents in a pot before lighting a half split log with a match. He then sat with Roman at the kitchen table.

"My name is Olav Markov. When you get home you can tell my story to your family and I hope you will be grateful that your parents were not like mine. I hope you will embrace your life and become someone the world will speak of for years to come."

Roman did not reply but certainly wished the same.

"My brother ran away when he was sixteen. He was an odd boy that rarely smiled. I don't know where he is but at night I think that if I had had the same courage, my life would be different. I guess now it is neither here nor there. I am what I am. You will sleep here this evening," Olav ordered. He glanced at Roman wondering why the boy was so tanned. Surely a blond hair-boy would turn red from the sun before browning so quickly. "I do not trust anyone in this filthy village and neither should you. Tomorrow you can walk home safely and if you wish I will accompany you to wherever you are going but only to a certain point."

For the first time since he awoke, Roman felt at ease although he wished desperately to be home with his family. "I am Roman Kharmalov and I live in Pripyat."

The man smiled and chuckled. "I have heard a story of two beautiful sisters with this name. Apparently they are the light of God's eyes... are you related?"

"You're joking... that's funny," Roman answered with a wide grin. "Mila and Tania are my sisters. I hear this often in my city, I could never imagine that anyone outside Pripyat would know of them. They'll find their celebrity status embarrassing."

Olav stood up and stirred the soup. The heat from the stove seeped through the filthy shack. "Perhaps one day you will introduce them to me and I can brag that I have met the two most beautiful sisters in the Soviet Union. It will be my sole defining moment."

Aside from everything else he had heard from this man, the young boy found this comment overtly depressing but nodded anyway.

"I would like that Olav. They would be happy to meet the man who kept their brother safe for one evening in the village of Kopachi."

Olav recognized that Roman was a good soul and thus would protect the boy. He would not tell his guest that he too had had nightmares of a large black bird with red eyes. He would not tell him that if any remaining villagers knew of his presence that they would most certainly try to finish what his mother could not, what superstition had foretold them to do. He too would be in danger. He had looked into the eyes of the stranger and that could only mean he was now infected. Olav thought briefly of what he would say to two beautiful women if he had the courage to even face them.

"My sole defining moment," he repeated, almost too sad to hear his own voice.

The Teacher's Assistant

At three o'clock Alex returned from his hunting trip and tracked down a sweating Yuri who was still shoveling sand into sacks. He told his friend that he and several other men had combed the woods and Roman was nowhere to be found. As far as Alex was concerned, Roman got on a separate bus and was probably in Kiev by now. Yuri was due for a break so the two men walked to a water cabin that had been setup hours earlier. Men were given a choice of water or vodka. Most took the latter, but both friends decided on water.

"How was it?" Yuri asked referring to the hunting of pets.

"Horrible... what else could it be?" Alex answered. "Dogs would run to us hoping for food or whatever and we shot them. When no one is watching, I will pray tonight for forgiveness."

Yuri wiped his eyebrows with a sleeve. His hair was soaking wet. "I hope God is listening because no one should have to live through that. We're shooting animals that were sleeping on our beds three days ago. It's a nightmare that we will never awake from."

Alex suddenly appeared distracted. "I know that guy," he said pointing towards a skinny man with black hair. "Valeri Markov... he was a teacher's assistant at the Security Academy. He's a psychopath; I am surprised that anyone would allow him here."

"If he was a psychopath he wouldn't be allowed within five feet of the academy."

"You don't know him like I do," Alex retorted. "Everything about him is weird. He stares at you like he's studying your life… it's hard to put into words. Plus, he is insanely organized and meticulous. The guy is also more of a communist than any KGB I know. Trust me when I tell you that he is not right in the head."

"We need anyone we can get at the moment," Yuri replied paying his friend little attention.

Alex was always judging people before he actually knew them and as far as Yuri was concerned, this was no different.

When Yuri's back was turned, Markov noticed his ex-student looking at him. He followed a long wink with a big grin before cocking his finger like a gun and aiming directly at Alex.

****

At five P.M. that evening, Valeri Markov and his accomplice, Stani Amatov, climbed the stairs to the top floor of the Ogneva street apartment complex. It was in this building and in the cottages along the river bed that the elite of Pripyat lived. On a normal day an armed security guard would be patrolling the grounds intimidating anyone who did not belong. Behind the apartment, only minutes away, motorboats of all sizes bobbed up and down in a small marina. Tied to posts forever like harbored prisoners, abandoned and left to the mercy of the seasons. Valeri would return one day to steal the engines.

"We should get back to work within the hour," Stani said with trepidation. The short man twitched nervously, certain that they would be detected by passing soldiers.

"Don't be scared Chipmunk. Fifty more buses arrived in the last hour with liquidators. Do you think they will miss us?"

"I guess not," the partner replied while rubbing the long deep scar on his left cheek. As was the norm he stared at the ground when speaking. His head bobbed back and forth whenever he spoke.

Valeri opened one of the front doors on the fourth floor and poked his head about. "Nice life they had here in Pripyat. No one locked their doors or maybe they left in a hurry."

The two walked in and immediately noticed the size of the apartment. It was easily twice the size of what the two were accustomed to and this incensed Valeri.

"Fucking Jews and rich pricks all living in luxury while we struggle in poverty hoping we have enough food on our plate at dinner time."

Stani picked up an ivory statuette of David and showed it to Valeri. "This is worth a few rubles. I'll get something to wrap it in."

He walked to the bathroom and picked a small dark brown towel off a shiny copper railing. It was plush, and he rubbed it on his cheek while staring into the huge mirror with the golden frame. The white marble floor tiles both impressed and angered him. These people lived in a luxury he would never know. The wallpaper in the main hallway was less impressive.

They may be rich but their design skills are worthless.

"In Moscow, these people would be burned on the stake," Valeri mumbled. He whipped out his pocket knife and sliced through two paintings on opposite walls. "This is not the communist life." He knocked over a vase before telling Stani to move onto the next apartment.

The two thieves went through every apartment on the floor before arriving at 414 at the end of the hall. Their two large sacks were getting heavy with the day's haul. Stani was anxious to get back to the Reactor but his partner had no intention of returning. Valeri opened the door, and it creaked with each inch. When he looked into the apartment he saw a woman lying on the floor with her head resting upon a heavyset man who was obviously deceased. This sight was secondary to the tall man as he noticed a fireplace in the apartment and to Valeri this was a most awesome appendage to an apartment. He made a mental note of its size and encasement. Someday he would own a replica.

The woman lifted her head suddenly. "Do you not knock before you enter someone's home?"

"You should not be here madam," Stani said politely, not daring to look at her. He stared at the floor, concealing his damaged face.

Valeri grabbed his partners shoulder and pulled him back with more force than intended. Stani came close to falling but grabbed onto a coat hook that protruded from the beige wall. Valeri rushed towards the grieving woman and stood above her like an angry parent.

"Why should I knock? I am a Soviet citizen and what you have is also mine."

The brunette realized she may be in danger and changed her attitude. "My husband spent the day yesterday on the roof. It was a warm day, and he thought he would get an early tan."

Valeri found her oddly attractive and was paying far too much attention to the gap between the woman's black dress and thighs.

"That was pretty stupid then, wasn't it? Even the privileged have moments of idiocy. I imagine the boils on his face are the remnants of radioactivity."

It was a cruel remark, but the woman nodded yes. Valeri knelt down on one knee while Stani examined the other rooms.

"Did his heart give up? He looks like a very fat man - probably had a large appetite."

The woman looked way from the dark-haired intruder and covered her mouth. He had gypsy skin and his breath was unpleasant. "Yes," she answered softly.

"The government will not consider him a Chernobyl statistic. They will call this a fat man dying from heart failure."

"Why are you in my home?" she asked.

Mascara and tears ran down her cheek and hung on her pointy jaw refusing to make the final jump. The skinny man was disturbing her, and she was too exhausted to fight.

Stani walked back into the main room holding a Menorah. "Hey Valeri, check it out. She's a Jew."

Valeri glanced at the woman and chuckled. He clapped his hands slowly, applauding his partner's discovery.

"How about that? Pripyat is the perfect place to hide."

"You are not soldiers, leave my home," the woman demanded hoping her influence would deter them. "Leave now or I will summon the Mayor."

She tried to stand but Valeri held her down. He straddled her with one knee on each of her arms. He wrapped his right hand around her neck and stuck his thumb in between her lips. She swiveled her head from one side to the other trying to break free. When she tried to scream, Stani tied a handkerchief around her mouth causing her to gag uncontrollably. Valeri removed a knife from inside his pant leg, above his socks. He slid the blade across her face gently before choosing to slit her left wrist in one quick unexpected slash. Stani likened the fresh gush of blood to a fountain in the middle of a park. The middle-aged woman shook violently until the assistant grabbed both her ankles. Valeri unbuttoned her top being careful not to allow the fabric to touch any of the blood that was spilling onto the wood floor. Her breasts were large and sagging. Valeri had never seen such large nipples on a woman and was uncertain if they were attractive or not. He lifted her skirt and stuck his hand inside her white panties. The woman tried once again to scream but her cries for help were nothing more than muffled wisps of air. Valeri waved Stani away and took off his pants. He then lifted the woman's legs in his arms and placed his limp penis inside of her.

"When you greet your Jew husband on the other side, make sure you tell him that you died with a Gentiles cock inside of you."

He thrust until she closed her eyes one last time. Blood made a path down towards his boot, which he consciously lifted. He dropped her body and pulled up his pants. "Does she have a pulse?"

Stani checked and answered no.

"Fix her up and make sure it looks like a suicide," Valeri demanded.

Markov wiped his shirt with the back of his hand and checked for spatter stains. No need to wash. He wandered around the apartment and buried within the woman's clothes drawer, underneath an array of laced panties, he found a hand carved jewelry box filled with pearls, bracelets and diamond rings. His face lit up with an excited sense of accomplishment. The tall man was ecstatic with the bounty and said just that to his partner. Back in the main room he noticed an oversized painting of a forest on the wall above a black leather couch. He slowly carved a large X from each corner and then scraped the canvas ensuring no one would consider repairing it. *Piece of shit*, he muttered.

Stani was fondling the dead woman's breasts, which strangely incensed Valeri. He said nothing, allowing his partner to further denigrate the Jew corpse. Her shirt now buttoned, Stani stood and smiled briefly before lowering his head to avoid eye contact with his partner. The two men took turns wiping the doorknob clean before exiting the apartment.

While descending the darkened apartment stairwell, Valeri mentioned that they needed to find a safe haven for their new found stash. Stani's head bobbed fiercely and argued they should return to the Reactor but could not reason with the more dominant Valeri.

"We will take the jeep into one of the surrounding villages. The buses have all gone by now and the liquidators are not scheduled to sweep the villages until next week."

"How do you know this?" Stani asked.

"You should pay attention Chipmunk. Read the bulletin board outside the Reactor. Everything has a time allotted to it. Business as usual, Moscow is treating this like a normal work day. To that I say what we have always said. *They pretend to pay us so we pretend to work.*"

Stani chuckled nervously. "Do you have a preference to what village you wish to drive to?"

"Kopachi. It was the first to be evacuated so there will be many empty homes."

At the bottom of the stairs Stani opened the exit door and the bright light made him squint. The jeep was covered with the same grayish white powder that all the streets were now blanketed with. He called the powder nuclear snow.

"So I guess then that we are heading to Kopachi. I hope you know what you're doing."

"Not to worry Chipmunk, you may witness a reunion of sorts."

****

"It's getting dark Valeri; we should turn into any of these homes."

Stani was tethering on impatient but had no input on any decision.

"Drive slowly and be silent. I don't want any stragglers to notice us. This is not Pripyat my friend. These people will poke out your eyes for soup and then feed it to you."

Stani did as he was told and a few minutes later Valeri ordered him to come to a full stop. To his right, Valeri saw a girl sitting outside in a chair holding what resembled a child but may have been a simple toy. Through the open door of the girl's small home, oil lamps illuminated her aloneness.

He knew this girl.

The sun had almost completely disappeared. Tree branches waved in the soft wind as if welcoming a long lost son home. A solitary owl hooted a warning. Crickets sang in no certain harmony and bushes moved for no reason. The village symphony was nothing new to him.

"I think we have found the perfect hideaway," Valeri said with a sinister grin.

April 28th1986

Yuri slept in the tents just outside the Pripyat city line. In the past twenty-four hours, five hundred tents were installed to accommodate the influx of men arriving from Kiev and Moscow. They were men of all ages who were told little other than they would help stave off a disaster. A camaraderie quickly developed once they realized the danger that each of them was now part of. On Monday morning at eight a.m., Yuri was on the Pripyat beach shoveling sand into potato sacks that would soon be dropped onto the reactor fire thus finally putting an end to the murderous emissions. It was already warm, but he insisted on wearing a long sleeve shirt with a surgical mask and cap. If he could find earmuffs he would wear them too. Mr. Kharmalov was all too clear with his insistence that Yuri protect his skin.

"Yuri," Alex called from street level. He walked down the tiny hill towards his friend.

"Hey buddy," Yuri said while wiping his forehead. Alex was browning too quickly, and it concerned the tall engineer. "Grab a shovel."

"No can do," the security guard replied. "I'm off to Kopachi."

"Kopachi? What the hell for?"

Alex shook his head. "You're not going to believe this. Last night, some idiot filled three buses full of stray pets and drove them to the Kopachi forests. He figured they would have a better chance of surviving. I guess he didn't know that Kopachi is a haven for wolves."

Yuri removed his gloves and wiped his eyes. "It's a nice thought but very stupid. The radioactivity on the animal fur would be more intense than what we are breathing. All he did was shift the problem somewhere else. So then, you're off on another hunting trip?"

"I'm not proud of it but yes. If we are ever to come back here, the animals have to be removed."

Yuri huffed. "That's my buddy Alex in a nutshell... always the optimist."

Alex shrugged. "I have to be known for something. Have you heard from Tania?"

"I talked to her father. They wouldn't let Edith on the plane to Moscow so they had to take a bus from Kiev. They won't arrive until Wednesday morning. Mr. Kharmalov told me that the plane was too full with patients and that the flight over would be too hazardous or unhealthy for the two women especially Edith whom they suspect is pregnant."

"That's just fucking wonderful," Alex muttered sarcastically. "Pregnant and her husband is probably about to become a footnote. And Mila; has anyone heard from her?"

Yuri put his gloves back on. "Nothing yet but if you're heading out there can you keep an eye out for the two of them? I asked permission to go, but I was given a flat out no."

"Of course I will. In fact, I'll patrol the entire village and ask a few of the guys to help me out."

Yuri said thank-you with a quick nod. "Hey, don't let me see you without a mask again. I'm not kidding; I'll knock out your teeth."

Alex smiled and headed back up the tiny hill to street level. "Yes mama. I finally got my real mother on a bus and now I have to contend with a new one. I just can't win."

Yuri shoveled sand into a sack and then tied it shut. He had thought of no one but Tania for two days but now felt a tinge of heartache for Mila and Roman. A feeling of self-pity was replaced by an emotion he was unfamiliar with: Hopelessness.

****

Olav was still sleeping when Roman snuck out of the tiny house. He closed the door quietly and sprinted towards the gravel road that he prayed would lead him to the outskirts of Pripyat. He knew he was lost but if he could just see the river then he could follow it. The boy was in panic mode thinking of the trouble he would be in. There was no doubt that he would be grounded for the entire summer and fishing would be out of the question. At this point, he didn't care. The warmth of his parents embrace was a safety net he would never again untangle.

He stayed off the main road and listened for the familiar flow of the Pripyat River. A gunshot caused his body to seize in fear and he found himself breathing heavily while crawling on the forest floor. His striped shirt gathered wet dirt as he inched towards the morning's intruders.

They were dressed exactly like the alien beings from Alien Conquest. It was true... the creatures from another planet had

142

landed and were shooting human beings. They would only keep those that would be good slaves, he was sure of this. Roman picked up a rock and thought of launching it at one of the creatures but then realized he was defenseless against so many.

Several gunshots rang through the air and the tall field grass rustled from animals darting in several directions. Roman took off in a hurry and when doing so his sudden movement attracted gunfire in his direction.

They found me.

If he had waited only ten more seconds he would have seen his future brother in-laws best friend, Alex, take off his headgear to wipe away the sweat that had accumulated on his entire face.

He backtracked to Olav's house, darting through the heavy foliage being careful not to run too close to the main gravel road. When he got within one minute of the home, he saw a plume of smoke over the shorter trees and heard angry yelling. Roman stopped, found a good hiding spot and peeked through a large bush towards Olav's home.

A dozen plus adults and teenagers were leading Olav towards his mother's body. A rope was lassoed around his neck and his hands were tied in front of him. His home was burning yet none of the mob cared about the flying pieces of fiery ash that floated above their heads. A teenage girl picked up a jagged rock and flung it at Olav's face striking him on the nose. He did not flinch. An older gentleman grabbed Olav's shoulder and forced him to kneel. The son of the onetime leader of Kopachi was now staring directly at Roman. He smiled realizing that the boy had come back for him. The longstanding superstition had come to fruition. He had looked into Roman's eyes and was about to pay

143

for his transgression. His eyes closed, accepting his fate. A bullet pierced his skull, and he slumped over dead.

Roman fell backwards and tried to shout but could not. Only a dry heave exited his mouth. His legs were mush as he grabbed onto a tree for help. He could not tear his eyes away from Olav's dead body. I just had dinner with him, he thought. These people are insane. I hope the aliens find them and burn all their homes. I hope they become slaves until their final breaths.

He had no inkling on where to dash away at this point but after five minutes he found the courage to exit the forest and cross the main street, a good distance from where the aliens were shooting. Roman paused for a minute under a small pine tree speckled with a grayish ash. Some of the pines were turning red, which he found bizarre. His lungs burned from running so fast for so long. There was no way the aliens would catch him this deep in the forest. He remembered an episode on television that said aliens needed their spacecraft because they could not walk long distances.

They are too slow for me. I am fast like the wind.

A creek flowed peacefully only a few meters away, and he bent down to cup some water in his hands and drink small amounts. The spastic coughing bout he experienced earlier had hurt his throat and running had only irritated it more. The cool water was soothing although it tasted peculiar.

He heard singing and immediately hid behind the same tree. A sparrow - only feet above him - tried to emulate the soft sound but failed miserably. The singing continued, and it dawned on the boy that no alien could sing so sweetly. Cautiously, he approached the owner of such a calming voice along the gravel path that doubled as a road. He found her sitting on a dirty white

144

kitchen chair outside her old, rundown home. There didn't appear to be anyone else there other than a girl with very short blond hair. As he neared, Roman guessed that she could not have been more than eighteen years of age, probably younger. She was holding a doll and singing to it. He accidentally stepped on a twig and the girl lifted her head. Her eyes were blue but as he would recount a few days later, they were void like deep black holes. They were alien eyes, and this initially scared the boy.

"Have you seen my baby?" She asked without questioning the boys' intrusion.

Roman had no answer and stared at the girl while pondering his escape. Her dress was a filthy mix of mud and blood stains and he speculated how it had become so sullied. She should change and look more respectable.

"He was here yesterday, but they took him away," the girl continued.

"Who took him away?" Roman questioned. "The aliens?"

The girl tilted her head not understanding the young boys' question. "Maybe, I didn't know them. They fought with my grandfather, told him he had to stay. Did you see them take my baby?"

"No," Roman said less guarded.

The girl rocked back and forth with a slow melodic motion squeezing the plastic doll under her thin forearms.

"They ripped him from my arms. I was breast-feeding like my grandmother taught me but she left. She left with the aliens. My grandfather stayed, but he's dead now. The bad men killed him. Maybe they were aliens too."

Roman stepped back not sure what to do. He looked in every direction and neither saw nor heard anyone but the soft voice of the crazy girl staring at the dry mud on and around her feet. She was now humming an old traditional song his own mother used to sing when he was much younger. He noticed the doll had no clothes and had one eye missing. A bug crawled out of the empty socket and fell off the face to the ground. Roman watched in disbelief and wondered if he had left one terrifying dream and entered another.

Is this entire village insane?

"The aliens cut my hair," she said. "My baby used to pull it and giggle. Am I ugly now?"

"No," Roman said comprehending his new situation. "You are quite lovely. My sisters are the Kharmalov sisters, the most beautiful girls in Pripyat. You would still look good next to them."

She stopped rocking and briefly smiled. "My name is Galina," the girl whispered.

"I'm Roman; it's nice to meet you Galina."

She said nothing for a few moments and Roman waited for her to acknowledge his greeting. "Something is happening, Roman. The aliens look like us but they are very angry and rushed. My grandmother went with them. She betrayed me. Maybe she is one of them."

"Yes, something terrible is happening" he answered nodding several times. "Two nights ago, I saw fire in the sky. It was stunning, like fireworks. I thought it was fireworks."

"It sounds wonderful. Maybe grandmother went to see this for herself. I wish she had brought me."

Roman was extremely tired and famished. If he could get this odd girl to feed him then he would have enough strength to return home. "I'm hungry Galina. Do you have any food to eat?"

The girl nodded once. "I have plenty of bread. I made stew but you cannot eat it. Only the bad men can eat it. You can have all the bread you wish. The milk has turned but I have vodka and water. I am not allowed to drink the vodka. Grandmother would be mad at me."

Galina stood slowly as if she was in great pain. Her doll fell to the ground, but she paid it no heed.

"Will you hurt me, Roman?"

"No," he replied surprised by the question. "Of course not."

"That is good to hear. Men hurt me often. The bad men hurt me last evening after the aliens took my baby. Can you take my hand?"

Roman sensed the girl's despondency, grabbed her elbow and then placed his hand in hers. They walked very slowly to her tiny home. Inside, the smell was nauseating and Roman held his free hand under his nose. There was very little in the home aside from a large wood table for eating and one brown rocking chair with loose paint chips hanging from each leg. A purple curtain divided the kitchen from what he suspected was a bedroom. There was a wood stove with a pot on it and above that a couple of empty cupboards. In the corner closest to the door, Roman noticed dry blood, and it curled his stomach.

"Sit at the table Roman. Please do not eat the stew; it is for the bad men. Promise me you will not eat the stew."

"I promise Galina."

She smiled and then brought a loaf of bread that was hard but still edible. She placed a dish of butter and a knife in front of the boy and he immediately began to devour the entire loaf. Galina laughed excitedly for a brief second and then stopped as

147

quickly as she began. She seemed very pleased to be feeding the boy, and this did not go unnoticed by Roman.

"Who are the bad men Galina?"

"I don't know…they came to my home and killed my grandfather. They dug his eyes out of his face with a jam spoon and let the cat play with them like little marbles. The little one took grandfather outside and shot him. He killed the cat too. One of them hurt me for many hours. I kept my eyes shut."

Roman felt dizzy with horror. The girl acted as if all this violence was natural as if it was routine. She seemed incapable of feeling pain.

"What do you mean?"

"He forced his penis into me," she said nonchalantly. "The village men used to do the same except the villagers gave food and money to my grandmother. It pleased her so I did as they wished. I would close my eyes and think of the meal I would eat when it was finished. They would bring chickens, beef, potatoes and milk. Sometimes, if there was both a man and a woman, we would get eggs and cheese for a week. This made grandmother very happy. She would not be satisfied if she learned the bad men did not leave provisions last night."

Roman knew exactly what she was talking about and felt a loathing inside of him. Mila once told him about a child molester and killer that was terrorizing the city of Rostov. This poor girl lived only twenty minutes from Pripyat and was experiencing the worst kind of hell. He could hardly wait to leave this village and never return.

"Why didn't your grandfather stop this?"

"He hurt me when I was much younger," she replied with an eerie smile. "Grandmother slit his penis when he slept. She

148

said that he deserved it and so did I. I understood. After that, he walked with a limp and no one spoke to him. When grandmother was away he still touched me but would give me chocolate if I stayed quiet. Men from the city brought many bars when they visited on weekends. I like chocolate."

"Come back with me Galina. My parents can help you."

She shook her head. "I have to wait for my baby. The bad men said they will return him to me but I can't tell anyone they were here or that they are coming back."

"I saw the aliens firing guns; I think they are killing everyone in the village. We should leave."

Galina stood up and brought the butter dish back to the tiny pantry it came from. "You are a nice boy. I have to wait for my baby."

"I don't think they're coming back Galina," Roman maintained.

"You can stay with me Roman. If you wish to hurt me like the other men, it's okay."

Roman placed his hand on his head in disbelief. "I will not hurt you. I wish to save you."

She spoke as if she did not hear a word the boy said. "You can stay here and be my friend. I have never had a real friend before. When you wish you just have to lift my skirt and I will understand. I will think of dinner. I deserve it."

"Galina, stop! You do not have to do this for anyone… ever! Your grandparents were horrible, horrible people. The villagers are horrible people. I just watched them kill Olav."

The young women stared at Roman with skepticism not comprehending why he would refuse to enter her. She sat down in the rocking chair facing the boy and began playing with her hair.

"Have you seen my baby? The aliens came and ripped him from my arms. They left with my grandmother. Why do you think my grandmother would leave me alone with my grandfather? He had no more chocolate. He has no more eyes either."

Roman stared back confused not knowing how to reply. She had disappeared inside of herself. Galina tilted her head as she did half an hour earlier.

"The aliens cut my hair. I had long hair past my shoulders. Do you think I'm still pretty?"

****

He should have left after the bread was finished but he felt a need to help the young woman. She was not right in the head and obviously defenseless. As she rocked in the old chair, Roman swept the floor and lit the oil lamps. He knew she was watching his every movement. The boy was hoping that she would recognize that he was no threat and that she should trust him.

"Galina, it will get colder in a few hours, do you have enough blankets? Where do you sleep?"

The girl pointed to the floor in front of her. "Sometimes in the work shack out back but it is very dirty."

Roman could not imagine anything dirtier than this very room. "Is that where you bottle jams and vegetables?"

Galina raised her eyes long enough to speak. "No, it is where they kept my bed. Grandmother sent the villagers and the

150

city men there when they visited me. She called it the work shack."

If it was the last thing he ever did, Roman would track down Galina's grandmother and have her executed. "If anyone ever tried this with my sisters I would kill them."

"The Kharmalov sisters… most beautiful girls in all of Pripyat," Galina said as if repeating something that had stuck in her brain since earlier in the day. The thin girl stood listlessly and walked towards the stove. She tossed a lit match onto the loose paper which soon ignited the wood. "Roman, the bad men will be here very soon. This stew is for them."

"Galina, we can leave now. They will never find us…" Roman stopped speaking. He heard the sound of a vehicle driving towards the home. *Shit*, he muttered.

"The bad men are here," Galina uttered with a deep sigh.

She pointed towards the purple curtain adjacent to the kitchen table. Roman had looked behind it earlier and found a simple unmade bed.

"You can hide there until they find you. I will not say a word… you must be a shadow."

The boy was now panicking. He could have left hours ago but chose to help this peculiar girl. His father had always told him about people less fortunate than them and that he should always lend a helping hand. He was only doing what his father expected of him. With nowhere else to go, he rushed first to a utensil drawer and took out a long sharp knife before running behind the curtain. He arrived without notice but only by seconds. He heard the deep voice of a man shouting, "Honey, we're home."

Roman peeked intermittingly through the curtain. The two men wore army fatigues and were not aliens. The leader of the two was average height, maybe smaller and very skinny with jet black hair. The second man was even smaller and wore glasses. He had a deep scar on his face that he consistently and unconsciously touched. It was so freakishly evident that Roman almost felt sorry for him. The skinny man called him Chipmunk. After a few minutes, the boy distinguished that the leader was named Valeri.

"Bring the stash from yesterday to the table and we will count our winnings," Valeri ordered.

Chipmunk strolled over with a green army bag and emptied the contents.

"Be careful you mongrel," Valeri yelled. "These are not your father's balls." The dark-haired man went through the loot and picked up a pearl necklace. "The Jewish bitch has contributed to our war effort. We will get a fine paycheck for this." He placed the pearls gingerly on the table and eyed Galina. "Hey girl, I did not get an erection for the Jew whore yesterday; I saved that for you. She was older but had beautiful tits Galina; much nicer than yours. Your tits are small and filled with nuclear milk."

Chipmunk laughed at his friends quip.

"How long before we get our dinner?" Markov questioned sternly.

Galina turned around almost shyly. "Not long."

She smelled the wooden spoon but would not put it in her mouth. The steam that moistened the base of her nose indicated that the dinner was almost ready. She began to calmly and quietly hum the same song she had been singing most of the afternoon. Reaching up into the cupboard above the stove, she took down two wooden bowls, which she then filled with stew. The bowls were then placed in front of the men and Galina chose to sit at the

152

table while they ate. Valeri asked for a second helping and this pleased her.

The leader took a short break from his meal and lowered his dinner spoon. "I spoke to another villager who decided to stay in his shitty home. An old man with no teeth; says he knows you very well. He told me you are known as the 'milk maid' because your hands and mouth drain men like they were teats on a cow. I defended your honour and had Chipmunk bash his head with a shovel but I will be expecting a demonstration of your skills this evening."

Galina did not reply but instead watched as the man took another spoonful of her stew.

When he was done, Valeri ordered his partner to wait outside and check for any signs of the army. Chipmunk was not pleased with this as the temperature had dropped several degrees. He walked outside holding a pack of cigarettes and muttering to himself.

"Come to bed Galina," the tall man commanded.

"No… we can do it on the table. That would be different." She looked directly towards Roman and smiled causing the boy to be paralyzed in fear of being caught.

"Cheeky girl," Valeri grinned. "I like the way you think."

Galina sat on the table and then lay down with the back of her knees resting on the soft edge. Valeri lifted her dress and winced before dropping his pants and underwear.

"Tomorrow you will wash your entire body. The smell is unpleasant, like rotting fish." He grabbed her hair and lowered her head to his penis. "Make it hard with your mouth, milk maid."

Galina took the man's penis in her mouth and did what her grandmother had taught her. Roman peeked through the curtains and could see the man's dropped scrotum hanging against the edge of the kitchen table. This man was a vile human being. Roman clutched his knife tighter.

"Okay, enough. I do not wish to finish too quickly."

He spread Galina's legs open and then entered her. The girl winced for a second and then closed her eyes. Valeri removed the girl's dress from her shoulders exposing Galina's breasts. He fondled her tiny pink nipples while speaking.

"You have been a good girl Galina. I will take care of you until I leave this hell hole. I found some iodine pills in a doctor's apartment. Stupid fool was probably frightened of being caught with them. You will take one of these every day. I do no not wish to fuck a radioactive cunt every evening, especially one that stinks."

Galina said nothing as if her body had departed into another room.

"You buried your grandfather as I asked. I am pleased that you are listening."

The girl opened her eyes and smiled. "I did not bury him."

Valeri stopped his slow thrusting. "I asked you to do this. Where's his body?"

Galina began giggling, which incensed Valeri. He yelled at her to stop but she could not. The man slapped her and the girls eyes turned from wild to raging.

"Where is the body?" he screamed one last time.

She paused for a few seconds before speaking. "Some of if it is outside next to the work shack. The rest of it is in your stomach," Galina said giggling once again.

Valeri stopped thrusting and stared at the girl in disbelief. When he raised his fist to hit her, Roman burst out from behind the curtain and jammed his knife into the man's dangling testicles, pinning them to the soft wooden edge of the kitchen table. Valeri yelped in pain and then, as if sensing a moment of freedom, Galina lunged forward and bit the man's ear, tearing off the lobe with one rabid gnash.

Roman ran out the front door and rushed towards the camouflage of the deep forest. Chipmunk was nowhere in sight. He could still hear Valeri screaming in pain as he raced through the deep foliage. When the twelve-year old recognized that he had arrived at the river bed, he exited the woods and saw the lights of activity around Reactor Four shining like a beacon. It filled his entire body with relief. There was a purple haze, an almost brilliant glow above Pripyat.

This is what happens when aliens hover, he thought.

****

Mila was cold and crying when she heard singing in the distance. It sounded like the Sirens from Greek mythology and she was drawn to it. Instead of an island of beautiful women she found a young girl with short blond hair and a torn dress sitting with her head down. She was holding a plastic doll between her knees and forearms. When the girl lifted her head to look at the intruder, Mila stepped back in shock.

The girls face had been mutilated. Someone had carved a cross on both her cheeks and forehead. The wounds were fresh

155

and Mila checked her pockets for anything that could clean the dried blood. A rush of pity and intense anger filled her body, and she wanted only to hug the poor child.

"Have you seen my baby?" she asked.

Mila glanced at the doll and tied to connect the girl's environment with her psychology schoolbooks. "Are you holding her?"

Galina squinted for a second. "This is a doll. Have you seen my baby? Aliens took her away. My grandmother went with them."

"No, I'm sorry; I haven't seen your baby."

The girl said nothing and lowered her head. "The aliens cut my hair. I had long hair, but they cut it. Am I still pretty?"

The girl is not right in the head.

"You are very beautiful, perhaps the loveliest girl I have ever met," Mila replied.

Galina smiled showing her yellowing teeth. "No... the Kharmalov sisters are the most beautiful girls in Pripyat."

"What?" Mila exclaimed. "Who told you this?"

The younger girl was oblivious to Mila's sudden anxious behavior. "My friend Roman told me this. He is a good boy. He did not want to hurt me like the bad men and the villagers."

"Where is Roman now?"

"He left last night after sticking a knife in the bad man's balls," Galina said nonchalantly. "He is such a good boy. He's my only friend."

Mila could not understand the girl's rambling and hoped that none of it was true. "Did these *bad men* hurt Roman?"

Galina shook her head several times. "No... he was like a shadow. I told him to be a like a shadow and he did as I said. He

156

hurt the bad man because the bad man was hurting me. Roman is my friend."

Although this news relieved her, Mila was suddenly heavy hearted knowing that her brother had gone through a traumatic experience. An anxious tremor rushed through her stomach.

"Do you know which way Roman went?"

The girl shrugged and then nodded several times as if once was not enough. "He went back to Pripyat to get help for me. I wish Roman had visited many years ago."

"Where is your mother or father? Is there anyone here to help you?"

"Many years ago I saw my mother hanging on the big tree around the corner. The women in the village were laughing, they seemed very happy. Grandmother went with the aliens. Grandfather is next to the work shack and in the bad men. Maybe one of the village men will bring me a chicken if I let him hurt me."

"I don't know what you are saying," Mila said entirely confused. "Come with me, we'll find Roman together."

"I have to wait for my baby. I cannot leave without my baby."

Mila wanted to help the girl but at the same time realized her priority was her brother. "I am going to search for Roman but I will be back for you," Mila said as clearly as she could.

Galina slid her hand beneath her left leg and took out a grey pouch. "The bad man said these were iodine pills and that I should take them. Please give them to Roman, he is my friend. I would like you to take them too."

Mila took the pouch graciously. It was an unselfish gesture but Mila was not certain if the girl was aware of how important

157

these pills were. For a moment she considered returning the pouch, but she thought of her brother and the notion quickly disappeared. Only the strong survive.

"Thank-you," Mila said softly.

The girl stared at Mila as if in a trance. "You're so beautiful. You're the most beautiful woman I have ever seen. Are you one of the Kharmalov sisters?"

"I'm Mila Kharmalov, I'm Roman's sister."

Galina smiled and her eyes changed suddenly from sullen to bright as if a body light was switched on. "Roman's sister… that means you are also my friend. I now have two friends."

Mila's eyes misted knowing her brother had such a profound effect on a stranger. "I would be proud to call you my friend," she said after clearing her throat.

This was surreal. It isn't really happening.

A flock of birds left several trees in tandem and dove above the women in perfect synchronicity. Dark clouds slowly pushed forward, preparing to dampen fields and spirits. Galina pushed her pinky finger into the eyeless socket of her doll and twisted. She hummed a few bars of the same song she loved to sing before lifting her newly scarred face to address Mila. In an unexpected moment of clarity that would quickly disappear, Galina uttered the words that Mila Kharmalov would never forget.

"I wish I was you."

****

It was close to midnight when Roman finally arrived at his apartment building. He sensed something was very wrong as not a single light was lit in any of the homes. Surely there had to be someone awake at this hour. He tried to open the lobby door, but it was locked. He was not aware that his building was shut down after dark. He banged on an open window of a first floor home and waited for the resident to answer. Several knocks later he was still waiting. He could wait no more. The boy was too tired and angry to be civil. Roman climbed through the window and tip-toed to the front door. He opened it ever so quietly and slipped into the hallway unnoticed. He then climbed the stairs to the eighth floor and turned the handle of his apartment door. Thank God that mama trusted our neighbours.

He immediately flipped on the lights and announced he was home. No one answered, so he crept into his room looking for Mila. His heart hurt when he saw that his best friend was not there waiting for him. After viewing his parent's room he realized he was all alone.

The aliens got them.

The events of the past two days overwhelmed him and he sat on the living room couch to cry. The tears poured out of his dehydrated body and fell on the soft creamy white pillows he often slept upon. How could his family leave him all alone? Did they fight the aliens or just give up?

It was then that he realized that he had to be strong. He had to rescue them no matter what.

Roman went to the kitchen and turned on the water tap. He drank two glasses of water before deciding to cook some potatoes and green beans. While waiting for the water to boil, he

159

flipped on the television and slumped back onto the couch. Nothing interesting was playing except the daily news...stupid Russian propaganda.

A noise outside distracted him. He peeked through the flowery curtains that his mother washed once a month. An army truck had pulled up in front of the building and two soldiers exited quickly.

Roman was running once again. He flew down seven flights of stairs to the first floor and checked for open doors that would lead to window facing the backyard. He found one almost immediately and crashed through the apartment without any worry of waking anyone. Jumping out the window, he fell softly to the soft grass below and ran as fast as he could. His belly ached, and he was tired of running but the alternative was not an option. He hated to admit it but the safest pace for him was the one place he hated more than any building in Pripyat. Roman ran directly to his school.

The two soldiers entered the Kharmalov apartment looking for the twelve-year old boy that had been reported missing.

He was gone.

Someone would have to tell the father that the boy had foiled them once again.

****

Roman sat alone in the classroom he once detested. The blackboard still had math equations from the previous week. He

160

didn't know the answer when his teacher asked him but as he stared at it this morning, the answer popped into his head. It was easy, and he wondered why he couldn't figure it out earlier. Actually, he was more than aware why. He was paying more attention to Natasha than his teacher. Sure she was stupid as were all the girls in his class but he liked her anyway. She sat next to him, which was not a good thing as far as his studies were concerned. Natasha smelled good and her face was so pretty. He pushed his desk within inches of hers. The noise of screeching steel against the hard floor echoed in the student less room. He lifted Natasha's desktop and took out her notebook. Her handwriting was neat and cute. On the inside cover she had drawn a heart with her name and Roman's. He smiled and his chest beat quicker.

I knew she liked me.

He was hungry, hungrier than he could ever remember. Roman strolled the empty halls to the Teachers' Lounge and walked in. Normally it was locked but not today. He imagined correctly that everyone left in a hurry. He had never been inside this room before and it dawned on him that he could be one of very few students that had ever crossed this threshold. There was carpeting throughout the room with two couches and three round kitchen tables. Roman went directly to the large refrigerator next to the sink. There was a bevy of different fruits, milk and a bar of cheese. He devoured the cheese on one of the couches. He lay on the sofa with his dirty shoes and chuckled thinking the teachers would be aghast in horror if they saw him. He farted and laughed out loud.

The milk was sour and he spit the tiny gulp into the sink. In one of the cupboards he found several cans of condensed milk. He located a P-38 can opener and punched a hole large enough to drink through. It was disgusting but wet his thirst. He drank the entire can and then opened another. He ate an old ham sandwich left by one of the teachers on the bottom shelf of the fridge. Not bad, he thought. If anything, it kills the taste of the milk.

They had a record player. Roman couldn't believe it but walked over to the far corner next to the back window. It was beautiful, much nicer than the one his parents had. He lifted the clear cover and stared at the LP that lay there waiting to be played. The writing was strange to him; it was not Russian. Surely, the teachers were not permitted to listen to this. Maybe it was one of those albums with a fat man singing in Italian. He hoped it was not; he hated that crap. The boy gently pushed the tiny lever that turned on the turntable. The arm moved, and the needle dropped effortlessly on the LP. The music was like nothing he had ever heard. It jumped off the black disc like a bouncing ball. He felt his head move to the beat causing him to giggle. He loved it.

Roman found a bicycle left behind by one of his classmates and rode it through the halls. He rang the bell and yelled out to everyone to come join him and dance. The door to the Teachers' Lounge was wide open and music was on as high as it could go. He drove without holding the bars and clapped his hands.

Come dance, everybody dance!

No one joined him and after a half hour he gave up. He wished Natasha was with him. He would dance with her. If Mila was here he would dance with her too but not in the same way. His heart ached. Roman could not believe how much it hurt not having Mila nearby. He missed her more than mama and papa and felt a guilty pang just thinking it.

He would return to school if he did not find anyone he knew. It was four p.m. and the boy calculated he had three hours of sunlight to investigate what was happening in his city. He rode the blue bike in between buildings being careful to dodge the military trucks that passed too frequently. After hearing how the soldiers were rounding up people and putting them on buses, he ascertained that they were working for the aliens. They shot Baba too, which in hindsight was not a bad thing.

Roman stopped at the ice cream shop and looked inside. As expected, it was empty and even worse, the door was locked. He found that silly as everyone knew that aliens couldn't eat ice cream. He suddenly felt like giving up and sat with his back against the store entrance. He no longer cared if he was caught. If his parents and all his classmates gave up so willingly then maybe it wasn't so bad. What was that word that Olav taught him? Oh yes, despair. Roman understood quite well what this meant. He was feeling it now, and it was awful.

A truck of men drove by and did not notice him or maybe they did but didn't care. Or maybe he was invisible now. Galina told him to be invisible, and that worked. Roman grimaced knowing his fantasy was impossible. Maybe everything was a fantasy, and he had been living in a dream that he could not wake from. That seemed more plausible. If it was a dream then he could do anything he pleased and control the outcome. The men that just drove by did not see him because they were only a passing billboard in his dream. The boy stood up and walked to the middle of the road. He yelled for his parents and waited. They did not appear. He lifted his arms to the sky and screamed for

Mila. He repeated her name several times. *Mila,* he shouted. *Come to me Mila!*

Only a few yards away, a shaking Mila Kharmalov stared at the brown-faced boy she loved more than life itself. Her face and clothes were filthy, spotted with radioactive dust. She called for him but her voice was overcome by emotion and only a wisp of his name exited. She exhaled quickly and called his name again. Her steps quickened as her brother turned towards her. Mila dropped to her knees in front of him and enveloped his thin body in her arms. *Stupid fish-boy,* she whispered. Roman's eyes moistened momentarily, but he did not cry. Mila was not as strong. She could not contain her emotion and cried openly. The twelve-year old held his sister not wishing to let go. His best friend was here, everything would be fine now. He could control his dream.

"I saw things Mila," he said almost too blasé. "I saw terrible things."

"I know you did," she replied while wiping tears off her cheeks.

His face was a dark brown and Mila knew that he had to be treated immediately.

Roman hung his arms on Mila's shoulders. "Is it the end of the world?"

His question was honest and Mila realized her brother had no idea what had happened at the Reactor.

"No Roman," she whispered, "Only the end of us."

The boy scrunched up his face not comprehending her reply. "I learned a new word… despair. I felt it Mila. Do you know this word?"

A wet drop of blood fell onto Mila's left hand. She looked at it in shock and searched from where it came. A slow path of blood was exiting out of Roman's ear and it frightened her.

"I know this word very well but I have never felt it when you are with me."

An army jeep drove quickly towards them and stopped within feet of the brother and sister. Two soldiers jumped out and at once asked if the boy was Roman Kharmalov. Mila answered yes and told the men who she was. The soldier said that he had been searching for two days. Neither acknowledged him.

"He needs medical attention," Mila said quietly.

Roman would not let go of his sister. "Will you stay with me Mila?" His voice trembled.

"What do you think fish-boy?" she answered, trying to calm him. "Whenever I don't, you get lost for days at a time."

They drove back to a field camp that had two doctors performing triage. On the way there Roman felt a surge of fatigue. He smiled when he recounted riding a bike through the halls of his school listening to illegal music. He babbled something in a foreign language. Mila had her arms around her brother and asked him to repeat what he had just said. His eyes were closed. The soldier in the passenger seat turned and said it sounded like a Beatles' song. Mila rolled her eyes and groaned that it was doubtful. Roman heard the man and grinned.

Yellow Submarine, he said before falling asleep.

April 30th : Hospital No. 6, Moscow

Soldiers arranged for Mila to catch a separate plane to Moscow at no cost. Roman was transported on a special plane with other radioactive victims. She was not happy with the arrangement but was thankful she would arrive the same day her brother did. She saw Yuri prior to departing Pripyat and he promised to call her parents. It never dawned on her that she would never return to the city she loved.

Mila was desperately tired and hungry. She paid one of the female custodians a few rubles to allow her to shower in the nurse's private locker room. She took her time allowing the water to wash away the filth of the last four days. Her discussions with Roman were sad; there was no other word she could use to describe what her brother envisioned. All he wanted to do was catch some stupid fish, and it cost him his innocence. And now he was here, in a hospital with hundreds of men waiting to die. It was incomprehensible to her that Roman was sick, and she was not. This is not fair, she thought.

Hospital Number Six is located on Novaya Basmanaya Street in the Basmanny District of Moscow. The beautiful architecture that lines the streets leading to the hospital is missed by those that grieve. There were soldiers staying in tents outside the front door of the hospital. This instantly worried Mila. The second that she entered the clinic she could tell that the influx of patients was taking its toll on the entire medical staff. Even the young ladies at the reception were withdrawn and overly fatigued. Mila's simple request about Chernobyl victims was met with a loud sigh and three fingers, meaning third floor.

166

It was noisy. That was the first thing the pretty woman noticed as she stepped off the elevator. Patients in hospital garb were gathered by each door chatting about the accident. They stared a bit too long as she walked by them. Even sick Russian men can be disgusting, she thought. She asked a passing nurse if she knew what room Roman was in and the woman responded 312. Mila read the door numbers as she sped towards her brother. She found it extremely odd that every second room was empty. When she walked into room 312 she was pleased to see that Tania was with Roman.

"Hi guys," Mila said in her best faked enthusiasm.

Roman looked worse than he did when she left him yesterday. Tania was holding his hand as the boy slept. Mila kissed her sister on the top of the head.

"He is in and out at the moment," Tania whispered. "The doctor will speak with us later. A nurse took Roman's white blood cell count three hours ago. They asked me if I'd consider offering my bone marrow and I answered yes."

Mila remained silent waiting for her sister to continue. Tania was very white as if she had not slept in days.

"Edith is here, a few rooms towards the end of the hall," she said, "I don't believe Yanush will survive another week. She requested a rabbi visit but none would come. He is sharing a room with twenty other sick men. The first day they got here they were in good spirits but now they are very quiet... it is an eerie hush. Yanush is the worst of of them. The day Edith and I arrived he began to vomit more and more often and this was then followed by extreme diarrhea. The nurses change him every two hours if they have the time. His bed is sealed off by a thick plastic sheet and the medical staff shove their hands through tiny holes to treat and clean him. Edith is not allowed to touch her husband and doctors have begged her to leave the hospital altogether. Of course, she has refused. He has difficulty breathing, he is always gasping for air. We are told his problem is due to damage to the mucosa of the mouth. I don't know what this means but someday I will research it. Someday when our time in the hospital is just a bad dream… I will research everything that I have seen here." Tania looked back at her sister and gave her a half smile before bowing her head gain. "David is dead. He did not survive the trip to Moscow and died on the plane."

Mila covered her mouth and paused before speaking. "He was a good person. After hearing Yuri describe what happened to him I expected to hear this. I am sorry for his family."

Tania was not sure how to react to her sister's nonchalant attitude. "Yes, he was a very good man," Tania answered solemnly. "The hair on Yanush's body has fallen out. It took three days until all of it was gone. He would barely wipe his head and the hair would stick to the side of his hand like it was a magnet. The nurses are scared Mila and I don't blame them. They are at risk and so are we just by being here. The man that was in Roman's bed died an hour before our brother arrived. He too was a firefighter. All the men in this room are firefighters. They have given me letters to give to their families in case they do not leave the hospital. The first two days when the victims were brought in, the hospital was not prepared so I helped however I could. I gave blood the first day and yesterday I helped with food trays, changing clothes and cleaning sheets. Clothes are changed twice a day. I was given rubber gloves as if that would help. I know it does not. A custodian told me that the medical staff has undergone a quick guide on how to comfort the patients. I don't want to say it is the blind leading the blind because the staff is performing an impossible job yet…"

"Go home Tania," Mila pleaded. "I have our apartment keys with me and I will stay with Roman."

Tania smiled. "He has been asking for you, he always asks for his Mila. I have to stay here, my sister. If not for Roman, I should remain for Edith. She has no one except me. I did not know this until yesterday. Her parents are gone and Yanush's parents have no means to travel to Moscow."

Mila's eyes circulated the room. There were easily fifteen beds, probably more. Most of the men were lying down, but a few were sitting upright on the side of their beds chatting quietly. Those that chatted still had plenty of hair and their skin appeared normal. The man next to Roman was sleeping. His head was patchy with hair and his breathing was erratic. Tania followed her sister's eyes.

"That is Maddy, a friend of Yanush," she whispered. "He is only twenty-two years of age. His wife was one of the few that were able to see their husband in our Pripyat hospital. His face was so puffy that she did not recognize him. He got here, and the staff gave him the proper fluids intravenously and suddenly he is fine again. When his wife got here in Moscow on Tuesday, he was full of energy. One day later, everything changed. Doctors spent two hours yesterday removing skin and tissue from his open wounds. He yells at her to go away and save herself but she won't leave. It breaks her heart and I am sure it breaks his. The head of radiology told her that Maddy's nervous system is deteriorating. I have spent a lot of time with her. She reminisces a lot about the love she has for him. Five days ago he was a healthy young man playing soccer twice a week and now he is a body of gelatin. The

169

burns started to rise to the surface like yeast in bread. The same has happened to Yanush. In Yanush's case, the burns were tiny lesions at first but they grew so fast, almost overnight. Different parts of his body changed color. His legs are grey, his face blue and his arms are a blotchy red. It is truly indescribable Mila and I do not wish you to experience this. One of the doctors informed Edith that extreme radiation kills in fourteen days. It has been five days and both these men are not long for this world. It is horrible for me to say this Mila but I want them to die. The pain that Yanush is suffering is unbearable for both him and Edith."

"There is no cure?" Mila questioned thinking solely of Roman.

"It is too far advanced," Tania replied. "I pray that many of these men will go home but I don't know how long they will live afterwards. If there is irreversible bone marrow damage then surgery is useless. I am told an American doctor is here just to perform this procedure. It doesn't appear to be working. Other than bone marrow, I don't know what else can be done."

Mila stared at Roman. She loved him more than anything in this world and it made her stomach queasy thinking that he too may face the same predicament. There had to be a way to save him.

There was nothing she could do.

Turn

Tania was understandably solemn while describing her first weeks in Hospital Six. I watched her facial expressions change several times, and she sucked in huge breaths more often than usual. Lena wiped a few tears from her eyes and I wanted to hug her but knew this was not the time. I imagine that many Kharmalov tears were shed in May, 1986.

"We stayed with mama and papa in our old flat. Mila and I took turns staying overnight, which was entirely unacceptable to the doctors but it did not take long for them to fall under the spell of my sister. We needed passes to be on the floor every day and trust me when I say that Mila and I never had any issues. Her blend of beauty, brashness and persuasiveness became a popular discussion amongst the staff."

"I guess that runs in the family," I quipped.

"Not now," Lena replied rather quickly and seriously.

Tania paid no attention to our side bar. "There was another little adventure that took place far from the hospital and involved my Aunt Vera. She, Uncle Georgie and Boris were back in Kiev trying to reassemble their lives. They were having a hard time as neighbors shunned them when they learned they had spent the weekend in Pripyat. If you are not aware Aaron, the citizens of our city took a great deal of abuse when they returned to their hometowns or even when they stayed in temporary hospices. The kids were bullied and called several names relating to nuclear accidents... stuff like bright light heads and glow in the dark dolls. We weren't Russians or Ukrainians anymore, we were "Chernobyls" and if people didn't fear us they wanted to know everything we knew. Even the adults were brutally unkind and worried that they too would be contaminated. It was a very difficult time and considering those that assaulted and insulted us were our own countrymen, made it harder.

In all honesty, we did not know much about Aunt Vera, she was an enigma to all of us including mama but at the same time, she listened very well and she adored papa. Papa was the most intelligent man she had ever known, which was not a stretch when you consider that Uncle Georgie was a nincompoop."

I chuckled wondering how Lena could translate Tania's words so colorfully.

"Kiev always had a May first parade. Hundreds of participants ranging from war veterans to student bands would march the streets of Kiev proper. On this particular day, Vera found it necessary to inform those that participated and those that watched that they were risking their lives. It was a warm day and the winds were coming directly from Chernobyl so if I can make a comparison I would say it was like standing on the Bridge of Death.

She had Georgie staying at home with Boris with all the windows closed. If one of those windows was opened there would be hell to pay. Anyway, the people of Kiev were oblivious. They had no clue what was happening because no one told them. The residents of Sweden knew more than the people who lived two hours away from Reactor Four. As far as the people of Kiev were concerned, we from Pripyat were contagious but that was as far as it went. They did not take into account that the wind that warmed their faces was carrying an invitation to the morgue.

Vera was on a mission. Papa had taught her a lot in just a few days and she decided that she had to save the residents of

172

Kiev. So… she ran through the parade holding a sign that read, "Radiation is killing you now!" For as long as she could, she shouted at people warning them of isotopes and a Russian cover up. Needless to say she was shouted at and taunted until the police arrested her. The newspapers made her look like a lunatic. Oh my, the Kiev's had a good laugh… for a few days. Then word started to spread that a lot of people and I mean a lot, were sick and getting sicker. Suddenly there was mass panic and the same people who threw apples at my aunt were now on trains out of the city. I heard a story that a scrapbook of photos for these parades was kept for every one of them except the parade from 1986."

"Was she in prison long?" I asked.

Lena thought it was a bizarre question at the time but Tania did not. "Interestingly enough, no she did not. In fact she spent no longer than three hours locked up, which further amazed us. Mama asked her how it was possible that she was at home on time for dinner when anyone else would be sent to Siberia. She just shrugged saying that the officers realized she was performing a public service. Again, Vera has always been an enigma or as my mama would say, "A Gypsy enigma".

Lena pointed towards my recorder and said it had stopped. I replaced the tape with a new one.

"Yanush died on May 2nd, eight days before the one doctor predicted. It was the only day that I had arrived at the hospital after nine a.m., which meant I had to wait for a doctor to allow me entrance. Mama was at home and papa was with Roman. I found Mila in the corridor with her arms around my crying friend. Maybe it was my breakfast that morning or perhaps I too was feeling the effects of radiation but for some reason –

today - more than any other day, I was terrified. It was as if I knew in advance that May 2nd, 1986 would be the worst day of my life.

****

"They just carted his body away," Edith sobbed. "They won't let me see him. I was gone for five minutes and he died. He waited for me to leave."

Mila wasn't replying choosing instead to listen quietly. Tania walked behind her sister and tapped her on the shoulder motioning to Mila that she would take over. Mila stood up, embraced her sister and returned to Roman's bedside.

"His pain is gone," Tania said while stroking her friend's hair.

"And mine continues," Edith promptly replied. "What am I to do without my Yanush?"

Tania consoled her friend for the next thirty minutes. There was little she could say or do that would take away or dull Edith's suffering. Time is the only shoulder any of us should cry on. She wondered what Yuri was doing at that same moment. Was he safe and was he missing her as much as she missed him?

For the past four days the two sisters did whatever they could to console their parents and Edith. Roman had good days followed by bad. He was the only child amongst the men. Mila once heard two nurses discussing what type of parent would leave their child alone after a catastrophe. The eldest Kharmalov sibling tore a piece out of the judging nurses real quick. Both

174

ladies helped soldiers clean the floors around the patient's beds when nurses became obstinate. They were demanding protective clothing and Tania agreed with them. Mila was less appreciative of their work.

Before long, the patients began to speak with Tania and Mila as did the soldiers. When wives realized the beautiful women were only being helpful, they befriended the sisters and often brought soup for the entire family. Two of these patients joined Yanush that week at the Mitino Cemetery and the sisters attended both funerals.

No one understood why Roman took a turn for the worse. The doctors claimed that a bone marrow transplant was a bad idea for Roman yet not one of the family members was given an explanation for why his diagnosis had changed. Mrs. Kharmalov blamed the American doctor. Anton Kharmalov had an idea of what was happening. When a new patient was brought into their room the linen was changed as per norm. The senior Kharmalov asked a doctor if the actual bed had been removed and was met with an answer of no. Anton was incensed and questioned the doctor as to why a radioactive piece of steel bedding would not be replaced with one that was not contaminated. In other words, his son had been sleeping on radiation since the day he arrived. His argument was returned with a reply of," Sir, you have been here for a week. You might as well be sleeping inside Reactor Four. What difference do you think a new bed will do?"

And he was right.

One day later, the family cried in unison outside in the corridor when Romans face developed blue marks and lesions.

They had left the night before and he was breathing rough but not more than that.

The proud son and beloved brother, was going to die.

Pripyat: May 1, 1986

"You're still brown," Yuri grumbled at his best friend.

"I know but I don' feel ill at all," Alex replied. "Why is that? Why is it that you're still pasty white and strong while others around you are falling like bugs in November? The hospital is packed."

The two were sitting outside their tent watching soldiers and reservists buzz around them. Yuri had lost a bit of weight but only because he had not eaten as much as he normally did. Both men were working ten to twelve hours a day doing whatever was asked of them. For the most part, they spent their days performing manual labour such as shoveling or carrying supplies from newly arrived trucks.

Yuri swallowed a mouthful of oatmeal and drank from a water container he shared with no one. The sun had yet to peek out of the bombardment of clouds that threatened to bring rain. It was cooler this morning yet still warmer than most early May mornings. The heat from the reactor ensured this.

"If I knew the answer to that, then I would be nominated for a Nobel Prize but to be honest, I have asked myself the same question. I guess we should be thankful. By the way, it's May first; will we be watching a parade this afternoon and fireworks this evening? I hope they don't come from the reactor."

"Yah right," his friend smirked.

Alex surveyed the makeshift camp. It was in a field of uncut grass close to the marina. The first night that he and Yuri slept here there were forty tents. That had ballooned to three hundred in six days and five more fields were filled like this one.

In the distance he saw Valeri Markov having breakfast next to the smallish man with the scar on his cheek.

"One of the older guys said he saw Markov leaving an apartment building holding a large bag. He thinks he was looting."

"Are you ever going to let this go?" Yuri sighed before lying on his back.

"No," Alex answered. "I believe the old guy because Markov is capable of such a thing. He is a worm and cannot be trusted. I am curious to know what he does all day and to whom he reports."

"Okay, when this crap is done, I will personally lead the investigation on this scumbag but for now please do me the honor of shutting the fuck up about Valeri Markov."

Alex dropped his head and then lifted it with a mischievous grin. "Fine, I'll talk about Yulia instead."

Yuri chuckled. He guessed that even Alex was aware that many were tired of his never ending pining for an ex-girlfriend. "You're an asshole."

"Speaking of assholes…." Alex said while pointing towards the man approaching them.

"Oh shit," Yuri growled. "We have another hour; I'm not going back to work so early, he can kiss my Ukrainian ass."

Colonel Breshevski was in his mid-forties and built like the army tanks he claimed to once drive. His brown hair was always cut razor short and never touched his oversized ears. He had a deep voice that was almost as intimidating as his barrel chest and he loved to bark orders. Yuri once remarked that the man was born to be a soldier. Well, either that or a circus freak, he would mutter as low as possible.

Both Yuri and Alex made a movement to stand but Breshevski told them to remain seated. He had a friendly demeanor this morning that Alex found odd and Yuri found suspicious.

"Good morning comrades," the Colonel began. "My superior wishes to speak with you both. There is a situation at the plant and your names were mentioned."

"We didn't do it," Alex blurted.

Breshevski squinted for a second before continuing. "You are not being questioned for anything Alex. When you are finished your meal, please join me outside the Officers tent next to the Reactor entrance." The Colonel tipped his cap and left as quick as he came.

"That wasn't so bad," Alex murmured.

"Really?" Yuri replied. "And you believe that something good can come out of this? As David once said, you are a naïve little chimp."

"Well maybe but I'm extremely adorable," the security guard casually added.

They waited half an hour and caught a ride on a jeep headed towards the reactor. The main tent was huge and more similar to an outdoor food market than what the enlisted men had been sleeping in. There was a least twenty desks lined side by side with an officer behind each. Breshevski noticed the two men, stood and walked towards them. He was followed by a taller, older man dressed like their Colonel, in full military uniform.

"This is bad," Yuri muttered. "He's Russian."

The taller men extended his hand and both Yuri and Alex shook it.

"Gentlemen" Breshevski smiled, "Major Asimov is from Moscow. He has joined us as of yesterday and reports directly to the Kremlin."

"Sir," Yuri saluted. Alex did the same but somewhat awkwardly.

"At ease comrades," Asimov grinned. "I understand that you are both very strong swimmers. Top in your class from what I am told."

"He's okay," Alex smirked. "I'm excellent."

The Major smiled, albeit briefly. He was trying his best to be less than military but was uncomfortable doing so as if he had forgotten how.

"I will hazard a guess that little information about the nuclear plant has been explained to either of you in the last week other than rumors."

Yuri was not intimidated by the officers ranking. "Sir, judging from the influx of men and officers we have made our own determinations."

"And I imagine you would be close to the truth," Asimov replied calmly. "You, comrade Larinov are an engineer in Reactor Four so you are familiar with the functionality. Comrade Mishkin, you are less familiar so I will enlighten you if I may. There are three floors below the reactor itself. The two bottom floors are what are known as bubbler pools and serve basically as huge water reservoirs for emergency cooling pumps as well as pressure suppression systems that condense or trap steam if ever a steam pipe bursts. Above them and below the reactor is what we use as a steam tunnel which is in simple terms, a pressure release system. The steam released by a broken pipe is supposed to enter the steam tunnel and then be vented into the pools on the bottom floors to bubble through a layer of water. The explosion caused several of the cooling pipes to rupture and to further exasperate our situation, too much of the fire fighters water accumulated below."

Yuri nodded as if he knew exactly what was happening. "The core is so hot that there is now a risk of too much steam thus causing an explosion."

"Yes comrade Larinov that is what we expect. The graphite and fuel have started to burn through the reactor floor. If they reach the bottom floors then the next explosion will be catastrophic for not only us but for all of Europe.

Yuri was now extremely uncomfortable. In his experience, Russians only talked to him when they needed something. "And what is it that Alex and I can help you with?"

"The drain pools need to be opened and we will require your strong swimming skills."

Alex chuckled. "Excuse me Major; your comment caught me off guard. The drain pools are below the reactor?"

Yuri knew what was about to be asked of him. His eyes were locked on the Major while he explained. "Yes, they can be drained by opening the sluice gates."

"Comrade Larinov would be knowledgeable in this area as he knows where the gate valves are located," Asimov said.

"The sluice gates are like a miniature dam Alex," Yuri continued. "Open the gates and the water will flow out. You and I could do this task with ease yet the Major is omitting a rather obvious detail."

Asimov raised his hand. "I am seeking volunteers' comrade; you are by no means obligated."

Alex was still confused. "Yuri?"

"The water is extremely radioactive, my friend, and we would be risking our lives." Yuri continued to stare at the Major. "If anything, it is a suicide mission."

"It is a mission that will save the planet," Asimov added. "There is no other alternative for us and the explosion caused by a fallen reactor would measure several megatons. Corporal Breshevski would be joining you."

Don't be a hero Yuri, Tania had begged him. Her words bounced around his head like an eight ball before it dropped into a side pocket.

You will be saving the planet.

"I will volunteer Major," Alex said with his shoulders pushed back.

"Alex, for God's sake," Yuri blurted. "You could die from this."

The security guard waved a hand in the air and harrumphed. No opportunity like this would ever arise again and he pounced on it.

"Six days later and I have not vomited once and neither have you. We are Supermen, you and I. Nothing can harm us."

Yuri closed his eyes and tried to breathe. His heart was beating faster than it ever had. He knew he had to do what was being asked of him but at the same time he could not bear to disappoint Tania. The engineer dropped his head before speaking. He did not want his superior to see him in a moment of weakness.

"I was to be married the day the reactor caught fire. If this task does not go as planned and I fall ill, I want you to promise me Major that you will arrange for my marriage to be legalized before I pass."

Asimov nodded several times. "Heroes of the Soviet Union are gifted whatever they please comrade Larinov. Your families will be taken care of for the rest of their days but as for your marriage… not only would I grant this request, I would be honored to be present."

Looking over the Majors shoulder, Yuri caught a quick glimpse of an older man on his knees vomiting violently. A co-worker called loudly for a doctor but none came. *That could be me in a few hours,* he thought. *I could have disappeared into the forests and no one would have known or missed me. Thousands of men surround me and yet I am the one God has chosen to be sacrificed. The invisible enemy was peeking around the corner waiting for me to poke my head out and I did just that. I am the lamb to the wolf.*

I am not Superman.

"I also ask that the Kremlin does not count casualties against those that are saved. I and those around me are not statistics to be leveraged."

Asimov put his hand on Yuri's shoulder and then took off his cap. "I cannot, as a man with family, look into your eyes and consider you a statistic. What you are about to do is beyond bravery son. If the world was ever to forget your name then the world was not worth saving."

Diving For a Nation

Tania and Edith sat on a bench outside the Hospital, a few meters from the soldier's tents. Tania had prepared sandwiches the night before knowing her friend would need nourishment. Edith had not slept since Yanush passed. Her eyes were sunken and tiny stress pimples fought for space around her chin. She had not showered or changed her clothes in a week and her body odor had become a distraction.

"My husband's parents are my only family," Edith began between small bites. "I was an only child and so was he. Did I ever tell you that I met him at my mother's funeral? She passed a month after my father. She took her own life but I am not ashamed to admit this. She said life without my father was useless. It hurt me but I understand this now. Yanush was working part-time in the cemetery to pay for school. A few friends joined me for the burial but left soon afterwards. It was Yanush who comforted me. He was a beautiful stranger. I think in our life we remember one beautiful stranger; he was mine."

Tania held Edith's hand and listened. She tried desperately to block out thoughts of Yuri and pay full attention to her friend.

"We began dating a week later and within a month he was living with me. His parents were not pleased that he was in love with a non-Jew and have never accepted me. They believed his association with me was a loathsome blemish as described in the Talmud. In anger, his father described me as non-human. Yanush was saddened by their posturing and denounced his religion...for a short while. To this day, I cannot fathom how anyone can say the words love and religion in the same sentence." Edith exhaled a long breath and moved on to a happier subject. "Coincidentally, we were studying in the same University and both graduated at the same time. A job became vacant at the local firefighter station and he was offered the position a day after graduation. Six months later we were in Pripyat. Life was perfect."

"Our lives *were* perfect," Tania added.

Soldiers began whistling at the two women. Tania was initially incensed by their rudeness until she saw a nurse signaling Edith. She tossed the sandwiches in her purse before walking hurriedly towards the front entrance.

"He's been calling you," the stout nurse advised Edith.

Edith turned from tired to frantic and ran towards the stairs leaving Tania alone with the nurse. Her face was flush with sweat when she arrived at her husband's room. The bed was empty. She called for a nurse and none came until she yelled. Two older women with stern expressions approached. Edith remembered their faces as soulless.

"We looked throughout the hospital for you," the head nurse claimed.

"I was gone for fifteen minutes," Edith replied with frustration. "Where is Yanush?"

With little expression or compassion the head nurse replied. "He died fifteen minutes ago."

Her head became light and her knees buckled. Both nurses grabbed an arm and supported her against the white wall. She could barely breathe. One of the nurses remarked on Edith's body odor and the other snickered.

"I was gone for fifteen minutes," she whispered.

****

Yuri and Alex sat on the edge of the bubbler pool with their fins above the water. They were dressed in dark diving suits that covered their entire bodies from the neck down. The security guard was much more gung-ho than his friend Yuri.

"I could piss in this suit and no one would know," he joked.

Yuri tried to smile but could not. He had thought of little else but Tania. He was ashamed to admit that few thoughts of his parents had intervened his longing for the woman he loved.

"If we get out of this alive, I'm going to buy Tania a magnificent home with a garden and a swing set for our children. I will plant flowers so that I can hand her one every morning when she awoke."

"Wow, that's the most romantic thing I have ever heard a man admit to another man. I think now is a good time to piss myself."

"You're an ignoramus," Yuri replied. "Tell me again why we're friends."

"Because you can tell me anything and although I may pretend to be laughing, I am, in fact, totally envious and extremely happy for you. That's why."

"Why did you volunteer so quickly Alex and don't say it's because you are a proud Soviet. I know better."

"If I make it out alive I'll be a chick magnet," Alex grinned. "Girls will flock to me and want to touch my irradiated body."

"So you're doing this for Yulia?" Yuri retorted.

186

"No man… definitely not. Give me an ounce of credit; I'm not a total loser. I'd like to say I am doing it for Mila because she is so freaking hot – damn she's hot - but she never paid much attention to me." Both men snorted a bit. "I'm doing it for my father. He tried to give me as much as he could but he had so little. I want him to know that he gave me more than enough and that what I do today is as big as a sacrifice as the sacrifices he made for me. I am my father's son."

Yuri looked at his friend briefly and nodded. He thought about all the times that Mrs. Kharmalov had chastised Alex about his father and how many times he himself had found it humorous. The guilt was crushing.

"You were never in Yulia's league," Yuri said quietly.

"This is what you have to say to me minutes before we plunge into a pool of death?"

"It's true," Yuri shrugged, "She was never good enough for you." Yuri paused before continuing. "You are such a good man Alex, not as good as me but a good man."

"Asshole," Alex said while rolling his eyes.

"I'm only joking, but I meant the first part. You're a great companion and someone who deserves the best woman possible. If Mila had known you better and hadn't married that strange little person then she would have had an awesome partner if it had been you."

Alex shook his head. "Can you believe it, we're so typically men. We're risking our lives and here we are talking about a hot woman. We should laugh at our farts next."

"Pull my finger," Yuri said sticking out his hand.

Breshevski walked behind them and asked if they were ready. He was holding a large flashlight in his shaking hand.

Neither Alex nor Yuri missed this, and both silently worried their superior would be a hindrance.

They lifted the masks and goggles and slipped them on. Yuri was breathing heavy and asked the other two to wait while he exhaled slowly. He grabbed Alex's arm and the two men nodded their love for each other. Yuri could not see that Alex was crying. He held his friends hand, and they slid into the pool.

Breshevski's flashlight died within seconds. Just like the cameras on the day the reactor exploded, the radiation ceased its components. Yuri motioned towards the men to follow him and they used the pipes below the waterline to guide them through the dark. Yuri was surprised they could still maneuver easily and debris was of little concern. The diving suits were useless and he could feel his legs tingle as if a thorn bush was being lightly brushed against his skin. The sluice gate and the valves were only seconds away but Yuri worried they would never leave the bubbler pool. The three men grabbed the valve to the left of the thick steel gate and pushed it upwards. The gate strained and made a haunting belligerent noise but thankfully began to dislodge. They pushed the valve harder. The sluice gate opened and the dangerous radioactive water flowed out.

The men rushed to hold on to the pipes and swam back to where they jumped in. Breshevski held on to Alex's leg, slowing him. Each required assistance from two co-workers to get out of the pond. Their bodies ached. In cities across the Eastern Bloc, parents and their children cheered proudly as soldiers, tanks and veterans marched the crowded streets honouring May Day. Hours later, parents and their children would cheer as fireworks danced against the background of a night sky. At Reactor Four, the news of the diver's success brought cheers from the hundreds of men that waited in anticipation.

The three heroes did not hear the cheers from men outside the reactor. They would not hear the sighs of relief from the Kremlin. All they heard was each other's groans.

In the first six days since the reactor explosion neither Alex nor Yuri had become ill. Within six seconds of leaving the bubbler pool both were vomiting. Breshevski was lying on the concrete floor barely moving. Strangers carried them outside the reactor next to the large tent where several commanders were waiting. Yuri thought he saw Major Asimov ordering a doctor to hurry. The last word he heard before losing consciousness was *Moscow*.

The Kremlin *did* count casualties and *did* leverage those losses against those that survived. Although the names of the three divers were printed in every major newspaper around the globe, the world soon forgot them. Instead of statues in major European cities they are no more than a single, solitary footnote in a story that precious few will ever know.

****

She watched as his body was inserted into plastic bagging like a weekday lunch. The soldiers then lifted Yanush and placed him in a wooden coffin which they nailed shut. The coffin was then gently dropped into a larger lead coffin which was soldered shut. Edith was mortified and her tired body buckled. Tania could barely stand herself. She was glad her mother did not join her.

189

A doctor explained that Yanush's body was so contaminated that the government could not risk the chance of radiation seeping into the water table thus he was to be buried in a lead coffin at Mitino cemetery.

"No, there must be some mistake," Edith pleaded with the soldiers guarding the coffin. "He is to be buried next to his grandparents, he is Jewish."

"He is a hero of the State; therefore his body belongs to us. He will be buried at Mitino and there will be no further discussion. Good day comrades."

An hour later Tania and Edith stood outside the guarded gates of Mitino.

"They say he dies a hero but they won't allow me to add a simple quote on his headstone. There are only his name, date of birth and death... nothing more. I want to add beloved husband and friend but apparently heroes of the state cannot be undignified by such triviality. I can't even visit him when I wish."

Tania held her friends hand and stared at the young soldier blocking entrance into the cemetery. He avoided her eyes as much as possible.

It is no wonder they drink so much.

An elderly woman walked in front of the two woman and spat on the pavement. "Your glowing bodies have polluted my husband's final resting place. I curse you. I curse you... bitches! Go back home, you don't belong here."

Edith buried in her face in Tania's shoulder. "I brought this upon him. I'm not Jewish. His parents were right."

This is inhumane, Tania thought while ignoring her friend's misguided remark. She stared at the old woman but did not confront her. If soldiers were disallowing entrance to Edith

190

then the same was happening to this elderly widow. The old woman left with tears streaming down her face. Edith was crying so hard she began to yelp. Back at Hospital Six her mother was inconsolable. A short block away, a small gang of students hung May Day posters and banners on lamp posts and store windows. She could hear their laughter and considered it a sweet denial. There is no happiness in this country.

May 2nd 1986

The front page of Friday's newspaper declared July 4th as a day to fight imperialism. Anton Kharmalov read it with disinterest and contempt wondering how such nonsense could usurp the disaster he was experiencing. Where was the news on Reactor Four? Anger rose through his chest and he came close to screaming the injustice being buried and ignored.

His family was upstairs attending to his only son. He wanted to pray for a miracle but did not know how to pray. Guilt overwhelmed him. It was his own selfish desire to leave Moscow years ago. His wife was content with their lives but he wanted more. He heard stories of beaches and exotic shops in the town of Pripyat. He would be a fool not to accept such an opportunity. They left their Moscow apartment in such haste and with so much laughter it angered their neighbours. They have returned in total misery. The neighbours avoid conversation and contact. Who's laughing now?

A soldier rushed in through the front doors and ran to the front reception. The desk attendant casually lifted her phone and called for a doctor to come downstairs. She said a code that Anton guessed had to do with another Chernobyl victim. The soldier disappeared outside, only to return seconds later.

A gurney holding a new patient was carefully pushed through the front entrance. The doctor had not yet arrived and Anton approached to get a closer look. The soldier noticed and held up his hand asking Anton to stay where he was.

"Is he from Chernobyl?" Anton questioned.

The soldier looked at his co-workers first and then nodded yes. He noticed the newspaper in Anton's hand and told him to look at the back page. A small article mentioned sluice gates being opened by a commander, engineer and security guard. His heart stopped. An engineer and a security guard. Not possible. *Please tell me this is not possible.* He neared the soldier.

"What's his name?" he said through gasps of air.

"Sir, it's confidential," the soldier responded.

"Is it Yuri or Alex?" Anton begged.

The soldier stared back quizzically before dropping his eyes. The doctor arrived barking instructions and gesticulating wildly with his hands. While leaving, the soldier looked back at Anton and saw the anxious concern in the man's eyes. He would be admonished later for speaking but he could not ignore the anguish he perceived.

"Yuri," he answered compassionately.

Anton returned to his seat. His chest hurt and he feared he was having a heart attack.

He no longer wished to pray. God paid no attention to Russians.

****

Tania did not remember where she was when she learned Yuri was two rooms away from Roman. She fainted and awoke hours later. He was sleeping the first time she sat next to him. His face was a deep brown, much worse than Roman's. His once thick blond hair stuck to the wet pillow his head lay against. Each time he moved, hair escaped his scalp like October leaves. His once ruby lips were a dirty white. It struck her that she was angry with

Yuri. This was not supposed to happen. They were supposed to have a happy life and a happy ending. He promised.

I begged you not to be a hero.

The American doctor could not recommend bone marrow transplant. No explanation was given but Tania realized it was because Yuri was too far gone. Nurses had already assembled the plastic curtains around his bed. This was the first sign of imminent death. She could not touch the love of her life and was warned that visits of more than twenty minutes were hazardous to her health. She didn't care.

"Hi baby," Yuri whispered.

Tania smiled as best she could.

"Do I look like shit?" he asked.

"You've looked better," Tania answered. "Are you thirsty?"

Yuri nodded and Tania handed him a cup of water through a hole in the curtain. He sipped the water through a straw with his head down as if ashamed to look at his fiancée.

"I'm going to fight this Tania," he said.

"And I will be by your side fighting with you," she replied. "Your commander is here. He mentioned you wished to marry me now just in case."

Yuri looked into her eyes pleadingly. "Please."

Tania nodded. "Just in case…right?" Yuri said yes and Tania half smiled. "We can't find your parents Yuri. They haven't registered in any city yet and they haven't returned to Kharkov. Commander Asimov is doing what he can to locate them."

"Alex?" Yuri questioned between a deep inhale and exhale.

"Asimov said he was fine." His concern for Alex over his parents did not go unnoticed.

Yuri closed his eyes and smiled. "That son of a bitch is a cat with nine lives." He coughed several times while trying to hide the pain it caused. "Do you have your ring?"

"It is always with me," Tania replied.

"I love you, Tania Kharmalov," Yuri said closing his eyes. Within moments he was sleeping again.

Tania stared at him while he slept. "I love you too, Yuri Larinov."

I begged you not to be a hero.

May 5th 1986: Goodbye

At two-thirty-five in the afternoon, Roman opened his eyes so suddenly that it startled Mila.

"Ok… that was creepy," Mila smiled. "How are you feeling?"

"Better," he said while Mila handed him a cup of water. He emptied the cup and handed it back to his sister. "Did grandpapa have a large mole on his cheek?"

"Mama's dad did… yes." Mila answered with furrowed brow. "That's a strange question Roman. Why do you ask?"

"I spoke with him a little while ago. He asked that I say hello to mama and that I should tell papa he's perfect for his daughter and that he's sorry for the unkind words he said."

"Roman… Grandpapa Vic has been dead for a decade. You never met him. Maybe you've seen old photos of him but you never met him."

"Well yah, I know this and that's why I asked the mole question. Pay attention Mila."

"You had a dream Roman," Mila insisted. "A very strange dream."

He touched Mila's hair and held her hand. "I'll be alright Mila, don't worry about me." Roman smiled. His breathing was labored but his voice was strong. "I saw Jacob, he is terrified and holding on. His eyes are so big, so filled with fear. I asked him to join me but he refused. I told him my pain was gone, but he wasn't ready to go. He's lonely. Maybe he needs a cigarette. Oh yah, that reminds me, tell mama and papa to stop smoking."

Mila looked at her brother and felt him squeezing her hand lovingly. He didn't look like he was recovering. If anything, it was the contrary. His face had blue marks, like gigantic bruises that were not there two days ago. Yet, his mind was strong and clear. He stared at the far corner and chuckled. Mila turned her head and saw nothing.

"Mama and papa don't smoke and why are you laughing?"

"Yuri just called me a punk. He said we can go fishing but only if I agree to swimming an equal amount of times."

"And where is Yuri?"

Roman pointed towards the corner. "He's over there with the teachers."

"I don't see him," Mila replied with opened hands. "What teachers Roman?"

"God's teachers, I think they might be angels, but I didn't ask. I met mine last night. She will teach me how to live in heaven. She's very attractive but obviously not as beautiful as you."

"Roman… you're not going anywhere. Stop this joke now."

The twelve-year old continued. "Mila, I was already in the light. It's warm and comforting like my bed at home. The light is God's breath. I felt God's breath, and it was as loving as your embrace. I only came back to say goodbye to you."

"You're scaring me. This is not an episode of Alien Conquest. Please stop this now."

He didn't reply right away and instead gazed at the woman he would miss more than any other. "You're my best friend Mila. There is no one in this world I love more than you but you must soon realize that others need you more than I. You're a

197

gift my sister. Papa always said, you're a rose in a field of dandelions and I thank-you for everything you've given me."

"Roman…"

"Don't be scared, I'm not. I was before but not now. I have no more pain, it's gone and you would agree that this is good. I'm going fishing but eventually… you and I, we'll be together again." He let go of her hand. "I love you Mila…"

"I don't understand why you're talking like this Roman?" Mila said more loudly than she cared to. His eyes were shut, and she assumed he was too exhausted to continue his charade. "Fine, go to sleep but I'll be asking questions when you dare to awake. Crazy fish-boy."

Mila was still shaking her head when her father walked into the room. He smelled like cigarettes. His eyes were teary when he told his daughter that Yuri had passed away ten minutes earlier.

He wept hysterically when he noticed his son was no longer breathing.

****

Mila remained in the hospital hours after her family returned home. The emotional outpouring was exhausting, and she wished only to sit on the bench outside her brother's room. She imagined him standing and walking towards her, laughing at the practical joke he was playing. He was always playing jokes on her, this was no different.

Doctors and nurses passed by, paying little attention to her. She heard moans from inside the room. A man cried out for his wife. No one answered. The lights dimmed momentarily and returned to normal.

There is no one in this world I love more than you but you must soon realize that others need you more than I.

Mila reached out as if Roman had repeated the words. The same man cried again. Mila stood and walked to his bedside. The other men in the room watched closely as she touched the distressed patient's shoulder.

"You're not my wife," he whispered.

"No, but I'll stay with you until she returns tomorrow."

The man quivered before speaking. "I've been here for five days and she has yet to visit. I am dead to her."

Mila closed and re-opened her eyes. "Then it is I who will return to you tomorrow."

He stopped shivering and gazed into the most transfixing eyes he had ever seen. "Are you an angel?"

Mila lifted the bedcover over his chest and then held his hand. "I'm Mila Kharmalov."

April 22, Present Day Kiev: Wednesday Evening

"Lena didn't seem very upset about not attending this soiree of yours."

"Hey Canadian boy," Bruno squint. "Do I look like I speak French? If soiree means event then no, she wouldn't be. It is with a bunch of old men so do you want your pretty lady being mentally undressed by a room full of men drinking vodka? Have you not noticed I am carrying three full bags of bottles?"

"Good point and yes I have noticed. I thought it was guys' night out with strippers. So who are these men?"

"Be thankful your girlfriend's cousin has connections because this would never have happened if you came here alone."

"As I have said several times since my arrival in your city - thank-you. So who are these guys?"

Boris didn't answer. We walked into an apartment building, rang a buzzer and then waited. A minute later the elevator door opened and Evgeni from the museum exited. He smiled at me as he opened the door.

"I bet you didn't think you'd see me again," he grinned while extending his hand.

I shook it and said no. "Boris is full of surprises," I added.

"Aaron," Boris interrupted. "I have to speak to Evgeni for a few seconds."

I nodded okay and walked to the elevator but was still able to watch the two men discuss. Evgeni initially seemed surprised by the conversation but then began shaking his head. He looked at me, spoke to Boris who replied by also shaking his head, which I deciphered as no. The museum director then stepped outside the apartment building and I watched through the glass doors as his eyes followed a car driving away. He then returned, and both men joined me by the elevator.

"Anything I should know boys?"

"No, I thought I saw his ex-girlfriend when we got out of the taxi," Boris said quickly.

He was obviously hiding something, but I wasn't concerned.

Evgeni shrugged his shoulders. "Stalker girlfriends…what are you gonna do eh?"

We stepped into the elevator and exited on the third floor. The apartment doors were all a dark gray which would have been fine if they hallway carpeting was not lime green. We walked to the second to last door and entered into apartment 303. The apartment itself was void of any furniture other than a few kitchen chairs and a very long bench pushed up against the main room wall. Sitting upon this bench and the available chairs, was a ragtag crew of more than a dozen men. A few others were on the floor leaning against one of three walls. There were several tall lamps scattered around the room aside from the one dangling light bulb in the center of the ceiling.

Boris handed out bottles from the three bags and the men thanked him graciously. I imagine this was payment for allowing me to be here although Boris never admitted to it. The men looked old to me and I don't mean that they had deep wrinkles or liver spots. I mean they looked exhausted, worn down as if they had been plowing fields for fifty years. The one man sitting directly in front of me had sunken eyes that I imagined dropping to the floor in front of his ripped shoes.

"Take this," Evgeni said handing me an ear phone. "I'm going to translate for you. If you have a question, raise your hand."

I was impressed to say the least. He had thought of everything in advance and I wondered if he had done this several times before my arrival. Evgeni turned to face the tired audience and introduced the three of us. Based on the looks Boris received when he was introduced, I gathered that there was a lot that Lena's cousin was not telling me. The men offered him an instant reverence as if he was a celebrity or priest. When I was introduced, Evgeni mentioned I was from Canada and the men nodded that this was cool with them. Boris made a joke that I obviously could not understand and the men laughed. He grinned at me and then turned towards Evgeni.

Evgeni spoke in Russian and then in English for me. It was not the ideal situation for these men but they were patient.

"Aaron, the men in this room are very educated on nuclear energy. They were not when they began working at Chernobyl but through the years they have learned much from these types of meetings as well as the Internet and papers published in Russia that made their way into their hands. When we were speaking a few days ago I mentioned that you should never ever believe anything published by the IAEA or WHO. If you do not already know, WHO is the World Health Organization. Remember a few years back in your own country when this association warned travelers not to travel to Toronto because of SARS? They did a real number on your economy for six months. Well, they have a very dubious agenda, one that is difficult to comprehend. Since 1959, the International Atomic Energy Association has had an agreement with WHO to veto any of their research into nuclear energy and the effects. I printed a statement from WHO in 1956 that I want you to read before we continue. The men in the room have read the Russian translation."

Evgeni pulled out a piece of paper from his jacket and handed it to me. I unfolded it and began reading:

Genetic heritage is the most precious property for human beings. It determines the lives of our progeny, health and harmonious development of future generations. As experts, we affirm that the health of future generations is threatened by increasing development of the atomic industry and sources of radiation. We also believe that new mutations that occur in humans are harmful to them and their offspring.

"That was in 1956?" I questioned

"That is correct," Evgeni replied. "In 1959 they agreed to never broach the subject again. Whatever the IAEA says, they agree to or make no comment. In present day terminology, WHO is the IAEA's bitch."

Boris chuckled making me speculate once again where these guys picked up their English.

"Now I am going to tell you something that is a disgrace to mankind and none of the men involved in these negotiations have ever apologized or even shown any snippet of remorse. The only participant that told the truth was a man from Russia named Lagasov and he ended up committing suicide two years later. The IAEA, some U.N. members and a few world leaders *negotiated* a deal on how many deaths would be attributed to the Reactor Four explosion. Yes you heard right… they negotiated a deal. The IAEA won and the amount of deaths was calculated as four thousand. Lagasov said a minimum of forty thousand and he was later ostracized in Russia and within the nuclear community. So after hearing this, what chance do you think the men sitting in this room had? The pains in their bones; their weak hearts; their children's weak hearts; cancerous thyroids... fuck man; I can go on for hours. If you're going to write Tania's story, you have to know *all* the events, *all* the side stories and you have to include them in the book because I gotta tell ya man - the Kharmalov sisters are precious to us."

What the hell is he jabbering about? Why would he bring up the Kharmalov sisters in mid-sentence and what in God's name have I walked into?

"Yah, I know, you have no freaking clue and how could you? No offence to you Aaron but do you honestly believe that I would have spoken to you at the museum if I had not of known who Lena was? Your girlfriend doesn't want you to know anything, and that's cool... but everyone in this room wants you to write it. To tell the truth... that's all we ask."

I opened my mouth to speak but Boris stopped me.

"Just listen Aaron," he hushed.

"These men Aaron are heroes; they are forgotten heroes dying a bit more each day. No one knows the exact amount because records were burned or lost but the estimate is that there were between seven and nine hundred thousand liquidators. The liquidators were called in to clean up the mess, plow the fields, bury villages and build the infamous sarcophagus covering Reactor Four. The first man who is going to speak is Ivan. He is visiting family for a couple of weeks but he was born and still living in Belarus."

A balding man with shaking hands waved at me and I waved back. I said hello in English and he grinned albeit very briefly. Evgeni moved from the center of the room and stood next to the half open window. He began translating in a low voice. Ivan chose to remain seated, and I soon learned why.

"I was raised in the town of Vetka, next to the Sozh River. We were a bustling town with a strong economy because of our wharf and abundance of arts and crafts. We had a large Jewish population although our town was founded by the Old Believers...Orthodox Christians. Throughout several centuries we have had a history of invaders but they were always eventually defeated. Our last invader has killed many of us and refuses to leave. You can guess that this conqueror is radiation.

Three days after the Chernobyl explosion, winds carried dangerous clouds towards Vetka and our lives changed forever. I was twenty and a simple reservist but when an officer of the administrative unit came to my home, I had no choice but to join fifty others from my town and head to Ukraine. I was married only three months earlier during the solstice celebrations so leaving my wife behind was very difficult for both of us. She feared for my safety and with good reason. There were many of our old folk falling sick in their fields. It was happening with such frequency that patrols would check the skies for circling ravens and scour the fields for wolf packs. My wife and I did not labor on the collective farms and stayed inside for work so we were fortunate in that respect. The crazy thing is that the fields on the west side of the main road were contaminated but the opposite was true on the east side, only half a kilometer away.

There are others who will go into detail about the impossible work we performed and the after effects on us. I was a liquidator that worked on the roof. I made three trips of two minutes over five days and was sent home. I met Albert there, and we have remained friends."

He pointed toward Albert and then continued speaking.

"I am forty-six years of age and incapable of walking long distances. I am a smoker as are most of the men here, but although my lungs suffer, I have difficulty walking because the bones in my legs and feet have degenerated. I have what is known as primary bone sarcoma and it is caused by radiation. There are tumors in both my leg bones and the only cures in most cases are chemotherapy and surgery. Doctors cannot give me chemotherapy...they can't give any of us chemotherapy, we are thoroughly toxic. The surgery alternative would be to install metal implants but my surrounding bones are too brittle and the metal will not withstand the radiation that my body cannot or will never excrete. The only solution is amputation."

I covered my mouth almost too methodically. I wanted to hide my shock but didn't fool anyone.

Ivan continued not perturbed as if he had told his story hundreds of times. "It is my future and I do not expect to live past my fiftieth birthday. My wife is also ill and not much better than I. She has advanced arthritis. The doctors told her that her case has nothing to do with the years of radioactivity that she breathed or ate. She is forty-five and can barely hold a spoon. I have to cut her meat and potatoes. There are mornings where I have to dress her and there are mornings where she chooses to remain in bed. I could not be here today without the help of a neighbour who graciously offered to help my Anna.

Thirty percent of Belarus land is now useless and the other seventy percent is monitored. We eat radioactive food and drink radioactive milk. Our children are tested for increased radiation levels every month in school. They are told to eat more fruit and vegetables but our soil is shit and contaminated. Merchants still sell fruits in outdoor stalls; they have to live too. Our air is contaminated especially after a rainfall. Most of Europe greets spring with hope and open arms. Belarusians pray for a cold winter with no snow. We are sold fish from our rivers and we cook it until it is burned. For some reason we believe this kills the radiation." Ivan lowered his head and paused. "Eighty percent of our children are unhealthy. Can you imagine this in your country? They study long hours to achieve average grades because we are all sick in our brains too. We are a population of nine and a half million yet we have over three hundred special hospitals for children with diseases like cancer, bone abnormalities or retardation. Many are orphans or have been abandoned. It is truly an abomination that is kept a secret from the world. It is as if we are censored. No one believes us anyway.

I am told that the effects of radiation normally take ten years but for us we could see the results fairly quick. Since 1993 our population is showing negative growth every year. People dying, silent abortions and low sperm count...all due to Reactor Four. We were once an agrarian society but now everyone has flocked to the cities because we cannot grow sufficient amounts of food and who the hell wants to dig their hands into radioactive soil for a living? After the explosion, Russia sent us their radiated food and milk. No one told us. They still do not tell us shit. Fucking Russian dogs.

A year after I returned from Chernobyl, my wife gave birth to a child with no limbs. He died within a week. We did not try again. I am impotent now and have been for at least ten years. Not that it matters, my wife is too brittle for any intimacy. We love each other and I am thankful for that. There are many more like me in Belarus. We are a quiet group because our leader is a dictator and there is little we can do to change this. I am happy to be here today and to sit in solidarity with my comrades."

Ivan looked at Boris and then directly at me. His stare was compassionate and for a moment I could see a glimpse of happiness erasing his previous dour expression.

"On June 23rd, 1987, a week after my son died, Tania and Mila Kharmalov visited my wife for an entire day. They brought her jams and new clothing but most of all, they brought comfort. My wife has never forgotten this. I have never forgotten this. We keep a photo of them on our wall next to our wedding portrait. That is my story."

Ivan was handed Vodka, and he took a long swig. The room was silent when Evgeni stepped three paces closer.

"We have a doctor in attendance Aaron who will frighten you with statistics. For now, let me tell you a bit more about Belarus. The capital city is Minsk and it is believed that Minsk is free of radiation. Of course, this is pure fiction. I will give you a case in point, which I call the Chernobyl Chain. The chain exists in every aspect of the lives of anyone residing in Ukraine, Belarus and Russia and across the world for that matter. The chain will never be broken and this is because of nature, because of the economy and mostly because of morally handicapped men... desperate and incredibly greedy men.

Belarus is a poor country as are most ex-Soviet countries. Its inhabitants do not earn fantastic salaries therefore they buy most of their goods from Belarus manufacturers. Let's use furniture as an example. The kitchen chair in a Minsk apartment may have been manufactured in Minsk but the lumber arrived from many miles away. There is an awfully good chance that the wood was cut from the Exclusion Zone. Where else are they going to get cheap lumber? So that there is no misunderstanding, milling lumber does not get rid of the radioactivity; nothing will. A husband and wife and their children will sit on their new kitchen chairs eating dinner having no clue that day by day their skin is absorbing small radioactive isotopes.

We hear stories - such as Tania's - of people returning to their villages in Exclusion Zones. We applaud their romanticism and wish them well. Unfortunately, these same people burn radiated peat and straw to keep warm. The smoke rises into the clouds and wind pushes the clouds into the cities. Rain deposits it on our skin, in our water and on our food. Maybe it is only small amounts, but it is small amounts every hour of every day. It is the Chernobyl Chain.

The good doctor will soon elaborate but for now I will allow Dmitry to tell his story." Evgeni returned to his spot next to the window.

A very short man with dark hair and dark eyes stood and acknowledged me. His face was flush red and the bluish veins on his engrossed nose were like tiny silk worms trying to dig out of their soil prison.

"Hello, I am Dmitry and I am also from Belarus. I live in Hrodna now, close to the Polish border. I was born in the province of Homiel, near Ukraine and Chernobyl. Two years ago I moved in with my daughter and her husband because I can no longer support myself. I have trouble breathing and my kidneys are troubling me. I have a list of ailments but I am told that I am pretending. My daughter has a lowered kidney that has pained her since the day she arrived in this world. She is barren and will never be able to carry a child to term thus I have no chance for grandchildren. When I die, my family name will die with me.

The government has cut off our casket money because they declared Belarus clean of radioactivity. It is now seven years that I receive no income. On the day that our administrators made this declaration, they removed the public Geiger's that counted the radiation in the air as if everything had magically returned to normal. Only the younger generation was fooled by this.

In early September of 1986 I was one of the liquidators that cleared the roof of graphite and concrete. During the evening we slept in tents on straw beds that of course were radiated. We drank our allotted vodka and bonded as Soviet brothers. Many of the men were not young. I was thirty but there were men there much older than me...women too. I stayed five days and had five shifts. Three shifts lasted two minutes and two of only a minute. To be blunt, we were like ants. One group would finish and another would begin. It was an assembly line of death.

For unexplained reasons, we had female names for each of the contaminated areas around Reactors Three and Four. Area K was named Katya, and it had 1,000 roentgens. Mina was a bit stronger and had approximately to 2,000 roentgens. Then, the strongest of all was Masha, and she was only twenty meters from the destroyed, open reactor. Most of us worked there, breathing close to 8,000 roentgens.

What many are not aware of is that the initial plan was to have robots clean the roof but their instruments melted so men had to complete the work. We were then nicknamed *bio-robots*. I had my soldier's uniform with a simple gauze filter covering my mouth and nose. We cut and hammered lead and then taped it under or above our uniforms to act as protection against the radiation. There was a commander - I forget his name - giving instructions on what we were to do once we climbed onto the roof. He had two television monitors to show us where to go and what our duty would incur. He was there all day and all week giving the same instructions to each group. I sometimes question if he remembers our faces and thinks of how he sent us up there knowing our lives would never be the same afterwards. Does his guilt match our pain...I wonder. Then again, he may be long dead."

Dmitry stopped speaking and grabbed a bottle of vodka from one of the other men. He took a long gulp, wiped his mouth and continued. The liquid wet his tongue and numbed his emotion. I circled the room with my eyes. The majority of the men were listening but not watching Dmitry. They hung their heads, reliving their personal tragedies with each guzzle from the bottles passed from one hand to another.

"On my last day, I wished to do as much as possible. Every tour of duty lessened the background radiation for the next group and the appreciation I possessed for my comrades had grown over the week. We were brothers in arms...heroes or at least, part-time heroes.

Masha was not an inviting woman; she was a hot and heavy beast. I ran as best I could to the nearest shovel and scraped up the graphite. The walk to the crater was ominous, but I did not look into the eyes of the monster. I threw the graphite into its mouth and ran back for more. In my head I was thinking of how I was helping to save all of Europe. I was saving my wife and our future child. I was saving my parents, my neighbours...I was saving me. Most importantly, I did this for Mother Russia. We would halt the imperialists' criticisms and our greatness would be restored. I guess then that my thought process matched the disorientation that crept into me. I felt sick as I zigzagged towards the monster for a second trip. Dizziness had engulfed me and my legs became weak. I lifted my shovel over the edge and when I tried to release, I stumbled and fell. My eyes were now looking directly into the burning gaping hole of the reactor. I cannot tell you how long I remained in that position. One of my comrades grabbed my shoulder and carried me away. I threw up immediately upon entering the long hallway. My face was brown and the taste of metal seeped into my gums. We were told that radiation had no taste... it's not true. The commander worried for my health and sent me to Hospital Number Six in Moscow. I was one of hundreds on my floor stacked like children's blocks into twenty rooms. I only stayed for six days as doctors feared my health would worsen amongst the men more badly infected.

I went home. Our fields were poisoned. Water was undrinkable yet we washed ourselves with the same water thinking it would not affect us. There was no work, and we struggled to survive. We hunted squirrels and rabbits until none were left. Families left the homes their forefathers had owned for generations. We looted them within hours and sold whatever we could to black market thieves that visited once a month. Within a year our government told us we had to move. How could I move when my parents were buried in a cemetery only minutes away? I took a handful of dirt next to their grave and apologized for leaving them. My daughter was only a month old and crying nonstop. My wife and I knew our girl was not well. We, as well as one hundred thousand others, moved to Gomel and the surrounding areas. I got lucky and worked as a trolley driver for two years. One day my arm fell asleep and has never awoken. The

212

doctors tell me I am imagining and I should seek psychiatric help. I lost my job.

My wife died of a heart attack three years ago, she was fifty one. She did not smoke or drink but her heart failed her.

Back when I lay in the Moscow hospital bed, my wife was permitted to stay aside me for only five minutes every two hours. One day she visited with a woman I can only describe as an angel in human form. I could barely tear my eyes away from her, she was so beautiful. She must have had a profound effect on my wife because it was the first time I had seen her smile since my arrival. I recognized this angel as did others I shared a room with. It was as if the entire floor had become electrified with excitement. My wife cried...but they were tears of happiness. Suddenly, I forgot the radiation that was living inside of me. I stopped worrying about my future and the struggles I knew would forever follow me. I just stared into her transfixing eyes realizing how special the moment was. She said her name was Mila Kharmalov. She took my hand in hers and said thank-you. And she meant it."

I felt goose bumps in my arms and legs. This was an entirely new twist to the biography that I was writing for Tania. Still, it was odd that Lena never shared these stories. As I listened to the other memories told this evening I became more and more confused or flabbergasted at Lena's secretive nature and even more curious as to how the Kharmalov sisters attained such notoriety.

"Aaron, this is Doctor Igor Gobachek." Evgeni said introducing the average looking man.

The doctor was wearing jeans and a black t-shirt, which was sort of contradictory. He had a thick black hair parted perfectly down the center as if Moses had commanded so. It was obvious the good doctor was extremely detailed. Even his shoes were shined. Amongst the other men in this rag tag group, he stood out like a sore thumb.

"I should warn you that Igor is very straight forward. If you didn't know him, you wouldn't like him and probably think him a condescending bastard." Evgeni shrugged and grinned like a schoolboy. "Just a head's up."

Evgeni winked at the doctor and took his place next to the window.

"I speak English Aaron but for the sake of our audience I will be conversing in Russian. I think I shall begin by explaining the word roentgen. The easiest definition would be that a roentgen is a unit of exposure dose that measures x-rays or gamma rays produced in dry air at zero degrees Centigrade. An acceptable dosage is 12 to 15 micro roentgens and you can find that in any major city. It is commonly known as background radiation. On a sunny day without wind, Kiev is measured at sixteen micro roentgens. One thousand micro roentgens equal one milli-roentgen. One thousand milli-roentgens equal one roentgen. In simple math, one million micro roentgens equal one roentgen. Therefore, one roentgen is approximately one hundred thousand times the average background radiation level in any major city. I will repeat that so that here is no misunderstanding. One roentgen is one hundred thousand times the normal level of radiation found in an average big city.

A dose of 500 roentgens over five hours is lethal to humans. During the first three days of the Chernobyl accident the levels were as high as thirty thousand roentgens. The firemen that climbed the roof in the early hours of April 26th were literally fried by gamma rays. Within minutes their bodies were decomposing while they still breathed. Within an hour, their organs were liquefying and anyone who came close to them was exposed to the enormous amounts of radiation that permeated their entire aura. The firemen unknowingly and unwillingly became killing machines.

Okay, now for the isotopes involved. I'm not going to get into a deep description of isotopes or we'll be here all night. In simple terms, an isotope is an atom where the number of neutrons differs. Ionizing radiation has enough energy to remove an electron from an atom thus destroying molecules. This in turn leads to DNA damage, cell death and thus tissue and organ destruction. The damage done by ionizing radiation is cruel and irreversible. What the IAEA tells you and what is indeed fact are very different. For one, the IAEA does not take into effect what Evgeni called the Chernobyl Chain. They have, in effect, erased this from the total equation.

Let's discuss the isotopes that were released into the atmosphere. We had the less dangerous iodine-131, but we also had the extremely dangerous plutonium, strontium–90 and worse of all we had a shit load of cesium-137. Each of these isotopes can cause different illnesses. At the beginning of this get together, Evgeni mentioned the IAEA insisting only four thousand deaths could be held accountable for the Chernobyl accident. Actually, that could have been probable if only iodine-131 was released. The fact of the matter is that of all the radioactive isotopes shot into the atmosphere only a maximum of fifteen percent was iodine 131. The rest was cesium and strontium.

Strontium is cesium's cousin, so to speak, and it resembles calcium so it gets into bones. It can cause leukemia and several bone cancers. It is strontium that has ruined Ivan's life as well as

215

his wife's. The percentage of leukemia cases in Belarus and Ukraine increased one hundred fold until nineteen-ninety-three before returning to normal levels.

Cesium... now, this stuff is some scary shit. Our body mistakes it for potassium so it is absorbed by cells and instantly becomes internal radiation, eating away and burning away at everything in its path. It will stay in your body for decades, heating or burning muscle cells and organs. Just ask the guys here about cesium.

What you won't hear the IAEA admit is that cesium can be a major cause of heart failure. Children that come into contact with this stuff develop holes in their heart. I often hear of young American athletes dying of heart failure... that's the effects of cesium. It lodges into soil and will remain there for centuries. You cannot get rid of it. If not for nuclear power plants or nuclear bomb testing we would rarely if ever come into contact with it but... the cat's out of the bag.

In case you are not aware, it was the American government that started this shit. Nuclear testing in Nevada in the late nineteen-fifties introduced cesium into the food chain. They fucked up that country real good. Breast cancer, heart attacks, diabetes... man, they're all the result of fall out. Diabetes hardly existed in the US before the Nevada nuclear tests. Then wham... hundreds of cases and then thousands. No one could pinpoint why. Well, we know now. What's worse is that the crazy bastards went ahead and introduced depleted uranium to the world. We call it a depopulation agent. It is now outlawed but George Bush Senior drowned Kuwait and Iraq in that stuff. Winds carried it around the world. Do you remember the soldiers that came back from the Gulf War with a mystery syndrome? That was depleted uranium and those men and women are either still suffering or dead. They have some real sick puppies in the U.S. military.

Anyway, I'm off topic. When I start thinking about the IAEA, Putin, the Carlyle Group, George Bush one and two and all those other elite mother fuckers, I get riled up and forget to remain professional.

There are hundreds of kids in Japan right now suffering heart disease. Cows eat grass that has been infected by the Fukushima nuclear accident and kids drink the milk therefore kids develop heart problems. There's another cover up by the way. Fukushima is a disaster on so many levels. All of the west coast of the United States and Canada is contaminated. You will now discover what we have learned the past twenty six years. The cesium is in your dairy, your wheat and… hell, what can I say, it is the beginning of a new Chernobyl Chain. Maybe in the future we'll call it the Canada Chain.

In Russia, scientists have diagnosed hundreds of cases of what is known as germ line mutations, which are basically changes in the DNA of the sperm and ovum. These mutations occurred in people living within one hundred and eighty miles of Chernobyl. That is one day of strong winds Aaron. Germ line mutations become genetic, it is passed on… do you catch my drift? It's an irreparable mutation that will multiply and multiply. Chernobyl has spurned what we call a biological legacy. We have mutations; early deaths; spontaneous abortions; inherited diseases and so much more. It's a never ending nightmare.

I have seen the grandchildren of liquidators being born without an organ. Both our adults and children are constantly sick. Their immune systems are hopeless and they cannot fight illnesses that someone in your country could shake off in a week. The men in Ukraine, Russia and Belarus have weak sperm. Many ignoramuses would find this comical but it affects the repopulation of our country, it affects the psyche of our men and it affects our economy. Less boys will be born; there are more instances of hermaphrodites… everything is linked together. Once again, it is the Chernobyl Chain, and it has been happening for twenty-six years and it is *still* happening. I see it every single day. You'd sob your eyes out if you knew how many women from Belarus and across Ukraine come to my hospital asking for an abortion. They have seen their unborn fetus and cannot bear the thought of bringing an invalid into the world. It breaks my heart over and over again.

The IAEA denies the increase of thyroid cancer in children. I hear this and I shake my head. It is rampant in Belarus and a serious problem here in Ukraine. Our studies show a five hundred percent increase in thyroid cancer since 1986. Have you ever heard of a Chernobyl necklace? It is a surgical cut from one end of the neck to the other. That's the everlasting scar when you remove a thyroid. These kids can't get jobs because of the stigma. They have problems finding partners and their lives are basically shit. The children who are inflicted spend so much time in hospitals that they have pet names for their nurses. Their immune systems have changed… their DNA has changed and this will continue with each new generation. In relation to healthier countries we have become a new species of mutants. It is truly a black mark on our history and our future.

I will end my little rant as follows: The problem won't be going away any day soon Aaron. Radiation hangs around in the atmosphere and when it rains that same radiation falls on us, on

218

our food and in our water supply. The Pripyat River drains out to Dnieper. The water from the Dnieper is what we wash in. Algae absorb radiation and small fish eat algae. Big fish eat the smaller fish and we eat the bigger fish. It is the Chernobyl Chain and as it stands now, we are only an afterthought. The IAEA has won."

Igor rubbed the back of his head and exhaled a long breath. "When I was six-years old, my father died in a Ukraine hospital that I eventually interned. Like the men in this room, he was a liquidator. On that day, I vowed to become a doctor and do whatever I could to not only eradicate cancer but to also put an end to nuclear power. I am failing on both accounts. A week after my papa died, Tania and Mila Kharmalov visited my home. They brought me some toys, and they spent the afternoon with my mother. I did not know these women although I do recall noting how strikingly beautiful they were. They did not have to console my mother, and they did not have to spend their money on toys for me but they did. An hour after they left our apartment, we were visited by the KGB. I screamed at these men and they left us alone. I was genuinely scared for these wonderful sisters. Until this evening, I had no idea that Tania was dying and I intend to visit her tomorrow. I will thank her for being who she is and who she was and then I will get on my knees and apologize for the heathens that took her away from us. I hope I do not cry but I am certain I will. That is *my* story."

I didn't respond but my only thought was as follows:

That is my story too.

****

"Igor," I said with hand extended. The doctor was on his knees next to Tania. His eyes were red, and he looked as he said he expected to look yesterday evening.

"Hello Aaron," he replied. He stared at Lena longer than I appreciated and smiled. "The last time I saw you, you were no higher than my mama's couch. Hello Lena, I'm Igor Gobachek."

Lena shook his hand and then stared at me curiously. "It's nice to meet you, Doctor."

"Excuse my intrusion," Igor said warmly. "I did not know until last evening that a family friend was in the hospital. I'm excited and honored that your Aunt remembered me."

Lena's eyebrows lifted casually as if she was accustomed to strangers lauding over her aunt. I, on the other hand, was impressed the man did what he said he would do and gave him a thumbs' up. Igor kissed Tania on both cheeks and before he bid us goodbye, he warned Lena that I was being taken away from her for the afternoon and would not be back until after dinner time. Lena nodded and sighed for longer than normal.

"You've become popular in just a few days," she groaned.

"I can't help it; I'm just so darn charming."

Tania looked good today. She was sitting upright in her bed waiting for us to arrive and the second we entered her face beamed with happiness. She told Lena that she had slept for almost twelve hours and felt refreshed. She took my hand, and I kissed her on the forehead.

"Such a gentleman," she smiled.

I smiled back and Lena rolled her eyes before giggling. Tania was in the mood to talk and rambled on to Lena for at least two minutes before facing me. I sat in my usual chair on the opposite side of the bed.

"My aunt wishes to know if you have any questions," Lena said.

I nodded yes. "I'd like to know if she and Mila were well known in Ukraine."

Lena glared back at me for what felt like an eternity before repeating my request to Tania. Tania lifted her eyebrows and shrugged before uttering a few words to her niece.

"Yes, it appears that my *boyfriend* has been researching on his own," Lena scowled. "Tania will grant you a reply. I, on the other hand, would not be so willing and will certainly be having a short discussion with Boris this evening. I imagine your doctor friend is also part of this."

Tania noticed Lena's facial expression and tapped her niece's hand lightly as if to say -"Don't worry".

"Our lives had been ripped away from us Aaron and although we knew the reason, we wanted reprisal. We wanted answers and we wanted closure. My parents were devastated; both Mila and I had our own personal traumas and it seemed to us that no matter where we travelled or where we visited, there were others in the same dilemma.

We felt there was little we could accomplish back in Kiev so my sister and I remained in Moscow. It was not what our parents wished but within a week they moved back into the Moscow apartment we dwelled in before Pripyat. It allowed us to be together while Mila and I figured out what we needed to do. At first we were angry and wrote anonymous letters to the underground newspapers but in time… in time our anger was replaced by compassion for the ever growing number of patients at Hospital Six. We saw things that were, in our eyes, not right. Doctors refused to visit the radiation patients unless they received more money, calling it Danger Pay. Nurses were phoning in sick or quitting; so many of the patients were lying on bed sheets soaked in their own urine. For us, we felt that helping these men was redemption of sorts and a way to cope with losing Roman and Yuri.

In the beginning, the hospital staff found our behavior odd as no sane person would choose to be there. Their attitudes changed quickly, and we were made very welcome. From the early morning to the late evening we did whatever we could to ensure that these men were comforted in their final days. We held their hands, we fed them and we sang to them. When nurses were unavailable we changed sheets, emptied bedpans and washed the open sores that seared their bodies. Most importantly, we comforted the families of these heroes and explained what should be expected. Since Mila and I had experienced this pain, the families were more accepting.

I did not mean to insult the doctors and nurses Aaron. They were doing an impossible job and risking their lives but even with increased staff, there were never enough of them. For three months, helping out at the Hospital was our daily routine. We did not take a day off and we ate meals that were given to us by the nurses and quite often by the families of the men we cared for. We attended funerals and comforted widows and their children. As far as we were concerned, these men and their families had to know that someone… anyone… cared about them and that we were thankful for their sacrifice.

Then our lives changed once again.

In mid-August my sister and I were sitting on a bench outside one of the hospital rooms and a young man asked to sit with us. He seemed pleasant enough and told us that one of the

Liquidator widows had mentioned how helpful we had been. I forget his name to tell you the truth. Actually, I am not certain he offered his name. He just started asking questions, and we answered them in between our duties. I recall that his face was pock marked yet he was not sensitive about it. Mila and I discussed on whether it was because of teenage acne or a childhood disease. He wore a black beret at all times as if it was fashionable. I found it rude to be wearing a hat inside a hospital but at the same time the man himself was nothing but courteous. He returned every day for a week with more questions. Neither Mila nor I had any idea that he was writing a huge story about the two of us. I thought he was more concerned with the men we were attending to. For some reason he believed it necessary to idolize us… to make us celebrities for some cause. It is true that we wanted the Kremlin to admit their errors but not at our expense. Our earlier rage had faded within weeks of working at the hospital. The idea of being the poster girls for an uprising was absurd but as soon as that article... that damn article started circulating across the Soviet Union, Mila and I were placed on some sort of freedom pedestal.

Strangers recognized us and stopped to chat. Half the time the words that came out of their mouths were frightening. They spoke of revolution and political upheavals as if we were going to lead them. Mila and I were only concerned with the radiation victims at Hospital Six. We had neither intention nor desire to fight Moscow. We didn't even want to be in Russia and I, personally, didn't consider myself Russian anymore. I was from Pripyat not Moscow yet there we were suddenly in the middle of some people's movement. That silly man wrote down all our thoughts. They were the same thoughts that most citizens of the

Soviet Union had but he put our name next to these thoughts. It was as if he was fine with sacrificing our lives for his cause, for his blind ambition."

"Forgive me Tania," I interrupted. "During that period, wasn't this type of notoriety extremely dangerous?"

"Of course it was; we were visited several times by the KGB. Our parents were visited, our neighbours were questioned…it was dreadful. There was a Major who commanded Yuri that became our guardian angel of sorts. He would not allow my sister and me to be prosecuted. Still, we continued to work at the hospital for no pay. We did so until it became unbearable for us and the staff. It was then that we began travelling to Belarus and across Ukraine to visit victims of the Chernobyl accident. If we could no longer help the patients at Hospital Six, we would help the men and women who were suffering in their homes. These were the victims with no lifeline, with no support or medicine. There was a doctor at the hospital that was sympathetic to our cause and supplied us with whatever we asked. Widows gave us clothes and toys to redistribute to the needy. Our fame became less of an adherence when shop owners donated food and blankets.

Yet, no matter where we went, we were followed. Mila was not a shy person, and she often vented her anger on KGB officers but not so much that we would be arrested. I trusted her judgment and for the most part she remained calm or calm enough. That changed when a quick stop in Moscow to see our parents brought us a surprise visit from an unexpected and unwanted visitor.

Lena was almost two by late December 1987. She laughed a lot yet was uncommonly quiet for a child that was constantly travelling from one city or village to another. For eleven months, we rode carts and hitchhiked across Ukraine and Belarus visiting ex-patients and treating those that could not fly to Moscow or Kiev. The hospitals in Belarus welcomed us with open arms and allowed us to sleep in their dormitories with interns who wished to be elsewhere. The atmosphere in these hospitals was dreadful, and we witnessed horrors that no human should. Children being born with no limbs or one too many limbs; legs swelling up to size of elephant trunks; a baby with no eyes…

There were nights when I closed my eyes Aaron and prayed to God to whisk me away to a different time, a happy time. If he was punishing us, I begged him to stop as our lessons had been learned.

God's classroom lights are never dimmed.

After fourteen months in Belarus, word spread that the Kharmalov sisters were preaching democracy to weak willed, susceptible patients and their traumatized families. The accusations that caused us to flee Russia had followed us like a hungry dog to a different country. It was as if someone wished us to fail. The propagandist newspaper articles devoted to us were as bitter as the Belarus winter winds. Hospital administrators avoided our pleas for reason and demanded we leave.

Children cried as did their parents. They tugged on our sweaters and begged us to stay. Two police officers escorted us to the Ukraine border. They gave us their money, blankets and a basket of food. One of the officers knelt and asked forgiveness. He cried openly much to the embarrassment of his partner who was ashamed of his government's actions but far less emotional.

The snow was heavy, and we had no boots. Lena was crying.

For the first time in over a year Mila and I were revisited by a feeling that we had hoped would never return. Yuri had felt it. My parents were still feeling it and now it was back in our lives.

We arrived in Moscow on a Wednesday night and mama and papa were ecstatically happy. I remember mama not allowing Lena to leave her sight for the entire day. There was no baby food in the apartment so Mila set out early Thursday morning to buy vegetables and fruits to stick in a blender. Mama had a good one she was quite proud of so in her own words, making pureed food was more convenient than buying.

Tragedy was our new name. We seriously considered that we were cursed. Mother mentioned that it was our Gypsy aunt, but that joke was no longer funny. Mila and I had spoken in great detail of the quiet life we would lead once were settled in our Moscow apartment. We agreed to allow the events of the last two years to be swallowed up like a sink hole by new memories... happy memories. It was not to be. The sink hole swallowed us instead.

After all she had been through; this was the worst day of Mila's life.

Thursday, December 17th, 1987. 9:30 A.M.

A snowstorm had passed through Moscow a day earlier leaving behind two feet of snow. The streets were still being ploughed in the well-known Sleeping Zone suburb of Moscow proper. Mila sidestepped many pedestrians as she weaved through icy patches on just about every square of sidewalk. The closest grocery store was owned by a husband and wife that lived in her building and she was looking forward to saying hello. A young man with a black beret recognized her and said hello. Mila smiled and replied the same before quickening her pace. She was in no mood to listen to radical rant. As she neared the corner two police officers were waiting for her. She was not surprised by this as it was happening all too often. Only one of the men spoke while the other leered at her very openly.

"Your papers please" he demanded.

Mila took out her citizenship papers and handed them to the officer.

"Mila Kharmalov," he said slowly while glancing at his partner. "You must be very proud of the popularity you have attained on the backs of those that protect you. Where is your sister at this moment?"

She knew something was astray as this was not their common procedure. Normally a police officer would look at your papers, ask a question and then let you leave. Mila accepted that she was not going anywhere very quickly.

"Why do you ask?" Mila replied frustrated. "We have told you time and time again, we are loyal citizens and wish to cause no change."

227

"Answer the question," he ordered.

"My sister Tania is with my child and parents at our residence."

"This would be the kidnapped child of one of our comrades?" the officer claimed. His breath formed a cold cloud and drifted into Mila's eyes.

Mila scrunched her face and a sudden anger rose through her chest. "Kidnapped? You are misinformed comrade. The cowardly father of my daughter Lena abandoned us at Pripyat for a slut in tight pants. I have not heard from him in eighteen months."

"You have not heard from him because he could not track you," said a voice behind the two officers.

Simon stepped around the men and faced Mila. He had changed little except for the round glasses that now rested on his tiny nose. His face was not as thin and she noticed a few white hairs hanging outside his fur hat.

She stared at him with disdain. "You piece of shit, how dare you show your ugly face to me? Go home to your whore."

"I want my daughter Mila and today I shall have her." He pulled his gloves passed his wrists and they immediately returned to where they had been.

"Fuck you," she screamed at him. "Leave us alone and go paint your bullshit dreams. You were never Lena's father and never will be."

The two officers abruptly grabbed Lena and pinned her violently against a storefront wall. Her white cotton hat fell to the sidewalk. Bystanders walked away realizing what was happening. The young man that Lena had said hello to earlier was watching from across the street, scribbling on a notepad. Cars slowed to catch a short glimpse.

Simon edged up close to his ex-wife and whispered in her ear. "When will you ever learn that you cannot defeat us? You are a servant to Mother Russia and nothing more. We are your Masters."

Mila's face was pressed against the wall and a protruding brick scratched her left eyebrow.

"He likes men… did you know that," she squealed at the officers. "You are following orders from a man that should be arrested. Listen to me you dumb fuckers, he's a sodomite."

Simon laughed out loud. "Nice try bitch," he said while spitting on her. "You can release her when the child is with me," he instructed the officers. "If she causes any problems, I give you permission to do whatever you please for as long as you like."

He walked away and was instantly followed by a car with two occupants. The door opened, and he hopped in. They drove away to the complex lived in by the Kharmalov family.

An hour later, a frantic Mila entered her parent's apartment. Everyone was crying.

Lena was gone.

****

"What are you going to do?" Tania asked. She sat at the kitchen table facing her distraught sister.

Their parents had long fallen asleep, exhausted by the day's events. It was near midnight and Mila had said very little over the past three hours. Tears had dried on her face and she refused to wash them away. Her normally rosy cheeks were a dull pasty white. A violent winter wind assaulted their balcony window searching for a way in. Neither of the sisters noticed.

"If I could fight them with ammunition, I would rain a barrage of death upon them. If I had the magic button that would launch a hundred nuclear warheads on this shitty country, I would press it in a heartbeat."

Tania said nothing hoping her sister would come up with an intelligent plan of attack.

Mila clutched her hands around the back of her head. "I'm so tired Tania. I cannot beat the communists. I am nothing more than a wheel on someone else's automobile. We are all the same and to whom will I plead my case? Will they listen to me over one of their own?"

"No, they will not," Tania replied angrily. "But you and I are not like anyone else, are we? Even if *they* do not listen, others will. Maybe we've never wished it but this destiny has fallen upon us. It has forced itself through our doorway and until we beat it down, it will hold us captive."

Mila lifted her head and touched her sister's face. "Destiny is an ice cold witch, my sister. The lines we cross will eventually be the lines that bind our wrists. Are you prepared to cross that line and are we in this together?"

"My life is your life," Tania answered without delay. "Shall I get the paper and pen?"

She knew me too well, Mila thought. "I don't want to be inspirational Tania. I only want to say what is on my mind… on our minds. It will be our voice and our words that readers will remember. No matter what happens - Yuri, Roman and Lena will

230

be proud of us. And... no matter what happens - we will always be the sisters Kharmalov."

"Always," Tania whispered and then repeated.

The next morning Mila awoke and slipped on her winter coat and boots. She told her inquisitive and worried mother that she would return in an hour. The temperature had dropped to below freezing and very few people were walking the main street. She followed the same path she walked yesterday and waited. As expected the young man with the black beret approached her. He was about to walk by but Mila grabbed him by the arm.

"Tell your editor that he did a real number on my life," she said very seriously.

"Excuse me?" the man replied.

"Give him this," she said unperturbed while handing him the letter that she and Tania wrote. "Next Thursday is the western holiday called Christmas. I want this piece circulated on that day. Is this understood? The following article on my arrest will also contain a reprint of what I have written and will be circulated the following week."

"I will guarantee this Mila," the stranger assured.

She nodded a few times not sure if she was pleased with his answer or if she felt a total and undeniable disdain for the young man.

"I never want to see you or your black beret again."

"I cannot guarantee that as I am loyal to you," he answered with a hurt voice.

Mila closed her eyes hoping this nightmare would go away. She did not want the burden, and she did not want the fame.

"Return my daughter to me and we will speak again."

This time the man smiled. He bowed his head slightly and turned away. She watched him as he disappeared around the corner. He is trying to make a difference, she thought.

He's wasting his time.

The young man's name was Petr, and he was the assistant editor of the samizdat, a monthly underground newspaper that was delivered to coffee shops and kiosks across Russia. Copies were dropped off anonymously in the subway and anywhere with heavy foot traffic.

Petr stopped in one of these local coffee shops and sat to read what Mila had delivered. A pretty waitress with short brown hair offered him coffee, and he accepted graciously. He removed his beret and placed it next to the cup and saucer. The handwriting was exquisite, but he expected no less from a woman he found to be extraordinary. Her eyes were so penetrating he thought he would never forget them. Petr took a sip of coffee and then read the words written by the Kharmalov sisters.

We are not who you think we are.

If you are expecting a sticky sweet soliloquy or some nauseating, incomprehensible poem about the Russian soul, then you will be disappointed and quite frankly, we don't care.

My sister Tania and I are products of good parents and the city of Pripyat. We were born in Russia but the jewel city of the Soviet Union whitewashed memories of our birth land. With respect to those of you living in the Sleep Zones or the towns and villages surrounding this

232

metropolis we call Moscow, there is not one citizen of Pripyat who has returned here willingly.

The Pripyat streets and apartment complexes were as pristine as the beach that welcomed us every summer weekend. The coffee served in our shops was brewed in machines delivered from Italy. Parks bloomed with hundreds if not thousands of flowers every spring. We were the elite, living a life that the vast majority of those reading this article could never imagine and will never attain. It is an unfortunate truth but also a call to arms for young Russians who dream of a better life for their families and future generations.

As many of you are aware, Tania and I spent several months at Hospital Six caring for and attending to men who died for all of us. It has been less than two years since Reactor Four of the Chernobyl Nuclear Plant caught fire and released millions upon millions of radioactive isotopes into our everyday lives. The men that fought the fires; cleared the roof or buried villages are already forgotten by those who naively believe they were not affected or are no longer affected. What horribly ignorant people you are. You are dying. Even as you read this I can assure you with great certainty that you are dying.

And you do nothing.

I watched my sister Tania cry a universe of tears while the man she loved more than life itself choked on his liquefied organs. His blood was pink. Are you unsure that you have read this properly? Let me repeat then. His blood was pink. Can you imagine the horror that Tania will dream every night for the rest of her days? I watched as our beloved and beautiful brother could no longer cry a tear. My hand is shaking as I write this. He was twelve for God's sake and his skin slid off his bones. He was the light of my life and taken from me because we are a nation of scared and desperate corpses. I say fuck you to each and every one of our citizens who chooses to continue this charade. We allowed Yuri Larinov *to die for us and we allowed Roman Kharmalov to die for no reason at all. I could give you a long list of widows who have nothing left to live for but I honestly question if you would care. Will you remember their names as you empty one more bottle of vodka into your bloated stomachs?*

Fuck you.

A century of history has claimed our souls yet we do nothing. Millions of Russians were murdered by a madman who stole our land and declared we were better off working for a Soviet Union. We accepted this as if it was our calling. To this day we fight in wars protecting a motherland that refuses to nurture its own children. It is always accepted as our lot in life. We are Russians thus it is our duty to be miserable bastards. We accept catastrophes as just another day or as expected. "Never be happy because tomorrow will bring more gloom." It is the Russian mantra. What a pitiful existence we lead and what a pitiful people we are.

Aside from working at Hospital Six, Tania and I crossed Russia, Ukraine and Belarus. The stories we heard could only be construed as unbelievable and we often believed the storytellers were exaggerating. It turns out that they were not. Every claim, every mountain of a story was fact. I will share some of these details with you comprehending that they will fall on deaf ears and that the majority of you would prefer to piss in the hallways of your filthy apartment buildings than to actually fight back and be real men.

Did you give your children milk today? Did you feed your family a delicious plate of beef at dinner time? I can only hope that you did not. Tania and I learned that a huge portion of ground beef from non-toxic cows has been mixed with the intestines and meat of radioactive cows and the practice continues to this very day. We ship the majority of our toxic milk to Belarus. "Give it to them cheap, they'll love us." The

Kremlin is well aware of this, in fact they signed the orders. Nonetheless, Muscovites have received a good portion of the deadly milk and beef. Tell me, does it hurt a bit more when you suddenly realize that you are also a victim?

Perhaps this knowledge will move your shiftless asses or perhaps not. That is your choice.

At twenty-three minutes past one a.m. on April 26th 1986, my life was disrupted not for a day or a week but for a lifetime. Why did this happen? The Kremlin will have you believe that this enormous catastrophe was the fault of two technicians. Bullshit. What our leaders will not tell you is that similar disasters have occurred in other nuclear plants across our country but not as massive. Almost every inch of our nation has been scorched by radioactivity at some time in the last thirty years.

Reactor Four in Chernobyl was constructed hurriedly and without proper inspection. The roof was built with combustible material. What brilliant architect would build a nuclear power plant roof with something that can burst into flames? What is even more incredible is that the roof was only one of a hundred infrastructure errors that were kept hushed.

Chernobyl was not an accident, it was a disaster with a timeline and the Kremlin knew it.

And now our leaders wait for a new generation of citizens to forget how they murdered us. The history books will not be rewritten, they will never make mention of the hundreds if not thousands of years we will be poisoned by this calamity. All will be mercifully forgotten.

You have already forgotten.

Belarus is a wasteland. Has anyone told you this? Tania and I saw children born with limbs on their back or with foreheads the size of footballs. We witnessed a mother scream in terror as her child's gigantic head snapped off its neck when she held her daughter for the first time. It is happening here too; do not be so sanctimonious as to believe that we are immune to these horrors. They are occurring every day in hospitals throughout Russia. The difference is that if a doctor in Moscow wrote about these experiences, he would disappear. He or she would never be seen again.

My ex-husband has convinced his superiors that he is worthy of a proletariat position. It is confusing to me how such a man could be offered a job requiring total loyalty. The day after the Chernobyl explosion he left my daughter and I to fend for ourselves and then boarded a bus with a woman who was desperate for a new life. He didn't even kiss his daughter goodbye.

Yesterday he took my girl from me claiming I kidnapped her. I did no such thing, but I have deduced that he needs a child in his home to distract from his latent homosexual desires. His name is Simon Danilova. He had police officers detain me on the street while he stole my daughter from the arms of her grandmother. Before leaving me, he made sure I understood that we could never defeat our communist leaders, and that we were nothing but servants to our masters. Those were his words, and he sincerely believed them.

So my dear servants, I ask you with humility if we are worthy of the blood that runs through our veins. Does the life of a Russian have any value or are we merely tiny pebbles to be skipped off the waves of a radiated sea? My sister cannot bring back her Yuri and I cannot wish my Roman to walk through the front door and flip on the television to watch Alien Conquest. They are gone from this world. I have no judicial court to listen to my pleas for the return of my daughter. So what exactly do I have?

What exactly do we have?

Within one week of you reading this, my sister Tania and I will be made to vanish. I do not know where we will be sent but until that time we will remain with my parents and enjoy their love for as long as possible.

Perhaps you will care what happens to us or perhaps not. That is your choice.

We are not who you think we are. We are you, no more and no less. When our voices are stifled, your voices are stifled. We humbly ask that you remember the sisters Kharmalov. We ask that you remember Yuri, Roman, all the men and children who have died because of Kremlin lies and remember the wives who leave flowers at the fence of a cemetery they are not permitted to enter. We ask that you open your eyes as wide as your hearts. We ask that you save Ukraine and Belarus. We ask that you save Russia if indeed it is worth saving. That is your choice.

Finally, we ask that you join us in telling the Kremlin, the KGB and their sympathizer's two words and only two words.

Fuck you.

My name is Mila Kharmalov and my sister is Tania Kharmalov. Perhaps one day we will meet or perhaps not.

That is your choice.

Petr read the letter a second and a third time. He then folded it carefully and placed it in the pocket of his winter coat. He paid for his coffee and then headed towards the secret office of the samizdat. For the last few years the paper had become a focal point for poets and philosophers. The newspaper had remained popular but since the seventies, readership had dwindled until the story of the Kharmalov sisters graced the front page. The original article about Tania and Mila was read by more Russians than any other issue. University campuses all over Russia plastered the article in their cafeterias, libraries and even washrooms. Although the sisters were unaware of the vastness of their fame, Petr was not. These next two press prints would be read around the world.

I will return your daughter to you, Mila Kharmalov, he promised himself.

****

"I find it amazing that someone can just take your child without any court order or doctor's letter...something." I said shaking my head.

"Russia trailed behind until recently Aaron," Lena cut in. "Before the Soviet Union was dismantled there was no such thing as Social Services. The final word was signed and delivered by a ruling member and rarely were the concerns of a woman considered when decisions were made. It is getting better but then we hear about Pussy Riot and dead journalists and the old beliefs resurface. Progress in Russia is a fragile old woman with no cane."

Tania smiled understanding only my facial expression. "It was our life Aaron, it was what we accepted. Two days after the letter was printed and circulated the KGB knocked on our apartment door and handcuffed Mila and me. Our parents were sad but strangely, not angry. They were proud of us, especially my mother, which is something neither of us expected. Even when I think of this today I cannot imagine the thought process of my mother during this difficult time. She stood up to the KGB and called them farm chickens frightened of the farmer's dog. She got up right in front of his nose and told him he was worthless. The

238

agent did not say a word as if he was unsure of what he was doing and as if he believed the words my mother was yelling were true. Neither of the men uttered a word to us while we were in their car. They would look at us in the rear view mirror and then lower their eyes like they were ashamed. Like the officers on our last day in Belarus, I am convinced that they knew what they were doing was wrong.

We were put on a bus and sent to a Siberian labour camp in Maryinsk. It was known as a Gulag decades earlier but we were not treated as harshly as the male prisoners of those days. There were three hundred women, about fifteen children and twenty male guards. The babies or children stayed in a different section but mothers were able to visit every day. We shared a room with thirty other female detainees and throughout our imprisonment neither Tania nor I slept more than six hours any night.

The day after we arrived, the word got out that we were the Kharmalov sisters. It would be hard for you to believe Aaron but Mila and I were treated as some kind of royalty within these walls. Inmates swapped their beds so that my sister and I could sleep next to each other. If a guard got too close, our prison mates would come to our rescue. You can imagine that many of the guards were not good men and they took advantage of the younger girls. We were not immune to their advances and their hands but we were never subjected to anything more than gropes. The other ladies would not permit this and would maintain abstinence to all guards if either of us was harmed.

It was a work camp and we sewed government uniforms for eight hours a day. Some ladies worked the fields in the summer growing vegetables that became the soups and meals we ate throughout the year. There were some nasty women of course.

239

I guess that is expected but they too let us be. If anything, they often acted as our security ensuring the prison guards did not watch us in the showers. The two years we spent in prison were for the most part, uneventful. News of the outside world came from word of mouth. Most of us were nonplussed about external events. In late February of 1989, things became weird and then seven months later a foreigner caused our life to become…I guess I can say, wonderfully weird. The weird piece started with a visit from a man that Mila would eventually hunt for years.

He called himself The Prince.

Chapter Two: The Prince's Imagination

Prison

Her orange jumpsuit was not entirely flattering but the new prison guard gasped silently when he saw Mila for the first time. He had heard stories but never imagined that any woman could be so lovely. He dropped his head and concentrated on why he was instructed to visit this dreary hell hole.

The space itself was a cliché dark with no windows. A six foot by four foot table was in the middle of the room with the customary light source above the table. Valerie Markov sat in front of his interviewee and placed a tape recorder between them. He pressed the Play button and began the interview.

"Mila Danilova?" he asked, expecting a harsh response.

"My name is Mila Kharmalov… never call me that disgusting name again." She closed her eyes realizing the man was toying with her. She would be more careful. "Call me what you wish comrade, it makes no difference in the long run."

He placed his hands on the blue folder he had brought with him. "I can call you Kharmalov if you prefer. As you say, it makes no difference and I personally couldn't care less."

He lightly touched his eyebrow and Mila found this somewhat effeminate. The man was average looking at best but appeared to be someone who spent a great deal of time in front of his bathroom mirror. His black hair, albeit too long, was washed and bound tightly in a ponytail. His security uniform was ironed and fit to perfection.

"You spent five minutes with my sister yesterday. Why do you feel it necessary to ask me the same questions?"

He shrugged off her inquiry. "Your sister is a delight to speak with but I surmised rather quickly that she knows much less than you. She is a soft soul and I could not bear to interrogate her."

Mila nodded appreciatively. "Ah, so you have deduced that I will have no issue in telling you to fuck off. Let me save you the wait time… fuck you. Will this make your interview more enjoyable now?"

"Bravo," he smiled while clapping listlessly. "You are exactly what I have been advised. Before we continue this pretense, would you like some coffee or tea? Maybe milk from a radioactive cow?"

"Oh... now it's my turn to say bravo," Mila answered followed by mocking claps. "That was very clever for a Siberian prison guard. How does one become a prison guard in Siberia? Is there a school program or do the Soviet brain trust throw you into a truck and dump you here? I would side with the latter."

Markov was having difficulty not staring into Mila's eyes and for a moment wondered why Danilova would ever leave her. She's a bit foul-mouthed but strangely refreshing. Nonetheless, he was here to do a job and would not allow the Kharmalov woman to garner any leeway.

"Neither actually. We come here to rape women who deserve to be raped. At night we swap stories and then write letters to the women's parents describing the experience. It is hard to imagine that we get paid for this too. I am looking forward to writing your parents."

"Big man with a little dick," Mila huffed, unperturbed by his vulgarity.

"And after I write your parents I will write the samizdat. If I'm feeling generous I'll accompany my article with a photo or two."

Mila shook her head and sneered. "Do you even have a dick? You seem to me as someone who has lost his penis. Did you lose your penis?"

No matter what she said, Valeri would not be swayed from his mission. He wanted desperately to burst her ego and hurt her in ways the pampered princess had never experienced before.

"Tell me about the samizdat Mila…why did they choose you? I mean - let's face it - who are you? I've read the samizdat articles and the subsequent dribble that followed. I've poured through the KBG reports and it has always struck me odd as why the men who write this sentimental slop are always hung up on your looks, as if you are some Greek statuette. You are really no different than most women but these pawns give you so much rope to play with and then forget the treason you have instigated. I, on the other hand, will take that same rope and wrap it around your neck. I'll have no problem whatsoever in defiling you over and over again to prove what I believe is true. You're nothing special aside from big tits and a decent face so why don't you shut that face and answer my questions.

Is it not true that you approached the editor of samizdat to write these famous articles? Did you embellish your stories to get back at a successful ex-husband who left you because of your extreme lack of culture?"

Mila found his diatribe pointless and the questions absurd. She had never backed down to any man and was not about to start now.

"So many questions... what's in the folder? Can I see?"

"Concentrate prisoner Kharmalov. Why did you approach the samizdat?"

"Aside from *man with no dick*, what do I call you?" Mila questioned, trying to infuriate the guard.

"You answer my question and I'll answer yours."

Mila laughed out loud. "What does it matter? I'm in jail. What the fuck can you do to me now that..."

She stopped talking and thought about what was happening and why this man was sent to visit her.

"This is interesting," she began slowly. "Why would a special - *prison guard person* - be sent from Moscow to speak with me when I have already been accused and sentenced? Stop me if I'm not on the right track here. Someone talked, and it got back to a pencil pushing worry wart in Moscow. Am I getting close? The elite need something to keep us here. That's it isn't it?" Markov did not change his blank expression. "My ex-husband needs to explain why he put me and Tania in this prison." She smiled and shook her head, disgusted with the Soviet Union communist government. "How is Moscow these days? Still teetering on the edge of a cliff? Counting down to the end?"

Markov took a handkerchief out of his pocket and wiped his hands for no reason. "The Soviet Union and our communist belief is very much alive comrade Kharmalov. Am I to believe you are a trader or perhaps a threat to our empire?"

"Well duh... that's why I'm here Einstein. What side of stupid did you wake up on this morning?"

Markov pursed his lips and released a scratchy kiss. "You are not like your sister. I preferred the company of your sister. She is angelic while you are a crass bitch. How did two completely

245

contrary humans come from the same womb? Was your mother a whore?"

"Oh tsk-tsk small dick man," Mila said feeling empowered. "We're going to discuss our mothers? I am looking at a mama's boy and you want to discuss mothers? Come on... relax, take a deep breath and try harder. Put your little handkerchief back in your pocket and be a man."

"The infamous Mila Kharmalov," Markov wheezed while gently rubbing his forehead. "I was told you were a vision of loveliness and every man's dream. To be honest, I am disappointed. Your beauty fades quite rapidly once your personality is revealed."

Mila shot back instantly. "I didn't ask to meet with you and I am not here to fill your fantasies or fuel your tiny erection. The samizdat approached me and asked me questions. They ruined my life, and they ruined my sister's life. If I could take back every word, I would in a second. That is all there is to this ignorant interview. There are no secrets, there is no underlying story. It is what it is and nothing more. So if that is all that you need to know, I would like to end this interview the way I began it. *Fuck you.*"

The well-groomed interrogator smiled believing he had touched a nerve. "This interview will end when I say it is over. I have not decided how long my letter to your parents will be or how many pictures I will send with my article."

At that moment there was a knock on the door and a short man with glasses entered the room with a coffee for Valeri. He was staring at the floor when he placed the hot cup in front of his co-worker. The shy man had a long deep scar on his left cheek.

Mila's jaw dropped, and she stared at him in disbelief. Roman had once described a man similar to the one she was looking at.

It had to be him. *It was him.*

"Thank-you Chipmunk," Valeri said half officially and half comically. "This is Mila Kharmalov close up; the woman of false lore in the flesh. Take a quick glance and try not to ejaculate."

The man named Chipmunk did not look at Mila and shuffled back to the entrance. Mila watched him leave knowing that he was a murderer. A brush stroke of frigid air passed through her prison uniform and she folded her arms against her chest.

She recognized his name.

She took a moment to compose herself as Markov sipped his coffee.

"Is he a friend of yours?" Mila asked coolly.

"He has this employment because of me. We have been acquaintances for a few years now."

"I am from Pripyat… did you know this?" Mila started. She would ask the prison guard leading questions hoping to dupe him.

"What fool does not know this? That is an inane question from someone who should be answering and not asking. Perhaps you are not aware of the roles of an interviewer and an interviewee. I will ask again Kharmalov… who did you approach to tell your lies?"

Mila paid no attention. "Your hair is very long for a prison guard… it is almost woman-like. Do you have complexes or insecurities about your appearance that you wish to discuss?"

"I will let you touch it later on when I straddle you. What was the editors name Mila?"

She leaned back on her chair with her hand against the side of her mouth. This is the man who carved that young girl's face with crosses. She was sure of it yet not at all frightened of the consequences of revealing her belief. He had much more to lose than she.

What was his name?

"When the reactor blew there was mass pandemonium. Soldiers and liquidators were everywhere. It was impossible to police such an influx of people. Were you a reservist or a soldier? You must have spent time at Chernobyl?"

Valeri glanced at the tape recorder and nodded yes. "Why are we discussing ancient history?"

Mila acknowledged his secrecy. "There was talk of enlisted men stealing family heirlooms and then selling them on the black market. Some of these thieves made small fortunes and were never caught."

"So then," Valeri said trying to push the conversation back in his favor. "You are saying your editor was one of these men? That would be fitting for a man who prints lies."

This was turning into a game of ping pong psychology, Mila thought. "For a short period – until the KGB insisted I halt – my sister and I tried to track a couple of these thieves. The story was documented in the first samizdat article but I will elaborate for you, small dick man."

"I wait with great anticipation," he replied sarcastically.

"Two of these criminals snuck away from Pripyat and drove to the small village of Kopachi. I have a tendency to believe that Kopachi was the home town of one of the men. I was close to confirming this but our brilliant government officials shut me down."

He pushed the tape recorder closer to Mila. "Thus, your editor was from Kopachi? Is this what you are alluding to and are you giving me a clue?"

Valeri was pleased with how he covered his tracks.

"Bravo," Mila applauded the man. "You are a worthy opponent and now lead two bravos' to my one. Did you know I studied psychology in university? I didn't finish because I chose to marry a homosexual. You can well imagine that my few years of training did not serve me well at the time." Valeri did not respond. "I had a fascinating course that delved into the minds of psychopaths and serial killers. My professor was an older gentleman who was very passionate that every madman was product of his mother's personality. It was *always* the mother's fault. I truly despised that belief but at the same time his proof was overwhelming if you were to believe the case studies he gave us. Mind you, these studies were biased and students were never treated or assigned cases that proved otherwise."

"You are boring me comrade Kharmalov, please get to your point so that we can continue the true nature of my being here."

"Well it is a very Russian character trait do you not agree? Russian sons are placed on pedestals well above their sibling sisters. I used to read these case studies and compare them to what I often viewed with my own eyes. Russian men struggle with moral dilemmas versus the pampering they expect from their wives or mothers. If they do not receive exceptional treatment they either turn to vodka or beat their women. Sometimes they kill their wives. I would hazard a guess that we have the highest rate of spousal abuse in the world although I cannot prove it. How do you feel about this?"

"I think you would make a shitty psychiatrist."

Mila disregarded his comment. "My mother did not pamper my brother Roman. Truth be told, it was me. He was my best friend, and I was his."

Valeri took a sip of his coffee. "I am losing patience Kharmalov."

"Why would you lose patience?" Mila asked with furrowed brow. "Do you have somewhere to go small dick man? I'm certain that you can't return to Moscow without some kind of reward from me. In fact, I'm certain that you have nowhere to go at all."

Valeri turned off the tape recorder. "It has to be pleasant for you to have special status knowing all along that I cannot take out my gun and pistol whip you. You must think me stupid, Mila Kharmalov. You had privileges in Pripyat and now you have them here in prison. A traitor to our communist brothers and sisters yet you are untouchable. I talk my game understanding that I can't raise a hand to you and you sit there smugly, knowing I cannot. I don't call this fair but I work with what I am given. What you haven't grasped - you faggot loving slut - is that eventually you will be released from these prison walls and I will be waiting for you. When your popularity fades from our short memories there will be nowhere for you to hide and believe me when I tell you this... I *will* find you."

Refusing to waver from threats, Mila tilted her head sideways. "Have you seen my baby? The aliens took her from me."

"Have you suddenly lost your senses woman?" Valeri responded, not following Mila's leading comment. He was more intent on bringing Mila down a few levels and would strike her

250

where it hurt. As he spoke he monitored Mila's facial expressions. "Your daughter is with her father and the skinny woman. I found it somewhat amusing to learn that you knew this skank very well in your rich town. Small world isn't it? I had my way with the skinny woman so that you know. Your ex-husband avoids her now just like he shunned you. He was in his home office and I fucked her on the kitchen counter. Oh, and it was a big kitchen with expensive accessories; very bourgeoisie for a bureaucrat in my humble opinion. And the little one… what's she called again? Oh yes, *Lena* was sleeping a few feet away. The skinny bitch kept screaming the name Alex until I slapped her a few times. Does that name mean something to you? It was the bugging the shit out of me but no matter. She was crying when I left and asked that I apologize to you. It would have been very touching if I could feel any kind of emotion. This is the woman your daughter now calls mama. How does it feel to know that your daughter is being raised by an ass-nuzzler and a whore? She's going to be a piece of work when she gets older. Next time I bump the emaciated wench, I will ensure that Lena is wide awake so that she can watch and learn."

Mila did not retaliate while the man's words sunk in. She realized that he could be lying but at the same time his comments came as validation to what she and Tania had often discussed.

"I am both surprised and not surprised. The fact that you have no emotion fits the criteria I have evaluated. Sex with Yulia is also no surprise. I would tone down your enthusiasm about it; her virtue was never her positive feature. What surprises me the most is that you are still able to achieve an erection. The odds are flabbergasting considering your past and considering the insecurity you must have about your small penis."

Valeri folded his hands and bit his lip. The Kharmalov woman was a worthy advocate but not prone to emotional outbursts. What upset him was that this prisoner may be smarter than him. It was upsetting to know that he would not accomplish anything today.

"Very well, based on our discussion, I shall return to Moscow and inform the powers that be that you are a danger to the Soviet Union and should be imprisoned for a minimum of fifty years."

"And what makes you believe that you will be leaving this prison?" Mila said while rotating her neck.

"I have no desire to continue this useless discussion unless you want me to stay. Have I turned you on? We can do it on this table if you wish."

The pretty woman rolled her eyes. "Hmm. You have quite the ego for someone less than average in every possible way. During several of your futile tirades, I've been trying to place a name; it's driving me crazy. My brother Roman went fishing in Kopachi on the Sunday morning after the nuclear explosion. He had this silly notion that aliens had landed in Pripyat and that was why soldiers were combing the villages. He ended up staying overnight with a man named Olav who was later assassinated by other members of that fucked up community. I'll get back to Olav as I am sure you want to learn more. The next day, Roman met a young girl who had been abandoned by her grandmother. Should I say the girl's name or shall we take it for granted that all is understood?" Valerie did not nod or reply. "Very well, her name was Galina. I met her the day after my brother stuck a knife in the testicles of the despicable piece of crap who was raping her. Anything you wish to add... *Valeri?*"

She knew his name. The filthy bitch knew his name. He thought of his exit plan while the conversation continued.

"Yes, I would be pleased to comment. She gave me a venereal disease. The little blond prostitute was awesome but her cunt reeked. It was a lesson I shall never forget. Smell the pussy first before entering. We should be teaching this in our schools."

"I imagine the pain was excruciating," Mila said proudly.

Valeri shrugged. "Right through the scrotum but I am pleased to say that it missed my balls. I had to get Chipmunk to remove the knife. What are friends for if not to remove sharp objects from their buddy's scrotum?"

"Let me see your ear," Mila requested.

"No," the man replied. "Let me see your tits. I guess not. I'm an artist Mila Kharmalov just like your ex-husband but I do not paint monuments to dead men. I paint dead women… women I kill. On the night your brother left me pinned to a kitchen table, I did not have my art material. I needed to paint Galina because I wished to kill her. Given the circumstances, I chose to carve symbols on her face and forehead. I chose the Christian cross because I believed Galina needed saving… like you. I very much look forward to the day when I paint your portrait."

"She was just an abused girl… a child. Why would you kill her?"

"You are not listening Kharmalov. I did not have my brushes so I could not end her life. She died the same way her mother died. The villagers hung her on the tree by the side of the road. The girl was a prostitute, and this is a sin."

Mila nodded very slowly, unsure of why this obvious murderer was alluding to religion. "And these are the same villagers that put a bullet in your brother's head? Did you not wish to exact revenge?"

Markov gestured his hands to show his disinterest in any revengeful act. "Why would I do that? Olav was a shell of a man. If I killed men, he would have been the first but I only kill what I fuck and I don't fuck men. I leave bestiality to perverts like your ex-husband but I will tell you a little story. One time after my mama drugged Olav, I took some garden shears from the shed and snipped off three of his fingers. He was in a coma-like sleep and momentarily awoke when I was about to snip the last digit. He laughed and went back to sleep. It was exhilarating and to be honest the beginning of a new life for me. We called our mother Baba and let me tell you, Baba was very proud that evening… very proud. Then I punched her in the head, lifted her skirt and dry humped her from behind until she cried for mercy. She always preached that women had to be trained like dogs. So I trained her. That was my last day living in Kopachi and my last day living as anyone's servant."

This man was not human; he was one of the disgusting aliens that Roman spoke of.

"You should not be allowed to walk freely."

Valeri laughed. "It's always the mother right? Isn't that what your professor taught? Listen to the older generation Mila, they have much to offer." He laughed again.

Mila was finished with surprises. "I found Galina's grandmother, and the kidnapped child. The old woman cursed me, said I would live the rest of my days in damnation. I told her I was a Gypsy and showed her all my teeth. Then I spat on her. She was executed. Fittingly, I should add. I watched as she dangled from a long rope. I expect you will face the same fate someday soon."

"Oh Mila Kharmalov, I am much too smart. There were conditions for me to make this voyage to visit you and I also have pictures of your husband in a less than flattering position. I won't get into details but I can assure you that no matter what you claim, none of it can ever tie me to the whereabouts." He smiled realizing the parallels of what he just said. "Look at me, I'm untouchable too. That never dawned in me until this very moment. We have something in common to remember until the day I get my opportunity to paint your portrait."

"This is the Soviet Union," Mila rebutted, "There is always someone screwing up. I am confident that some KGB loser will enjoy the opportunity to investigate a psycho."

Markov grinned. "Now, now, let's not get vicious. Please take into account that while you are in here…I am out there and Lena is out there too. I'm just making a point of reference that you might find important."

He played his best card last. As with most demented psychopaths be could be lying so she would relay her information to one of the guards later on this evening. She was Mila Kharmalov after all and that should account for something.

"And one last bravo goes to you, small dick man. You saved the best for last. Congratulations, you have truly won this battle."

Valeri stood up and stretched. "The battle has only just begun Mila," he answered emphatically. The man paused for a few seconds before continuing. "I would never harm your sister; I want you to know that. I *will* paint her portrait but she will not be aware of my proximity." He made an awkward bowing

255

movement that confused Mila. "It has been a rare pleasure to be sitting with you today, comrade Kharmalov. You are a raunchy liar and I cannot wait for the day that I screw you repeatedly until you beg me to end your utterly useless existence. I promise to wrap you in a Russian flag and sing the anthem while you embrace death. Your portrait will be a crowning glory... my Da Vinci if I may."

"And I cannot wait for the day that I loudly applaud your execution," Mila shot back but with minimal exuberance. "I guess we both have something to dream about."

"Please allow me one last question Mila Kharmalov." She stared back at him without answering. "If you were standing in front of God and he blessed you with one wish, what would you ask for?"

Mila shrugged as if the answer was obvious. "I would ask him to give Lena a long and healthy life."

Valeri was clearly unhappy with her reply, hoping for something vainer. He bowed once again.

"Orange is not your colour. It makes you look fat," he said before leaving.

Erasing Evidence

The downtown Moscow apartment complex had ten floors but unlike the apartments in the Sleeping Zone, this one was occupied by lower echelon KGB officers. Valeri had been monitoring the building from a coffee shop across the street for the last two weeks. There was only one caretaker and both he and his wife slipped out of the complex every day at two p.m. The large wife with her thick legs would line up for bread and milk while the smallish balding husband bought vegetables and a large bottle of beer from kiosks in a park adjacent to the Bakery.

Outside the apartment building, a well-built security guard with an outlandishly large mustache would light up a cigarette every half hour and stroll around the building looking for anything out of order. Judging from the burly man's pace, Valeri deduced that the guard was not altogether worried about foul play.

He would have approximately two minutes to dart across the street and slip through the unlocked window of the custodian's basement apartment. When inside, he would hide wherever he could from the husband and wife team and then take care of them after their workday was complete. He needed the Master Key but would have to attain it without allowing the caretaker and his wife to see his face. Once they were tied up he would wait until after nine p.m. to make his way to the fifth floor apartment of Simon and Yulia Danilova. If he did not veer from his plan, he could be out of the building by ten p.m.

It was four degrees centigrade with a mild wind on this particular Friday in late March. Rain had fallen in the early

257

morning but the streets were now clear with heavy foot traffic in all directions. The ladies had replaced their fur coats and boots with sweaters, short skirts and high heels. Taxi drivers drove slower to admire the return of spring in Moscow. It would be simple for Valeri to cross the intersection without being noticed.

Valeri voided his bowels and then hid under the double bed when he heard the unlocking of the apartment door. For several hours he listened as they discussed specific residents in the building. He had to stifle a chuckle when the wife mentioned Yulia on several occasions. Even in her new environment, the thin woman's past indiscretions had tagged along. The wife was harsh with her husband and for most of the evening her tone never dropped below a sneer. Every time she walked, her heavy feet caused floorboards to creak. Valeri felt a kind of pity for the caretaker and silently hoped that the man would lash out at some point but he just sat at the kitchen table for three hours and took the abuse. It was painful to listen to but as far as Valeri was concerned it was not his fight. He had another mission. As luck would have it, the two were early risers and fell into their bed well before nine P.M.

The man was snoring within ten minutes. Valeri inched his way out and then stood over the two sleeping residents. With rope and black stockings in hand, he lifted his leg over the husband and knelt between the two. The woman budged first and Valeri dropped the rope and stockings to place his hand over her mouth. He then took his gun out of jacket and slipped it into the husband's mouth. The man awoke choking for breath.

"Do not struggle comrades or this will not end well," he quietly ordered. "I want both of you to turn over on your chests very slowly. I am not here to hurt either of you, I just need information. If you give me what I need, you will wake up tomorrow to continue your gloomy routine. Nod your heads if you understand what I am saying."

Both nodded, but the wife was omitting a whispered shrieking noise. Valeri stroked her hair and whispered that she need not worry. He bound the husband's hands first and then tied one pair of stockings around his eyes. When this was completed he did the same to the wife.

Markov left the bed and turned on the bedroom light. He threw off the bedcovers and looked at the couple. They were younger than he expected. The husband was smaller than he first anticipated and wearing white long-johns but the wife, who was now on her side, was easily fifty pounds overweight. She had abnormally large breasts that crammed a mini pink night shirt. For a moment, Valeri forgot why he was there. He strolled over to her side of the bed and began speaking.

"Please turn over onto your backs comrades," Valeri commanded. The two did as he said. With their hands tied behind their backs they were in obvious discomfort. "Good… very good. I will ask you a string of questions and you will answer honestly and without pause. The first question is what your first names are?"

The husband responded Theo and his wife replied Rena. Valeri thanked them and stroked Rena's hair. She did not shy away, which Valeri found titillating.

"How long have you been the custodians of this building?"

"Two years ago today," Theo responded.

"Happy anniversary," Valeri said nonplussed. "Where are the listening devices in each apartment?" He stuck his finger in Rena's mouth and then rubbed her saliva across her lips.

Theo did not pause at all and answered dutifully. "They can be found in all the phones and some lampshades. The bugs in the lampshades do not work well, they are not passive resonant."

"How many are in this apartment?" Valeri dragged his gun gently down Rena's pink night shirt and rubbed it softly against the front of her panties. She opened her thick legs invitingly causing Valeri to breathe rapidly.

You're here for a reason, don't be stupid.

"We are non-KGB so only our phones. I am in charge of installation of all listening devices. The higher floor you reside in, the more listening devices your home will have. The officers on the top floor cannot speak in any room without being recorded."

"That is indeed interesting," Valeri said while lifting Rena's pink nightshirt passed her swelled stomach. "So everything is recorded meaning there is no one monitoring real time?"

"No, of course not," Theo replied. "That would be too costly and would require three to four KGB officers to monitor their co-workers. Even the Kremlin is not that suspicious."

Valeri quickly slid his tongue from Rena's protruding bellybutton down to her beige panties. She let loose a short gasp and then faked a cough to cover her excitement.
"How about video equipment?" he asked.

Theo was moving his head hoping to see the intruder but could see nothing. "This building is too old for video. It would require every home and wall to be rewired. There is no

260

surveillance here other than the security guard who patrols the stairs and hallways."

"Thank-you Theo, that was very informational," Valeri said with a content tone. Rena had a smile on her face exciting him further. He had a full erection. "You are a younger couple, why do you not have children." The intruder was confused with his own question. This was not what he planned.

What are you thinking, stop now while you can.

Theo did not return an answer and after thirty seconds of waiting, Rena spoke instead. "Tell him, husband, why we have no children."

"It is not his concern," Theo replied defiantly.

"Yah right, it is because I repulse him. He does not wish to touch me."

"That's not true," he shot back. "I was one of the first liquidators in Chernobyl. I spent two weeks - not a week or a couple of days - but two weeks clearing the debris from Reactor Four. My wife cannot comprehend the toll that the radiation has taken on my entire body. She will only believe it when I die, which probably won't be long from now."

"Always the same excuse. He can't get an erection for me. I'm sure he can for the slut on the fifth floor but not for me."

Valeri tickled Rena's stomach and then slid a hand inside her panties. She was instantly wet and responding. She pushed her tied hands against her lower back to lift her hips. It had been a long time since he did not have to force himself on a woman and his heart was pounding wildly.

This is really happening.

"What are you doing?" Theo demanded to know.

"I have to be honest with you liquidator. I have an erection for your wife at this very moment. It is very hard and I am worrying that I will explode before I enter her." Valeri pulled down Rena's panties and slid his tongue into her vagina.

Theo turned on his side and started kicking wildly hoping to strike the intruder. He kicked his wife instead thus infuriating her. Valeri had an extra pair of stockings and wrapped them around Theo's ankles. He was too far gone; his mind was controlled by a lust he had not experienced for years. Markov pushed the man towards the center of the bed and then kissed Rena on the lips. Her mouth opened, and she stuck her tongue into his mouth. An incensed Theo began shouting so Valeri stuck a pillow on his face. He then whispered to Rena to sit on the same pillow. The heavy woman did so while giggling and Valeri kneeled on Theo's chest while he fondled his wife's breasts. Her exaggerated moaning drowned the sound of her struggling husband. While Valeri's fingers played with her clitoris the rhythmic motion of Rena's heavy frame suffocated the man she had married thirteen years earlier. Valeri dropped his pants, stood on Theo's lifeless chest and guided his erection into the widow's mouth.

Their lovemaking lasted another thirty minutes and when all was done Valeri lay on top of Rena.

"He has been having an affair with a woman on the fifth floor since the day they moved in eighteen months ago. I can't prove it but I am a woman... I can feel it." She heaved a large sigh. "It's nice to have a real man touch me after so long. How does it feel to be on the other side of cheating Theo?"

There was no response, and this further angered her. "Hey I'm talking to you. It doesn't feel good does it? I had a very strong orgasm Theo, probably the strongest I have ever had. Doesn't this make you want to fight?"

"What are you doing?" Valeri asked nonchalantly.

"I want him to acknowledge that infidelity hurts."

"Hmm, okay," Markov grunted. "What he said before was true."

Still blindfolded, Rena kissed Valeri on the lips while he stared at her flushed chubby face. "What was that darling?" she asked.

"What Theo said about the liquidators and Chernobyl, I was there. It was pure hell. A lot of these guys can't get erections anymore. It's probably just as well because their offspring are plenty fucked up."

"He's not lying?" Rena quickly questioned.

"Maybe he was, maybe he wasn't… I don't know, but the guy loved you so I would say he had a terminally limp dick."

"Loved?" she said panicking. She reached for him, found his shoulder and shook it. "Theo… Theo wake up."

Valeri immediately held his hand on her mouth muting the cries that he knew would soon come. "Rena, you killed him. Your fat ass and the pillow you were sitting on suffocated him. Theo is dead." He was unsure if he was feeling an emotion but suddenly he felt a bit weak. She used him. "Murder is a sin Rena."

The large woman began struggling, trying to push Valeri off of her. He had hoped that this would not happen but given the circumstances he swiftly came to terms that his fantasy was too one-sided. Valeri calmly reached to the floor beside the double bed and picked up his gun. In a few short movements, he lifted both pillows, shoved them against Rena's face and then fired his gun in the centre of the top pillow. Rena women stopped struggling and Valeri stood up slowly. He was disappointed but not surprised. He walked into the bathroom, took a quick shower and then dined on leftovers from the tiny refrigerator.

Borscht… only peasants eat fucking borscht.

The master key hung on a hook next to the front door. Valeri stuck it in his pocket and exited the basement apartment. He climbed the back stairs to the fifth floor and opened the apartment door of Yulia and Simon Danilova.

The first thing he noticed was Yulia sleeping on the couch. Her short beige skirt was pushed up revealing white panties. Valeri had brought Rena's stockings with him and he moved quietly towards the sleeping woman holding his gun against the bridge of his nose. He gently knelt on her ribs and when she awoke startled, he placed the pistol on her cheek.

"Choose to live or die Mrs. Danilova," he whispered.

Markov tied her arms behind her back and then did the same to her ankles. He took out a handkerchief from his jacket pocket and shoved it in her mouth.

"I will blow the child's head off if you make one stupid mistake."

Yulia's eyes were all he needed to confirm that she would not be causing him any trouble. He unbuttoned her blouse and examined her tiny breasts before continuing his mission.

Valeri did not have to go far to find Simon. The KGB statistical advisor was in his office fast asleep with his head on a paper littered desk. Valeri sneered at the man's disorganization.

He sat down on the beautiful chair with the soft grey cushions facing the man he would soon terrorize. He grabbed a fistful of paper, rolled them up in a ball and tossed it at Simon. The man's eyes opened slowly and then quickly. Simon stood up and was about to yell before Valeri aimed his gun menacingly.

"Why are you in my home?"

Markov grinned. "I would not call this a home; it is simply a living quarter. A home is something that everyone can hardly wait to get to. Your wife is sleeping on a living room couch and her husband is sleeping in his office. Is there trouble in paradise?"

"My personal life is not your concern Markov. I repeat my question; why are you here in a superior's *home*?"

Valeri chuckled at the superior remark. "Relax agent Danilova and address me as comrade. You are not my superior in any sense of the word. Before you utter another word I should make you aware that I have photos of you with your boy assistant in the back of a government car. I took them before the windows steamed up. He is young this boy, is he not? Maybe sixteen years of age at most? I did some research, and he is the son of a very high ranking officer. I cannot imagine how you would suffer if I let these photos become public property."

Simon's mouth was wide open, and he suddenly had difficulty breathing. He took off his glasses and wiped his eyes.

"What do you want?"

"Did you do as I asked comrade? Valeri Markov is now dead and I am now Olav Markov?"

"Yes, I did this the same day you left for the prison. So that you know, Valeri Markov died today in a car accident. It will be published in tomorrow's journals."

"Very good… I am pleased. This young boy you've been buggering - is he your first or have there been others? It must be difficult to find homosexuals to play with considering your governmental position. You would be surprised of how many of you exist. I have seen them with my own eyes and then heard of their gruesome deaths. A priest I knew was tossed into a burning furnace as if it was the fires of hell. Do you expect the same to happen to you?"

"I am very careful," Simon whispered.

"Umm…not really… no. Let me ask you something comrade that no one else has ever asked you." Valeri was leaning against the table with his hand under his chin. "How in God's name did you land a spicy little number like Mila Kharmalov? You're not a handsome man nor are you strong. You're an artist, which in many less cultured countries is considered the lowest form of shit. And the most compelling mystery of all… you're a homo."

"Why should I bother answering a question that you are incapable of understanding?"

"I'm willing to give it a shot. I'm listening… I'm all yours but not in the way you would wish."

Danilova lowered his head and would not make eye contact with Valeri. After a half minute of silence Valeri sighed.

"Okay fine, I'll be nice, no more tasteless jokes. I am sincerely curious about your relationship with Mila, please tell me about it."

"I did love Mila," he whispered.

266

"But how comrade?" Valeri interrupted. "Like a man loves his dog or like a man loves his woman?"

"Like a partner loves his partner."

"Good answer… well worded. I will write that down when I return home tomorrow evening."

Danilova shook his head in disgust and in pity. "You and others like you chastise me for being who I am but show no empathy for the anguish I suffered for well over a decade. It would be impossible for you to comprehend the wave of emotions I dealt with on a daily basis."

"I do not feel emotion nor can I empathize so I can't help you."

"Having known you for only a short period I can still say without any hesitation that I'm not surprised to hear this," Simon answered as clearly as possible. He looked at the man with the pistol and wished he had never made the initial call to hire him. "Mila was incredible with me. The woman you interviewed is not the woman I fell in love with. She was so pure and yet so… worldly. Any room became electric the moment she walked in. It wasn't just her beauty, it was her entire aura. She would listen to anyone and soak in their entire conversation as if every second was a learning experience. Tania was the same. It was almost eerie to have them in the same room because crowds of people were drawn to them. Can you imagine the popularity that I attained by dating and then marrying a woman like Mila Kharmalov? I was a total loner before she came into my life and then all of a sudden I was being invited to dinner parties. My artwork was being showcased and seen by people who had previously never given me a second glance. I cannot sit here and tell you that I charmed Mila; I did not have the charisma to do so. For some reason she was attracted to me, perhaps out of pity. Perhaps it was she who loved me like a man loves his dog."

"Yes, I get all that. The pity angle is very likely but Simon... *you're* gay. *You...* like men."

"And in the Soviet Union that is unacceptable. I married Mila to be accepted, hoping that my urges would disappear. They did not."

"So why did you decide to run away with the skinny thing with small tits... or did I answer my own question?"

Danilova would not answer.

"Oh come on," Valeri said waving his gun. "Let's hear it. Trust me; there is a sense of relief when you share secrets. I felt great when I told your ex-wife some of mine... it was truly an unburdening."

"Her hair used to be very short, and she reminded me of someone," Simon whispered. "Another man."

"I knew it," Valeri exclaimed. "It doesn't say much for me but I had an inkling that was the reason. And now that her hair is long she no longer resembles the man you dreamed about. Well that's all I need to know."

"Don't kill me in front of my child," Simon requested.

"I'm not going to kill you. I never said I would. Did you hear me say that I was going to kill you? I only kill what I stick my penis into. I don't have sex with men therefore I do not kill men unless of course they are trying to do me harm. Will you be attempting to upset my life Simon?"

"No, I swear to you," Simon said with a raised and hopeful tone.

"Okay great - that is wonderful to hear. Now you sit there and I'll be back in a jiffy. Don't make me do anything I don't want to do Simon. Stay where you are."

Danilova dropped his head on the desk relieved that he would live another day. He dared not move but after five minutes he wondered what was taking Markov so long to return. Music was now playing in the middle room. Finally, he heard footsteps and he cusped his hands on his desk like a good student.

Valeri returned to the office with a tearful Yulia ahead of him. She was holding a gun with a plastic container taped to the end of the barrel. Markov had another gun pointed at her head.

"What is this?" Simon said gulping back a deep breath.

"As I said comrade, I don't kill men, so I have asked Yulia to put a bullet in your head. You can't believe that a card carrying communist like myself would allow a homosexual to remain in a position of command within our ranks did you?"

Simon stared back at Yulia who was sobbing uncontrollably. "Don't do it Yulia," he begged.

"He's going to kill Lena if I don't," his wife stuttered. "I can't have Lena harmed."

"Don't trust him baby, he will kill you too."

Tears raced down her face. "I don't care what he does to me; I don't wish to live any longer."

"Yulia please… look at me honey."

Valeri bent over and whispered in her ear but loud enough for Simon to hear. "Do you know why he left Mila for you? It's because you reminded him of a man he was in love with." Markov chuckled. "I can't imagine how that makes you feel. If that isn't a good enough reason to kill the bastard then I don't know what is."

Yulia pressed the trigger and the gun barrel clicked. No bullet exited. She lowered her head and her body shook wildly while Danilova sighed with great relief.

"Fuck me!" Valeri yelled. "Wow, what a rush. Did you all feel that? You should have seen your faces."

"You're an animal," Simon shouted in anguish. He pissed his pants and hoped Yulia would not notice.

Valeri stuck his gun against Yulia's head. "Do it again."

She shook her head no but Valeri calmly reminded her of Lena. She lifted the gun with her shaking hands and aimed it at a terrified Simon Danilova. This time it fired. The bullet struck Simon on the side of the head and after his head launched backwards his neck rebounded within a fraction of a second. His head hit the desk with a thud. Blood drenched the unfinished paperwork he had promised for the end of the week. Yulia gasped and then fainted. Lena awoke and began crying.

"More paperwork," Valeri muttered. "It seems that every homo I've ever met dies in a gruesome manner." A trail of blood dripped off the desk and onto the polished wood floor. "I'm not cleaning this," he voiced before dragging Yulia into the main room.

When Yulia awoke on her favorite couch the first thing she noticed was Lena sleeping on the adjacent matching couch. Markov was sitting on a chair next to the child with an easel, paint and brushes.

"Do not speak too loud, you will wake the child," he said quietly.

"What the fuck…" Yulia began before being interrupted by the artist.

"I took the liberty of cutting off your hair and returning your style to what it was when you lived in Pripyat." Realizing that Yulia may try to attack him he took the gun off his lap and pointed it at Lena. "The baby," he warned.

She grabbed the back of her head and glared at Valeri. "You're crazy… you're fucking insane."

Markov paid little attention to her barbs. "Yelling will wake the child, is that what you wish? Try not to move too much. Let the artist create."

"I want you dead," Yulia said tersely. "I want to see you hang from the tallest building so that all of Russia can dance on the streets under your swinging corpse."

Valeri stopped painting and looked momentarily at the skinny woman with short hair. "That was original…quite imaginative too," he responded, continuing with a placating tone. "You missed your calling Yulia. While I have your attention, I will tell you more about myself. I was visiting your friend Mila a couple of weeks ago and she managed to coax a few stories from me and after doing so I felt much lighter… it was like a cleansing of sorts. I told your dead husband the same thing before you murdered him."

"Fuck you," she interjected.

"Yes, I hear that more and more often," he said matter of fact. "Your husband had good taste in art material. The brush hairs are exquisite; I am not used to such perfect strokes. Let's return to me. I made a small fortune off your misfortune. Well, not just your misfortune but the whole Chernobyl bit. After officials ordered all families to leave, I pillaged as much as I could. I found

271

gold jewelry, gold coins, pearls and a crap load of money under mattresses. You wouldn't believe me if I told you how much money but it was more than your husband could make in a decade. So I bought an older house in a Ukraine village and began rebuilding."

"You're a man of many talents," Yulia growled. "How proud you must be."

"Yes, I am proud of my accomplishments. Do you have any accomplishments Yulia other than stealing a homosexual from his straight wife and moving into this grand apartment? I will tell you an achievement you may not have even considered. You are partially responsible for the Kharmalov sisters becoming so famous. If you had not seduced Simon with your part girl – part boy charms, Mila would never have travelled the Soviet Union nor done any of the things the samizdat articles claim. Are you not proud of this? On top of that, you have cared for her daughter while she toils in prison, which of course we could blame on you if we so inclined. I don't think anyone will write songs about Yulia Danilova but you're certainly a great background character."

Yulia lay back on the couch and closed her eyes. "Fuck you, you're a maniac."

"The women from Pripyat curse far too much," Valeri chuckled. "It is unbecoming of a lady. Mila's sister, Tania… she did not curse; she is a fine specimen of a woman. So as I was saying, I rebuilt my aging home by tearing down walls and adding another thirty feet. I wanted a full kitchen and living room as well as a bedroom and an art room. While I was doing this I noticed that the flooring in my bedroom was warped so I tore off every tile and discovered I had a basement. It was just dirt, foundation and poles but I fixed it up just enough so that it could become useful to me."

"I'm very tired Markov."

"As am I but you don't hear me grumbling," he replied, uninterested in the woman's complaint. "Maybe if you listen you'll perk up real quick. If I was listening to the same story I would be on the edge of my seat." He bent his head around the easel to take a quick peek at the girl whom he found quite lovely, with or without her long hair. "I was rather uneducated when I left my village at the young age of sixteen and within days of leaving I decided to do whatever I could to augment myself to a level most Soviets could not be bothered to reach. I am an enigma of sorts Yulia. I believe in our communist agenda yet I strive daily to fulfill the spiritual needs that all humans must attempt to attain. Our Soviet ideology wishes to eliminate religion but I find this legislation entirely unnecessary. If anything, religion and communism would be the ideal match if the foundation of catholic sins was strictly implemented. Are you aware of the seven sins?"

Yulia snarled. "If boredom and misery are a sin then I need to be saved."

"Misery is most definitely a sin Yulia but I am afraid it may be too late for you to be saved. Did you know that there are fifty million believers in our empire but less than ten thousand churches? I find that a travesty yet I travelled throughout Ukraine visiting these hospices with the intent of knowledge and spiritual enlightenment. Our one-time leader, Vladimir Lenin called religion the opium of the people. There is truth to this because the more I learned, the more I wished to know.

In September of that first year I arrived in Lyiv and sought refuge in the parish Dormiton Church. I found its towers to be strikingly powerful against a backdrop of ugly homes and businesses. Beholding the beauty inside is an act I can only wish all Ukrainians could partake. The frescos and their meanings, the Armenian construction, wall paintings and color choices were intoxicating. I rarely feel emotion Yulia but that day... I knew I was home." Valeri rinsed his brush in the small bottle of water and then blotted the damp hairs on the couch next to Lena. "I was soon introduced to the parish priest who welcomed me, fed me lunch and had me working within an hour. It was here that I learned how to toil with lumber and more importantly, how to paint. I helped in the restoration during the day and I studied at night. On weekends after service, I would sit alone in my tiny room and recreate paintings from books that I borrowed from our library. It became my sole passion."

"All this talk about church," Yulia huffed with a scornful tone. "One would assume a holy place would teach you morals and compassion. It did nothing of a sort; I see a monster in front of me."

Markov pondered on her words for a few seconds as if confused. "But... I'm not a monster. I am a loyal communist with an education based on the teachings of Christianity and European scholars. The parish priest insisted I study several hours a day, and he assigned the secretary and his assistant to help me. I would not dare to disappoint them as it could mean my expulsion from my new home. Nonetheless, I was fascinated by Christian history and tradition thus needed little coercion. I created my own interpretation of a better society and eventually shared it with my leaders. You see me as a monster yet my goals Yulia are for the betterment of Mother Russia and its citizens. If you were as well read as I, you would be in a better position to judge or at least argue. Are you familiar with Niccolo Machiavelli?"

"Only by name," Yulia grumbled. She pondered several means to escape but none were viable. Lena's life was too important yet she fretted for her own. "I suppose you are a fan."

Valeri shrugged and his face twitched as if surprised by the question. "Of course I am. He was highly misinterpreted but his work is symbolic to me and has changed my very being. Order by force; purge the community of those stronger than you or in better standing. These are words to live by metaphorically if you wish to achieve your goals. I have merged his work with my Christian belief in the Seven Sins and our Marxist foundation. To be an empire of strength and morality we – the citizens of the Soviet Union - must purge ourselves of those that do not belong. It is not survival of the fittest but instead survival of the intellectual in a society that is presently drowning in vanity. I consider myself to be the rebirth of Machiavelli and a Russian savior. I am a supreme product of the Soviet Union… and I am The Prince."

Yulia was no longer afraid of the conceited man with long hair. She leaned forward as if to make her message clearer.

"You're mad Valeri… a veritable lunatic. If you're a prince then it is the Prince of Darkness."

His painting was done, and he dropped the brush into the dirty water. Pushing the easel to his right and away from Lena, Markov looked directly at the exhausted woman when he spoke.

"Then so be it. You are in a place of reverence Yulia; you should acknowledge me and beg for mercy."

"I will say these few words to you Markov so that you can return to your fantasy world understanding that you have accomplished nothing this evening. A few hours ago, I was not a happy woman but with Lena in my home, I was content. I never for an instant pretended to be her mother nor would I insult Mila by claiming I was, yet I was satisfied in raising her every day in a manner that would make Mila proud. I understood my role in this household and I understood that my husband was not the man I married. I didn't care anymore - not a bit - but I peacefully retained a hope for the future. In a few years I could move on and meet someone who loved me for who I am."

"That would be someone like Alex?" Valeri interjected.

"Yes, like him. I wish I could go back in time and beg his forgiveness. He would have forgiven me…and I would have rewarded him every ounce of my love." She stared at Markov curiously. "What do you know about Alex?"

Valeri smirked and then leaned over on the edge of his chair. "I am sure you know that your security guard was in the newspapers for his bravery. There was a photo of him standing over his best friend who was being carted away on a stretcher. He was despondent, bawling like a five-year old child. I'm sure all the babushka readers were touched by this unmanly display. That evening I managed to spend a few minutes with him and he told me all about Yulia, the love of his life and how he wished to find you. If I remember correctly, his girly eyes were almost teary just speaking of you, but of course he was also pleading for his life. Close your big blue eyes and imagine my knife circling his neck while I pulled back his greasy hair. He was at fault Yulia; I did not initiate this encounter. It was not enough that the country was applauding him; he had to try to expose me for doing what I felt

276

necessary to fund my own aspirations. If only he had let his foolish new ego subside for a while then perhaps the two of you would be together today. He was a hero for a short period until I snapped his neck and felt his last shuddering gasp on my lips. The moment itself was surreal because I opened my mouth and swallowed that final breath. It was as if I had caught his soul and he is now trapped inside of me. Trust me when I tell you this, I was not happy to end his life as I do not murder men. Killing him was contradictory to everything I believe in but he left me no choice. I spent several weeks in penance to cleanse myself of guilt."

Yulia had been aware of Alex's demise but was told it was in a fire. Hearing Markov boast of his crime made her want to do the same to him. She remained silent but contemplated crying. Markov paid her no heed and continued his story.

"I always paint my subjects as I see them in their past, present and future. Before I walked into this home I had a general idea of who you were in Pripyat and who you are now although you have presented me with moments that *almost* made me rethink my decision. You pity yourself don't you? You accept your situation but not without a loathing towards others and a need to search for anything better. When I say anything, I mean Alex. The boy was never what you wanted yet for a fleeting moment he was superior to what you have...or had."

Yulia said nothing but her eyes showed a woman who was seething inside; a woman who was ready to pounce on the babbling mad man.

"You love the sound of your own voice. You're an asshole."

Markov contained the excitement that was building inside of him. "Admit it; he wasn't good enough for you two years ago when you trapped a homosexual alternative. You're someone who uses pity as an attraction rather than an opportunity to recreate yourself into a more worthy person. There are many who will want to hug you and take you away from your destitution but then there are those like me who don't give a fuck and would rather lead you to a tree and hand you a long rope. The way I envision things, if you had found Alex you would have used him until a new man came into your shadowy excuse of an existence."

He turned his painting towards Yulia and her face went totally blank. Markov had drawn a long green snake topped with Yulia's face and short hair. Her reptilian body slithered around a tree branch like a depiction of the Garden of Eden. It was a frightening illustration that turned her stomach. It was too much for her and she rushed Valeri with a fury of punches. The painter avoided her blows and swung her tiny frame around with ease.

Markov wrapped his right arm tightly around her neck and squeezed hard enough to cease her struggling. Yulia's large round eyes were bulging. He fell backwards onto the couch.

"The women who choose to attack me are always shocked at how powerful I am Yulia. I begin each morning with a health regimen of exercise and can boast that I often do one hundred consecutive push-ups without breaking a sweat. Do not resist, it will only increase the pressure on your thorax." He lifted her skirt with his free hand and forced his hand into her panties. "I told Mila that I had sex with you in your kitchen. I was only trying to get a reaction from her but she showed little. I was disappointed by her nonplussed response but as I recounted our conversation on the drive back to Moscow it occurred to me that Mila had

278

taught me a great lesson. I learned that sometimes the biggest lies are not as harmful as the tiny ones."

"Please let me go," Yulia whimpered through multiple gasps for breath.

The crazy man lowered his captive's panties to her knees and stuck his middle finger inside her dry vagina causing her to quietly sob.

"I have had an entertaining evening. The custodian's wife was very hospitable until she touched her dead husbands shoulder. And now I have you in a precarious position. I am at odds with myself on what to do. Truth be told, I find you very enticing and strangely beautiful. In a different circumstance, I might have mulled over the possibility of a relationship with you. Let me ask you a question Yulia that will have a substantial effect on how this evening progresses or ends."

His grasp loosened and Yulia exhaled a long breath. She was shivering. A nervous release of urine trickled off Markov's fingers and down her thigh. Valeri's lips touched her ears as he spoke.

"If you were standing in front of God and he blessed you with one wish, what would you ask for?"

Yulia's head was hung low. Her eyes hurt from the tremendous pressure of blood that had splashed around her pupils. She was deeply ashamed of having Markov's hands fondling her genitals but said nothing, hoping he would let her be if his desires were satisfied. This is what she had become.

"I wish that Alex's life had been spared."

"So that you and he could have a happy life together?"

"Yes," she replied with her eyes closed in disgust, "So that I could have one iota of happiness in my life."

Valeri was not pleased with this answer and applied a great deal of pressure around her neck. Yulia did not expect this and tried to lift her body off Markov's hips. With one quick jolting movement he snapped Yulia's neck, and she breathed no more.

"Dumb cunt," he said louder than expected.

He dropped her on the couch leaving her dress hiked up over her navel and then knelt over her to speak to her rigid face. He had hoped she would want to be with him.

"I ended your life in the same manner I finished Alex's life. I believe this is a rather poetic, and a fitting means to discontinue your inane subsistence. If you see Alex wherever you're going, tell him you died with my finger in your skinny pussy." Markov was acting more strange than usual as if very upset. He shook his head before addressing Yulia's lifeless body. "Did you think for a moment I was not aware of your dalliances with the burly doorman every Tuesday and Thursday? I was scoping your building for two weeks. You left Lena with a neighbour just to wet your loins. You're a tramp and you disgust me." He walked away and circled back to the corpse. "One last comment skinny woman: Usually I only kill what I screw but given how much I have fucked up your life already, I'll consider this as one and the same."

He stood and wiped the piss off his fingers onto Yulia's skirt. There was much for him to do before he left this apartment. First off, he would have to return the painting material to its rightful place and wash the bottles of any fingerprints. The exquisite brushes went into his jacket pocket. Markov calculated that it would take at least thirty minutes to wash fingerprints off the furniture and doors the way he was accustomed to cleaning.

He gently picked up Lena and returned her to her bedroom. She did not awake, and this greatly relieved him.

A half hour later he sat at the kitchen table with three white bed sheets. He tied them together to create one long sturdy rope. When certain they would not come loose, he strolled calmly to the couch and tied one end of the elongated sheets tightly around Yulia's neck to form a workable noose. He pushed her off the couch and then dragged her to a window above the wrought iron radiator that he used to knot the other side of the sheet. Yulia's panties were still around her ankles and Markov chose to keep them as such.

I want my comrades to see her as she lived… a whore.

The window was difficult to open, and he wiped his fingerprints before staring out at the empty streets. Valeri lifted Yulia's limp cadaver and pushed her out the window. His makeshift rope worked flawlessly, and he admired his work for longer than intended. He was in artist with life and death.

With all the lights now turned off, Markov leapt down the backstairs two at a time to the first floor where he re-entered Theo and Rena's apartment. He then crawled out their open window and joined the drunks that zigzagged on the empty sidewalks. One of the inebriated men pointed up towards Yulia but Markov kept walking. He was untouchable and today he did his communist brothers and sisters a great service.

I am the rebirth of Machiavelli and a Russian savior. I am a supreme product of the Soviet Union… and I am The Prince.

Mila's Prince

At ten o'clock on a Tuesday morning, Chris Langley sat behind his expansive desk, smoking a cigarette and trying to decide what to mull through first. Three years earlier he had quit his job at an uptown Calgary law firm and opened his own small practice specializing in human rights and abuse litigation. His dream of being the voice of the people had disappeared quickly as he found himself buried in employee dismissal cases and PETA claims. Occasionally he worked on spousal abuse but that law had a way of protecting drunken husbands and scamming mistresses. It was distressing to say the least.

He butt out the cigarette he knew he should not be smoking and picked up the manila envelope that his administrative assistant had just dropped off. The edges were taped, and he did not recognize the stamps that adorned the upper right corner. Instead of tearing the envelope open, he took out a pair of scissors from a side drawer and carefully cut the top of the envelope. Inside he found a letter and two newspaper articles.

"Hey Jen," he called out to his assistant. "Can you take a look at this please?"

A short and somewhat heavy red-haired woman in her forties strolled in and stared blankly at Chris.

"What do you think this is?" he asked lifting the letter and the two articles.

"Well, my years of experience would say that I'm looking at a couple of newspapers and a handwritten letter."

Chris grimaced knowing the woman was teasing him. "Is this Russian?"

Jen shrugged. "Couldn't tell ya Chris, looks like it but I imagine it could be Polish too."

"Yah, maybe. Why the hell would someone send me this? Do we know any Russians?"

"Sure, you defended that Olga woman six months ago; the one that got fired for *not* sleeping with her Russian boss. Remember? She said this was Canada, she didn't have to do that crap anymore… ring a bell?"

"Okay, yes I remember. Nice looking girl too, couldn't speak a word of English. Beats me how we won that case, I still don't understand the full story. Can you call and ask her to come in today? Doesn't matter what time or tell her I'll go to her mother's house."

"I'll try. Hope I can find someone in that household who has actually learned English."

"Thank you darling," he replied with a bad Russian accent.

Chris gazed at the first newspaper article. There was a blurry photo of two women sitting in what looked like a hospital hallway. They looked very attractive yet very… opposite. One wore a dress and one wore what looked like jeans. The woman wearing the dress had light hair, and the other was much darker yet their faces were similar. They must be sisters. He looked closer at the article and noticed the date was 1986. *That's three freaking years ago*, he mumbled. The second article was dated 1987. He attached the letter and articles with a paper clip and set them aside at the far corner of his desk before resuming his normal work day.

283

Ten minutes later Jen re-entered and told him that Olga would drop by at lunch time. She was only too happy to help her favorite lawyer any way she could.

"Are you sure she didn't say something like, he's so handsome, I'd love to go out with him?"

"I'm very sure she didn't say that," Jen shouted back, "Or anything close to that. You're ten years older than her so keep your brains out of your pants, please and thanks."

****

Olga arrived at noon wearing a short flower patterned skirt and high heels. She looked like an old childhood memory. Chris had grown up watching Rocky and Bullwinkle cartoons and Olga reminded him of the female villain, Natasha but a very sexy version of the animated character. She was tall, a bit too thin with pale skin and black hair.

"Hello Christopher," she said with only a hint of an accent. "It's wonderful to see you again."

"You too Olga," Chris replied noticing the girl's lack of accent.

"You will be happy to hear that I have been studying English and I owe this to you. After the court case, I forced myself to separate from the chains of my language and learn English. I went to second language courses every day, and I studied eight hours a day without fail. After the second month I began reading novels and watching television. Six months later I am pleased with my advancement. What do you think?"

Chris was nothing less than shocked. This girl could barely say hello half a year earlier.

"Olga… this is unbelievable. I'm in awe of you right now. Congratulations."

Olga was very pleased with this comment and her face lit up. "Thank-you, Christopher."

"Yah well, you deserve it. Anyway, thanks for taking the time to visit," Chris began. "I don't know anyone who speaks Russian, and I was hoping you could help me out with something that I received today."

He handed her the first newspaper article, and she read the first two paragraphs. She then turned her attention to the letter which she read silently.

"This is very sad," she whispered slowly.

"What is sad?"

"I have heard of these two women. My father once mentioned that he met their father on several occasions."

"Who are they?"

"They are Tania and Mila Kharmalov. Their family is from Pripyat, close to the Chernobyl nuclear building. I am from this city too. On the night of the explosion, my father did not wait for news. We got in our car at two in the morning and drove to the Polish border. He gave the Russian guards twenty thousand rubles and they let us pass. The Polish guards then arrested us but only for a day. Three months later we were here in Calgary."

"Why did the Poles let you in?"

"Lech Walesa had gained momentum and as far as the Polish were concerned, they were steps away from independence. I think that was why the Russians were guarding the border. The

Polish people will be voting soon so I imagine it is just a question of time that they break ties with Russia."

"Okay."

Olga wiped an imaginary stray bang as if one was out of place. Chris could have told her that her hair was near perfect.

"These two girls were very popular after the Chernobyl accident. I know this only because I have read the article once before. Thousands of Ukrainians, Belarusians and Russians have read this story and many of us believed it to be fiction. I have heard that the writer was imprisoned but in the Soviet Union it is difficult to distinguish between truths and lies."

"And who are they? What is it that they did?"

Olga tilted her head and exhaled a short breath. "It is my understanding that they were compassionate angels that asked for the truth. I will read you the first article but it is very long and I will have to pause to think of the translation."

"Your English is incredible; your studying has not betrayed you."

Chris found her gorgeous but made an effort to keep his demeanor professional. Olga once again tossed a stray bang aside and commenced reading.

"In my lifetime I will never meet two more beautiful sisters than Mila and Tania Kharmalov. Studying their faces I am left breathless and I have convinced myself that I am gazing upon two Renaissance masterpieces. Surely no replicate could ever be created on any canvas and surely no sane man would dare to try.

A normal person could never have survived the same pain Mila and Tania have suffered in the last two months but then again, they are not normal. They are God's paintbrush, and every stroke brings empathy, love and hope. I am sitting in Hospital Six on the floor designated for radiation victims of the Chernobyl disaster. Tania has long flowing blond hair that caresses her simple dress. Mila appears stronger than her sister and possesses a wild beauty that is altogether intimidating. She wears jeans and a white sweater that fits her to perfection. In less than an hour I feel as if I have fallen in love with both and would lay down my life to protect them.

I am not alone with my emotion.

The nurses treat them with reverence and the doctors ask for their help. The wives of dying men embrace these young ladies as if they were close family. Strangers bring them food and drink. When I asked to sit with them, they shared their food with me. I offered cigarettes, and they took them, only to hand the same cigarettes to one of the older impoverished nurses. I am dumbstruck not only by their beauty but by their kindness. I want to believe I am blinded by their appearance yet every passing minute sheds my doubt.

I ask them questions and they respond courteously. 'If you must write, then write the truth,' they tell me. 'See these men for yourself. Listen to them and write what you see and not what you are told to see.' I promise them that I will do this and today I have honored my promise because as a Ukrainian I cannot help cherishing these sisters even though they are Russian. I cannot help writing as I see the truth because each and every one of us owes the sisters Kharmalov this bidding. We must treasure them and when all is said and done - when the world returns to a new normal - we cannot allow ourselves to forget them.

Ukraine and Belarus love the Kharmalov sisters. I love the Kharmalov sisters."

Olga placed the newspaper on her lap. "Did you follow the Chernobyl accident Christopher?"

287

"In all honesty, I did not. I was aware of it but since it did not affect me and because it was a Russian problem I unconsciously ignored it. I was raised to be wary of communists."

The twenty-three-year old nodded and smiled briefly. "This attitude is very prevalent in Canada. I have tried to follow the accident but news is difficult to attain. My cousin Anya lives in Odessa and when we speak on the telephone she tells me about the children that lived in the city of Pripyat. They are sick yet the government will not admit their illnesses are due to Chernobyl. Anya has mentioned the Kharmalov sisters, and that there was a song written about them by one of the men that Tania and Mila visited. She said it is a very moving melody that will make you cry."

She paused, reached for the newspaper and continued reading. Chris listened in total fascination and when the girl was finished he could not ever recall listening to a story so enthralling. It was a story that touched his heart to the point where he could not bear to hear it again. When she read the second article written eighteen months later he became angry.

"Sons of bitches, this absolutely appalls me. Why do they do this shit to their own people, it blows my mind," he said. Olga did not reply as if she had heard this before. "Would you mind reading the letter Olga?"

"Not at all," she replied while picking up the thin white paper. "The handwriting is bad."

"Dear Sir, My name is Anatalov Khizhinski and I am the father of Katerina Khizhinski. My daughter Katerina is imprisoned in the Siberian town of Maryinsk. I am not writing to you about my daughter

as she has indeed committed a crime that is worthy of her present punishment.

Last month I visited my daughter for an allotted time of one half hour. Although guards patrolled the prisoner cafeteria, Katerina managed to tell me a secret she was forbidden to speak of. She did so out of a friendship that she has established with two sisters whom she believes are heroes of the Soviet Union.

Katerina believes their lives are in danger as guards have become quite ambitious in their advances. My daughter fears for the safety of these wonderful women. If you or your government can help in any way, you will be performing a service that will be applauded by the citizens of our decaying empire. The sisters are Mila and Tania Kharmalov.

If you please open your heart to their plight, I personally will plant a forest of trees in your name.

Thank-you."

Chris nodded his head several times and then called for his assistant. "Jen, can you get me the phone number for Amnesty International?"

"It's in your Rolodex," she yelled back. "It's been there since day one."

He glanced at Olga who was watching him closely, pleased with the turn of events. "Well Olga, looks like we have a big job in front of us. How many Russian speaking friends do you have in this city and how many of them have the balls to be part of a demonstration at the Russian Consulate in Edmonton?"

She grinned and then out of nowhere winked at Chris. "There are several hundred in our church and even more in

Edmonton. Every one of them will go to Edmonton; this I will guarantee you."

He lifted his phone and placed it in front of Olga. "You start dialing and I will order the bus to take us there next Saturday. Deal?"

"You were my hero six months ago Christopher. Once again, you have not disappointed me."

"Yah well… I've always wanted a forest named after me."

****

There was not just one bus that left from Calgary on a three hour drive to Edmonton. There were fifteen and they were followed by a parade of single vehicles. One call to Amnesty International and the word was out. When they arrived in the northern city another eight hundred demonstrators were waiting with bull horns and protest signs.

Free Mila and Tania.

Mr. Gorbachev, are you sleeping?

I love the Kharmalov sisters; and so many more.

The translated article was printed in newspapers across Canada, the United States and the United Kingdom. Similar protests happened in Ottawa, Toronto and Vancouver. University students broadcast the translated article several times a day. In one week, Chris and Olga had organized a rally that would reach the eyes and ears of the Kremlin.

One week and three days after the Canadian rallies, Mila and Tania Kharmalov were released from the Maryinsk labor camp and returned to their Aunt's home in Kiev, Ukraine. Prime Minister Gorbachev insisted he had no previous knowledge of the sisters and was disgusted by their imprisonment. It was one more nail in the Soviet Union coffin.

Mila and Tania were free.

Stage Two

"They just let you go?" I questioned. I found that very odd and frankly, unbelievable.

"Yes," Tania replied. "It is my belief Aaron that Gorbachev was preparing for the inevitable. He was reaching out to the populace with this small olive branch of peace. He was demonstrating to the world that Russia was not without compassion."

"Then what happened," Lena inquired as if she had never heard the story.

"Coincidentally, the day after we were released, the Berlin Wall was toppled. It was November ninth, if I remember correctly. Kiev was abuzz, and it seemed like everyone on the streets were discussing when Ukraine would follow suit. The movement for an independent Ukraine was now in full gear."

"Yep, I've watched the videos on YouTube," I said, not realizing how inane the comment was.

Tania had no clue what I just said and Lena rightly preferred not to translate.

"Mila was curious how someone in a faraway land knew about us and she asked many questions to many people yet no one could answer. She also wished to meet the man who arranged the rallies in Canada. A kindly administrator sent inquiries to a Canadian Embassy and eventually – many months later – reached Christopher Langley."

I knew that name. "Isn't that your step-father?" I said to Lena. She smiled and answered yes.

Tania smiled but this time she understood her niece. "Mama and papa joined us. Lena had been with them since a day after Simon was found dead. Mila was overjoyed to say the least to hold her precious child. We were seven people in that tiny apartment but we were happy. Uncle Georgie had passed two years earlier so the company was welcomed by Vera. I don't recall Uncle Georgie earning a large salary but Vera had plenty of money to support us.

Our fame, as you would call it, had not entirely faded. The youngsters knew nothing about the Kharmalov sisters but their parents continued to stop us on the busy streets of Kiev. KGB officers followed us on occasion but never asked for our papers. Valeri Markov had called Mila untouchable. I was beginning to believe it true. Aside from family, our only true constant was that Ukrainians had this conviction of sort that Mila and I would save them from the evil Soviet empire. There was nothing further from the truth but fate kept pulling us on a path we did not wish to tread.

Nineteen - ninety was a year of upheaval in Ukraine and Russia. Workers went on strike and the Ukraine government was leaning towards a partnership with Russia. It was called perestroika, but this was not acceptable to the populace as we wanted full independence. A rally was organized for September 30th and Mila was asked to participate. Well, both of us were but I flat out refused. Mila initially said no because that was the same day that Christopher Langley was arriving. Imagine him flying in to see a woman that may have been arrested the second she walked off the stage. It was pure craziness but once Mila put something into her head, she would not let go."

"What do you mean?" I asked.

"The organizer was a good man who would lay down his life for Ukraine but those that surrounded him were misogynists. All Russian speaking men are misogynists, even today. To these guest speakers, Mila was little more than a celebrity for the striking workers in attendance to gaze upon. Her opinion meant nothing but a type of nostalgia. She was just a beautiful woman someone once wrote a song about. Those poor deluded men, they had no idea how wrong they were."

September 30th, 1990

Tania estimated that two hundred thousand workers were on hand to hear comrades fight against perestroika. Mila shrugged but the butterflies in her stomach were well hidden. Truth be told, she was informed half an hour earlier that her Calgary lawyer was in a taxi on his way to see her speak. This made her more nervous than public speaking. She shook her head in disgust when told that it took two hours for him to clear customs.

Many of the demonstrators waved to Tania and Mila as they stood outside the tent where the guest speakers or wannabe politicians waited. Mila wanted nothing to do with these men and preferred to breathe the autumn air. The sisters returned all salutations. Small children walked up to them and asked for hugs. When a twelve-year old boy with blond hair did the same, Mila held on a bit longer. She was visibly emotional for a few minutes afterwards and had to turn away from the crowd.

In the distance, a tall man was approaching the sisters. He had a huge smile which in Kiev was deemed as something only fools did. She grinned back realizing this handsome man was not Ukrainian. He was tall, she thought. *Thank God he's tall.* The man next to him was many inches shorter and introduced as the translator.

The blond man stuck out his hand and introduced himself as Christopher Langley. The two women did not bother shaking hands. Mila hugged him and then kissed the grinning man on both cheeks. Tania did the same but less enthusiastically.

Mila looked him over and gave a slight hint of approval. "You come to meet us wearing jeans?"

Chris returned the once over and his lips twitched, unnerved by the gorgeous woman. "Oh Mila Kharmalov, I knew you would be wearing the same, so I wanted to blend in."

Tania laughed but realized quickly that the conversation would not include her. A stranger touched her shoulder and handed the younger sister an envelope. She turned to say thank-you but the man with the black beret had disappeared.

The guest speakers were filing out of the tent indicating that the inspirational piece of the rally was soon to begin. Mila cursed the timing and apologized to Chris.

"No problem," he replied with a wry grin. "Please ensure you don't wear jeans at dinner tonight."

This time it was Mila's turn to smile like a fool. "Mr. Langley… I accept your extremely forward invitation. Please make sure you are well-dressed and shaved." She pointed at his muddy shoes. "And be certain to shine your shoes."

A member of the stage crew rushed her off, but she looked back at Chris to see if he was watching her. Her heart beat rapidly when she saw that his eyes had not left her.

The workers knew who she was before she spoke. Wearing a turtleneck and a jean jacket, she was exactly what the audience had imagined she would be. When it was her turn to speak, she waved to the throng with both hands and then walked along edge of the stage shaking hands with those that stood close by. She worked the crowd like a rock star. The wind picked up and blew her long dark hair across her face. While introducing herself, she took an elastic band out of her jacket pocket and tied her hair into a ponytail.

"Hello my countrymen, comrades, brothers and sisters, I am Mila Kharmalov.

What an incredible turnout. I would embrace each one of you but we'd be here until December. To the mothers in the crowd, when I lift my hand in a few minutes, I want you to put your hands over your child's ears.

It is cold my comrades but addressing you today is like a warm summer breeze on an Odessa beach. Thank-you for allowing me to be here with you. Believe me when I say that it is entirely my honour to be among such courageous Ukrainians. You will return to your homes this evening knowing that you are making a difference, not for a community or a city but instead for an entire nation.

Two years ago my sister Tania and I began a letter with the words, "We are not who you think we are". I still believe this because what you feel, we feel. We feel every frustration as well as every heartache. Yet, we also sense hope, comrades, and hope is something that until recently so few of us has ever inhaled. The words you wish to say are the same words that Tania and I wish to shout from the rooftops. But my friends, I can tell you straight up that I am not anything like any of the others who have spoken in front of you today. Listening to speeches in the last hour, I would swear that we must take up arms and prepare for a fight against our enemies.

What utter bullshit.

It's as if none of these gentlemen learned a bloody thing over the last century. Sure, let's start another fight; let's begin our own Cold War." She paused and looked at the men sitting behind her. "It is futile and never the answer. Comrades… I am tired of death. I have seen more than my fair share and I'm sick of it. I am totally, unequivocally exhausted with the anger and hate that desperate politicians conjure up with such ease like it's their birthright to do so. I am certain that the ladies in the crowd are in agreement.

I am so glad that I'm a woman." Mila laughed and dropped her head. "I apologize my brothers, I couldn't resist."

When I was a child in school I read books that taught me that capitalism was evil. I remember how frightened I was turning the pages and believing that most westerners were poor. I would stare long and hard at photos of beggars on every street corner and wonder how any society could allow this. My family was not rich, but I left my home in the morning with a meal in my stomach and I went to sleep every evening never considering that others could be hungry. How lucky I was to be living in the Soviet Union.

And then ladies and gentlemen I began to think for myself and you want to know something? I like thinking for myself.

Now, we are all aware that in a collective society this is frowned upon yet there comes a time when each of us must think for ourselves. *Hey Dmitri, you don't like what I say?* Well, that's fine but I still have the right to say it and guess what, I'll listen to your opinion if you have the balls to express it. We are here as brothers and sisters today expressing an opinion against tyranny…against men who wish to continue their vice grip control over us." Mila paused, raised her arms and shouted, *mothers.* "You're voicing your opinion…doesn't it feel fucking amazing? Is it not a liberating sensation that you wish you could feel every single day of your life? We are human,

298

we have our own opinions. We have our own likes and dislikes and we most certainly have dreams that we have never shared with the people closest to us. You have listened to arguments and rousing speeches this afternoon but when you go home to your families this evening it is up to you and only you to formulate your own opinion. It is your obligation as a citizen of Ukraine and as a citizen of the world to do so.

Glavalit ensured that everything we read denounced the west and portrayed the Soviet Union as a triumph of civility. We were supposedly the peaceful empire and what the rest of the universe should aspire to be. We watched the same themes ad-nauseum on television and in movies and believed the party line was the best way… the only way.

I stand before you today to assure each of you that our parents, uncles, aunts and teachers were all wrong.

The man selling beer or the women you met in bread lines were wrong.

We were wrong, and it is time to accept this. You now have the opportunity to say out loud… we were wrong! And that's cool… it's fine. There is no shame in being wrong my countrymen but there is incredible shame in walking the same road knowing in your heart that it is not the direction you should be heading.

Many of you know my story. I watched hero after hero die in Hospital Number Six. There is no need for more death. The new heroes are before me now. Some of you are old and some of you are barely shaving yet you are the future and you are the new heroes of Ukraine if – and only if – you work together. The liquidators worked together as brothers and staved off a disaster. It is time for all of you to do the same. Look to the west and see what Poland and Germany have accomplished. The Soviet walls have crumbled leaving behind simple stones that we – we, the people of Ukraine - shall use to build homes and new businesses instead of walls. Not one bullet will be fired and not one child will be orphaned. The only death will be communism. We will watch it breathe its last breath and then we will dance on our streets and raise celebratory toasts in our homes.

But we will remember… we will never forget.

To the students who have joined us this afternoon… listen to me closely. Do not heed one word from war mongers, they are your enemies. You are the future and you are the future without guns. No government in the world would dare harm you. This day and this rally will come and go but your day is now upon us. I stand before you offering the torch that neither I nor any old man can keep burning. You must band together as schoolmates and as Ukrainians to save us… to save yourselves. These men behind me are not the answer you seek because the true answer is within you. Discuss in your classrooms and in your libraries and grab this torch before it dims forever. Grab it now… do not wait any longer my children. Open your strong, uncluttered minds and use history to your advantage. Gather inspiration from lands we have never travelled to and gather inspiration from the pure heart that beats within you.

And students… most importantly, when the communist sympathizers attempt to influence you, I do not want you to argue with them or even to discuss their lies. I want you stand proud and tell them two words and only two words. Do any of you know what they are?"

A young man yelled and several in the crowd repeated the words. The samizdat articles were good for something, she thought. Mila raised her arms and shouted *mothers* again.

"Yes comrades… let's say this in unison. Tell them these two words… fuck you!"

A plane appeared seemingly out of nowhere and circled several times. It was flying too low causing a nervous stir throughout the crowd. The engine cut and a lower hatch opened, dropping a load that at first looked like a cloud of blood before the wind dispersed the contents in several directions. People in the crowd lifted their hands to catch the thousands of rose petals swirling and dancing in the cold air. Many in the crowd began singing, *Our Nations Rose,* the song written for the Kharmalov sisters.

The fearless sister raised her arms to catch one of the petals. They fell on her head and shoulders and littered the stage. Warmth engulfed her. She shook hands with several men who rushed the platform before waving goodbye. More of the crowd joined into song during the chorus. The other guest speakers would not look the dark haired icon in the eye and she didn't care one iota. She was quite pleased to believe they fully regretted inviting her.

Mila looked for Tania and Chris but there were too many bodies blocking her vision. Suddenly, she saw someone she did not expect to ever see again. He simulated taking a photograph and walked away. Mila's face dropped in shock and she quickly stood, pointing towards him. Her body was trembling while yelling for a security guard but the crowd was singing too loud.

Valeri Markov disappeared into the crowd.

301

A Madman Reborn

"This paintbrush was a present of sorts from a KGB bureaucrat. His wife was in love with me so she murdered her husband. I begged her not to follow through with her threats but she was obsessed with me. When I made it clear that I wouldn't sleep with her, she killed herself. Sad story really but I hold on to this brush to commemorate their tragic lives. It's a fine piece of equipment. The hairs on the brush don't allow for streaking, which you can probably determine is important and tantamount for impressive results. My paintings are shown in galleries across Europe, have you heard of me? I try to emulate the Renaissance painters to some degree but it is much too time consuming.

Art is not as respected today as it was in centuries past. Today it is considered a hobby by most but in yesteryears it was a vibrant industry. There was a period in history where popular artists had their own factories to create paint, paper and framing. Developing a new shade of paint was comparable to someone in today's Kiev inventing new technology. Then of course there is the argument that legendary artists used optical aids to trace their masterpieces. It is a disturbing theory that I hope is false. I could try this today but given our present whereabouts, using the sun and a paper bag will not be an option.

So where was I? Oh yes, my semesters in Lyiv. Like any common university, I was given exams to write and pass. Anything less than ninety percent was unacceptable yet I never once received a failing grade. In easy terms for you, my teacher was the assistant priest. Even now I shudder when I think of him. He was a very unattractive man in his late thirties with little or no

302

hair left on his opaque skull yet an abundance of fur sprout like wheat fields on his shoulders, back and especially in his nose. I used to silently calculate that his snout was a minimum of ten centimeters long. It was indeed a snout and I imagine a family of birds could nest inside with relative ease. His name was Auger. It was a surname that ensured a great deal of bullying from an early age and the reason – I believed - he sought the sanctuary of a church.

His room was next to mine yet I was never allowed to visit. I found this odd to say the least as he had no issue in knocking on my door whenever he pleased. Almost on a daily basis, he would ask me many personal questions and my response would always be a lie followed by a visit to the confessional. I had washed away my previous sins through hours of prayer therefore I found no need to feed the curiosity of an ugly assistant that the entire congregation found repulsive.

The relationship between Auger and I was one of silent disdain. I believe he disliked me because I was better than he in all respects. I arrived at Dormiton to learn. He arrived there to hide. I was good looking, and he was hideous. He asked me many personal questions, and I asked him none. I had no interest in his past life and anything I learned about him was offered or by chance.

My artwork was excelling and noticed by the parish priest. He hung many of my works in the infirmary and library. Needless to say, Auger was jealous of this. He briefly attempted to replicate my success but his weak hands could barely hold a brush let alone master one. In time, he turned to a more insidious means of lowering my standing with our leader.

My bed sheets were checked thoroughly for months when the priest was told that I was an excessive masturbator. No evidence was found. I had no need to fondle myself. Every Wednesday, Thursday and Friday afternoon, I was commissioned by the parish to paint murals on the walls of a local school. It was tedious and idiotic work because I was required to create stirring portrayals of Soviet leaders. I say idiotic based on my belief that our leaders required no further enhancements to their legend. The church, meanwhile, had an agreement with local administrators to advertise the communist party line simply to remain in existence so I did what I could for my benefactors.

I was one of two altar servers during Sunday morning services. I would dress up in a glorious gold and white robe with detailed stitching that was worth more than the home I grew up in. My tasks were to light candles, wave incense and ring the bell before consecration. My counterpart, Adana, would do the same under the ever watchful eye of our assistant priest, Auger. Adana had a seventeen-year old sister named Yana. In confidence, he divulged that she had become a growing concern for his parents. They would drag her to church every Sunday hoping to instill morals they believed she revoked with increasing frequency. Adana had no proof of such other than school hall gossip. At the time, it sounded to me that Yana was suffering the same false attacks I was.

On my first day at the secondary school, I started to etch a mural of Leon Trotsky riding a white stallion. As tasteless as that sounds, the portrayal was chosen from a long list of tacky ideas by the administrative unit. It was mid-afternoon and students began to file out of class and return home. Yana approached me from behind and poked me in the back. I did not recognize her at first as her long blond hair was tied up in a ridiculous bun. Her face was pretty, but she had one leg shorter than the other and walked with an unmistakable limp. She told me once that her handicap affected every facet of her life including her desire to be popular. It was imperative for her to achieve social standing but why was never explained. After a few awkward moments, we calmed down, and she watched as I worked my magic on the solid grey wall. I was nearing eighteen years of age but aside from the prostitute in my village, I was lacking any real skills with members of the opposite sex. Yana sensed my inexperience and used it to her advantage.

She giggled for no reason and touched my arm when she spoke. The halls were empty and our voices bounced off the whitish lockers. The bulge in my loose pants became a humorous distraction that the teenaged girl stared at with no shame. Yana's voice changed from bubbly to seductress and I was soon under her spell. She grabbed my hand and led me to a room in the lower bowels of the school. She whispered that very few knew of this hideout or lair as she referred to it. There were old chairs and torn books scattered on the dusty foundation. In the far corner I was able to distinguish a large hole in the wall where concrete bricks had been removed. Yana said that the previous janitor hid whatever he stole throughout the school year in that very hole and then brought it home at the beginning of summer holidays. One long brown table stood alone, empty of any debris.

Yana kissed me with her open mouth. Her tongue searched for mine and saliva dripped down the side of my lips. She released her hair from its constriction and then did the same to my penis. Her hand slid up and down my shaft and she massaged the head until I could no longer withstand the mounting pressure. It took only a short minute. She giggled but kissed me anyway. With her wet hand pressed on my shirt I was led me to the table where she promptly lay down, dropped her white panties and opened her legs. She softly ordered me to kneel and then stick my tongue in her vagina. I was a year older than the blond-haired girl and her thin body had yet to fully mature, yet she was schooling me. Yana instructed me on what was necessary for her to achieve the same shuddering climax that I had experienced. I eagerly followed her precise coaching. For the first few minutes she moved her hips in slow circles but as she approached orgasm her hands pushed the back of my head and her hips pushed upwards. I was enjoying the ecstasy but selfishly; I was worried of suffocating. She whimpered and released me. I inhaled a precious breath and then stood to watch Yana do the same. My chin and mouth were sopping wet, but I did not wipe the moisture away. This was a prize I earned. The smell on my fingers was her personal fragrance. I would not wash them.

Yana was pleased.

There were conditions.

Yana met me three days a week, and we enjoyed each other's bodies. Condition One was that I was never allowed to enter her but for the time being, this did not bother me. I no longer ejaculated within seconds thus allowing Yana to try new techniques. I dared not ask where she learned her tricks but one day she mentioned in passing that she was reading books that were banned by the communist party. I didn't believe her but if it was indeed true, I wanted desperately to read these books.

I was never permitted to speak to Yana in church. I was older than she and her parents would grow suspicious. I had no issue with this although I admitted to her that I often hid an erection beneath my robe. Her parents appeared strict. I watched them fidgeting in the pews and marveled at how they never smiled. Yana's mother was still attractive with large uncontrollable breasts. I imagined that Yana would have the same in a few years. The mother wore large hats in church, ridiculously large hats. I don't know why she chose this fashion but men would jostle before service began just so that they could sit behind her and hide from the priest.

The most telling characteristic of Yana's father was his brutish nature. He was muscular, perhaps the strongest man I had ever seen. His hands were like giant hammers. Any blow from this man would have to be fatal. If ever he sought me out, I would run like a proud coward and brag about it later.

I didn't catch on to his suspicion at first because I was too busy staring at Yana and dreaming of our next encounter. The father never looked at the priest. In fact, I doubt he listened to one word during the sermon. Instead, he watched Auger and followed Auger's line of vision. This made Adana nervous.

The last condition that Yana made clear was that I was to spy on her brother. She despised him. Her parents placed his future far above her own and he was thus showered with praise and gifts that were never awarded to her. *There was something not right about him*, she told me. Many of the girls in school had made suggestive advances towards him but he refused or shied away. *It was not normal.* Although being naturally muscular like his father, Adana had no wish to participate in any sports. Yana found a book of his poems stashed beneath his mattress. They were confusing. Much talk about love but no mention of a woman. She repeated that this was not normal. I asked to see these poems but

Yana denied me. I silently questioned if she was lying again. Yana lied often.

But maybe not this time.

I had never met a homosexual before and had no clue what distinguishing features they may have. There was one older man in Kopachi who never married. The village women gossiped that he liked roosters and then they'd cackle like hens. It never dawned at me that each time he smiled as I passed him on the road he was hoping I would smile back. He looked no different than anyone else. Yana once insinuated that I was a village boy misplaced in the city. Perhaps there was truth to this.

Adana was a good person but maybe too genteel. He stayed after church to mop each aisle of pews. This should have been my task, but he insisted each week that I do my painting. I was an aspiring artist and should not be wasting my time with menial work. The kind act was appreciated even though I soon learned it was a ruse to get me to leave.

Services finished at twelve noon and by one p.m. the doors were locked and everyone had gone home. The priest was always invited to lunch leaving the church empty except for Auger and myself. I, of course, was normally engrossed in my painting but not this day. Yana had recently implied that Condition One could be changed if I found incriminating evidence on Adana. If ever I needed inspiration, this was it.

He finished his mopping and then for no apparent reason sat in the third aisle pew. I was hiding in the very back aisle on my knees. The floor was dirty, suggesting that Adana did a very poor job. I peeked whenever I heard a new noise. One arrived within minutes and I was not as surprised as I expected to be. Auger sat next to Yana's sixteen year-old brother. Neither of them

308

spoke and instead just looked ahead. I found this incredibly curious thinking that maybe it was religious meditation. I was indeed a village boy misplaced in the city. Auger's head suddenly tilted back. I dropped to the floor and waited a few seconds before looking again. Adana had disappeared. Auger raised his arms and placed them behind the pew as if to hold on. He let loose a bizarre and eerie howl that rebounded off the high ceilings and echoed for several seconds. Adana reappeared.

Yana was pleased with me.

The following Wednesday, I told her what I had witnessed. She was not shocked or disappointed. I inquired about Condition One and she said not today. I felt cheated until she put my penis in her mouth. I forgot about condition number one.

The village I was raised in was not clean. We had no means to move the heavy rusted tanks left behind by both Germans and Russians. They sat there for decades as a monument to lost comrades. Or so we told ourselves. No one had indoor plumbing, and it was common to be hunting and then suddenly step in a neighbor's turd. When the twelve-foot wide by six-foot deep hole we dug for our population's excrement was full, we burned our waste in a field of dandelions and small snakes. The snakes would crawl across our boots as if we were friends. If we were fast enough, we would trap it under our soles and then cut its head off for entertainment. It was bad luck to keep the head, so we threw it into the fire with the rest of our garbage. When a fire was started other villagers would join and throw in their debris until a huge plume of smoke filled the sky. The smell was disgusting as dozens of men, women and children would toss in bucket after bucket of feces. I often wondered how they could store so much of their body waste for so long without vomiting incessantly from the smell. We would bat fat flies out of the air with ease. Their expanded bellies were too full of our crap. The villagers had a superstition that a summer of flies was an omen for future richness. It's hard to believe we were so poor.

Lyiv smelled like a burning fire of shit. There were an abundance of plants and factories and every afternoon the sky above the city would transform into a huge cloud of smoke. From a distance you could swear that every corner had a smoke stack billowing grayish white pollution. On humid summer days, the smoke rested above us like it was enjoying a long deserved nap. The stench was choking.

Yana's father worked at one of these plants. It was open twenty-four hours a day and that meant the furnaces were working nonstop. She said he melted steel that would be shipped to other factories and manufactured into cars and buses. He was paid well in comparison to others. I didn't believe her. I believed that he melted steel for a living but as for making decent money, it was plain to see the family struggled. Maybe all his money went into buying strange hats for his wife.

I arrived back in my room on Friday afternoon at five p.m. An hour later I ate dinner with the nice middle-aged lady who cooked our meals. She didn't live with us. No woman was permitted to stay past nightfall. I was finishing my plate when she asked if I had seen Auger and I replied no. I wanted to add that it was a good day when I didn't see him but resisted the urge. Since his perverted dalliance in the church pew, I made a concerted effort to avoid the assistant priest. The cook mentioned that no one had seen him all day, which in itself was unusual because the ugly man rarely left the church grounds. If I looked like him I would be a hermit too.

The conversation halted there but was restarted again the following morning. Auger was missing. The priest gave me a key to Auger's room and asked me to search for any clues of his whereabouts. The assistant would be fuming when he learned that I had finally viewed the inside of his secret den. He would be absolutely seething when I described what I saw. In the bottom drawer, underneath his Sunday robe, was a bevy of personal history that Auger purposely kept hidden from our small community.

I sifted through hundreds of pictures of naked men and boys. I had never seen a naked man before and never wished to see one again. I dropped the photos and ran to summon the priest. He asked that I remain quiet and demanded I burn the photographs. I didn't even wish to touch the pictures but followed the order as requested. We waited for Auger to return but he never did.

On the following Wednesday, Yana was in good spirits. She didn't bother with idle chit chat and rushed me as best she could to our secret love nest. She threw off her skirt and panties and lay on the table. Condition One was finally being altered. It was her birthday, and this was my gift to her. I needed little coaxing and slowly pushed my penis into her tiny hole. She made a yelping sound like a surprised dog but adjusted quickly. I, on the other hand, was overly excited and ejaculated in record time.

Yana was not pleased.

We tried again and this time she groaned and screamed. I was nervous of being caught by anyone within a mile of us. Her moaning was like a train at high speed. She wrapped her legs around my waist and dug her nails into my back. I winced in pain. She saw my face and thought I was finishing. I continued.

My heart beat faster than ever before and fatigue began to set in. She let loose a shrilling scream, buckled and came to a full stop. My only thought was that we had arrived at the station. I was still erect. She didn't care. Yana pushed me away and got dressed.

I was thanked for the information I supplied the previous week. She was now queen of the household and her brother was not allowed to leave the house. Her father beat him and called him a queer. He was disowned. The happiness in Yana's voice was in a word, disturbing. Her brothers plight meant little to her. All that mattered was her new status. Tonight, she was to receive a gift at dinner and possibly cake. She kissed me goodbye and left me with my pants around my ankles. I still had an erection.

Yana wasn't at school on Thursday or Friday.

I was worried that she ate too much cake, and it had made her sick. None of the family attended church on Sunday and the priest took notice. I couldn't tell him that Yana was also missing from school without raising suspicion about my clandestine meetings. There are many secrets in churches. It is something I learned over three years of seminary education. Everyone has a secret. Except the lady who cooked for us, she was an open book. I wish she wasn't.

After service the priest was called away in a rush. There was a distress in his face that I had never seen before and wanted to ask why. For two hours I swept the aisles between the pews. I wished Adana was there.

That same evening I was shocked to learn he would never be returning to our church. After Yana's birthday dinner, Adana slit his wrists in the family bathroom. I was not aware someone

312

could die like this and I later researched how it was accomplished. I was not distressed about his death, only curious on how he did it. He was successful in taking attention away from Yana, that much was certain. I'm sure she was more mad than sad. It was then I realized that Yana, and I shared a common attribute. We didn't care about anyone else but ourselves. We didn't even care about each other. The priest asked me if I was depressed about Adana's passing and I answered yes. I lied.

Another secret never to be revealed.

There was no funeral for Adana. He was cremated and forgotten by everyone except his mother. She returned to our church the following Sunday but Yana's father did not. Neither did Yana. It wasn't until a full month later that she went back to school. We talked for a few moments but she left afterwards. She did the same the following day. On Friday we went to our secret room, and she lowered her panties but kept her skirt on. She ordered me to please her with my tongue and I obliged. The young girl seemed to take great pleasure in pulling my hair and took a long time to climax. She raised her underwear, gave me a friendly kiss on my cheek and left. I was totally confused with her attitude but considered she was still in mourning or at least abiding by some rule or silly Russian superstition.

The same scenario played out three more times and Yana was progressively rougher. She believed herself to be in a position of power over me. Baba believed this too. The next time we met I continued the charade and did as she asked. When she was fulfilled, Yana patted me on the head. I grabbed her wrist and twisted causing her to scream. She looked into my eyes for a brief second and her haughty expression quickly changed. I turned her around and bent her supple body over the table. In a matter of

313

seconds I had ripped off her skirt and panties and plunged my penis into her. She screamed again so I put one hand over her mouth and pulled her hair violently with the other. *Who's the lead dog now*, I yelled. Weeks of frustration forbade any gentleness. I was hurting her and didn't think twice about it. She tried to bite my hand, so I struck her hard across the back of the head. She submitted after that. *Good little gimp*, I told her and then patted her on the head. The sweetest revenge is a pat on the head.

"My father killed the priest," she said in between moans. I stopped my thrusting and asked her to repeat. "He wrote a letter to the priest pretending he was my brother. They were to meet at our apartment. Augers believed it. My father tossed him into one of the gigantic furnaces at the factory. He made Adana watch and that's why he killed himself."

I pulled out of her and lifted my trousers.

She goaded me saying that once her father finds out what I did today, he would do the same to me. The brazen girl turned to face me. Yana sneered when she said that this time, she'd be the one watching when her father tossed me into the furnace. I said nothing, and she attempted to limp around me. The priest would be ashamed and I could not allow that to happen. Yana pushed me hard, but I stood my ground. I punched her directly on the nose and she fell backwards. I grunted that I was not done and grabbed her by the scruff of the neck. Once again, I bent her over but this time I slammed her face into the table. She screamed loudly but her pain had no effect on me. Each thrust was harder than the one before. I slammed her face again and a splotch of blood creased on her forehead. She begged me to stop and promised she wouldn't say a word. Now it was me who was laughing. I pulled her scalp hair upward, wrapped my forearm

314

around her neck and squeezed. Her fingernails dug into my outer thigh only increasing my excitement. I could feel her energy dissipate with each passing second. I whispered in her ear that when she sees her brother, tell him that she died with my cock inside of her. I ended by asking her to remember the seven sins. One quick jerk later, the girls fingers unleashed and her arms hung lifeless. Any power she once had was now inside of me.

I was still erect.

She did not fit perfectly into the gaping hole in the wall. I had to push hard until every inch of her rigid body was stuffed within the opening. I heard her neck and both legs snap. The sound was no different than the sound I make when I crack my knuckles, only louder. As strange as this may sound, I believe if Yana's left leg was not an inch shorter, she may not have fit. I found the missing concrete blocks in a corner with two living and three dead mice. I dropped one of the cinders on a mouse that was stupid enough to watch me. Then there were four dead mice. In twenty minutes time Yana had a resting place where she would never be disturbed. I wiped my pants as best I could but my hands were filthy. From that point on I would always carry a handkerchief in my right pocket for moments like this.

When I arrived back at the church I had a quiet dinner with our cook. She was in a solemn mood but I did not ask why. I didn't care to know. I wanted to inquire if she knew any teenaged girls with loose morals. In a little over a month's time, the parents of Adana and Yana were childless because of their offspring's affairs with men at a cathedral they believed offered structure, forgiveness and hope. There are many secrets in every church. I had them too."

Valeri stood and stretched his arms as high as they could reach. His neck was a bit tight but not because of any increased tension. He twisted it side to side and listened for the small pressure releasing crack. Like most of his models, this girl had long dark hair. She was by far the heaviest girl he had ever painted and moving her into the basement was no easy task. She reminded him a bit of the caretaker's wife.

What was her name again?

The young woman had been crying. Valeri grew weary of crying models and wished that just once one of them would smile. He approached her and she began to squirm in her chair trying to break loose of the rope that entrapped her. He was more concerned that the chair would split into several sharp fragments under the weight of his guest. He had removed her top believing her large sagging breasts to be a metaphor for the art he was creating. Her areolas were the size of tea coasters, which he noted as something he liked. Valeri circled a finger around the woman's left areola and then pulled on her nipple. He wished to see how pointed it would become. It took a few moments, but the nipple protruded a good half inch. Valeri took a mental note and would paint his victim with erect nipples.

"I've watched you for months," he said while exhaling a long tired sigh. "On the day that three hundred thousand of your freedom fighters held hands for independence I was briefly holding yours. I could have taken you then but I waited. I have plenty of time on my hands. You live with your mother in a shit hole of an apartment. I went in when no one was home. It's a pig sty, you are better off here in this dark basement. Does your mother know you have condoms in your underwear drawer? She is very young…your mother, I mean. She must have had you when she was barely a teenager. Are you aware your sweet mama has several boyfriends and no real job? I have not seen her doing anything that could be construed as work. From what I gather, these boyfriends pay your rent and food for time well spent. I can only imagine that the word whore was introduced into your vocabulary at a very young age." Valeri walked behind her and gently grabbed both of her breasts. "I commend you for trying harder but you do tend to use food as a crutch. Earlier this week in the lunch diner you had a plate of Perogies with two bowls of sauce. Seriously, it was a small mountain that would have been three meals for me. Your bowel movements must be legendary.

From Tuesday to Saturday you work at the grocery store next to the new Laundromat. Your boss's wife is an unsightly wench. It is rare that we, in Ukraine, see such an ugly woman. That neck of hers must stretch for two feet; she looks like an ostrich. Is that why the owner has such fun with you in the back room? I believe he stores the canned beets and pickles on the first shelf. They're lousy pickles, the worse I have ever tasted. Does he buy the condoms that you hide from your mama? You're very loud; I think you should know this. I was in the store once with another customer when he was having his way with you. Yana moaned and wailed like you. I compared her to a train. You are more like an airplane on a runway preparing to take off. An older lady in the store at the same time as me was frightened by your moaning and ran away as fast as her fat little legs could move her. I don't think she wanted to be around when you landed."

He walked in front of the girl and grinned. Her face was suddenly very flushed and Markov could not deduce why.

317

"I am need of some nourishment. When I return, I'll regale you with some more tales of my conquests and experiences. Don't be missing me too much."

Valeri climbed the ladder and squeezed through the opening into his bedroom. He used to keep the floorboard shut but in recent months he had become more bold, more sure of himself. As always, he visited the bathroom and washed his hands thoroughly. Looking into the mirror that he himself built, he stared at his rapidly aging face. The Crows Feet around his eyes were deeper than only last month. Approaching thirty years of age he still believed he was too young for these devil lines and would have to remember to buy cream the next time he visited Kiev. His hair was still long, and he had no wish to cut it short like most of the men in his small town. Samson would not cut his hair so why should he.

The girl's father died when she was fifteen. Valeri knew this because he saw a small newspaper clipping hanging on her bedroom wall. He was a liquidator at Reactor Four during the first two weeks after the explosion. The family needed the money, and he volunteered. Every trip onto the roof was another paycheck. The girl kept a diary under her pillow, which he unlocked with a pen knife. The father was a good man but his wife loved money. He was too weak; he should have beaten her when she came back with bags of groceries and perfume. The girl wrote that men would visit their apartment during the days her father was working. Her mother ordered her to stay in her bedroom but she heard everything. Sometimes there were two men and once she peeked out to see three. They were naked and in unspeakable positions. Her mother would laugh and then scream and then laugh again. When the men left, her mama would go shopping for clothes. As best she could, the young daughter would make dinner for her father and they would eat it in front of the television.

She loved her papa and spent every free moment with him. They took long walks and kicked soccer balls in the park. He didn't want to be apart from his Angelika and that is why he didn't leave his cheating wife.

Angelika… such a pretty name.

His daughter was his world. The money from Chernobyl would pay for a new life and they could say goodbye to the woman who purposely shamed them. He died on January 7th, New Years' Day, in Hospital Number Six. Her mother was busy and could not make the trip to Moscow. She wished her mother was dead and papa was alive. Life had everything backwards.

Valeri contemplated what he was doing to this pitiful creature. Like the others before her, he had ravaged and broken the young woman. He wished he had chosen someone else. Although he would feel no remorse when all was done, he did feel that this time, he had erred. She was fat but her disease was not gluttony, it was sadness. She fornicated with a married man but he was old. Markov considered that maybe she was seeking the affection of a father figure.

If he let her go she would surely tell the police and his face was forever etched in her brain. He could drug her with the root and then drive to Odessa. It was seven to eight hours away. This would confuse her and the police. Perhaps she will say something to change his mind, to prove he had been right. She was playing tricks with him trying to influence her release. This morning when he woke up he stepped outside and saw an apple tree in bloom across the street. He had been living there for three years and never once noticed this very obvious tree. He deliberated if some cheeky sot was playing a trick on him. All morning he had recounted minute details of his experiences and travels to this overweight woman yet he could not recall seeing a huge tree fifty feet from his house. He was much too astute. There was without a doubt some kind of deception in the making.

He ate a tomato sandwich and poured black tea into an expensive teacup he had pillaged from Pripyat. Most of his cutlery and plates were courtesy of the residents of that once thriving town. It would please him if he knew they missed their belongings. While in the fat girl's apartment he stole some of her mother's expensive jewelry. He sold it all to his black market connection in Lugansk. Until now it never occurred to him that the mother would blame her daughter. He didn't care; it was just something he believed to be unfair. He would ask the girl about it when he continued his artwork.

He liked his new painting. The girl was large and the people from her life were tiny toy-like characters displayed as satiric cartoons. She was anti-communist, so he painted a small orthodox Jew dangling from an erect nipple. Her fleshy breasts were partitioned off as if they were sides of beef to be sold in the market. As always, the face he drew was not the victim but instead resembled Mila Kharmalov. An ostrich was burying its head in the girl's bushy pubic hair and a tiny depiction of the older storekeeper was lying on her tummy with a napkin tucked into the neck of his shirt. Hundreds of protesters were feeding off her thick thighs.

He finished his sandwich and placed the plate in the kitchen sink. Returning to the basement, he sat and sighed when seeing his hostage was slumped over. He continued his story anyway.

"I am a strong believer in God and a loyal follower of communist methodology. That makes me an enigma of sort because other than within me, the two have never melded. If given a chance the two could work together rather nicely but political aspirations have always conspired against the marriage of church and state.

During the hostile beginnings of the Soviet regime, the Bolsheviks and Tsar Families were murdered en-masse for having conspired against the Soviets. For years, the Bolsheviks were well known to be anti-Semitic and were responsible of the deaths of thousands of Jews. The priests of this era preached that the Jews murdered Christ thus killing the Jews was payback for taking the son of God from the real chosen people. The Soviets claimed the Bolsheviks were Jew lovers and thus joined forces with Muslims. It was classic who said what and who do you believe. The Soviets as you are well aware, won handedly. Nowadays, the Russians are trying to annihilate Muslims in their own country and Georgia. Jews fled Russia during WWII and they continue to seek refuge in Israel and other Jew loving countries. As I read through several history books it appeared to me that Russia – again like me - is an enigma and a huge contradiction. Soviet rule with a background of Christianity would uphold a long lasting peace. The Russian people have rarely known any era of uninterrupted peace. The opportunity for wide spread Christianity in this land is now upon them yet they have discarded one working class for three separate entities that can never balance each other.

Christianity offers hope while democracy offers greed and never the two will meet. I have the solution but no means to spread my beliefs. Russia has the means but no desire to return to one class. So, do you understand now what I am saying?

Russia will never find harmony and neither will I.

As it is now, there is no manner to spread my doctrine. I am not an orator nor do I wish to be. Instead I have written journals that someday will be released to the world. The readers of these journals will do so initially thinking they are reading the ramblings of a serial killer. Instead, they will quickly decipher that they are in the process of devouring an intellectual buffet that will change their lives. The word will spread of an important manifest that will save Russia, Ukraine and all the CIS countries from the shackles of western media mind control. I will be remembered as the Russian savior… the Prince.

When the time is right, I will offer myself to the police or militia, whichever is more reliable for my purpose. Until then it is my duty as a lifelong communist to rid the world of self-indulgence and weakness.

The priest believed me to be the strongest young man he ever met. He admired my work ethics and my willingness to learn as much as I could about Christian ethics or morals. Although my concept of morals was different than his, I never shared my secret ideology. He was better off believing I was the person he wished me to be. I, on the other hand, was not comfortable in my skin. I saw things I did not agree with and I acted on my solid values. It was my second year in the parish and I was a few months past my twentieth birthday. Yana was never found. Her parents posted photos across Ukraine hoping she had run away. They left the church, and I never saw them again.

I have seen governments tumble and crops fail. I have watched the strongest men beg for their lives. Change is a certainty and nothing is as it seems. There is only one unwavering fact in this world. No matter how the universe turns or how your position in life finds you, there is one constant. Women are a man's true opium. No herb or chemical is as intoxicating or addicting. Once you inhale a female's aroma you will always return to her bosom. I was a twenty-year old man and needed the warmth of a woman's curves. I found one twice my age.

Everything about her was wrong for me and I welcomed her. She taught me more than I could ever imagine and more than I cared to know. She was evil incarnate. I was weak.

Iona was her given name. She was named after a grandmother who was trampled by a German tank three days after the woman gave birth to Iona's sickly mother. At five feet ten inches, Iona was the tallest woman I had ever met. When hunting the city streets she purposely wore heels to tower over men who dared approach her. During our infrequent quiet moments I would lie on top of her and my feet barely passed her knees.

If not for Yana's father I would have never met the Amazon lady. There was no longer an assistant cleric therefore when the priest was not available it was my duty to listen to confessions. Iona visited on Tuesday afternoons, coincidentally the same time our priest disappeared every week. Where he went I did not know nor did I care to ask. The middle-aged woman would sit cross legged in the confessional with the first three buttons of her shirt hanging loose and then brag about her rendezvous' with strangers she met in parks and bars. It certainly did not appear to me that she was asking forgiveness or was ashamed of her actions. I would respond in my lowest voice that penance would be served with a certain amount of prayers and a donation to the church. Although I asked her to attend, Iona never made an appearance on Sundays.

I had grown very inwards since my altercation with Yana. I did not beg forgiveness as I felt no remorse. Instead, I pledged to forego the flesh and immerse myself in religious study. Iona was responsible for me renouncing this resolution. There were many attractive girls at Sunday service and many more on the streets of Lyiv but I abstained. There was this one time when the urges were so strong that I whipped my back with a thorn bush until the pain in my trembling body sent me into a deep slumber. By the fourth week, Iona's visits had become a primal necessity for me. I found her raspy voice shamefully erotic and decided that this week I would ask more intimate questions. She was not fooled by my amateurish inquiries and left the confessional. I was disappointed and thought for sure she would never return. To my surprise she waited outside my half of the confessional to view the man listening to her secrets. I was not dressed in any priestly garb, which resulted in a more satisfactory conclusion for me. Her face was ordinary but her long legs were splendid. I imagined how much time it would take to slide my hands up from her ankles to her thigh. She read my eyes, grabbed my hand and placed it under her skirt. I protested saying we were inside the church and I would lose both my job and residence. She asked if I wanted more and I whispered yes. She asked if I wanted to experience a world I had never before witnessed. My penis was bursting. Yes, I said with authority. She would return at seven p.m., before the sun set. I was to wait outside for a green Lada. She unzipped my pants and held my erect penis in her palm. I was terrified of being caught but at the same time mesmerized by this totally fearless

324

woman. She stared into my eyes as if to gage my fear. *You'll do fine*, she said. Iona turned away, and I was thankful. The last time someone ejaculated in this church they were tossed into a furnace. I compared it to the burning fires of hell. In a round-about way, I believe Iona was thinking the same.

The hair on her roundish head was dirty blond like Tania Kharmalov's but she was not near as good looking. The few times I awoke in her home, I would catch her staring into a mirror wondering how much longer her creamy complexion would remain clear of wrinkles and age spots. I was fascinated by how comfortable she was with her thin body. Inside her locked home, Iona would strip off her shirt and pants and prance around on cold floors wearing only underwear and slippers. She insisted I do the same, but I was less proud and would pretend I did not hear her request.

The tall woman was raised in a village outside of Lyiv. The stories she told me were eerily similar to my own upbringing therefore creating an instant bond. She would lie on her back with a bottle of vodka between her tiny yet perky breasts and recount one horrifying story after another until the bottle was empty. She had an older sister with a cleft lip. The sister, Aida, was avoided by other villagers at all costs and believed to be the spawn of the devil. Children threw stones at her and babushka spat on her shoes. They would threaten to burn down the family home if she came too close.

As I mentioned before, her mother died giving birth to Iona. No midwife would visit the home because of a superstitious fear that Aida would count their teeth. If she were to count all of them, the villager would die within a fortnight. The mother bled out after the fatal delivery ripped apart her insides. Aida told her

325

sister that Iona lay in the blood for hours and this is why her complexion was so perfect. Iona believed her.

We drove without speaking. For the first six months, I would become dependent on her driving skills as her village was forty-five minutes from Dormiton. The highway turned into mud roads with steep inclines and holes that caused me to leave my seat. Iona drank her vodka never once spilling a drop. Corn fields dominated the horizon and went on for what seemed like miles. I saw horses running free, stopping only to harass the cattle that ignored them. There were many log homes but very few people outside. I questioned Iona on where everyone was and she did not respond. Finally, I saw a man wearing a faded jean jacket pumping water from a huge well. When he saw our car, he dropped his head and turned away. The sun was disappearing under the last rows of corn. I wondered if my loins had made a very poor decision.

We arrived at her expansive plot of land. There were three homes per se. The first was a brick structure in very good condition. Iona lived here. The other two, several yards away, were more of what I was accustomed to seeing in villages. They were gray wood with rotting doors that barely closed. Rows of cut logs lay against the west wall of the middle home. Grass patches were scattered amongst hardened clay and a block well was perfectly centered between of all three houses. I asked who lived in the other homes. Iona looked blankly at the homes and then me. Once again, she did not answer. I followed her into her residence as if I had no choice.

Everything was clean. Her floor was polished wood with throw rugs under the kitchen table and at the main entrance. I was told to remove my shoes. The house was warm with the distinctive smell of burning wood. The kitchen cupboards had brass handles. I had never in my life seen a village home so beautiful and welcoming. She watched me closely.

Iona asked when I last bathed. It was a peculiar question and one that no one had ever asked before that evening. I responded that the priest insisted we bathe every morning. She nodded contently. She took my hand and led me to her bedroom. It was separated from the main room with a large oak door. There were Latin words carved into a wood plaque that I did not understand. I cursed under my breath for not beginning the language courses the priest ordered me to study. Her bedroom was uncluttered with no hanging photographs or paintings. Aside from a sturdy bed, a cherry oak dresser and a beautiful mirror centered above the dresser, the room was barren. Iona requested I sit on the bed and watch her disrobe. I was nervous as she dropped her checkered dress displaying small breasts and smooth thighs. Pubic hair poked out of her silky beige underpants. She had a small belly that lay over the top of her panties as if tired. She removed her bra, and I stared at the deformity she knew would alarm me. Her right nipple was missing, replaced by a deep red scar. She whispered that it was burned off, and I was not to touch it.

I was clumsy at first but soon relaxed, recalling the tricks that Yana had taught me. Iona was a quiet lover, making it difficult for me to guess when she was spent. It was midnight when she finally rolled over and briefly smiled. She asked if I had plans to remain in the priesthood. I explained that I believed in Christ and was fascinated by the history yet had no wish to become monogamous to a church. My response satisfied her, and she turned on her side to look at me. Before she would divulge

327

anything about her past she needed to know everything about mine. She would know if I was lying, so I was to speak openly and not prepare my responses.

To this very day, I do not fully comprehend why I was so talkative with this woman but realized soon after, that being truthful about whom I was most probably saved my life. I told her about Kopachi and my domineering mother. I spoke slowly when describing minute details of the village and its citizens. Iona had never heard of Kopachi but to her it sounded like any other small back-wood town she had briefly visited. She asked me leading questions and as a test I fibbed with one response. She asked the same question while grabbing my testicles. I answered truthfully. The questions were nonstop. As soon as I responded to one another was asked. I would not be leaving this home without revealing a detailed description of my last day with Yana. Her eyes never left mine and when there was nothing left to tell she kissed me full on the lips and wrapped a long leg across both my legs, trapping me.

I had done well. She assured me that in time I would know everything about her and she would teach me things that would guide me through a life of unparalleled pleasure. I believed her. Unlike Yana, Iona never lied. She had no need to.

We didn't sleep and Iona dropped me off at the church at approximately seven a.m. I was exhausted but knew there would be no slumber until later that evening. I had breakfast with the cook who had arrived only moments after me. She said I looked tired, and I replied saying I hadn't slept a wink. She made me a strong coffee and started jabbering about her experiences with sleepless nights. I thought of killing her. I was hungry, so she was spared.

328

Iona and I met on Wednesday nights until my visits increased to include Friday. Bit by bit she told me stories of her youth until one evening over two bottles of vodka, she recounted the full dark history.

At a very young age she would walk two kilometers to the closest school accompanied by her older sister Aida. Iona did not understand why the people in her village steered clear of them. The two sisters were ordered by teachers to sit in the back of the class and none of the other children would play with them. In time, the bullying became so extreme that their father decided to keep them at home. He would curse loudly and swear revenge but never did. In fact, he rarely left the property. Aida was his angel although even he found her facial abnormality to be unsightly. It was Aida who always sat on his knee and it was Aida who shared his bed. Iona was jealous of the attention she was denied. She had just turned eleven years of age when Aida's belly began to grow. Every week it grew a little larger until she could barely walk. Iona was terrified that it would burst but at the same time wondered if she would finally be left alone with her father. The night her family life began its slow disintegration was so cold and windy that the cries from inside the home were muted by the wind slamming against bending windows. Iona ran into her father's room and saw the man pulling a head out of Aida's vagina. It horrified the young child, and she screamed. Her father screamed back telling her to get warm water and dry rags. When she returned he was holding a baby boy. The father kissed his favorite daughter and handed her their son. Iona knew then that she would never receive his attention.

The snow had melted earlier than normal and by the end of March the sound of passing trucks on mud roads became more apparent. Aida had named her child Vera after a storybook hero. Iona did not remember the book it came from. She cried all the time. She awoke the rooster each morning and would not stop until sundown. The neighbours were curious about the newborn and on one early March afternoon while Iona was picking berries from the forest, a trio of village women wearing heavy coats cornered the young girl to ask who the father was. She answered honestly. Iona never lied.

A few hours after Iona's admission, a gang of fifty or more villagers were yelling death threats from the front yard. Young and old men held rifles while woman hurled large rocks through the windows. One woman was tossing cow feces with her bare hands. She would reach into an aluminum milk bucket, grab a handful and toss whatever didn't stick to her fingers.

The father stormed outside with an axe. Aida was not far behind holding her daughter. The father began waving his axe wildly frightening the intruders. A tall bearded man stepped forward, aimed his rifle and shot her father in the knee. The bullet tore through his leg and passed in between Aida's legs before it lodged in the front door.

He fell to the ground grabbing his wounded leg. The crowd descended on Aida and forcibly removed the baby from her weak arms. She tried desperately to run into the house but a teenager grabbed a fistful of hair and then pushed her towards the barn. Iona was dragged in to witness. Other men followed and closed the barn door behind them. The father yelled in desperation and this was followed by a boot to his head. Inside the dirty barn, the men were laughing, giddy with excitement.

330

Two of the stronger villagers tied Aida hands to the first post they saw and then ripped off her skirt. One by one they raped her from behind making sure she could not face them and count their teeth. A bucket of goat's milk was lifted and emptied over her head. She begged for mercy but none was given. Iona tugged on the tallest man's shirt asking why her sister was being hurt. He answered that she was a demon, and this was her exorcism. Iona had no idea what he meant but nodded as if in agreement. She felt no empathy for her older sister. A teenaged boy no older than fourteen could not perform and was thrown to the matted straw floor. The others laughed and spat on him. Iona did the same, which led to another round of laughter.

The tall man pushed her gently to the entrance, asking her to leave. Iona did as asked and returned to the front yard. The women had backed away from the blood soaked carcass of the man that Iona called father. She stood over him and pulled out the hanging ligament that was lodged in his mouth. The women screamed at her but did not approach. She did not know from where this appendage came and threw it on the ground. She tried to awaken him but soon realized her father would never again open his eyes. His pants had been pulled off and blood was seeping from something that had been snipped. She wanted to cry but could not. The only thoughts that came to her were those of self-pity.

You should have paid more attention to me, she whispered.

She didn't bury her father. Wild dogs dragged him away that same night. For five difficult years Iona lived alone and learned day by day how to hunt and cook. Neighbors had long ago stolen the family goat and the two sheep that Aida had named Pitter and Patter. Two years ago, Iona finally cut down the fly

331

infested corpse of her sister that hung in the barn. She burned
what was left off the gray carcass when she noticed a pack of
wolves circling her front yard. She lived on berries and the rabbits
she learned to trap and gut. She stole corn from the farm fields
she would soon be expected to work in. Occasionally an
empathetic villager would bring her milk and tea.

At fifteen her body had developed new curves. She
thought herself cursed when her vagina began to bleed every
month but told no one, fearing an angry mob would hang her in
the barn. Boys began to speak to her when she picked the field
berries. Iona found this strange as very few people had
approached her in such a long time. She blushed frequently, not
understanding the sudden attention.

One of the teenagers named Marcus stayed with her
longer than the others. He helped her around the house and
cleaned the fly infested barn. She liked him, or so she thought. He
was the son of the richest man in the village and was groomed to
one day lead the community. Their lot had three homes and
relatives resided in two of them. The family had thirty head of
cattle and fifty sheep. He was an inch shorter than Iona and
during their first kiss, stood on a rock to be level with her eyes.
Much to the chagrin of Marcus's family, they were married one
week after Iona's sixteenth birthday.

****

She had heard whispers that her husband was sleeping with a girl
who was barely thirteen. He grew inward and angry. Iona fretted

late afternoons when he would return from the corn fields. He'd storm through the front door and sit at the table, waiting for his dinner. If it was late, he beat her. If she burned the stew, Marcus would become enraged and strike her. She did not fight back; always worried a mob would hang her in the barn. Her shoulders ached from the deep bruises she was ordered to cover. He never hit her face; it would leave an evident mark.

In mid-April, ten months since their wedding, Iona was invited to travel to the neighboring village of Samaski. She gladly accepted but Marcus was not pleased. She would understand if he wished to hit her later. The voyage was only thirty minutes by horse and cart but it was the first time she had ever left her own borders. It was as if she was travelling to an exotic far off land. And it *was* exotic.

Samaski was more a town than a village. It had a restaurant and vendors stood behind wheeled carts selling beer to a lineup of thirsty men. The center of town was a hub for citizens and visitors from other villages and even the city. Those from the city wore clothes she could only wish to own. The fabrics were colorful and vibrant. She wanted to touch them just to remember how wonderful they were. She strayed from her village group and walked around mesmerized by the chatter and laughter. Merchants behind stalls of fish, meat, vegetables and trinkets called her to purchase their goods. She had no money, and they shrugged. Maybe next time, they smiled. They all smiled.

A drum roll signified an event about to happen only feet away. A man wearing tight orange shorts and socks that rose above his knees summoned visitors to come watch his act. He lay a hat at his feet and with sparkling eyes and a wide grin mentioned that if the spectators were happy with his performance it would nice if they left a few coins.

Iona was enthralled with the magician's powers and smiled the entire act. Many in the attendance dropped money in the hat but some threw their coins. One of the coins was tossed too hard and rebounded off the magicians boot back into the crowd. It rolled towards Iona and she bent slowly to retrieve it. The simple act of bending caused her to wince in pain. She handed the coin to an old man standing next to her and he walked it over to the magician. When the act was finished she clapped enthusiastically. She loved being in this town.

She was free.

There were three of them. The more talkative man had no hair on his head whatsoever but had a strong handsome face. She guessed he was in his late twenties. He wore a white undershirt that showed off his muscular arms. The second man was small, portly and wore glasses that slipped off his nose when he lowered his head. He had short brown hair parted in the middle. The third member of the group was an enigma to Iona. She was not sure if it was a man or a woman. Noticing her perplexed face, the bald man said that she was a he that wanted to be a she. Iona did not fully understand but chose to stay silent. *She* had very long blond hair and a complexion more lovely than her own. Her eyelashes were longer than any Iona had ever seen. Iona told the men her name and politely asked theirs.

"We no longer address ourselves by our given names," the bald man replied. "I am Doctor. My bespectacled friend is Chemist and our ladylike partner is Teacher. We each have a skill

334

that when combined is extremely… powerful. Chemist can create powders and liquids that can heal or hurt. Teacher is brilliant. You need only to ask a question and she will answer but to garner any response from her, you must ask a question."

"And what do you do?" Iona asked the bald man.

He smiled broadly. "I may or may not tell you the answer, Iona. Much depends on how you explain the cuts and bruises on your back and shoulders."

Iona gasped at his directness. She glanced at her long sleeves checking for rips or holes that may have revealed her predicament. There were none. How did he know?

"Teacher," Doctor said, "Will you please inform Iona how we knew of her distress?"

Teacher spoke softly with a feminine voice. This creature was very confusing to Iona, and she was fascinated by her… or him. The blond-haired person stared into Iona's eyes as if daring the girl to not look back.

"You are a young woman two inches short of six feet and you enjoy your tall stature. Today you are walking with a slouch that would not be apparent to the norms but it is to me. The few times you have attempted to correct your posture has resulted in you wincing as if in pain. This could be surmised as back pain except you do not move slowly. When you lowered your shoulder earlier to pick up a loose coin, you did so mechanically and chose to bend your knees instead. It is a warm day yet you are wearing long sleeves. This amongst other telling signs is why we know you have been beaten. Your dilemma is unfortunately, common."

"Teacher sees all and knows all," Doctor bragged.

Iona was impressed while at the same time unsure if she should remain seated with the trio. She looked passed the picnic

335

tables and across the square and saw none of her group. For a brief second she hoped that they had forgotten her.

"So Iona, this is your opportunity to tell us who you are and why you choose to live as you live. One chance my lady... this is your one chance."

Marcus once showed interest in her and now he didn't. These strangers could very well do the same. Nonetheless, she relished the opportunity presented to her and for the next forty-five minutes told them as much as she could remember. Her thoughts were scattered but Chemist and Doctor asked careful, genuine questions and she replied concisely, albeit, with little passion.

Iona answered a final query and exhaled. She had never revealed so much or spoken for so long to anyone. Communication was fun but totally tiring. Doctor was leaning on the picnic table examining his friends' expressions.

"Teacher," he began, "Is Iona a weak person?"

Teacher flipped her bangs before speaking. "No, she is not. She is incapable of being frail yet she is understandably naïve. The trauma Iona has experienced from a young age has left her insensitive to inner pain. Given the proper environment this woman would be a force to be reckoned with."

"And on a personal level Teacher, what are your thoughts?" Doctor asked.

"Her potential scares the shit out of me," she answered, strangely nonplussed.

"Chemist, do you concur?" Doctor questioned while staring at Iona.

Teacher was not pleased with the attention the muscular man was giving the tall woman. She grimaced and shot the bald man a look of displeasure.

"Most definitely," the smaller man answered. He pushed his glasses up his sweaty nose but hey immediately slipped again.

Doctor nodded several times before speaking. He slid one hand over his bald head and then rested both hands on top. "The question remains Iona as to what it is you will do about your circumstance. Will you return to the beatings or shall you enlist our help?"

"Help?" she squawked. "Gentlemen… and lady, I appreciate your time in listening to my problems but I am not in need of any help. I simply fulfill my duties as a wife." As if to save her from an uncomfortable situation, a woman from her village waved from a distance signaling that it was time to leave. "I do sincerely thank-you for your time."

Doctor grabbed her wrist. "If you change your mind Iona, we are always here. We hope to see you again."

He stood as did Chemist. Teacher made no movement whatsoever. Iona bowed her head and returned to the group of nattering women waiting for her.

She arrived home a half hour before Marcus' normal return. Fearing a thrashing she beat several eggs and tossed in vegetables and leftover turkey for an omelet. Marcus did not show at his regular hour. She ate her dinner and waited. Three hours later her husband threw open the front door and yelled for dinner. He was not alone. Following him into the narrow home, were two of his childhood friends. They too had been drinking heavily. One of the men, an average sized twenty-year old with a gigantic nose asked Marcus how he could move into this shithole after living in luxury. Marcus hissed and replied that it was a mistake. All three sat at the table and the husband ordered Iona to make more dinner for his friends. She did as asked but only had two more eggs. She added more vegetables and turkey to make it appear as enough. The men took turns at swigging vodka from two near empty bottles. With each gulp they became more boisterous and Marcus began to call his embarrassed wife offensive names. The friends giggled at each hurled insult. He pushed away his plate and stated that dinner tasted like shit. Iona was sitting on the only settee with her head in her hands. Hours earlier, three strangers made it clear that they would help her out of her awful life and she walked away. Marcus stood quickly causing his chair to tip. His drunken body ambled towards his wife and he fell on top of her causing the woman to yelp. He grabbed her hair and turned her over on her stomach. The two friends joined, and he instructed the big nosed boy to sit on Iona's ankles. Marcus lifted her skirt and pulled down her panties. He pointed at Iona's buttocks and commented on how skinny they were. He slid his hand under her stomach and then stuck a finger into her vagina. She begged him to stop and he in turn shouted at her to stay silent. He laughed loudly and welcomed his friends to take turns. The big nosed loaf did not need to be asked twice and dropped his pants. Marcus spread his wife's legs and then held her ankles when she tried to struggle.

The abuse lasted two hours, and the men took turns doing what Iona would one day describe as unspeakable. Marcus was not done with the evening's torture. He grabbed a large iron meat fork and heated it on the hot stove. His eyes were wide and wicked as he turned Iona over, ripped her blouse and singed her right nipple. Marcus laughed and blurted that the sound and smell was not unlike slabs of beef in a frying pain. The sudden sting was excruciating and Iona screamed in horrific pain. The three men laughed so hard that the big nosed boy vomited on Iona's hair causing the three to howl even louder.

They left the dark house with arms around each other's shoulders. They were proud comrades in an insignificant village.

Iona could not move. She remembered Aida tied up in the barn begging for mercy. Aida's sobs for help were ignored by her younger sister.

Iona did not cry for help. She knew none would come.

Marcus did not return, and she was thankful for this. Iona stood on shaking legs and hobbled towards her bedroom. She could not bear to look at herself in the mirror. She would just change her dress and leave. Her anus was bleeding.

It was a brisk evening and her escape would require her to walk a long distance on dark roads. She put on a heavy coat and flat shoes. Doctor would probably not be surprised to see her, she thought.

She was right.

The following morning she hid within the forest just outside Samaski. She drank from a small creek and then washed her face. Iona wet her tangled hair and then brushed it as best she could. Small chunks of dried vomit impeded her brush. She tried to sit, but the pain was too much to endure so she knelt with her arms folded beneath her breasts.

She waited patiently until noon. Hunger had set in and her stomach was rumbling. Slowly but surely and averting eye contact, Iona neared the happy sounds of the market. The three were sitting where she left them less than twenty-four hours earlier. It was Chemist who noticed her first and ran to Iona realizing she was in distress. Doctor soon followed but Teacher did not move.

They did not remain in the center square and instead brought Iona to their tiny domain. It was well hidden behind a line of trees, off the main road. Unless you knew where to look, there was no way you would find this home. They lay her on the couch and Chemist gave her a cup of water. Iona told them what happened. They listened with invisible venom pouring out of their eyes.

Doctor shook his head and left for a few seconds before returning with a jar of cream. "We will step outside for a few minutes. Rub this on your nipple and other sore spots. It is Friday; you will stay here until you are well. There is a possibility your body will flush out your trauma with fever so lie on this couch and rest. I shall return with blankets."

The trio disappeared outside but Iona could still hear their muffled voices. She felt safe around Doctor. Everything within the home seemed to have a purpose and nothing appeared out of place. It was much tidier than the domicile she had left and would never again reside in. The cream was milky soft and stung the blistered hole where her nipple used to be. Iona cried for the first time in her life and lay on the soft couch. Long red drapes had been left open allowing for sun rays to envelope her frigid frame. In just a few minutes she was fast asleep and would not wake until Saturday noon.

****

"How many live in this village of yours?" Chemist asked.

"A little over one hundred," she replied. "One hundred and eight to be exact."

"It will be one hundred and five by Tuesday," Doctor grunted. "We have driven a buggy through your village before. There are long rows of corn and fields of sunflowers. I recall a butcher shop of some sort with cattle in the back. One of the houses had many sheep, and another had wild turkey imprisoned by wire fences. If I recall correctly there are stray dogs everywhere. In Samaski these dogs would be shot."

"For some in my village, the dogs are dinner during long winters," Iona whispered.

The bald man closed his eyes and nodded. "Today is the 24th of April; next Saturday will be the May Day holiday. Are there any celebrations in your village on this day?"

"Yes of course, there will be an open field dinner. Half the families will lug their kitchen tables to an arranged spot and the entire community will eat and drink until no one can stand. I have never been to one. We were never invited."

"Oh, my dear, this year you will be the guest of honor. Chemist, what do you have in your bag of tricks that can fuel the ultimate revenge?

The shy man shrugged. "It will take a few days of uninterrupted work but I will produce what I like to call, Vengeance in a Bottle."

"Teacher," Doctor continued, "Do the fields of this town offer possibilities of another product or two?"

"As I have made clear several times before," Teacher sighed, "Only one of your desired products can be grown in our country but we will have a short germination period. It is indeed

possible and the reward would be high. There will be
a requirement of one dozen workers for a maximum of three
months if we were to use most of the available acreage."

Iona was listening to the trio not comprehending any part
of their discussion. "What are you babbling about?" She asked
with a small grin.

Doctor gazed back at her with an entirely serious face. "We
are discussing the legend you will become."

Teacher and Doctor left early on Monday morning. Iona
did not hear them leave and when she awoke she was alone. A
loose calendar claimed it was the 26th of April 1961. Chemist was
out back in his large shed with the door locked. He left a note on
the kitchen table that he was not to be disturbed but would be
grateful if she were to leave him lunch outside his workplace at
around noon. Just knock to warn him.

She decided she would clean whatever she could or at
least dust. The thought was generous but in this pristine home
there was little that needed to be washed or dusted. Teacher had
done most of it the night before. Each of the three insisted on
cleanliness and order as if it was necessary to their survival.
Clutter is an ignorant man's undoing, Doctor emphasized. She was
as usual unsure of his meaning but based on their secretive nature
she believed he was saying that proof had to be hidden.

It had been three days and fifteen hours since Marcus and
his friends defiled her. The anger still existed but the physical pain
had subsided. The medication that Chemist prepared was
miraculous and even the deepest bruises had faded yellow. The
hole where her nipple used to be was healing nicely and even that

342

was not overly uncomfortable. These men were the smartest she had ever met. She had heard of city people studying in large schools and wondered if her new friends were originally from Lyiv or even Kiev.

There were only two beds in the home. She was always the first to fall asleep and the last to wake. If there were three of them, why were there only two beds? Did Chemist sleep in his work shack? She walked into the larger bedroom and had a quick glance, worried that Chemist would catch her snooping. A double bed with two of the largest pillows she had ever seen was surrounded by one armoire and one dresser. There was a mirror on the far wall next to the door with a table below it. The polished table had makeup and two bottles of white powder. She had never worn any makeup in her life. This was without any doubt where Teacher slept. Iona was still confused why a man would want to act like a woman. It was too strange to even imagine. The one closet had a few dresses, sheer bed clothing and men's clothing... clothing for a larger man. Doctor slept here too? Iona backed out of the room and leaned against the adjacent wall. This was too much for her to grasp. Doctor was an attractive man that she had quickly become fond of. She had heard once that men such as this were imprisoned or executed. When the time was right she would inquire about his relationship with the smallish, long-haired androgynous being known as Teacher.

A black, three-tiered bookshelf in the darkest corner of the narrow home held large volumes she could not decipher. She had not read a book in over six years and the words inside the covers were incomprehensible. They had pictures of vials as well as body organs and skeletons. On the bottom shelf she picked out a photo album that she carried to the couch.

She stared at the photos with curiosity and awe. There were black and white pictures of men and women in different poses. She smiled when viewing the toothy grins; toothless grins; men holding trophies and women holding babies. Pages of pleasant photos were then replaced by pages of gruesome photographs. A succession of men and women were hanging by their necks on trees like light bulbs on the road to her village. Another photo had naked bodies stacked in crater sized ditches not dissimilar to the logs on the side of her home. Yet another had soldiers laughing while molesting struggling women. One photo had a priest tied to the door of a church that was set on fire. These were not random photographs, these were childhood memories. Iona closed the book not wishing to observe another reminder of how cruel life could be. She wished she could feel different, and she wished that she could experience happiness. The villagers in the market square laughed and sang. It would be nice to do that. She wondered if she was capable.

How does one purge a lifetime and start over?

Doctor had writing paper. At first the words came slowly, and the spelling was childlike but in the days, week and months ahead she improved. She would return and rewrite what she had begun weeks earlier shaking her head at how trivial her thoughts had been. This was her version of a purge and this was her new start. Teacher reluctantly taught her grammar and how to contrast her thought process by using emotion as a guide. It was difficult for Iona as she rarely felt emotions of any kind but she forged ahead. She started reading books that Teacher hid in her personal vault and these books enthralled her. Philosophy and psychology, religion and sociology… they were all fascinating.

She was still writing when a disheveled Chemist appeared before her at dinner time. He looked at Iona apprehensively but then shrugged as if glad that she found a hobby. Iona apologized and rose immediately to begin dinner. He stopped her and said that she could start dinner when she was ready to start dinner. This made no sense to her but at the same time it pleased the woman to no end. She wanted to hug Chemist but instead stepped back and held her nose. He smelled horrible. He grinned and explained his rotting egg stench was the culmination of a successful project and then promptly filled an iron tub in the back room with hot water. He shyly asked Iona not to watch him undress. Hearing this made her giggle while she shuffled the several pages of writing she had completed. Doctor and Teacher will probably return soon and would appreciate a warm meal. They did not arrive until early the next morning.

Neither Doctor nor Teacher described their completed task in graphic detail. What was explained to Iona at that moment was that her husband and his two accomplices were no longer living. Iona was neither happy nor unhappy and she would write this later that day. On the day before the May Day dinner, Doctor sat her down and verbally illustrated how Marcus was slaughtered. A hot flush of excitement descended from her chest to her genitalia. She blushed realizing she was mildly aroused. Doctor and Teacher had tied him to the same post in the barn that Aida had been strapped to. They started a small manageable fire and stuck hot pokers in his anus. Teacher followed this torment by burning both his nipples off. The two men that had joined Marcus the previous Thursday evening were made to witness the torture, and the same was done to them. Doctor castrated Marcus and forced the big nosed boy to swallow one of the testicles. Teacher asked Marcus if he wished to die. When he said no he was sodomized once again with the burning poker. When the young vile husband finally said yes to death, Teacher deep kissed him full on the mouth and proceeded to cut his heart out. The bodies were brought back to an associate in Samaski and disposed.

Iona said thank-you. She had no idea of what else to say.

Chemist displayed his work that afternoon to an awestruck group. Doctor was so pleased he picked up the smaller man and gave him a bear hug causing Chemist to blush awkwardly. The vodka at a village celebration was tapped from a barrel. An ounce of the concoction Chemist had created would slowly burn their insides like a plague. By morning, every adult and child in the village would be dead. Just to be certain, salt, pickles, cabbage and salad dressings would also be spiked hours before serving. Iona explained that most of the food was prepared and stored at the butcher's home.

She would be participating in mass murder and could hardly wait. It would please her to see the frothing mouths of the men and women who once threw rocks at her. To see the men who raped and killed her sister breathe their final breath would be like eating a piece of Teacher's sweet cake. When asked if she approved of the plan, Iona replied only with a large grin. Her senses were filled with a blend of hope and finality. For the first time in her life she felt that she belonged. She enjoyed the taste of kinship, hate and revenge.

For the first time in her life, she felt the addictive seduction of power.

And she liked it.

Samaski, as Doctor enlightened, was not a typical Ukrainian village. They were not an agrarian society and had no desire to become one. Kremlin agents rarely visited, and those that were considered threatening were decapitated in the main square for all to celebrate. Communists were hated by this community of thieves, murderers and black market pirates. They welcomed visitors with open arms and treated them to a day like no other in their dreary lives but when night descended and coins were counted, the secrets of Samaski were exposed. The Ukraine Independence Movement met here twice a month. Opium from the Far East was bought and sold several times a week. Body organs were boiled, crushed and marinated for Chinese sexual remedies. Female and male prostitutes plied their trade from midnight to the early morning hours. Men from across the Soviet Union, including top dignitaries, gambled until they had no money left. In some instances they would never return to their homes and became powder in a Chinese bottle. Huts were rented out for nights and sometimes weeks to western Europeans who risked the dangerous trip. Every member of the village had a role to play and to stray from this role meant certain death.

Annexing a neighboring village for land was well received. The drug trade was growing faster than ever imagined and the opportunity to grow the plant locally meant windfall profits. Independence required guns and soldiers. Better margins on opium sales would provide the movement with ample cash. It was decided that thirty men would accompany Doctor, Teacher and Chemist to Iona's village. The contingent was to wait until the sun had completely set before they appeared with their rifles. Chemist had guaranteed with his life that the inhabitants would be incapable of fighting back. The dead villagers would be returned to Samaski to be chopped, dried, crushed and sold. Any worthwhile belongings would be sold at the market the following week. Everything in Samaski was treated as an opportunity for money and everything, except death, was negotiable. The town was a collective in their own sense of the word. All for one and all shared in the wealth. In their own words, they were what communism failed to accomplish. As Chemist once bragged, if socialism had a true name, it would be Samaski.

Saturday began with heavy rain but cleared by noon. The deep holes in the sand and gravel roads were filled with muddy water and Iona worried that an unsuspecting cart would overturn outside their door. Cherry blossoms unfurled in the front yard and Teacher picked them lovingly. She said that they would be added to the next batch of soap. Chemist and Doctor had left in the early morning with several vials of the liquid needed to perform what the entire town of Samaski now deemed necessary. By three p.m. that afternoon they had returned claiming their task was completed. Every bottle of pickles, beets and sour cabbage had been tainted. Poison needles were injected into hanging slabs of pork, veal and beef. The barrels of beer and vodka were now wooden containers of death. They dropped off the body of the village butcher with Samaski's own version of a butcher. The long bearded man was pleased to have work on a Saturday. Chemist had one vial in his shirt pocket he claimed was an antidote. Iona was confused on why he bothered.

At seven p.m., it was time to leave. When Teacher appeared from the bedroom, Iona could not tear her eyes away. The half-woman wore a short white dress and dress shoes with small heels. Her eyes were outlined with mascara and her lips were adorned with bright red lipstick. Doctor took her by the

348

hand and walked the transsexual to the horse and cart that had been waiting for them. It was the only one with a board for sitting. Some men whistled while others turned away. Iona wished she had such a pretty dress. It had become obvious that her three friends held important positions in their community. Such a brash display would never be accepted in her village or any other.

The sun was near set when the caravan of ten horse driven carts arrived outside the village. They lifted the plastic cover off the lead cart that successfully hid their rifles from curious strangers they had passed on the gravel road. Ammunition was distributed and loaded. No one spoke.

Iona did not look at her house when the gang marched by. It was no longer her home and she would take the opportunity later to burn it to the ground. The smoldering ash would eventually disappear and with it, her past. The sounds in the distance were not of celebration but instead of agony. The group arrived to find men, women and children slumped over on the picnic tables or semi-cached behind long stalks of golden grass. When seeing the gang, one of the village men stood and stumbled towards them pleading for help. Doctor met him half way and plunged a dagger through the man's neck. The look of surprise remained on his face until he was gutted the next day.

Doctor asked Teacher what the next step should be. She answered that guns would not be necessary and to use their knives instead. Iona pointed at the men she wished to watch as their necks were slit. The parents of her dead husband begged for mercy but none was given. She ripped a necklace off her mother-in-law's neck before a dagger was thrust into the older woman's brain. Iona's eyes widened with glee as a fountain of blood spurted out. Once again she found herself aroused by devastation. Her one remaining nipple was fighting to protrude through the red top Doctor had given her two days ago. She had one of the men cut off the penis of Marcus's father and shove it in his mouth. *I remember what you did to my father,* she said angrily. When the village patriarch lay dead, she kissed the man who did as she asked and guided his hand beneath her dress.

You will be justly rewarded this evening, she promised.

A single villager was spared. When the killing ended, each corpse was tossed into one of the ten carts and then covered with a plastic canvas. The horses would be tired but not as tired as the Samaski butcher. Every home in the village was visited and looted. Teacher was not happy with the result except for what was looted from the expansive lot with three houses. She found plenty of makeup and perfume as well as necklaces that would sell for a handsome price. The village houses would soon be occupied by fresh recruits and a few existing Samaski citizens. It was not a war; it was a business acquisition.

Chemist was carrying a six-year old girl over his shoulder. She was introduced to Iona as her sister. The woman stared at the child for a few seconds and nodded.

"The child will stay with me," she whispered.

As they were leaving, Iona jumped on one of the moving carts and surveyed the village that made her what she was at that very moment. For some odd reason, it suddenly felt like home. Within the week, she and her three friends occupied the homes once owned by the richest family in the village. Iona was now the matriarch of a new village they aptly named Independence.

Valeri dropped his paintbrush into the dirty water glass he kept next to his right foot. He had been speaking and painting while paying little attention to his one person audience. He took a quick glance at his model and sighed loudly. Her head was still dropped, and she appeared to be sleeping. He summoned her to wake up, but she did not budge. He shook his head while lifting his tired bones out of the chair, walked a few feet and raised the girls chin. Her eyes, nose and mouth were bleeding. The chubby girl was no longer breathing. Fuck, he yelled. *The fat pig died on me*. This was inexcusable and at the same time impossible. She was just a kid, how could she die? Markov scratched his head and began the process of eliminating the evidence. He dragged the body to his wood saw and then went upstairs to change his clothing. He had hoped for one more night of depravity. If he hurried he might have time to drive to Lyiv. Remembering the size of his latest victim, he knew Lyiv would not be an option tonight.

Maybe tomorrow, he grumbled.

****

The rain was relentless as he made the two hour drive to Kiev. He always loved the feeling of anticipation and found it more exciting than the sexual gratification. His plan was flawless and unlike other kidnappings, this one would satisfy the pangs of regret he had been holding for the last two weeks.

His victim had a steady routine, which usually culminated in her returning home at approximately eight-thirty every

351

evening. It was still only May and the sun would be setting a few minutes before her arrival. This, combined with the rain, would ensure he would not be recognized.

He parked outside the building and waited. The five floor complex was on quiet street just minutes away from downtown. It was an older beige brick building with multi-colored wooden balconies that had withstood the ravages of fifty winters. In front of him, an unshaven middle-aged man leaned against a red Lada, taking quick gulps from a sopping wet brown bag.

He stepped outside and opened his umbrella. The front door of the complex was only fifty feet away. He would stay there until she arrived. She was late. He saw her walking briskly, holding a bag from another shopping trip. She was wearing a red mini skirt, which he always characterized as a hooker uniform. He raised his hand asking her to stop.

"Are you the mother of Angelika Podborski?" Valeri asked.

The women suddenly looked concerned and answered yes.

"She is being detained in Lyiv madam," he lied. "Your daughter was involved in a car accident two weeks ago and has lost her memory. We are sorry for the delay but we could not locate you. If you would follow me madam, I will drive you to our holding cell."

"Oh my," she whispered with a hand over her mouth. "Yes certainly. Why was she in Lyiv and more importantly why is she being kept in a holding cell?"

Markov had to think quickly. "Angelika became violent with two of the nurses at the hospital. The authorities felt it necessary to keep her in solitude."

"My daughter was violent? She is such a calm child. Is she taking her heart medicine?"

This comment caused Valeri to pause and remember the dead girls flushed face and bleeding eyes. She needed her pills.

"Yes ma'am but it took a while before an idiot cop realized she required them." The two walked to his car, and he continued to speak. "I am a psychologist and I ascertained that Angelika was a good girl but scared. She will be fine but in my opinion she needs her mother to be by her side for a few hours. The police will remand her in your custody."

They shook off their umbrellas and entered Markov's car. As they were leaving the parking lot Valeri asked the woman if she was hungry. When she replied that she had not eaten since noon he handed her a sandwich from the back seat. The pretty redhead took several large bites and commented that it had a tangy taste. In ten minutes she was sleeping and would continue her slumber until the time she woke up in the dark basement that would be her prison until the day she died. Baba's home concoction had never disappointed him.

Valeri drove slowly and watched her sleep. The woman's mini skirt was hiked up to her thighs revealing a slim pair of long legs. Compared to the daughter, the mother was a piece of art. Valeri acknowledged the woman was a whore and deserved to die a horrible death but looking at her excited him. She did not share the usual characteristics of his victims but he would keep her alive for as long as possible.

And why wouldn't he?

She was a special case and one that he would document explicitly, much more than the others. Angelika's mother was a milestone and aside from the palpable contempt he felt for her, she would be treated with an elevated degree of respect.

She would be his fiftieth victim.

****

"There was train that left Lyiv at five o'clock every Friday evening and stopped at a smaller city thirty minutes from Iona's newly named village of Independence. If it was raining the walk was a chore but on beautiful days I quite enjoyed the trek. The train ride was almost always entertaining as half inebriated workers would play their guitars and sing traditional songs. There were never many women, which was probably a small blessing as the men were ruffians. They cursed without reprisal and pissed through the open windows of the slow moving train. After a few rides I overheard that several would spend the weekend in Samaski. They were spending their wages gambling and whoring. Asked if it was worth it, they would reply that it was all they looked forward to.

One of them once questioned me on why I got off at the same stop. When I told him where I was going, he never spoke to me again. I thought perhaps he was a bit of a snob but as it turned out, he had heard the stories spread about the tall matron of Independence and feared I would speak of him. Iona was the legend Doctor had expected her to become. If I were this gentleman on the train, I would be frightened too. What he did not know was Iona's flame had dimmed many years earlier and her legend had faded almost as quickly as it grew.

The economy in 1964 Soviet Union was excelling and outranking anything the western world bragged about. Russia sent cosmonauts into space, embarrassing the evil Americans. Nikita Khrushchev glorified socialism and the empire while at the same time opening our doors to the west little by little. Everyone was working, and in villages, even the children had full-time employment.

Fear of rockets and missiles from the bastards in the west meant that Soviets had to re-arm in a hurry. Our military grew at lightning speed, which was understandable as the soldiers were paid better than scientists and even rocket technicians. The military should have been a sense of pride for the residents of Samaski and Independence but in truth, they were a nuisance. They would visit on weekends and act as if they were better than anyone. Their pants were filled with loose coins, much more than the commoners that sang songs on the train. The workers were dirty with wind burned faces so when it came to the women who waited at doorways, these men were no match against the young cherubic soldiers.

The first successful crop of opium was harvested in late August of 1964. Three years earlier, Teacher had estimated that a dozen employees would be required to cut, score and melt the pods. She underestimated by fifty. The operation was enormous thus when combined with the regular residents, homes in Independence were fully occupied. Chemist was working double shifts, teaching a dozen assistants' how to refine the raw opium into a morphine base. He finally tied string around the arms of his glasses to keep them from sliding off his sweaty nose.

The operation grew every year. Doctor would complain of initial costs each year and then bask in the incredible profits a few months later. A plan was made to extend Samaski into Independence. Houses and merchant malls would be built halfway between the two villages and then year by year more houses would be built to satisfy the number of visitors who never wished to leave. Iona built a long hall for gambling and a motel for the prostitutes to ply their trade for the overflow of customers from Samaski. In time, an equal amount of visitors flocked to both villages. Opium was sold with tobacco, in teas, in powder form and in herbal remedies. Employees often worked for nothing after spending their wages on their new addiction. If they fell too far behind in debt, their bodies were chopped, dried, grounded and sold to the Chinese who in turn sold their sexual remedies to Russians travelling to Samaski.

Iona was responsible for debts and was feared more than the KGB. Meanwhile, KGB officers escaped their wives and spent weekends in her motel and occasionally with her. To spend an evening with Iona was considered an honour and never taken lightly. If your performance was less than adequate you never spent another evening in her village and that included KGB agents.

What I found mystifying when listening to her was that no one, other than Chemist, knew how evil she had become and he was too frightened to inform his lifelong friends. To look at Iona from a distance you would consider her as an attractive older lady who smiled more than the normal person. I read magazines writing about how women can tell a man from the shoes he wears. Men claim they can spot a whore a mile away. None of this is true and appearances are and have always been a vain self-deception. We are so tightly wound in a world of generalities and profiling that we allow the most devious of people to dine with us never

356

considering for a second it could be our last meal. Iona taught me to be invisible. I can walk any street in this country and no one would notice me unless I stopped to speak with them. I don't make eye contact unless I have a reason. I do not give away my real name and I never pay with exact change. I tell only small lies that I can remember with ease.

After one year of living on the same lot as Iona, Doctor and Teacher returned to Samaski with Iona's half-sister. They missed their home and privacy and wished to raise the orphaned child away from a woman they felt was on the verge of breakdown. This event was tiny in effort but huge in effect. Iona was changing. For her, power was the ultimate aphrodisiac and more powerful than any herb that Chemist created in his tiny hut. She wrote her journals for hours on end describing in great detail her plans to dismember specific types of males and when the task was complete she would catalogue if the event was as she imagined it would be.

Chemist was a eunuch, castrated by soldiers after they raped and killed his mother. It was why he was always so shy around her and why he wished to kill every army brat that visited Samaski. Iona would lay dismembered penises on her kitchen table to convince Chemist her killing spree was done for him. He would thank her but know she killed because she liked it. He was not a fool; he had read her binders of loose leaf when she travelled to Samaski. Teacher had been right when she once said Iona scared the shit out of her. She kept some of the cut appendages and hardened them in a clear wax she ordered Chemist to produce. They lay waiting for her in the bottom drawer of her dresser on nights when no suitable men were available.

Drunk and horny men would willfully follow her into the home that Teacher and Doctor once shared. The comfy house had been renovated into a hall of horrors. The main room was similar to any other in this village but once the victim was drugged he would be carted off into one of the two bedrooms converted into torture chambers. The first room had a long chair with posts for handcuffs or chains. The backboard was upright at a sixty degree angle allowing Iona to sexually manipulate her victim if she chose to. There was no furniture in the second room.

Against her better judgment, Teacher found a book on medieval torture that Iona inquired about based on a conversation she had with Doctor a few months after Marcus was murdered. Sensing a need to have several of the devices in her home, Iona seduced the Samaski blacksmith. After a couple of sessions enjoying Iona's long legs, he was only too happy to recreate the devices from the borrowed book. He asked questions at first but soon realized that the more inquiries he made, the more distant she became. He kept his mouth shut and received the expected rewards.

His first creation was a Knee Crusher and Iona used it on an unsuspecting prey only two days later. Built from two spiked wood blocks, the knee splitter is placed between the knees of a terrified victim. Turning two large screws that connected the blocks would cause the spikes to close like a vice. Iona squealed in delight listening to the first young victim scream as his knees splintered into dozens of useless fragments.

There was a Head Crusher, a Judas Chair and her favorite device called Crocodile Shears. No man was spared the Crocodile Shears. On the fateful day she removed a dangling limb from her father's mouth she had no idea it was his penis. With his

358

reproductive organ he had impregnated her sister, and it was why she lost both of them at the hands of superstitious villagers. Ten years later she had deduced without any doubt that men were spawns of Satan and their penis was the Devils hand.

Crocodile Shears are two iron-cast sides of a tube with rows of spikes which are heated and clamped on the penis. The pincers slowly and painfully cut through the limb like a broken buzz saw. Iona would put the man's penis in her mouth beforehand to ensure an erection thus ensuring a clean burn. The exhilaration always shook her body and she would masturbate as she watched her victim's faces change from pleasure to pain. The orgasm was always stronger than anything a man could give her.

I was her male counterpart and we both knew this. The odds of us meeting each other were fantastic, and I was always cognizant of that fact. Without Iona I would not be the man I am today. She would recount her stories while I pleased her and when I told of her of any new exploit she would do the same to me. Within a few months we were sharing victims we picked up in Lyiv. The lovemaking that followed was like nothing I would ever again experience.

Iona taught me that only a select group of humans deserved to live, although without the worthless, greatness could not be acknowledged. The men and women that cared for families and for each other could remain but the dregs of society were to be purged. The whores that waited for weekend cheaters or virgin soldiers were not women or even human beings. They were simply vessels to trap the devils semen. Iona believed that both the prostitutes and their customers were perfect victims for her torture and during her life ending performances
she would remind her sufferers why they were chosen.

I had to have a quiet abode - that was first and foremost. Iona listed the dos and don'ts to being a serial killer. My home had to be sterile without any trace of what was occurring in the room I chose to hide my victims. Burying the bodies on the same property was a mistake and to be avoided at all cost. Chemist would burn her victims and then dissolve the bones in a special liquid he imported from Kiev. He could never have known that he too would one day swim in this same chemical.

Victims must not come from the same city or village. She learned from this mistake and I was not to do the same if I were to become successful. In the early days of Independence it was easy for her because all her victims were strangers from all across Russia and Ukraine but during my sojourn with Iona, we would drive to Kiev, Lyiv and Kharkov or sometimes as far as Odessa to handpick one or two worthy participants.

I was never to depend on force when subduing a potential victim. There were plenty of drugs available that could disable the strongest man or woman within minutes. The hardest part was transporting them into your special room. Being less than muscular, Iona always had straps close by to tie and drag victims to where she wished to perform.

If I could, I was to always kidnap women wearing expensive jewelry. If they were single, return to their apartments and loot whatever possible. Gold brought enough money to survive on for several months. Iona would have been better off not to tell me this but I'll explain that later.

By her own admittance she had crossed the imaginary line between sanity and insanity. Doctor and Teacher would no longer visit her home and insisted she visit them in Samaski so that they were not in harm's way. Stories of tubs filled with blood had circulated amongst the thieves of the northern village and the number of visitors to Independence dropped substantially. Only the desperate would work the opium fields, leaving Iona with sparse pickings for her treacherous deeds. She depended on their addictions to feed her evil desires.

Yes, she bathed in the blood. Aida once said her complexion was beautiful because she lay in her deceased mother's blood for hours after birth. Iona believed this to be Ponce de Leon's true fountain of youth. Her victims were drained before and after their demise. For a short while she would drink the blood of her victims while they begged for their lives. If they protested too loud she would straddle their mouth and urinate. She claimed this was her way to mock the Devil. She took his blood and replaced it with piss. I would never do this. I hate the Devil but would not disrespect him knowing the consequences. God would not forgive me for such a revolting act.

Her unraveling began when one of her workers could not get the drugs he requested. He was too far behind in wages and Iona refused him. Detoxifying and delusional, the skinny man strolled through the opium fields with several cans of gas and lit it on fire. He could not run fast enough to avoid the flames and his barbecued corpse was discovered days later. Doctor was incensed and struck Iona several times. He called her names she never expected to hear from his mouth. As far as he was concerned, Iona was no longer a member of their group.

They were her family. She had already lost a family and could not stand to lose another without her agreeing.

Doctor left her home in a tiff forgetting that Chemist was still working a few feet away. Realizing her desperate situation, Iona had to do what was necessary. She brought the reclusive introvert a large dinner and kissed him on his forehead before leaving. He had been so loyal to her and it would be difficult to continue without him. Iona returned half an hour later and found him slumped over his lab table. Beside the drool that has culminated around his mouth, vials of serums were encased and ready to be delivered. Chemist had become obsessed with curing disease as opposed to contributing to thieves and death. As much as Iona had veered towards one extreme, Chemist had chosen the opposite.

She would not despoil him in any manner; he was too good a man. Iona dragged his limp body to the front yard and with one swing chopped off his head with the axe she used to cut wood for her stove. She did the same with each of his limbs before dropping them in the vat of acid that he himself had prepared behind the middle home. His clothes and shoes were then burned in the fireplace as were several of his healing remedies. Iona had to make sure the inventor's disappearance appeared as if it was by choice.

Deciding to strike while the iron was hot, Iona travelled by horse and cart to Samaski the next day and convinced an unsuspecting Teacher that Chemist was ill. Teacher preferred to wait for Doctor to return from his usual duties at the market square but Iona acted as if in a panic. On the way over Iona offered the petite she-male sweet water that had been prepared before her departure. Teacher awoke in chains.

Iona was not as empathetic to Teacher as she had been with Chemist. She took her time and used the devices that had made her legendary. The Judas Chair shred through Teacher's anus and blood seeped down the back of her legs. Teacher screamed but would not beg for sympathy. She gritted her teeth and bit her tongue so hard that a small piece slipped off her lips and onto her flat chest. This frustrated Iona but at the same time convinced her that Teacher had betrayed her. *There is only one way you can become a real woman*, she sneered at the girlish boy. The Crocodile Shears were heated and placed on Teachers limp penis. Pain from the smoldering incision was too much for the transvestite and she mercifully fainted.

Eventually you would have been hanged; I only advanced your fate.

Within hours, Teacher joined her longtime friend in the hidden steel vat behind the middle home. Iona chuckled thinking how the two were now an acid broth.

To her surprise, Doctor never visited. She never understood this as he was in love with this thing called Teacher. It was as if he had accepted Teacher's fate as redemption for stranding Iona. Either that or he too was dead. There were rumors he had moved to Lugansk with Iona's daughter but she could never substantiate anything said. She never saw Doctor again.

I appeared in Iona's life fifteen years later. She claimed that during her five years as matron of Independence she tortured and killed over six hundred men and women. I believed her. Iona never lied. Not a week passed without one victim. Since then her count has been much lower but her desire never decreased. Sitting in Lyiv teashops, she would imagine different scenarios with those that served her, and those that sat nearby. Everyone without wrinkles was a prime candidate. She wore wigs and revealing clothing to attract lustful boys or cheating husbands. To approach her lasciviously meant certain demise.

The priest grew wary of my constant disappearances and finally insisted that I stay or I go. The motherly cook baked me a pie, and I packed a small bag of my belongings. I chose to live with Iona. My era as an altar boy was over.

In late 1985, she introduced me to a man who ran an academy for future security guards. The man was forever grateful to Iona for deflowering him when he was a teenager. He had no idea how lucky he was to still be alive. If ever I needed work, I was to go directly to him. The bonus was that I would escape any further investigation of why I had never enlisted and more importantly, I would be paid for easy work. Five months later, I was knocking on his door.

Iona should have listened to what she preached and that in itself was a valuable lesson for me. It was much too obvious that the tall woman was incapable of love so I was often left confused when she so willingly confessed her love for me. She would leave in her car for days claiming she was searching for viable part-time companions for the two of us but I knew she was on sado-sexual expeditions. For some reason, Iona assumed this mattered to me. While she was away, I would check every nook and cranny of all three homes looking for anything I might find worthwhile. I was not disappointed.

In the middle home underneath the kitchen sink I found a treasure of trinkets. Gold, silver, pearls, watches and even teeth were stashed below a loose plank. This particular area was filled to the brim, so I successfully guessed there had to be another spot with equal gains. Again, I was not disappointed. Iona had thousands of rubles stashed away below the kitchen sink of her own home. I found more jewels underneath her bed floor boards.

Iona was rich beyond belief.

I was rich beyond belief.

Perhaps I would have reconsidered taking Iona's stash had it not been for her inability to hide proof. I shook my head in disbelief when I found the binders of loose leaf paper in her closet. There were ten thick binders detailing her miserable life and her grotesque fetishes. Unfortunately for my lady friend, I found pages dedicated to me and what she had planned for my eventual termination. I won't tell you that I shuddered in fear or that I was sickened by her fantasy. If anything, I was impressed. Still, there was no way in hell it would ever come to fruition. I would reverse the table and do the same to her.

There were only forty people living in the village and none of them spoke to Iona. She was effectively ostracized. In her own words, it was no different than when she was a child. She missed the days when she ruled over the populace and often dreamed those days would return. When she spoke these words I wanted to slap her out of the delusion she could not free herself from.

The corn fields were now managed by the government and the men who toiled over them. Iona was never offered a dozen ear of corn or anything else from her neighbours. All her food was bought from other villages west of Samaski or in Lyiv. Rifles were cocked when she passed occupied homes. I was amazed the neighbors did not consider a hanging just to get rid of her. I am sure Iona had the same thoughts but then again, life in this specific area of Ukraine had changed. Years ago there was no one to overlook the villages but things had changed. Soldiers asked questions now. There was a head count every year and homes were inspected for known thieves. Even Samaski could not avoid the long arm of communism. The haven for criminals and gamblers had been dismantled half a decade ago in a bloodbath still talked about by those that survived. It was now a government

365

owned brothel. Only chaos could return their lives to a time of lawlessness and chaos was nowhere to be found. The single most heinous murderer in Ukraine history would have to die at the hands of the man who would ultimately replace her on the throne.

Iona returned with new clothes she believed would increase our kill rate. The older she got, the sluttier she became. I found that oddly sad. Iona was falling into the category of a group she insisted on annihilating. The irony was laughable, but I did not voice what I was thinking. She kissed me and opened a bottle of vodka from the cupboard. I watched her swallow large gulps knowing she would be sleeping in a matter of minutes. The powerful drugs she used to disable hulking men were now assimilating with her blood stream. She lifted her skirt and straddled my lap. I rubbed her where she asked until her eyes glazed over. I think she knew what was happening. As if the sky was delivering a stern warning, a crack of lightning shook the front windows. Mother Nature could not save Iona that evening and instead would only succeed in muffling her screams. She whispered an incoherent curse and a tiny puddle of her saliva dribbled onto my shirt.

The universe repeats itself in so many ways and does so as if vent on revenge. Species are exterminated and new species are born often preying on those that once hunted a lost genus. Men will kill men and women will breed new men. This was once explained to me as the circle of life. I call it God's complacency. Three masters graciously taught Iona everything she needed to know to thrive in a world that had been terribly unkind to her. She rewarded their thoughtfulness by murdering two of them. As if following the rules of the universe, Iona spared my life and taught me everything she had learned.

I let her live for two more days. She begged me to kill her after one.

The Unraveling

"You make it sound as if you're successful," she said with her head lowered.

The thirty-eight-year old woman refused to look Valeri in the eyes. She estimated it had been three days since she was fooled into believing her daughter was in jail. Not fully comprehending her situation, the petite redhead was concerned this man's semen would impregnate her.

"I am dreadfully successful," Markov contested. "I am incredibly rich and have done so without laboring for twenty-five years. You suck cocks to put food on your plate. Tell me who is better off."

She did not reply knowing she could not win this argument. Her only way out of this mess was to charm the sinister piece of crap. She had spent many afternoons role playing with her paying customers and those skills could be what saved her from the maniac who held her captive.

"You are right, I am not proud of what I have done or who I have become. My ego always outweighed my moral obligations and now that I am older, I find myself in a cycle I cannot break. I only wish for love and happiness, like any other real woman. I have been a stupid whore; a sacrilegious blight on our communist society."

Valeri did not expect this and dropped his brush into a can of filthy water. He stood and walked over to his prisoner. She had suddenly decided to look at him. Her pale white complexion and green eyes meshed wonderfully with her fiery hair. Although he felt nothing inside, he was intrigued that the woman confessed her sins with such honesty.

"Are you hungry?" he asked with a hint of compassion.

"Yes, very much so," she replied.

'What do I call you?"

She was veering him in her direction, she thought. "Vladamira but you may call me Vlaska."

Valerie nodded. "I'm Valeri. Would you prefer tea or milk?"

"Tea would be better, thank-you. My stomach does not digest dairy products well."

He went upstairs and prepared a small meal for his captive. Upon returning he asked Vlaska if she knew anything about religion. Valeri untied one arm, allowing Vlaska to eat while he sat in his regular seat. She replied in between bites of the tomato sandwich Markov made.

"My father was converted to Christianity when he was a teenager and met my mother at a church gathering. He was a strict authoritarian and tried very hard to instill the Bibles' morals within me. While other kids were enjoying their lives, I was holed up in a kitchen every evening reading scriptures and discussing the unholy nature of the kids I dearly wished to join. When I went to my bed every evening I prayed to God to save me from my parents. My prayers were answered when I met my future husband, Konstantin. It took three months before I was a pregnant sixteen-year old. My parents disowned me soon after that, citing that I required an exorcism. I believed at the time that God's answer was not well thought out and perhaps he had a very poor understanding of Russian. If that was the case then an exorcism could be disastrous. I moved in with Konstantin and his parents until we found an apartment eight years later."

"You sinned, and you paid for your sin."

"But what is sin?" she argued. "Who decides what is sinful? Am I to follow a template created thousands of years ago by a delusional man wishing to police his people?"

"That is blasphemous; I should cut out your tongue. The Ten Commandments are the backbone of every culture. If we combine it with the Seven Deadly Sins, we have the making of a perfect society. Do not fabricate conditions to create your own atonement."

"You shall not bear false witness," she retaliated. "Lust, Anger, Envy, Greed...I ask again, are you without sin? Are you not the same as me? Your semen is still inside of me, I did not ask for it to be there."

"I am the Prince. God has chosen me to lead the people towards their rightful destiny. I have been given a free pass in order to succeed."

"How fortunate you are," she sneered. "My father also believed that some men were put on earth to lead the masses. For a brief period he thought it might be him. I was invited back into my father's life after a family tragedy. My mother died because a man in the parish kidnapped her. Familiar circumstance... yes?" She looked at her roped wrist before raising her eyes. "Thou shall not kill. He repeated that a lot but in his heart he wanted to bludgeon my mother's murderer. He told me those exact words while cursing the path he had walked on for too long. He wondered if God was testing him as the parish priest explained. He later told me the hate in his heart was so strong that he considered beating the priest for lying to him."

"Most of my models rarely if ever spoke," Markov interrupted. "Suddenly, I miss that. Are you going somewhere with this?"

"I have much to impart but since I am your prisoner, I am left to ask permission."

Valeri grinned and nodded his permission.

"Thank-you," she began. "My father left the parish but continued to read the bible searching for solace as well as clues to guide him. He was suffering through a depression when, purely by accident, he met a man from Latvia. He had dropped his bible in a local park and the stranger picked it up. The first meeting was not clarified in great detail to me but in brief they met several more times over the next month and my father returned to Riga with the man. The stranger, I eventually learned was named Jaromir, had access to books my father had never heard of and was certain even the parish priest knew nothing about.

You would have liked Jaromir. He considered himself a liberal communist, a Marxist with a heart."

"I highly doubt it," Valeri uttered.

Mila continued, disregarding her opponents comment. "If anything, he taught my father a simple life lesson that was relayed to me on many occasions. I wish I had paid more attention because it is something that every person on the planet should acknowledge."

"The Secret of Life… I wait with bated breath."

The redhead ignored the sarcasm. "Jaromir was self-educated and spent most evenings and weekends in libraries. He discovered that every non-mathematical question had many answers or at least possible answers. Once you found one answer it often led you to another question related to the same subject. Most important to his research, he learned that every belief, be it religious or political, was open to several interpretations and never complete, meaning pieces were strung together to suit those in a position of power. In a nutshell, whatever you are told is the truth may be the truth to the one who spoke it but not necessarily true. It is up to you to find the truth or your truth."

"If this is the meaning of life, then if you don't mind, I will speak my own truth."

"Isn't that what I just said?"

Valeri chuckled and wiped his mouth with the back of his hand. "The meaning of life, dear Vlaska, is that God has a few shepherds and many sheep. Once you accept which category you fall under, your life will never be confusing. Let me hear you say *baaaaa*."

"And you bow to no one?" Vlaska asked with a ring of sarcasm.

The man thought of the question and his ensuing answer. "Some shepherds have many sheep with guns. I accept their wealth but not their ranking next to me. I am the only true messenger of God and the others are temporary at best. They are like musicians. Popular one day and forgotten the next. I will be remembered by generations of Soviets. My manifesto will be a rallying call for centuries of proud Russians and Ukrainians. We will rule this world using my principles."

"Yes of course, a clever blend of Communism and Christianity," Vlaska replied. "It is as I said earlier. The truth is what you believe it to be and not what someone else tells you it is. Both communism and Catholicism have been manipulated by men or groups of men to suit their own needs. How can you not acknowledge this?"

Valeri was now standing in front of his easel. "You are uncommonly opinionated for an early afternoon prostitute. Most whores only know the difference between circumcised or not. Do your customers let you read while they're pounding you? It must be difficult to turn the pages."

"How clever you are," Vlaska sighed. "If my other hand was not bound I would applaud your witticism. Is this how your future benefactors will be treated when they voice their thoughts?"

Listening to her reminded him of Mila Kharmalov, which for a moment enraged him. Still, she was intriguing. Her hair had not been washed for a few days and was stuck to her head like a package of wet noodles. He would wash her later and treat her to a nice meal. Regardless of her profession, he found her beautiful. Not Tania angelic, but nonetheless, beautiful.

"One for all and all for one," Valeri quoted. "To think otherwise would be blasphemous."

"So everyone will be taught to think the same? Who or what will determine what we think?"

"You're not paying attention," Markov grunted loudly. "The manifesto Vlaska… the manifesto."

"You make my head hurt Valeri," she said while sighing. "Perhaps you will allow me to read this epic proposal. What have you named it?"

Valeri had chosen a name a few years back. Many titles were attached to the first page. *The Soviet Agenda* was his first choice, but it was too bland. *God's Gift to Us* was another choice, but he found that to be something hard core communists might immediately denounce. He decided on naming it after an event that changed his life and something all citizens could relate to.

"I call it, *23 minutes past 1 A.M.*"

Vlaska didn't need an explanation. She finished her sandwich and bowed her head.

Markov washed her hair before untying one of her hands to allow Vlaska to wash her body underneath the red dress that was now filthy with dust. He then combed as gently as he could being careful not to hurt her while untangling the many knots that had accumulated over three days.

"Why did you choose this path, Valeri?" Vlaska asked courageously.

"I despise psychiatrists, Vlaska. Mila Kharmalov studied Psychology and I hate her."

"Don't compare me to someone I can't equal. It was a sincere question," she responded. "And I am not in a position of judgment. We all have unreasonable thoughts and make choices on whether to follow those fantasies. You have a dream of some kind and have chosen a bizarre method in which to accomplish it. Why did you choose this particular path?"

"Nothing I do is unreasonable," he said sternly. "Nor is it bizarre. I tread this path because it is the one less travelled. I prefer to remain invisible for the time being."

"Did you learn everything from Iona or did you always feel the need to kidnap and murder?"

"What is it you are trying to gain, Vlaska?" Valeri said while holding her wet hair.

Vlaska had spoken this conversation silently for the last couple of days. If she could earn his trust he may drop his guard long enough for her to escape. She waited for him to continue and he did not disappoint.

"Have you ever killed a goat, Vlaska?"

The question seemed incredibly odd, but she exhaled slowly, trying not to change the tone of her voice.

"I was born and raised in Kiev; I had no need to kill for meat."

"Yes, of course. You depended on people like me. My father taught me when I turned ten years of age. He explained it as my step into manhood. To be a man I had to learn how to kill." Valeri paused a few seconds before continuing. "We always had a couple of goats in the field behind our home. We fattened them up during the spring and summer and then butchered them in late fall. I would first take a hammer and strike the goat's temple as hard as I could to stun him into unconsciousness. My father would then help me hang the animal upside down so I could slit its hind legs down to its throat. Next we would cut round its anus and remove the colon and all of its shit. Then we removed all the skin, organs and anything that could spoil the taste of the meat. The best part was chopping off the head… it was easier than I thought it would be."

"Why are you telling me this" Vlaska asked with closed eyes.

"Let me tell my story," he quickly replied. "While we were gutting the goat, my father would tell me stories told to him by his father. My grandfather was a farmer when Stalin instituted his five-year plan and he survived the famine that Stalin imposed on all of Ukraine. Every bushel of our wheat was sent back to

Moscow and Ukrainians were left with nothing. Soldiers would ransack homes looking for food and if someone looked like they were eating regular meals, they were shot in the back of the head in front of their family. People were dying in the middle of streets and horse drawn carts would carry the bodies away. Some of the bodies packed into these carts were still alive but the Russians didn't care. My father would hold the heart of the goat we just butchered in his hand and say, "See this heart… we would never eat it because that would make us savages." Then he told me how his grandfather ate his sister's heart after she died from hunger. Not just her heart but most of her body. He wasn't the only one. Each of the neighbours in their village that survived did so by eating human flesh. No one talked about it… but they did it."

"A ten year-old boy should be not be told stories about cannibalism," Vlaska gasped.

"Ahh, but he should. It taught me survival and how the strong always outlast the weak. I hate Russians, I won't lie to you, but I don't hate Russia. I admire their power and their will to do anything to ensure that they remain on top. My father complained that Ukrainians were slaves to Russia, and I dreamt of doing the same to them. To accomplish such a task, one must think like a Russian. We were Stalin's goats. He slit us open and used our meat to feed his people. I document everything I do Vlaska… every victim has a purpose and a story. If we wish to bring Russia to its knees then we must follow my doctrine… my manifesto. Don't bother with western philosophies or fucking crybabies like Mila Kharmalov, they cannot hurt Russia. Without knowing, my father taught me all I needed to know. If we ever wish to defeat Russia… we must fatten them up, colonize them and then slaughter them like goats."

Vlaska stayed quiet while Markov continued to unknot her hair. Strangely, she had no qualms about killing Russians and in fact wished it would happen. In a few minutes he spoke again but changed the subject.

"What else did your father learn from the Latvian?"

Vlaska's eyes were closed, expecting her keeper to tug too hard on her hair. "Jaromir claimed there were forty or more gospels written and not just the four in the bible."

"More sacrilege nonsense…" Valeri said before Vlaska cut him off.

"Including one written by Mary Magellan."

Valeri stopped combing and walked in front of Vlaska. "And you believe this to be true? That would give you a role model of sorts wouldn't it? I mean, you being a prostitute. Maybe I'm your Jesus."

"Jesus didn't bind Mary to a chair in a putrid basement. If you read your Bible you'll realize that Mary was a common name and there is no reference to Mary of Magellan being a prostitute. This was a fabrication created by misogynistic priests trying to dissuade women from leading parishes. They had to put women in their place. Burning witches on a stake was a powerful symbol that the Catholic Church miscalculated."

"As you said Vlaska, the truth is what you believe," Valeri mumbled.

"Do you know why Constantine chose Mark, Mathew, Luke and John as the gospels for their bible?"

"My heart can't wait, please tell me quickly," Valeri replied sarcastically with his arms folded across his chest.

"Because they portrayed Jesus as the son of God, or Godlike, or not human. Every other gospel, including Peter's – the right-hand man of Jesus – described Jesus as a normal man. Mary was his girlfriend or perhaps his wife according to other writings. She was integral in his decision-making and Peter hated this."

"This Jaromir fellow... he still has these books?"

Vlaska felt a sudden concern that Markov would go so far as hurt the man. "I don't know. I never met the guy and my father passed away last year. Why do you ask?"

"The Prince likes fire," he responded.

"Oh get serious Valeri. Even the existence of Jesus has been questioned. No less than two hundred similar resurrected characters are depicted in stories from other countries before Jesus was even born. The same exact story existed in Egypt, India and Greece... the list is long. The messiah is born around Christmas and resurrected in the spring. It's based on astrological charts telling the history of spring and winter solstice. You need to walk through different aisles in your local library, you're stagnating. But once again, the truth is what you believe, and it defines you... until you pick up a new book."

Valeri returned to his chair and stared at the painting illustrating his impression of Vlaska. He liked her before this last discussion and had been enjoying his time with her. What if she was telling the truth and that stupid priest at Dormiton was wrong? It's not possible, that Jaromir person had a hidden agenda and Vlaska's father was ripe for picking. He would visit a library in Kiev this afternoon and do his own research. He'd put an end to Vlaska's crazy ramblings. He had eight hundred pages of instruction for the people of the Soviet Union that depended on accuracy and a solid religious belief. To start over would be an unacceptable catastrophe.

The painting was quaint and showed him having dinner with Vlaska. His face was hidden and all that showed of him was the back of his head while Vlaska sat across the table. Her face was partially hidden by a candelabrum he stole from Pripyat. She was smiling.

Vlaska waited for him to reply but he remained quiet. His chair tipped over when he stood abruptly.

"I'll be back," he said.

He did not return to the basement until the next morning.

Valeri checked both buckets under Vlaska's chair. The pee bucket was half full, and he brought it upstairs before returning to face her.

"Have the decency to pull my skirt down," Vlaska barked.

Valeri complied but reluctantly. "A shy hooker… how original."

"I'm hungry," she said while avoiding her captor's eyes.

Vlaska was exhausted from four nights of limited sleep. Last evening she had tried vehemently to release herself from the immovable chair. Her wrists were bleeding from her attempts to loosen the rope.

"You haven't earned a meal," he replied uninterested.

Vlaska shook her head in disgust. "Then untie my wrists and get it over with. I promise to pretend you're my best ever."

Valeri ignored her remark and stepped in front of his painting to examine what he considered an error in judgment. He then pulled his chair to sit directly in front of Vlaska. It was the first time he had ever done this with any of the women he kidnapped.

"I spent over eight hours in a library yesterday reading books, articles and even theses that critiqued the Bible. I would have stayed longer, but I forgot to bring money for dinner. These writings angered me at first and I believed them to the ranting of overzealous atheists. With a bible at hand, I began to reference everything I was reading and bit by bit, my heart hurt a little more. They picked apart passage after passage and referenced them to errors in translation or actual events based on science, local legend or archeological finds. The priest at Dormiton omitted these facts during my three-year education. I feel deceived and he will pay for his lies. I owe this to you Vlaska. You spoke your mind, and I have been humbled."

Vlaska did not acknowledge him until he repeated his thanks.

She didn't lift her head to look at him. "I am too hungry and too tired to think. I beg you... give me some food and water."

Valeri nodded. "You've been trying to escape. The rope around your wrists is red. The chair won't budge Vlaska, it's in the floor and the legs are fortified with steel tubing as are the arms. When you struggle, the rope gets tighter. I was well trained at the Academy."

Vlaska began to cry and this upset Markov. Not because he found it annoying but because he didn't wish to hurt her. He crouched before her and placed his hands softly around her ears.

"I will make you a big breakfast with a pot of tea. When you're done I'll put pillows behind your back for comfort."

Vlaska stopped crying but refused to look at him. If he was falling in love with her, she still had a chance to escape. When Markov went upstairs, she surveyed the dim basement to remember every horrific detail. If she ever tasted freedom, she would ensure he suffered the same torture.

He didn't return with a plate and this discouraged his hostage. Instead, he untied her from the arms of the chair and then retied her wrists close together. He did the same with her ankles but with more slack, allowing her to walk slowly.

Vlaska's chest was heaving; worried she was soon to die. "What are you doing?" She asked in between nervous breaths.

Markov smiled. "Isn't it obvious? You're going to eat breakfast with me upstairs and then sleep on a bed. When you awake, we're going to rewrite my manifesto. You and I, Vlaska, are going to create a new religion."

Her plan was working and suddenly she had hope of surviving. She didn't care what the crazy man wanted to do as long as she could regain her strength and possibly overpower him. Her father always told her that every man succumbs to a woman, no matter how powerful or weak he is. Her father was right. She had succeeded.

Six weeks passed and Vlaska grew accustomed to the daily routine of sitting at the kitchen table, pouring through books by obscure authors while taking notes. She learned how to sleep with her wrists bound and one ankle handcuffed to a bedpost. She learned how to bathe while Markov watched. There were times when she yearned for the privacy of the dark basement but not for long. She wore his shirts as clothing. They were comfortable and clean but Markov found her more attractive. She did as she was told. She bathed as often as she could to remove his scent and semen.

She found Markov's writing skills to be above average and feared that he may gain an audience with the passion he created on paper. His manifesto was violent and hard line communism. The need to purge the Soviet Union of elitists and intelligentsia was front and center. Money or wealth was a measure of greed and the rich would be hanged in public squares. His religious ambitions were tailored after a Japanese religion that worshipped their emperor. It sickened her, and she wished she had never criticized Catholicism. Markov was both the most frightening and egotistical man she had ever met. He promised to include her as an inspiration and tutor. She faked appreciative smiles.

She was pregnant.

Vlaska told him that she wished to go home to her daughter. He replied that she will be with her daughter soon. This pleased her and she continued her charade. It was a Friday afternoon when Markov baked a special chocolate cake. The religious portion was for the most part, completed. He was entirely gracious for her effort and the cake was a symbol of his respect for her. He cut her a big slice, and she wolfed it down in just a few minutes. He did not eat the slice he cut for himself and watched as her eyes glazed over.

When she awoke, she was back in the basement.

"What the hell…" she said groggily.

She smelt gas and looked around the basement before sniffing the red dress she had worn when Markov first kidnapped her. He had washed and ironed it.

"You poured gas on me? Are you insane?"

Markov was sitting in front of her, watching her eyes closely. "We're finished our project Vlaska, there is no reason for you to remain with me."

"What are you talking about? We're partners and lovers. Stop this madness, I beg you."

Valeri's lips curled up just above his nose. "Hmm…partners," he sighed. "Partners are never a good idea. My father was my mother's partner, and she killed him for sleeping with the village whore. Iona was partners with Doctor, Chemist and Teacher before she killed two of them. Hell, Iona was my partner, and I had to get rid of her before she cut me into tiny pieces. Partners are a bad idea. I do wish to add that I am entirely grateful for your effort and the time we shared."

"I'm carrying your child," Vlaska confessed.

This caught Markov off guard but only momentarily. She could be lying but what if she wasn't? An heir to his Machiavellian throne was intriguing.

"One of the books you made me read insinuated that Mary Magellan had a child named Sarah. It would be a fitting name if we had a daughter. The comparisons put together by future scholars analyzing our manifesto would be tantalizing…but it cannot be. If I am to save this declining society I must sacrifice my life for Ukraine and forego family."

"And if it is a boy, we'll name him Valeri," Vlaska interrupted with a hopeful tone. "I know you care for me, I can feel it."

"In an odd way, I do very much care for you and you have enlightened me on many levels. You are the last of my decadence Vlaska and lives will be spared because of you. I have thought about how to pre-market my manifesto and raise the curiosity of the masses that are close to making a choice for democracy in a land that cannot support such a choice. My problem is that removing prostitutes and anti-communist girls from my equation has proved fruitless.

No one cares Vlaska if you don't return, other than the men who pay money to defile you. The parents of daughters I have eliminated will search forever, hoping that one day their child will magically reappear but their neighbours or the newspapers don't care. They would care or take me more seriously if I kill someone in the spotlight; someone they look up to. A celebrity, a politician or a priest would be beneficial to my plan. Even better, if I had control of one of these personalities, I could spread my doctrine through him."

"I can help you accomplish your dream," Vlaska pleaded. "You know this…"

"The real character of any person is truly revealed seconds or minutes before they die. Stop begging Vlaska, it's ruining my imagined portrait. I will document your stay with me in great detail and future generations will consider you as my Mary. Unfortunately, I don't expect you to ascend to the heavens three days from now."

"You promised me I would see my daughter again," Vlaska yelled. "You promised!"

Valeri took a box of matches from his shirt pocket and lit one. He then tossed it on Vlaska's lap. Her gas drenched dress immediately caught fire

"Your daughter is waiting for you," he mumbled.

Vlaska squirmed, trying to smother the flames that were rising to her face. It was no use. Markov sat facing her, listening to the screams of what had to be horrendous pain. He deemed the

384

fear and panic in her eyes as educational. Her hair burned off her scalp and her nose and eyes melted. This had to be similar to the death that the hideous assistant at Dormiton experienced. Within two minutes, she screamed no more. The flames that had peaked over her head like a Bishop's hat had now rescinded to tiny embers. What remained of her skin was charred and smoking.

He returned his chair to its rightful position behind his easel and began painting. He didn't enjoy the smell of simmering flesh; it reminded him of burnt peas. The hostage chair would have to be rebuilt, and this annoyed him. She's at fault. It was Vlaska who put the idea into his head.

In hindsight, a witch burning was a bad idea.

Chapter Three: Mila Kharmalov

April 24th 2013: Ukraine Tourism

"Ok, hurry, we don't have much time," Boris urged.

Lena had just left to go shopping leaving Boris and me alone in the apartment. He stood at the balcony window looking down at the street.

"Time for what?" I answered.

"Oh my God, Canadian boy, get your camera and your coat and hurry. If we rush, we can make it back for dinner."

I knew I was expected to go somewhere this afternoon, but I was very comfortable on the couch hoping things would be cancelled. I dislodged myself and groaned while standing. Boris had a look in his eyes that told me I should move faster. I collected my coat and camera and we went outside. A blue van door opened and Boris hopped in first. I was hesitant but followed. Evgeni was driving and Igor sat in the passenger seat.

"Another surprise, gentlemen? I immediately questioned.

Igor turned to face me. "Most western men spend their time in Kiev drooling over our women. We are giving you a learning experience. Sit back and enjoy."

I stared at Igor and then Boris. "I like drooling. I like drooling a lot. Drooling is very underrated."

Traffic was brutal but Evgeni managed to find a route to the highway in less than fifteen minutes. No matter how many times I asked, our voyage destination was not told to me until we reached the highway.

"Aaron," Evgeni began. "We don't have a Disney World or mountain resorts or famous museums. Tourists don't flock to Ukraine except in the summer and mostly to spend time on

387

Odessa beaches. Strangely, out of the grinning mouth of disaster, a different genre of tourism has begun to fill our coffers."

"For the cost of one hundred and fifty dollars," Igor cut in, "You can spend a glorious five hours in the Exclusion Zone... as long as you sign a waiver."

"We're going to Chernobyl?" I exclaimed. "Are you guys out of your freakin' minds?"

"Well yes," Boris snorted. "Anyone who goes there is a lunatic to some degree but we'll take precautions. We're not going to be part of any tour group so make sure you don't wander off."

"Where the hell would I go?" I replied. "Oh man, Lena is gonna flip. She's gonna go all Exorcist on us."

Boris tapped me on the shoulder harder than he wanted to. "Don't know what that means Canuck. Relax and grow some balls. We're taking you on an excursion of a lifetime. You want to learn what Lena thinks about daily? This is it."

Evgeni looked back briefly. "This is exactly what bothers your girlfriend. I know why she's cautious with you but I'll let her explain when she's ready."

"What is it?" I returned curiously.

"Seriously?" Evgeni replied. "I just said Lena will explain. What are you... five?"

I ignored his remark and thought what the evening would bring. Lena will be pissed, that much is certain.

I remembered something.

I don't know why I remembered it but I suddenly felt this trip would be worthwhile on so many levels.

"Maybe this is not a bad idea. I need to take a picture that will make someone really happy."

Two hours later we arrived at a checkpoint. There was bus full of tourists ahead of us so we waited an additional ten minutes.

Evgeni looked in the rear view mirror and caught my attention. "Welcome to the Exclusion Zone," he said.

I bent forward to look out Evgeni's window. Aside from trees and bushes, I saw nothing that would burn in my memory. A soldier or someone resembling a soldier knocked on the driver window. Evgeni rolled it down and handed the short man an envelope. He read the contents and then waved for his partner. A second man appeared, read the same document and grinned. He looked in the back of the van and waved to Boris who in turn, saluted the guard. They told Boris if he needed anything he just had to ask at the information center. Oh, and lunch was free for us. When this was translated to me I knew there was more to Boris then he let on. I didn't broach the subject. Evgeni was still watching me in the rear view mirror, trying to gauge my reaction. I'm guessing he was disappointed.

"Evgeni and I have been here at least a dozen times," Igor stated. "I once wondered why a foreigner would want to visit such a dangerous environment. My hunch is that they want to put a face on Armageddon. My friend welcomed you to the Exclusion Zone. I welcome you to Armageddon."

I sat between the two front seats to see as much as possible. The ride was bumpy, so I held Igor's seat for balance. There were some houses, but they were lost underneath the vegetation that grew over and in them. Evgeni pointed out a village that had been entirely buried by liquidators. It was impossible to tell if he was telling the truth as all I saw was fields. He told me we wouldn't stop here because I could make an easy evaluation of what existed. I asked about animals and he answered that they were everywhere. I didn't see any.

The travelers in the bus we were following exited at the information center. We headed straight to the Reactor, a good twenty minutes away. The first things I saw in the distance were two half-finished projects. Evgeni said these were the beginning of Reactor Five and Six.

Igor said something in Ukrainian and Evgeni pulled over.

"You have to see this to believe it," Igor smiled.

We got out of the van and walked towards a pond. A couple of elderly gentlemen were throwing bread and potato skins into the water. Igor was right. If I hadn't of seen it myself, there was no way I would believe anyone telling me. I gazed in wonderment.

"They're catfish," he exclaimed. "Look at the size of these monsters."

"Those are sharks… that ain't no catfish. I've caught catfish… those are sharks."

He chuckled. "No my friend, they are most definitely catfish. No one is fishing anymore so they live longer and I think the radiated water has turned them into freaks. That's my opinion; don't put it in your book."

I was still shaking my head in awe. "I read once that a guy in Thailand caught a nine-foot catfish. Every one of these things measure five or six feet easily."

"What's that fool doing?" Evgeni asked while pointing towards Boris.

Boris slid down a small hill feet away from a dozen catfish awaiting more bread. He was holding a slice given to him by one of the older men.

"Let's see if they'll eat from my hand," he said, enjoying the attention.

"Very bad idea," Igor whispered to me. "But every man must be humbled."

Boris put one foot into the water and held a piece of bread by the surface. A couple of catfish swam by waiting for him to toss in the food. They wriggled as if squirming in anticipation until one could no longer wait. It jumped, missed the bread and bit Boris on the finger. The big man stumbled back, falling on the edge of the hill.

"The son of a bitch bit me," he yelled. "Fucking hell... they're crazy."

He picked up a small rock and flung it at the perpetrator.

"I told you it was a bad idea," Igor chuckled. "Let's go, Boris, we've got lots to see."

"I have to get checked," he yelled back. "You're a doctor, check my finger."

Boris rushed up the hill and Igor examined the finger. "Correct me if I'm wrong Aaron but I believe in the west you call this a boo-boo. Have your mother kiss it when you get home."

"That's very funny," Boris steamed. "Those may be radioactive fish. Have you never watched Spiderman? A radioactive spider bit him... remember?"

"You're gonna turn into Catfishman?" I joked. "I'd pay ten bucks to see your super powers. The ability to grow to enormous sizes... hey, it's already working."

"That's very funny," Boris grumbled. "I never liked Canadians; you're Americans with penis envy."

I wondered how long he had been waiting to say that little gem. I laughed and wrapped my arms around his shoulders. He called me an asshole and sniggered.

We got back into the van and drove to Reactor Four. Evgeni thought it necessary that I see it up close to get an idea of what I was writing. It was entirely covered by a sarcophagus and I thought that anyone who knew little about what really happened here would be bored. I was fascinated. I knew the dangers the liquidators took to cover the reactor, and I knew of the deaths and health problems this caused. It was a monument to courage. The Geiger counter rose to a very unhealthy level and then dropped again.

"Don't worry," Igor said. "It's weird but radiation seeps into one spot and stays. Any time we get close to moss, the Geiger will go nuts because moss absorbs the radiation. As long as we don't stick around for days, we'll be fine."

Evgeni stood next to me and explained how a new sarcophagus was necessary. The one we were looking at was in dire straits and needed to be replaced. He said that no one wants to pay for it. I couldn't understand how the IAEA wouldn't contribute to a new sarcophagus.

"If that structure was bombed, we'd be dead in a week," Evgeni noted. "How many madmen do you think have planned on doing just that? All of Europe... gone."

I never considered that and I wish he hadn't said it.

"Let's go. I brought you here to show you where Tania and Mila lived and to give you a sense of how incredible their lives once were."

We stopped temporarily at the Bridge of Death. I briefly touched the railing and imagined Mr. Kharmalov and Yuri walking home on the day Tania was to be married. The image of a radiated child crossed my mind.

"It's hot in this jacket," I whined.

"Imagine how hot it was when the winds blew across this bridge," Igor replied. "Stupid bastards. Don't let anyone tell you that ignorance is bliss. They're dead now. How blissful is that?"

Evgeni had remained in the van and beeped his horn. "We don't have all day, let's go."

"When we get to Pripyat, I'd like to go to the recreation center close to the Kharmalov home and I also want to see the ice cream parlor."

"Why?" Boris asked.

"I'll tell you when we get there."

"Tell us now," Evgeni demanded.

"I just said, I'll tell you later. What are you... five?" I laughed as did Igor. Evgeni nodded as if he deserved it.

We drove for fifteen minutes and stopped about one hundred feet from an apartment building. If not for the rust on balconies, the building still looked rather modern. The white brick was dirty from years of neglect but in all honesty, it didn't look much different from the inner city apartment buildings of Toronto. Trees around the side of the building hid a pathway that circled around to the front entrance. Evgeni pointed towards an elderly man standing on the sidewalk holding a rifle.

"That's curious," the Director said. "I've met him before. He's a good man with a sense of humor. I usually bring him some canned goods and he is always appreciative. He lives near to where Tania stayed in the Zone. He's always willing to discuss Pripyat before the explosion as long as the guides supply food. I guess he considers it his job."

"And the rifle?" I asked.

"First time I've seen him with one," Evgeni replied. "Come, we'll find out what's going on."

"Whoa," I answered. "The guy has a gun. We should have a safe word or something. What if he's insane?"

Boris chucked to himself. "He lives in the Exclusion Zone, Aaron. It's accepted that he's a fool. No offense to Aunt Tania."

"Car... if anything goes wrong, the safe word is car," Igor cut in while opening the passenger door.

The rest of us joined and walked towards the thin, older man with the scruffy white beard. The man, I soon learned, was named Drovy. He was a liquidator from Kharkov who decided to stay in the Exclusion Zone after his co-workers returned to their homes. I wondered if Drovy was hiding from someone or something. Looking into the man's wide, laughing eyes, I quickly understood his decision. I considered yelling car but Evgeni seemed to have everything under control. He pointed towards the rifle and Drovy nodded before answering.

"He says the dogs have been very aggressive lately," Evgeni told me. "If they get too close, he fires a shot and they run away."

I asked Evgeni to question Drovy on why he chose to stay in the Zone. The man replied that most people live in Slavutich, which has little contamination. He chose to stay in a smaller community because it would be quiet and he could live off the land. I then asked how he could live off contaminated land and he rolled his eyes. I figured this question got asked a lot, and he was tired of answering it. His response was a curt, "I'm still living." Not impressed, I thought of telling Evgeni to give his canned food to someone else as Drovy was shit at his job. Igor whispered in my ear that he would explain the choice to live in the Zone later.

Boris tugged on my jacket and pointed towards the side of the building. Neither of us could see much but there was a cloud of dust in between the trees.

"Looks like a truck or something is driving too fast," he deduced.

Evgeni turned towards me and stated that Drovy wished to apologize for his terse answer. I was told that he hadn't met many Canadians and that most visitors were from Germany and America. Evgeni remarked that Canadians came for the women and beer. He was in mid grin when Boris cursed loudly.

The dust we saw seconds earlier came from two horses who were now galloping full steam on the same path we stood on. Boris grabbed me by the arm and pulled me twenty feet towards our van. Evgeni, Igor and Drovy moved the other direction, choosing to stand behind a concrete block. The terrified horses passed us and we exhaled a collective breath.

I rushed towards Evgeni and Igor with my arms flailing. They were staring at each other in disbelief. Evgeni looked at me and shrugged.

"This place just gets weirder and weirder."

Boris was still standing in the same spot watching the horses as they disappeared in the distance. "Car!" he yelled. None of us moved, and he yelled it again, this time with his arms spread wide.

Igor raised his hand. "Oh crap… we have a new problem."

Horses don't run for nothing and we soon learned why they were panicked. A pack of wolves appeared from the side of the building and approached cautiously. They chose to stay a good distance away and we could see a few of them growling. I counted eight in total. Boris would later recount that there were twenty. The lead wolf stood a foot ahead of the others and approached one slow step at a time.

"Car!" Boris screamed again.

Igor raised his hand again before lowering it slowly. "Quiet, Boris. You have to walk calmly towards us. If they attack they will attack the weakest member. You're by yourself and they know it."

Not needing any prodding, Boris walked sideways until he was next to me. I wish someone had filmed this so we could watch it over and over. He looked like an overweight Charlie Chaplin. Drovy fired a shot in the air and the wolves dispersed but only for a moment. They reassembled and moved closer before stopping. Evgeni took the rifle from Drovy and asked for a couple of bullets. He checked the barrel, loaded and cocked. We said nothing as he bent on one knee and aimed the rifle at the lead wolf that had made several steps towards the men. His first shot echoed, and I barely heard the short yelp. The wolf slumped over on the road. Evgeni fired at the next closest wolf and it too fell on the road. The remaining within the pack fled behind Tania and Mila's old apartment building.

Boris yelled *car* one last time and started running to the van.

"Did you have to kill them?" I shouted at Evgeni. The blasts from the rifle were still ringing in my ear.

"Probably not," he answered. "But a few dogs and cats will live longer because of me. I never liked that survival of the fitness bullshit, especially when I can control it."

There had to be some deep meaning or metaphor in that but I didn't pursue the conversation as I was anxious to return to the van in case the wolf pack returned with backup. Boris was already opening the side door summoning us with wild arms to hurry. If it wasn't crazy, I'd be laughing. Evgeni was trying to analyze why a wolf pack was in the heart of Pripyat but said he needed outside help. I was just happy to be in a moving vehicle.

We drove for twenty minutes and stopped at a medium-sized forest in the middle of nowhere. Igor pointed at me and we got out. Evgeni and Boris remained in the van. We didn't say much until Igor found a patch of grass he was satisfied with and sat. I joined him.

"When you look at this section of forest you'll see a tree dense land that serves little purpose. The liquidators didn't bother with this part because it couldn't serve as shelter for animals. They didn't consider that someday this patch of forest could catch on fire. Eventually, a dead branch will reach the ignition temperature and start a rebirth of sorts. The fire will release nutrients into the soil allowing for new plant growth, a return of smaller animals and then larger animals preying on the smaller. Nature takes care of itself Aaron. It always has and it always will."

"I didn't know that," I said politely.

"Yah, it's true and it would be a great story if it were in another country… but not here. If the soil in that forest is burned it will release the plutonium that is buried underneath and a new chaos will develop. We'd be back to 1986 levels. That's why humans are banned from here, Aaron. They'll till the soil or dig lots for new homes. The second they do that, they seal their own death and those nearby. It's why Tania is dying. Once the isotopes are in you, they are there to stay. Do you understand what I am trying to tell you?"

I said yes but judging from the almost pained expression on his face he didn't think I did. He was trying to tell me something, and I wasn't grasping his intent.

"We had several scientists come to the Exclusion Zone theorizing on the effects of radiation on the local wildlife. The results have varied but I'm sure that comes as no surprise.

"Not really, no," I answered. "Every positive has a negative. The same type of thinking."

"Agreed. During the first half decade after the Chernobyl exclusion, scientists found mutants and deformities among the animal population but the problem... went away. Mind you, this was in the areas with low radiation. In the infamous Red Forest, the animals are still weak and have short lives. Low level radiation over an extended period of time doesn't seem to have had any effect on the wildlife. Different species have migrated here in tremendous numbers and they're breeding successfully or at least this is what's written.

The IAEA reads these statistics and uses them as proof that fallout radiation diminishes quickly and has no harmful effects on humans. I don't know why animals are not showing adverse effects nor can anyone prove otherwise and there's a reason for this. The animals aren't being tagged and a great deal of the research has conveniently disappeared. Ukraine has no budget to fund more research and western scientists are being denied access. I'd like to know how long they live in comparison to animals living in non-radiated forests. Some scientists claim that the populations are increasing because they're healthy but there's also the argument that the majority of wildlife migrate here because there are no humans. It explains the growing number of species as well as total growth. Couldn't we explain the growth as simply the influx of animals from across Ukraine and elsewhere instead of assuming they're reproducing? My belief is that they come here but they can't leave. It's like a roach motel."

I clicked on to what he was saying. "So, within their present environment they're still stronger than those beneath them in the chain but if they were to return to the environment they came from, they would be weaker."

"Exactly, and this explains why Drovy stayed. He knew his life would be shit if he returned to Kharkov. Never judge a book by its cover."

"Igor," I cut in, "I have to ask… your English is impeccable. How is this possible? Where did you go to school?"

Igor smiled as if he knew the question would be asked. "Boris, Evgeni and I have been friends since a young age. I went to medical school in London and did my internship in Bristol. Evgeni went to Montreal and stayed there an additional year after graduation."

"Okay, but how could either of you afford this type of education on a single parent salary? If I'm prying, just tell me."

"No, it's an honest inquiry. We were funded by Boris's grandfather. He saw potential in us and paid for our entire educations. We've been studying English since we were pre-teens."

"The plot thickens," I added.

"He is known across Ukraine as the Doctor. I'm not sure how rich he is but if I were a betting man I'd say he is in the top five of the wealthiest in this country. That's not saying much but you know what I mean."

"Mafia?" I asked.

I looked for some indication of truth from Igor's face but he remained stoic.

"It's not for me to answer but I've heard those rumours," Igor lied.

I nodded my head and recalled my conversation with Boris a few nights earlier. He clearly stated he survived because of mafia connections.

"We survive however we can Aaron but it's all relevant and no matter the situation, the story remains the same. Your benefactor owns you and your life can be turned upside down in a heartbeat. When the Doctor summons, I run. I've cared for some very shady characters in the last ten years. If I was ever to choose to say no, the repercussions wouldn't be positive. The same applied to the citizens of Pripyat. Their benefactor was a nuclear plant that needed their assistance. When the technicians screwed up, the plant turned on them… metaphorically, of course."

"I get your gist, albeit, it's a fairly broad metaphor."

Igor wiped his forehead with the back of his hand. The sun had peaked its way through the grey clouds and we suddenly considered removing our protective layer.

"Here's another metaphor in the making Aaron. I'm sweating and extremely uncomfortable. We're cooking under an extra layer of clothing but we're wearing that layer for an obvious reason. Do we remove our jackets and assume the risk? Tania lived a mile from here. Kiev was her protective layer, and she chose to remove it to come here. If it brought you happiness or a degree of relief, would you remove your jacket?"

"That won't be happening and I'm not a risk-taker," I answered, bluntly.

400

"So you say but whether it's subconsciously or even naively, you are most definitely, a risk-taker."

"You may want to elaborate Igor," I sighed. I had a feeling I was about to learn yet another surprise.

Igor shrugged. "You're fifty yards from the Red Forest… that's a risk, don't you think?"

"You guys kidnapped me, I had no idea I was coming here," I answered with half a smile.

"Maybe so," Igor quickly replied, "But you're glad to witness this. You have your own business. That too is a risk."

"More necessity," I said.

Igor shook his head. "You're not going to make this easy on me. Ok, fine. You're in love with Lena… that's a huge risk."

I let out a short harrumph. "Lena's not a risk, she's just difficult."

"Aaron… excuse me but I find it both inspiring and curious that you love someone you barely know. I don't want to worry you but you should be aware of the following: Lena is the daughter of Mila Kharmalov. I'm going to give her the benefit of the doubt that even she has no clue how influential her mother is or could be in this country. Mila is despised by the Ukraine government and the old boys club that calls the shots… and others." His voice trailed for a second as if in deep thought. "She's not allowed to set foot in Russia or Belarus for that matter. By association, you're with a woman who is considered a possible threat, and that makes you Aaron… a possible threat. It does the same for me, Evgeni and Boris. Do you think for a moment that your background hasn't been checked since the day you met Lena at the airport?"

"How do you know that I met Lena at the airport?"

401

Igor's face scrunched, and he sighed. "Get real man… we knew your story an hour after Lena told Boris you were visiting. You're a small blessing to us Aaron and we want you to tell our story. You write biographies for families. We're asking you to write a biography for a country. We planned your vacation while you were still on the plane."

"So you're using me," I answered with a fake dejected expression.

"No… well, yes in a way, I guess we are. Let's not get weird here… ok? Don't think for a moment we haven't enjoyed our time with you. You've been great and frankly, we need you a lot more than you need us."

"Ok, I'm just messing with your head," I grinned.

Igor shook his head several times and exhaled heavily. "You're a prick. Are all Canadians pricks?"

I leaned my head to the left and slid my tongue across my teeth before replying.

"Yes," I joked.

The small talk ended quickly. "After the explosion, the pine trees absorbed radiation and turned a ginger like colour. That's why it's called the Red Forest. Liquidators bulldozed most of it. They buried the trees in trenches and covered it with sand. The trees you see now were saplings twenty years ago. The buried trees are decaying and the radiation within them will eventually contaminate the ground water. It's probably already happened."

I shook my head and sighed. "This will never disappear."

"No, it won't and very few seem to understand this. Whether it's Three Mile Island, Fukushima or even the atomic bomb test sites… it doesn't go away. It keeps coming back and people are dying because of it." Igor stood and wiped the knees of his pants. "The only winners are the rich criminals we call the atomic elite. My wish is that someday we'll have a tribunal of sort to judge them. Maybe as a jail sentence we can have them live here for twenty years."

I uncrossed my legs and Igor grabbed my hand to help me to my feet. "Why do you stay in Ukraine," I asked. "Doctors as accomplished as you are needed anywhere in the world."

Igor shrugged and dropped his eyes. "Who would take care of Boris?"

It was then I understood that this doctor was owned by The Doctor. I didn't press further.

****

"It's there!" I yelled. Evgeni stopped the van and questioned what I was talking about. "I'll show you soon. Let me out."

We had backtracked to the recreation center that Tania and Yuri had met three decades ago. I stepped outside and asked if anyone wished to join me. Boris looked around and saw the horses that had raced by us an hour ago. He said he would wait in the van as he needed time to think of a good story to tell Lena when he returned to Kiev without me. Judging by the half bottle of vodka in his hand, Boris wasn't going anywhere.

It was kind of hard to miss as it was still enormous amongst the other tall brush that grew unattended within this children's park. The tree was as spectacular as Tania described it.

The trunk was massive, and I guessed the circumference to be at least fifteen feet. The new leaves would have blocked the sun if it hadn't disappeared behind ever darkening clouds. I would have to rush or risk getting drenched by a certain rainstorm. I heard Boris screaming at me to hurry. I didn't acknowledge him.

To be honest, I wasn't sure what I was looking for until I found it. I expected it to be covered but after scraping away a bit of moss I saw the carved heart with the initials Y.L + T.K.

Yuri Larinov and Tania Kharmalov.

My heart tugged while I unzipped my jacket to get to the camera hanging around my neck. I took several pictures from different angles. With a big smile plastered on my face, I returned to the van.

"In Ukraine, if you walk around with a grin like that, you're considered stupid," Boris advised.

Evgeni stared at me as if he knew I had done something special. "It is nice to see smiles. I think our lives would be better if we had more stupid, grinning people."

I handed the camera to Boris with my photos ready to view.

"Son of a bitch," he whispered.

It dawned on me that Boris said son of a bitch a lot.

He handed the camera to Igor who acknowledged my act with a smile. Evgeni nodded while staring at me. Nothing was said as he gently tossed the camera to me. He started the van and drove about twenty feet before stopping and looking into the rear view mirror at Boris.

"Tell him," he ordered.

Boris hesitated and wavered. He responded in Russian but everyone knows what nyet means.

"He needs to know," Evgeni insisted. "He has to know the danger he's in."

"Say what?" I piped.

"It's not bad," Boris huffed. He took a swig from his bottle and wiped his mouth with the back of his hand. "What the fuck? We've all benefitted from our association… just be content we're not on the other end of the stick. Either one of you could be homeless if it wasn't for your ties to me."

He hesitated before releasing a long burp. Igor and Evgeni remained quiet but their faces were stern after the last remark.

"Fucking idiots," Boris grimaced. "Do you take pleasure in my shame?" He shook his head several times and directed several Russian curse words at his friends before speaking. "My grandfather is the leader of a large group of thugs considered as Mafia. He's been in Lugansk since the early seventies. He's not my real grandfather. Just want to make that clear. All I know is that my mother's parents were both killed during some ethnic cleansing. I've never found any proof of this but I have to believe what I'm being told." He took a gulp of vodka and placed the bottle between his legs. "You better not tell Lena this or I'll hunt you down."

"Boris, for Christ's sake," Evgeni responded loudly.

Boris raised his hand as if to apologize. "He doesn't kidnap our women nor does he condone it. He assassinates the bastards in the sex trade. Most Mafioso have ties in this activity and hate my grandfather for his interference." Boris inhaled and exhaled. "I'm not saying he is some kind of criminal angel with a conscience. He is neither of these, but my mother is a woman and his love for my mother is unparalleled. He would never physically hurt a woman. His orientation is different and I'll leave

405

that as it is. What you need to know is that he is very protective of what is his and if anyone poses a threat to his kingdom, he will have them eliminated and it doesn't matter if they're related…" His voice trailed and he dropped his head. "I am his grandson but the line of protection stops there." He took another swig of vodka from the bottle that was now near empty. "Fuck," he grunted while wiping his mouth.

Boris looked at Evgeni and Igor before glancing at me. He was obviously disappointed in them and his glare lasted longer than either could withstand. They both looked away. His head soon rested against his chest as if he was embarrassed look into my eyes.

"He killed my Uncle Anton."

September 1992

She was called Teacher. They were all called Teacher, and they all looked the same. Blonde hair, thin, effeminate and short. She spent four hours a day reading books that Grandfather insisted she read. I say she loosely because they were boys who wanted to be girls. Grandfather supplied them with hormone pills he bought on the black market. Wearing a dress and high heels, she sat as prim and proper as she could on the couch facing the skinny visitor forced to sit on a wood chair. Not a word was spoken as she studied the man's every movement. She paid no attention to the smaller man who rarely lifted his head. He had a long scar on his face and appeared very conscious of his injury. Throughout the upcoming conversation, he did not say one word.

I was hiding behind the thick burgundy curtains that were drawn in the afternoon hours. I frequently hid here watching Teacher. She knew I was there and never said anything. I think she believed I was the ideal video tape that could never be destroyed. I saw things I should never have seen and will never forget. I hate her for that.

The skinny visitor had a ponytail that he kept stroking like he would an indoor cat. He was by no means effeminate like Teacher but in my early teen years, everything was very confusing to me. I could tell he was questioning the sex of the person in front of him yet he said little, as if he had seen it all before. My grandfather entered and sat next to Teacher.

"Thank-you for coming," he said to both visitors. The shy man nodded.

The skinny man was not amused and replied as such. "I didn't ask to be here nor was I politely invited. What do you want?"

I had never heard anyone speak to grandfather like that and expected the worse to happen but the warranted response was left alone.

"Should I call you Olav or Valeri or... should I call you Stani?"

Valeri Markov was now nervous understanding he was not dealing with any of the run of the mill thugs he was accustomed to working with.

"Who the fuck are you?" he replied anxiously.

Grandfather crossed his legs calmly and put his hand on Teacher's leg. His voice remained tranquil and clear. "Mr. *Markov*, if I hear another curse word from your mouth I will have your testicles removed and cooked for dinner. Is this understood?"

Markov's eyes opened wide, trying to survey his surroundings. "May I ask with whom I am speaking?"

Grandfather nodded appreciatively. He studied the other man for ten seconds before concentrating on Markov.

"Thank-you for lowering your tone. I will tell you our names, Mr. Markov, and I am confident you will recognize them. You may call me Doctor and my partner is named Teacher."

The visitor said nothing for several seconds trying to collect his courage. Even from where I was standing, I could feel his temperature rising. He placed his hands under his legs to hide his trembling. The edge of Teacher's lips rose slightly when she recognized a change in the man's demeanor.

"I take it then that you have heard of us?" Grandfather pressed. Markov nodded yes. "I wish first to thank-you for finishing a job I was not able to complete. Iona was my worse failure yet because of her I became a proud father. What did you do with my money, Mr. Markov?"

Markov coughed spasmodically, not expecting such a question. "I didn't know it was your money sir. It's been almost ten years, the money is gone."

Grandfather had been in these situations many times and I had witnessed a few of them from behind the same curtains. The shift of his body weight and the change of facial expressions were rehearsed to perfection. Markov was an easy mark. The smaller man showed absolutely no change in demeanor. I found that strange as did Grandfather.

"That's unfortunate for you. Teacher, from your ten minutes with Mr. Markov, what can you tell me about him?"

She was pleased to be able to speak and leaned forward but only marginally. Her tone was deliberately whispered to hide her masculine voice.

"Mr. Markov is meticulous. His face is carefully shaved, his shirt and pants are ironed and his fingernails are filed and clean of any dirt. He is average in looks but believes he has the face of Christ. His intelligence is above the norm but only because his self-imposed reclusion has allowed him to delve into subjects most people care little about. I know this because he stares at me as if he is staring into a mirror. Obsessive people do not waste their time with trivial pursuits or the company of others and when faced with enigmas, will study the subject with blind intensity."

Grandfather grabbed Teachers hand. "And what say ye, Mr. Markov?"

Markov had a momentary burst of courage and glared at Teacher. "You speak well for a dead person."

"Your testicles, Mr. Markov," Grandfather uttered. "Think of your testicles. In the future, if you wish to obtain a response from Teacher, you must ask a question."

"Why am I here, Doctor?" Markov asked.

Grandfather stood and walked behind the couch. He rubbed Teacher's shoulders before crossing his arms.

"I'm sure you'd agree Mr. Markov that I have a nice home. I'm not crazy about the security required but it is a necessary inconvenience for Teacher and me. When I first arrived in Lugansk in 1968, my daughter and I had very little money. I was reasonably well-off years earlier but my wealth dwindled after travelling from town to town for four years. I didn't wish to restart the career I had in Samaski but my options were few and far between. Within a year I assembled what remained of my team from my home village and moved them to Lugansk. Accumulating money was fairly easy from that point on. Samaski had always been a success because it was a Brotherhood of Thieves. We shared our profits and worked together. What I created in Lugansk was the same blueprint. At the time, there were many petty thieves and pimps with no organization. I gave them the option to join us or die. The smart ones chose to join our Brotherhood.

You, Mr. Markov, are a loner. I know much about you so don't bother to argue. You depend on surprise or disaster to accumulate wealth. Left alone in a strong economy with a strong police force, you could not survive. I am the opposite. I surround myself with talent and education. Nothing we do is spontaneous or unprofessional and we have secured ties to other groups across Ukraine and Russia. Our Brotherhood meets three times a week to discuss present and future projects.

We traded many types of goods, including stolen jewels, art and medicine. You should know that you have sold your stolen goods to my employees. Mostly though, we controlled sex and drugs. When Khrushchev turned a blind eye on independent businesses we started charging protection. If you didn't pay, your business was gone the next day. We have no patience for negotiation. In the mid-eighties, I opened my first night club and eventually owned twenty in Lugansk and Kiev. I had girls from across Ukraine working in these clubs and they served foreigners and government officials. The clubs were called Sam's, short for Samaski. Have you heard of them Mr. Markov?

Markov shook his head, no.

"That surprises me," grandfather responded, "Because a few of my girls disappeared. The same car was linked to their disappearance."

Valeri's face turned from stoic to concern. Grandfather grimaced before continuing.

"When the Soviet Union was dismantled last year, a new opportunity popped up out of nowhere. It basically just landed in our laps and we couldn't believe our luck. Ukraine had military equipment in warehouses that were manned by soldiers making shit for wages. They were starving and had no problem with selling guns, rifles and nuclear warheads to us. We bought them for a pittance and sold for millions.

That is the beauty of organization Mr. Markov. You learn things from a multitude of sources instead of from word of mouth. The more money I earned the more untouchable I became. Police were paid off as were politicians. Today, I can humbly say that I no longer follow the rules set by our fine police force or politicians. They follow what I tell them. I am the law in half of Ukraine.

I had you followed Mr. Markov. Once I learned that you were selling trinkets I had given to Teacher and Iona, I put two and two together. Days after you butchered Iona, my sources informed me on how you carried out her murder. Did you take her writings with you?"

Markov nodded yes.

"She was a product of her environment and an after effect of communism, as are you Mr. Markov. You would disagree but you are a square peg living in a round hole. I have no desire to change you but in order for you to see tomorrow's sunrise, you will temporarily dispel your notions and side with my concept of capitalism." Grandfather uncrossed his arms and leaned on the couch with both arms. "I will admit that I am intrigued with your theories for a new Soviet Union and empathize with the conflicts you must be presently feeling. I am well aware of your dealings with the Kharkov priest and the politician you have recently encountered. In time, we will discuss your essay and consider the attributes that could benefit my empire. That being recognized, if you knew me well Mr. Markov you would know that I have scum like you killed. I am not insinuating that I am perfect or have led a moral life but when I have someone murdered it is because they have been disloyal to me. You take pleasure in kidnapping and mutilating women. I find that deplorable. My daughter is a female, and she is my world aside from Teacher. You're the lowest form of shit on this earth but strangely, I find you fascinating and even more strangely, I need you. This would be a good time to ask me why."

The thin man was bolted to his chair, fearing for his life. "Why?" he mumbled nervously.

"We have a mutual enemy Mr. Markov. She has fanatical support from neo-democrats who want to dismantle what has taken me two decades to build. The Americans have thrown support behind her. She cannot be harmed but her decision to withdraw from politics must be hers. Who am I speaking of sir?"

"Mila Kharmalov," he answered scornfully.

"Yes, the one and only, Mila Kharmalov. I supply a large portion of medicine to the Chernobyl victims; heart medicine, lotions and pills to numb their pain. Chernobyl was a boom to my business and still is. I became wealthy because of it. She is running on a platform to dismantle the black market. I can't allow this to happen. Look at me and listen carefully. I cannot have one of my men do this task as it is risky on many levels. She is not the intended victim Markov, don't get a hard-on. If one hair on her head is harmed, I will personally chop off your dick. You will murder her father."

Upon hearing those words I wanted to shout out my disapproval, but I knew the consequences. I remember Teacher looking at the curtains waiting for my reaction but I stood frozen in the runners that grandfather had purchased only a few hours earlier.

"He leaves the apartment he shares with my daughter and grandson every afternoon at three p.m. to collect the afternoon newspaper. Don't get caught Mr. Markov. If you do and my name is mentioned, your life will end. Iona taught you many gruesome tricks. Take into consideration that she learned from me and I will take great pleasure in using them on you. When this job is completed you will suspend your kidnappings of women. I will fund your livelihood and supply you with women within this compound or at one of my clubs. You will visit on the fifteenth day of every month to collect your wages and… fantasy. Together we will study the social opportunities you write about but understand the following: If I hear of any future murders and tie them to you, Teacher will be the last person you ever see. Will you take care of the Kharmalov father?"

Markov nodded his head but then looked at grandfather with a puzzled expression. "I don't know what he looks like?"

"That is not a problem," grandfather replied. He then pointed towards the curtains as if he were looking directly at me. "My grandson will point him out to you."

****

"Oh man," I said, not knowing what else to say.

Boris was dangling the empty bottle of vodka in his right hand. His head was down the whole time, refusing to look at me. I couldn't imagine having to live with the guilt he was dealing with. At that moment, I realized why my life was in danger. I was with the daughter of Mila Kharmalov and now understood why I was being watched.

"I want to get home to Lena. We should never have left her alone."

"He wouldn't harm a woman," Evgeni mentioned.

"What about Markov?" I said, spitting out my words.

Boris waved the bottle back and forth. "He's out of the picture. The last I heard is that he has some form of dementia. My grandfather dropped contact with him six months ago."

I wasn't appeased. "So basically what I'm hearing is that if anything bad were to happen, I would be the target."

Boris cleared his throat. "I explained the reason you are here to my grandfather, and he guaranteed that no harm would come to Lena or you. You're not here to squash his livelihood so he is not too interested. He's on Teacher Number Five now and seems to have mellowed."

"Oh well… as long as he's mellowed," I fired back sarcastically. "That doesn't fucking comfort me Boris!"

"I know," the big man whispered. "I wouldn't allow anything to happen to you Aaron. I swear on my life."

I massaged my palms across my forehead trying to halt the surge of blood rushing to my head. Igor mentioned earlier that the three of them knew all about me before I stepped off the plane. It was because they had to give a report to The Doctor. That's what he meant and intentionally failed to reveal. This is insane. I've never hurt a soul in my entire life. I was only in Ukraine to help the girl I was in love with.

"What happened to Teachers two through four?" I questioned, breaking the silence.

Igor and Evgeni looked at Boris briefly before staring out the front window.

Boris shrugged and gave me an answer with no introduction or explanation.

"The Samaski butcher is older now but always busy."

I didn't need an explanation.

415

Imprints

I had to hold Lena. More than anything in this world, I had to hold Lena.

We arrived at Boris's apartment building and I was the first one out of the van. I didn't bother thanking Evgeni or Igor for the learning experience; the thought never entered my mind until much later. I rushed to the front entrance but had to wait for a slow moving, somewhat intoxicated Boris to find his key. My patience had long disappeared, and I told him to hurry. The door opened, and I ran up the stairs to see Lena.

She smiled when she saw me and was totally surprised when I rushed to hug her.

"Aaron?" She questioned with her cute smile.

"I'm just happy to be with you," I answered as best as I could.

I kissed her on her forehead several times and she didn't push me away.

Boris walked in and threw his keys on the kitchen counter. He smiled at Lena and lowered his eyes. Lena picked up on his drunken stagger and sighed loudly before noticing he was quiet for other reasons other than alcohol.

"Should I ask or will someone be telling me?" She inquired.

I looked at Boris hoping he would respond but he had turned away from the living room couch leaving me undefended from Lena's inevitable questions. *Coward*, I thought. I didn't like the man at this moment.

"Where have you been?" she whimpered.

Her eyes told me that she thought our afternoon jaunt had more to do with women than what actually happened. I am a lousy liar and Lena knew this. It's never a good idea to lie to an Eastern European woman but then again, the truth wasn't my friend either. I should've realized well in advance that I would be in a no win situation. I wasn't going to tell her about the possible danger I was in with a mafia person I have never met so I chose the second worse truth.

"We were in Pripyat," I said with a lowered head.

In hindsight I probably should have led with the gangster scenario. Lena stood immediately and her eyes opened so wide I thought they would burst out of their sockets. She hovered over me like an angry hawk.

"You idiot," she screamed. "You *fucking* idiot. How dare you?"

I tried to stand, but she pushed me back down. I had never seen her so furious. Her body was visibly shaking with fury.

"You learned nothing…"

I tried again to stand, but she slapped my cheek. I placed my hand on my face and Lena stared at me in shock realizing what she just did. She stepped back two steps before leaving towards her bedroom.

"Lena!" Boris yelled.

She stopped and pointed towards her cousin. "I never want to speak to you again."

The bedroom door slammed behind her and I slumped onto the couch. Boris took out two beers from the fridge and sat next to me. He handed me a bottle. I could barely grasp it in my trembling hands. My world was shattering.

"Wait five minutes," he said calmly.

"I'm done Boris," I replied, gasping for breath.

His large hands pulled my head towards his and he put his forehead on mine. "You will walk into that bedroom in five minutes and you will tell her to tell you the truth."

"I don't know what that means anymore..." I trailed. "I stumble into wall after wall with no door in sight. What is the truth, Boris?"

Boris took a long gulp from his bottle. "The truth Aaron is that our lives here in Ukraine are shit." His eyes were misty. "My life is shitty and there are days I want to jump head first off this apartment's roof. Others have done it, why not me?" He paused to exhale. "Your life is not shit. You have Lena and she loves and needs you more than you could possibly imagine."

"I have a hand mark on my cheek that says otherwise."

"Don't ask her for the truth Aaron. You will walk into that room and demand it. Don't ask... demand. And don't leave until she tells you everything."

He let me go and stared ahead as if lost in a trance. I lifted myself off the couch, placed my beer bottle on the kitchen table and walked into the bedroom.

"Get out" were the first words I heard, but I did not move from the foot of the bed. Lena was curled up with her head on both pillows. She noted that my face was expressionless. If I'm not mistaken, this was the first time she had seen me like this and was probably confused on how to deal with me.

"Tell me the truth," I said with little authority.

Lena leaned against the headboard with a pillow in her hands. "What? Shut the fuck up. Get out of this room immediately!"

Lena rarely if ever swore, and she had cursed me twice in the last ten minutes. I inhaled some courage and stared directly into her eyes.

"I will leave this room and your life after you tell me the truth," I said with much more authority.

She realized I wasn't bluffing and threw a pillow at me. "Then go asshole." Lena dropped her head briefly before glaring at me.

"Last chance Lena," I said while reaching for my luggage.

Her head tilted, and she looked into the dresser mirror. "If I tell you, will you leave me alone? "

"Isn't that what I just said?"

I didn't like where this was going but at the same time if this was our swan song, then so be it.

"Fine, I am as curious as you to see who you are." She studied me before continuing.

I think she was gathering enough courage to tell a story she had never told anyone. She took a while to begin, much longer than I anticipated before I witnessed a weird metamorphosis from anger towards me to self-pity.

"I love my mother with all my heart but… but she was so stupid. She was blinded by an impossible ambition…a revenge for her loss. She trudged me across Russia, Ukraine and Belarus without thinking for a second that her child was breathing the same shit she was fighting. I slept in hospitals and homes blanketed with radiation. I ate food from fields that are now fenced with forbidden entry signs."

Lena covered her face with the remaining pillow for a good twenty seconds. I'm not sure if she was crying but if she was it didn't last long.

"I arrived in Canada on June 8th, two days before my eleventh birthday. The customs officer checked my medical certificate and called a supervisor. I was terrified when they took me away from my mother and brought me to a room where a doctor and nurse were waiting for me. My mother had Chris paged and he was allowed to stay in the room with me. They took my blood and checked my thyroid gland not once but three times. Chris protested a lot but I didn't understand a word he was saying. Two hours later I was allowed to leave. My first impression of Canada was not pleasant.

The blood results came back a week later. My thyroid was *crumbling*, but the doctor suggested a specialist in Calgary. I didn't attend school that first year. Instead, I was placed on a special diet and given thyroid pills that made me irritable and tired. Very tired. They told my mother and Chris the possibilities of illnesses that may appear in the coming years. I was a kid and my mother was explaining to me that I may get this and that and whatever."

"But you're fine Lena," I interrupted.

She looked up for a second and then stared at her feet. "You think Aaron? I was eleven and my mother was telling me in simple words that there was a good chance that I could never have babies. I would never be a mother."

And there it was. The truth was finally delivered.

I suddenly remembered what Igor told me outside the Red Forest. He was giving me a hint.

Once the isotopes are in you, they are there to stay. Do you understand what I am trying to tell you?

I should have said something right there and then but I remained quiet.

420

"Your silence answers my doubts," she said while wrapping her arms around the pillow.

I nodded several times before speaking. "Oh really now… and you had the gall to call me a fucking idiot. You wasted three years of our life."

'We've had a wonderful friendship. It's callous to say it was a waste."

"Really?" I at once replied. "It' a friendship that should have been a love affair. Did you think you were protecting me? What kind of friendship did we have if you couldn't have the guts to tell your *friend* the truth? You're the idiot."

"Not having you was better than losing you," she whispered.

I leaned my hands on the mattress worried my wobbly legs would give out. "Is that you think? You drive me nuts, you're bordering on lunacy," I said while shaking my head in disbelief. "Whether we have our own children or whether we adopt is not a concern to me and never was. Lena, oh my God… are you blind? I am… I'm desperately, *desperately* in love with you and have been since the day we met. I go to sleep at night thinking of you and I awake in the morning, thinking of you. I dream of marrying you…"

I raised my hands as a symbol of surrender and started packing my suitcase. "Forget it," I grumbled.

I had to get out of that apartment as soon as possible. My legs were quaking as were my hands, and I tried hard not to let Lena see my distress. My stomach was tied up in knots and every breath I exhaled was short, deliberate and painful.

I didn't see her move from the front of the bed to where my luggage was placed. I was throwing in tee-shirts when her hand held my wrist. I raised my head and looked into misty eyes.

"Yes," she said softly.

I stared back confused. "Yes to what Lena?"

"I am also desperately in love with you and can't imagine a day without your laugh. We were born to be with each other. So yes Aaron... I will marry you."

The First Midnight Visitor

Tania did not awake when the visitor sat next to her. He was not allowed to be there but decided the risk was worth the effort. At midnight, there were only three nurses, and they were chatting at the main desk. As long as no patient screamed in pain, he was safe from being discovered.

He stared lovingly at her thinning face realizing she was not long for this world. The woman he had dreamed about for the last twenty years was leaving his life. He recalled the first time they had met. She smiled at his awkwardness and answered his questions understanding he was there only to complete a required task. He didn't wish to offend her in any manner and allowed her to leave hoping one day they would meet again. He did see her many times afterwards, but she never saw him. He painted her from a distance and wrote pages in his journals about her soft skin and welcoming eyes. He idolized her, and she was the only person in the world he had ever felt any emotion for.

I wish I had told you.

He left a solitary red rose on the checkered blanket that covered her sick body and kissed the frail woman on the forehead.

I love you Tania, he whispered.

Valeri Markov stood and left the hospital. Moments later, while sitting on a bench outside the front entrance, he cried. He could not recall the last time he cried or if he had ever felt his own tears on his face. He was truly alone in this world. It should have been the other sister lying in that hospital bed. For some odd reason he could not remember the woman's name but she would pay dearly for his heartache.

If he had waited an hour, he would have had that chance.

September 1992

Lena passed out somewhere around midnight but I wasn't as fortunate. My day had been topsy-turvy to say the least, and I was relieved that it ended on a good note. If I had my way, we would have been on the first flight out of Kiev the next morning but obviously that wasn't going to happen. I thought it might be a good idea to email my mother and let her know I was going to marry the girl of my dreams so I got out of bed quietly, hoping not to wake Lena.

Boris was still in the living room, spread out on his lounger.

"You're still awake," I said casually, while grabbing a beer from the fridge.

"Who could sleep with the noise coming out of your room? Make sure you clean the sheets tomorrow. I'm not kidding, I'm not touching them."

I sat on the couch next to him and grinned. "We're getting married. You're the first to know."

Boris nodded several times. "And all it took was a slap across the face. Most couples just kiss but if that's your version of foreplay, then who am I to judge."

"Thanks for the congratulations," I sneered.

Boris waved me off with a quick hand gesture. "Congratulations. You make it sound like it's a big surprise. I knew it before I met you but good, it's done and you can now dive into marriage misery. You realize, of course, that we are officially, family. You and me… family."

"My short lived happiness is now ruined."

Boris nodded causally. "Yah, well an American in the family would have been pretty cool. A Canadian… it's like cold soup on a cold day. Good for my hunger but my feet are still freezing."

"Are you done?" I asked.

"I could probably go on," he said while chuckling at his own humor.

I took a sip of beer and placed the bottle on the glass table in front of me. "Boris, I've been wondering about Mila's political aspirations. You mentioned something to that nature in the van and it stuck in my head."

"You can't take a break from your questions? My cousin just offered her life to you and you're wondering about her mother. "

"Hey," I continued, "It's you and your friends that insist I tell the whole story. Based on what I've been told, I may be in a morgue this time tomorrow."

Boris sighed. "Stop talking nonsense Aaron. This time next week you'll be back in your igloo cooking whale meat."

"Apparently, you're not finished."

"I never said I was," he said while rubbing his neck. "Mila, Mila, Mila. I love my cousin but at times I wish everyone would just forget her. If I could hug anyone in the world it would be her husband for taking Mila to Canada. Don't be looking at me funny for saying what I'm thinking either. You'll be remembering this moment five years from now once she's your mother-in-law."

"I thought she was an icon of sorts… someone to be admired."

"Oh yah, she is," Boris retorted. "That's the problem. Imagine being a family member of someone who's famous and

adored. No one wants to know about you. They wanna
know about your cousin. I dealt with this for years. It was fucking
tiresome."

"Boris?" I questioned.

"Oh fine… it had its benefits too but… people lost their
lives because of her. There is a very dear cost associated with
fame. We say we want it until we have it."

"What happened in 1992?" I asked.

"It snowed and then it rained, which was followed by a
bit of sun, then more rain and more snow. Same as last year."
Boris seemed pleased with his version of hilarity.

"Seriously?" I responded, less impressed

The big man yawned before speaking. "Didn't start in '92,
it started once she gave that speech the previous year. Word
spread about her take down of the old men's club of politicians in
Ukraine. You have to understand that Mila is a very open person.
Warm, passionate and way to astute for her own good. She can
read you before you even get a chance to say hello and if you
think you're winning a battle of wits against her, you're sadly
mistaken. She'll slice and dice you like a master chef.

Mila's Achilles heel is not her intelligence, it's her mouth.
Her mouth can get her in trouble while at the same time endear
her with thousands. In one day, she'll make a couple of enemies
while making a hundred new friends. It never computes in her
brain that those two enemies could be more powerful than twenty
thousand new friends. That, in a nutshell, is what happened. She
spoke her heart and in turn pissed off people that would
eventually break her heart."

"Can you elaborate? I asked.

"Can you get me a beer?" He replied quickly. "You were in the fridge and didn't even ask if I wanted one. I thought Canucks were supposed to be polite?"

I sighed, went to the fridge and brought back a beer. Boris smiled, showing his teeth.

"There's a beautiful woman in your bed and you're out here talking to me. Its ok, I understand. You're probably worried that your sled dogs are eating each other."

"Did you write a list of some sort? Give it a rest Boris," I answered.

"We're family now, I don't have to worry about what I say to you," he replied. "And yes, I wrote a list."

"We were talking about Mila."

"As always," he said. "Before that first speech, Tania was handed an envelope that she didn't bother opening until later that day. The samizdat characters were always keeping track of the two sisters and the envelope was from them. They claimed they were responsible for the letters sent to Chris Langley. They claimed they were responsible for Lena being dropped off at her grandparents when Simon was killed. He *was* killed, I have no doubt about this. I think it was Markov but grandfather would never confirm. Anyway, they made a bunch of claims and then asked if Mila would meet with them. I guess they thought that Mila owed them something, which was of course, wildly inaccurate. Keep in mind that the Soviet walls were crumbling everywhere and Ukraine was only months away from cutting ties with Russia. The samizdat was preparing for an entrance into politics and Mila was their golden ticket."

"And she told them to f-off?"

"At first yes," Boris answered. "The Russians did a shitty job at Chernobyl. The sarcophagus was flimsy and Mila was adamant with whoever would listen that it was still a hazard. Her focus was always on Reactor Four, it was what *you* Frenchies call her raison d'être. Promised payments to the Ukrainian and Belorussian liquidators were slow and there were whispers that they would stop altogether. There was no money. The banks were owned by the Mafia and the government was struggling to pay its employees. This incensed Mila and eventually it was the beginning of her platform into politics.

She decided to run for Mayor of Kiev, which is tiny compared to all the other shit that was happening but it was like a stepping stone. I know that Chris wasn't pleased about it but Mila promised she'd do it for a few years until her job was done. I was young and even I knew that was a long shot at best.

She flipped when she heard that medicine for the men and women who needed it was passing through the black market. As you already know, my grandfather made a fortune off this so you can imagine his first reaction when he saw Mila on television calling for an end to his moneymaker. She went overboard if you ask me. It's never a good idea to call the local police, "mafia prostitutes". And yes, that's exactly what she said. Man, she had people riled up but I gotta tell ya… she had a huge following. She had foreign investors from Europe and America backing her, which was unheard of in Kiev. I guess they figured her mayoral candidacy would turn into a national platform. And that song… man, they played that song so often that I began to hate it."

"I haven't heard it yet," I interrupted.

"Whatever," Boris said, wanting to change the subject. "I was eleven when this part of the Kharmalov saga took place. I had

429

a crush on Tatiana Kristhov but she liked Igor. Fucker. So instead of cuddle time with Tatiana, I spent a lot of time with Mila because we were both learning English. She was better than me because she had a love incentive in upper America."

"Still not done…" I sighed.

Boris continued as if I didn't interrupt. "My incentive was money from my grandfather, which was never enough. He spent more money on his fluff bunny than his own grandson but disappointing this man was never an option so every day after school, I studied. Mila spent the days at home and left only to pick up Lena from school. Tania found work in a government office but was let go when Mila became more and more outgoing. Tania wasn't angry. In fact, she was relieved to be out of the spotlight.

After six p.m., Mila became candidate Mila. She talked at schools, on the radio, in train stations of all places and of course, on the street. She was invited to dinner several times a week. It was craziness, and we knew she was going to win. We had army soldiers outside our apartment just in case one of Mila's enemies got over enthusiastic. Had to be soldiers because the cops weren't gonna protect her.

The election was slated for the end of September. The present mayor was packing his stuff, and that's no word of a lie. He was expecting to be slaughtered in the polls. He told a journalist that if he was still in the office following the elections it would be to deliver mail to the staff."

Boris stopped speaking and downed the last of his beer. "You know, our authority figures dictate how our lives will turn out. There are those that shake it off but they are the few. Uncle Anton played soccer with me. I realize it was difficult for him to do because he would have preferred obviously to be playing with

430

his son but he made the effort to be a friend. My dad never played sports. He sat on the couch and watched television. Uncle Anton was very different. He liked being outside… he needed to be outside. That day… his final day, I told him I was going to tag along and get the newspaper with him. I wanted to cry. I wanted to whisper in his ear to run away and never come back. I knew the consequences. It was him or me. When we took the elevator down, I told him I loved him. I told him he was best uncle ever."

Boris grabbed the hair from the back of his head and gently tugged. "We walked maybe thirty feet after we left the apartment and the short, masked gunman was waiting. Three shots… no mistakes. Uncle Anton fell to the ground with his hand still in mine. I was still holding his hand when my mom and Mila rushed outside. Aunt Tatiana died three years later. I was never told how or why. She was never the same after that day. Uncle Anton was everything to her. I took her man and her life away from her. In a way, I think I killed my aunt too."

He stopped talking. I think that day has been relived several times and is probably one of the reasons he drank so much.

"Sorry bud and I'm not proud to ask this but what happened with Mila? Did she quit that day?"

Boris stared straight ahead and did not look at me. "She thought of it and she had nasty words to say after the funeral but she went to another event a week later. She quit a few days after that."

"I don't understand."

"Mila received a letter. It said the next victim would be Lena."

"Whoa," I uttered.

431

"It was from my grandfather," Boris ended.

The Doctor's Dilemma

"Mama!" Lena shouted far too loudly.

She rushed to the woman sitting next to Tania. Unexpected as it was, this was a big moment for me but I could barely see the infamous Mila Kharmalov as she was still sitting when Lena embraced her.

And then she stood to greet me.

I am not ashamed to say that I was nervous to meet the tall, slim woman but I am a bit embarrassed to admit that I gawked at my girlfriend's mother. Still, let's be fair. I had heard many stories in the last few days about this dark-haired beauty but they were older stories dating back two decades. Mila Kharmalov was probably pushing fifty by now. She wore black jeans, which I guess was no big surprise yet even at mid-age they fit her perfectly. She was more than beautiful. Lena is a stunning woman but her mother is a goddess. Her eyes… my God, her eyes are entrancing. I could not tear my gaze away from this spectacular woman.

I stuttered. Yah, you heard me right, I stuttered. It wouldn't matter if you're a man or a woman. When you see Mila Kharmalov, I guarantee you'll be doing a double take. I have never seen a more splendid human being in my entire life and it took every ounce of concentration I had to lower my eyes, regain my composure and say hello like a normal person. Tania noticed my awkwardness, she didn't miss a beat and I think she was trying hard not to laugh. This was doubtless something she had experienced a thousand times.

"So, I finally meet Aaron," Mila said, looking me over. "I have heard hours of good and bad conversation surrounding you. More good than bad if that's important to you."

"Well yah, it's kind of significant," I replied sheepishly.

She was only a couple of inches shorter than me and to be straightforward, the lady was intimidating. Aside from the obvious appeal and liquid blue eyes, she oozed confidence. It was then I realized that the stories were true and nothing was embellished. I knew in that instant that I was standing in front of a hero. I'm pushing six feet two inches and I felt small and mediocre next to Mila. She might as well have been wearing a t-shirt with a big *S* on it. Oh and since I am a man, I do want to mention that she was wearing a black t-shirt that fit very, very well on her slim torso. Incredibly well.

Mila hugged me and casually whispered in my ear. "She's in love with you. Don't doubt it for a second."

"Thank-you," I whispered back. She let go of me and I exhaled. "I am entirely honored to meet you."

"You say that now," she chuckled. "Give it a couple of days."

"A couple of hours," Lena giggled.

I brought a second chair for Lena to sit on and my act was met with compliments from the two sisters.

"Is there anything special you wish to talk about Aaron?" Mila asked while tenderly grasping her sister's hand.

There were questions I wanted answered and Mila was the best one to solicit a response from. I didn't waste any time and went for the direct approach.

"Galina… what else can you tell me about her? I know you met with her and I gathered that she was hung soon after."

Mila nodded and glanced at her daughter. "Yes, the poor child was murdered by the peasants who had yet to leave that awful village. She was just a wisp of a girl who had no clue what she was doing and why she was doing it, other than to appease her grandmother. There was this Major who was very fond of Yuri and felt that he owed him and our family a great deal."

"Asimov," I interrupted to let Mila know we had touched on his part in this story.

"Yes, Major Asimov. We hear stories about the Russian military and they are always depicted as cold robots. This is a western invention and very untrue and Asimov was proof. I relayed my information to him and he sent men to Kopachi. They found Galina swaying on the same tree her mother hung from. The villagers swore up and down that they had no part in her death and that they never visited the girl's home. The soldiers interrogated the best they could but not one of the villagers confessed. Eventually, the Major was led to believe that the murderer was Valeri Markov. Have you discussed this wretched scum bag yet?"

Lena and I both nodded.

"Yah well Markov has been a thorn in my side for two plus decades. From our house in Calgary, my husband and I have been researching as much as we could and it was not until recently that we have broken some ground so to speak. There is no doubt in my mind that Markov is responsible for murdering my first husband and his wife. The KGB passed it off as a murder suicide especially once they found photographs of Simon with a young man. I received a letter two weeks later with the words, "You're welcome but don't get comfortable." The letter was not signed, but I knew it was from Markov. Major Asimov tried to track him down and thought that he did when he read a death certificate indicating Markov had died in a car accident. The date of his death was a day before he murdered Simon. That told me that he had a deal with my ex and he had made mention of sort when he visited me in prison but it never struck me that he would be given a new identity. I, by no means, believed he was that smart, and this is what has been hurting my efforts for the last twenty years.

Let's get back to Galina for a minute because I've strayed. My brother wanted the grandmother to pay for what she put that child through. Given that Roman had little time to live, I wanted desperately to tell him that this horrible woman was arrested. With help from Major Asimov we found her in Moscow and subsequently put the bitch in jail. Needless to say, I made sure to visit the old woman and give her hell.

When I got there, I thought I would find someone deeply despondent or ashamed of her actions but that was not the case. She was chatty with her inmates, joking as if she believed she was untouchable. This pissed me off, so I decided to knock her down a few notches by publicly recounting everything I had heard from Roman and from what I too had seen. That hateful woman had left Galina alone to fend herself. Make no mistake Aaron, Galina was stupid. I'm sorry for the terminology but there is no other word to justly explain the girls mind. She was not right in the head and unless Roman or myself had gone back to get her, she was destined to starve or to be abused until she was killed. I mean, who does this to their own family?

The old woman's cellmates had no clue of the atrocities this woman had performed with her grandchild so the tables turned real quick on the wrinkled bitch. Her fellow inmates withdrew lightning quick and their eyes were filled with an instant hate. The grandmother yelled and tried to spit on me. I told her how sweet karma was and that she was soon to face the same fate her daughter and grandchild had faced. I had one of the guards take a photograph that I could take back to Roman.

Russian justice is not a drawn out court battle when the facts are in and Asimov made sure of that. I was in that jail house for two hours when the old woman was led outside. They didn't shoot her; normally they would have but not this time. It was if every cop and guard had no interest in a quick ending. They hung her by the neck so that the inmates could visualize what death was. It was the only time that I was proud to be Russian. I was asked if I wanted a photograph of the woman dangling in the wind and I declined. When you have seen the things that I have seen, memory does not fade as fast as a five by eight photo."

"An eye for an eye?" I quoted.

"No man," the woman responded. "A neck for a neck. There was no burden on taxpayers that day."

Mila Kharmalov was one tough bird. Maybe it was a good defense mechanism and considering what she has lived through I had to respect that her beliefs derived from these experiences. Still, I was grateful that Lena was less worn and still fairly innocent in comparison to her mother. Mila continued speaking, and I listened attentively to the ascents and descents in her tone. Her English was astonishingly good, and she later explained that her husband was invited to many dinner functions so she was forced to study long hours to converse with other guests. Lena mentioned later, that in time, many of the invites were from groups that wanted to meet her mother. I believed that.

"Valeri Markov was obsessed with my sister. I wouldn't call what he had for Tania as love because the man was or is incapable of emotion. I am speaking to you in English at the moment because I don't want my sister to understand what I'm about to say for obvious reasons. About ten years ago, I was home in Calgary doing some translations for a Russian corporate website. The doorbell rang and there was a courier with a very large package for me. I thought Chris had bought me something as a surprise. I opened it to find a painting of my sister outside her home in the Exclusion Zone. It was an exquisite, extremely intricate painting and I won't deny this but it freaked me out. I searched for a name or something that would tell me who the artist was but I couldn't find a signature. In the back of my head I was thinking it was Markov, which was worrisome because it meant he knew where Tania was staying and he also knew where I lived. Days passed and neither Christopher nor I could find any hints until I stared closely at two birds in the upper left hand side of the canvas. They were totally out of place among the scheme of the artwork. One was flying with wings up around its head at a forty-five degree angle and the other with it both its wings and feet down. It was peculiar to see a bird flying with its feet hanging like it was standing in mid-air and this was the tip-off I was searching for. His initials were right there. V and M. That bastard knew where I lived.

He would never hurt Tania, so I wasn't worried about her. It was me he detested, and he had made it clear, face to face, and with threatening letters, that I would be his greatest conquest. To be honest, I didn't know why he hated me so much but his letters to me were so barbaric that I had to forward them to the police. He wrote about the torture I would endure and my inevitable ending. Even more strange, he would add these quotes from someone else's memoirs and mention that he had learned from the best. The quotes were horrific, but I was smart enough to keep his letters and this allowed me to do reopen my investigation with Christopher's help, and most importantly, with Major Asimov's help."

"You lost me there Mila," I said with a questioning face.

"I received another painting six months ago. This one was not lovely like the first but instead morbid. Lena was standing in front of five headstones. One each for mama, papa, Roman, Tania… and me. Tania's plot was adorned with dozens of roses and hand angel wings on the side. Mine had a severed head on top of the headstone. It was my head."

"Oh mama," Lena blurted.

"Christopher burned the painting in our fireplace and I decided to put an end to this charade. I called Major Asimov who is still alive and vibrant and asked him to trace the package. He was more than happy to do this for me and did so very quickly. The package came from Moscow so he went to the postal office from where it was sent and started asking questions. A clerk remembered who brought it but only because the man was easy to remember. He was short with a long scar on his left cheek. He was introduced to me as Chipmunk but his real name is Stani Pilov and he is Markov's friend.

"Ok, that's creepy," I added.

"Sure it's creepy, but it was a huge lead that would soon pay dividends or at least put us on the right track. Asimov was happy to be doing something other than playing chess with buddies in the park so he dived into his own investigation. Pilov was working in an admin position for a government dairy department and the Police had him arrested. Initially he claimed that Asimov had the wrong guy but bit by bit his association with Markov started to show up in registries and data bases. They worked together in the same academy that Alex had studied at before the Reactor Four explosion. Then of course, the prison records proved they knew each other. They had cornered like a scared cat and he sang like the canary the same cat was trying to swallow. Firstly, it was Pilov that mailed the packages. He did the research to find me. Asimov was out of breath when he recounted how the tiny man went on for hours detailing Markov's psycho rampage. It was horribly gruesome."

Mila switched to Russian at this point to appease Tania. The subject had turned away from anything that would disturb her sister. Lena, as always, translated as best she could.

"There were many kidnappings of young girls who fit my description or who were anti-communist. Pilov emphasized that Markov claimed to be a staunch believer in both religion and communism and that he had a mission to educate the world on the benefits of a blended society. If we found his notes there would be enough evidence to put him away forever while at the same time, allow the parents of these missing girls to grieve appropriately.

As has been the case since day one of trying to find info on this killer, there was a problem. Pilov had no idea where Markov lived. Asimov found this difficult to believe but Pilov reiterated that he had told the officers everything he knew and that he himself was terrified of Markov. If he had any hint of where the madman was residing he would drive the cops there as a public service."

"Also," I added, "According to Russian records, Markov was dead."

"Exactly," Mila exclaimed. "Very good, Aaron. When Asimov told Pilov about the car accident the man had no clue what the Major was talking about thus leaving everyone in the room confounded. Markov always sought out Pilov; it was never the other way around. Fearing that he would be left with a dead end, Asimov called a few people to find the death certificate and locate the coroner that signed it. There was no such person; the certificate was falsified by my ex-husband."

I wondered why the police weren't involved. "So now you have no address and no name. The cops could circulate a photograph."

"Sure they could, if we had a photo and Pilov had a suspicion that Markov was in Ukraine. I think he gave the cops a description but not much was done with it."

"What is this obsession he has with you?" I asked. "Other than the information you have on his exploits in Kopachi, it makes no sense."

"Well, that would be sufficient I think to any psychopath but yah, there is more, and it was Pilov who explained it in more detail. Markov sees me as a threat on many levels and as the person who stole the spotlight from Tania. In his eyes, it was Tania who was the true Chernobyl angel, and I was instead the red-eyed monster from the forest."

"And how were you a threat?"

"There were several things he despised about me. I publicly denounced communism, and I spoke against nuclear energy as well as the Kremlin. I wear clothes that are deemed very western-like but most of all, I did not adhere to the persona or image of the atypical Soviet woman. This drove Markov nuts as we say in Canada. In his eyes, I was the undoing of his ideal blended society. I was too much of a feminist and he believes that it is because of me that many of today's Russian women are boisterous or too opinionated. If I was taught a lesson then maybe his image of life would return to normal. Aaron… I'll try to put this in words we can agree to. When your space of comfort is so tiny there's no room for a variance of opinion. The best example I can give you would be someone in your town or in Toronto. It is so multicultural yet you take it for granted. You walk the streets of downtown Toronto and you're going to pass Whites, Blacks, Asians and Indians. It doesn't faze you; they are part of your life at work and play. They're your friends, family or even rivals. Lena is Russian yet she is your best friend. This is because your comfort zone is large. Men and women of different races intermarry because they have grown comfortable within this extended zone."

I nodded to signify my agreement.

"Ok, so you understand my description of comfort zone. When you're dealing with a psychopath, you're dealing with someone in a miniscule zone. They are only comfortable in their environment and thus prone to delusions. They're social misfits and suspicious of absolutely everyone. I invaded Markov's zone with my letters and speeches. He could have centered his attention on thousands of other people just like me but it was my association with Tania that reined his spite. My sister could do no wrong and I was everything wrong. Tania's the angel and I'm the devil. The devil was invading his comfort zone therefore the devil had to be eliminated."

"Wow," I interrupted. "Surely, after all this time his hate would have diminished."

"For you and me it would because we are accepting of societal changes. Markov is not as accepting and only wishes to live in the Soviet Union of years gone by. Every time he notices a societal shift it enrages him and his brain converts this into something that he believes I inadvertently created."

I then said something that made Lena wince but I had to voice what was on my mind at that moment.

"Mila, is it safe for you to be here?"

"I doubt Markov knows the coming and going of travelers."

"Well, I've been informed Lena has been followed since she arrived."

I wished I had said that in private to Mila but my loose tongue is nothing if not a good rabble rouser.

"Oh really," Lena immediately replied, perking up on her chair. "And how do you know this? Never mind, I know how."

"Relax children," Mila said with her hand in the air. "With my husband's help I bought a ticket two weeks ago. Lena, I never told you this but I need special permission to enter Ukraine because of the time I spent in prison. I am considered a threat to political stability or something like that. You're being followed by government lackeys not Markov."

"Mama, I was worried."

"I'm sorry darling, I never considered my child would be tailed but maybe it's a good thing just in case Markov has longer arms than we imagined. I'm here to see my sister and not to reignite a dead passion. So the answer to your question Aaron is yes, I believe I'm safe here. I do not wish to be anywhere else at this moment."

For the first time since she arrived I thought of what Boris spoke of yesterday. Maybe he exaggerated. I decided to forget that nonsense and concentrate on the radiant woman in front of me.

"Other than what Pilov said, do you know anything about Markov's life history?"

"He grew up in Kopachi with a brother, a domineering mother and an unhappy father. They're all dead except Markov."

"Maybe he took his brother's name," I blurted.

Mila stared back at me with a blank face. I wanted to look away because I couldn't gauge whether she was mad at me for saying something so obvious or mad for not thinking of it. It was the latter. She reached into her purse and took out a cell phone before leaving the hospital room.

"Did I piss her off?" I asked Lena.

My girlfriend shook her head. "I think you gave her an idea. She gets like that. Forgets everyone else and then leaves. It's not her best character trait." Lena turned away from me and explained to Tania what had just occurred.

I twiddled my thumbs for a few minutes until Mila returned. She patted me on the shoulder as she walked by.

"I called Major Asimov. He'll get back to me as soon as he can. I am ashamed to say that neither of us considered Olav. That son of a bitch may be collecting a pension off his dead brother. I've got to give him credit, he certainly is resourceful."

"Ok, well that's hopeful," I added. "It would be cool to end years of looking over your shoulder especially if it happens while you're here."

Tania poked her sister to get her attention and said a few words that made Mila grimace.

"You went to Pripyat yesterday?" Mila questioned. "Are you intentionally stupid or just stupid?"

I sighed loudly. "I received my scolding yesterday, thank-you very much."

Mila nodded. "Good, don't do it again or the next scolding will be from me."

"Really, and this is what I have to look forward to? You're not making it enticing... just so you know. On that note, there is something I want Tania to see, and *it* was the number one reason I visited Chernobyl."

I stood and handed Tania the photo of the tree I took yesterday. The look on her face made my adventure and the subsequent yelling well worth the time. It seemed like an eternity before her eyes veered away from the photo towards me.

"You're a delightful man. I have no words to thank-you for what you have done."

I walked a few steps and kissed Tania on the forehead. "Tell her please that I am entirely grateful for the time she has given me and I am incredibly proud to be sitting in this room with her."

Lena did as I asked while I checked my watch. Perfect timing on my part.

"I have one more surprise for you, Tania."

I told the three ladies I would be back soon and left the room.

Outside, next to the reception and waiting for me were Boris, Evgeni and my special guest, Boris's mother, Vera. She was a bit on the heavy side but her eyes were vibrant and the smile on her face was inviting. Her hair was entirely silver and cut short thus making her round face more pronounced.

"Aaron," Boris began, "This is my mother."

I shook her hand and then followed that with a peck on both her cheeks.

"Leave my mother alone pervert," Boris said with a silly grin.

"Yah… I'm the pervert," I answered sarcastically while rolling my eyes. "Come on; let's make a dying woman happy."

I had a good conversation with Boris after our Mila discussion. He told me point blank that it was Tania who believed she was responsible for Georgie's early demise. If she had arranged her wedding a week earlier or a week later, Georgie would still be with us today. Boris always felt that was nonsense and when Vera found out she made sure to take an early train from her new home in Odessa to see her sister-in-law. In Boris's own words, Vera could never forgive herself if she did not spend some time with Tania before she passed. I did not tell any of the three that Mila was also inside so the surprise caused an outpouring of emotion. I had managed to endear myself with the Kharmalov family just by doing what came naturally.

For the most part anyway.

Five minutes into the reunion, Boris pushed me outside the room.

"This is not good."

"Boris," I said wishing to placate him. "Maybe you're exaggerating our situation. Just tell the Doctor there's no reason to worry."

He said something in Ukrainian and I asked him to translate.

446

"The wind does not take requests," he said. "It blows in the direction it started from."

Charting My Map

I should sidetrack here for a quick minute. On the way back from the hospital, I was in a taxi with Mila and Vera. I let Mila know I was going to marry her daughter. She pecked me on the cheek and said thanks for the warning but she knew this a couple of years ago.

I wanted to have dinner at a nice restaurant but Boris pulled me aside and informed me Mila was still very recognizable and thus my suggestion, albeit thoughtful, was basically not a good one for a myriad of reasons. I watched my future mother-in-law closely throughout the night, not because of her good looks but because I noticed a fatigue or an exasperation of sort. She sat very closely with Lena, hugging her or holding her hand. At first I put this down to a mother missing her daughter but then I thought maybe there was more to her affection. Maybe Mila herself was suffering from some affliction? Or maybe she knew that her presence in this apartment was dangerous to all.

We were now five people sleeping in the large apartment and I found myself sleeping on a couch as Mila took my spot in Lena's bed. Vera and Boris had their own rooms. I wasn't complaining, the long couch was extremely comfortable. Unfortunately, on the day after Lena confessed her love for me, I was sleeping in the living room. Maybe that was an omen for years to come. At midnight I was left alone as everyone shuffled off to sleep. I had my laptop out and was surfing through YouTube for good videos on Fukushima. It was my first opportunity since yesterday's trip to Pripyat to do research and surprisingly, I was wide awake. My solitude did not last long

448

when Mila soon joined me. She wore the same t-shirt but her black jeans had been replaced by a pair of sweat pants. She still looked good, which is hard to pull off in baggy cotton pants.

"Do you love my daughter, Aaron?"

I looked back at her and a strange sound came out of my mouth. I think I spat out a few droplets and wiped my mouth just in case.

"Yes, of course I do," I answered. "I'm not gonna marry someone I'm not in love with."

Mila nodded a few times and studied me like a mother bear for a few seconds. "After a few dinners with Christopher, I knew he was the man I had been waiting for. We needed a translator for a good year but being with him and listening to his enthusiasm for life I was… for lack of a better word, mesmerized. I made sure to study English every day for three years until we finally married. The Internet was not in full bloom so we wrote letters and again with the help of translator, he called twice a week. I think one of the reasons I studied English so diligently was that I wanted to express my intimate feelings to him without anyone else in the same room. I was a mother with a child yet around him, I was a schoolgirl all over again. My heart would beat like crazy for days before his visits to Kiev. When I watched his plane land on the runway I was so nervous I feared I would faint."

"I don't worry about fainting when I'm about to meet with Lena but I think I would die inside if I knew I wouldn't be seeing her again."

"Are you saying she fills a void?" Mila questioned.

I shook my head wondering if Mila was trying to ply something out of me that didn't exist.

"There is no void that I know of. The void would appear if your daughter left me. Listen, I get the protective questions and I accept they have to be asked but you can relax. I've been crazy in love with Lena for three years. Let's also acknowledge that I have been the one who has never had any problem demonstrating my affection. My heart has belonged to Lena since the day I met her and she is well aware of this."

Mila smiled and I think I caught a second of her chuckling to herself but wasn't sure. "Fucking Kharmalov women... eh?"

"Damn straight," I answered. We both grinned simultaneously.

She asked what I was doing before she sat and nodded when I replied.

"I have probably seen many of the same videos you are about to watch," Mila commented. "I'm glad you're taking the initiative but just don't get caught up in websites that sell conspiracy for hits. In your book it would be helpful if you could tie the disastrous long term effects of this reactor accident to Lindsay Lohan's lesbian adventures."

"Excuse me?" I said before laughing out loud.

"It is the only way to get media coverage or to make the average reader give a shit," she replied.

"Evgeni and Igor gave me the rundown on Fukushima yesterday but I am not following you. Can you explain?" I requested.

Mila rubbed her eyes and then stretched out on Boris's lounger. I was forbidden to sit there but I he wouldn't dare tell Mila to move her butt elsewhere.

"I'm not a tyrant Aaron," she began. "I'm not the super strong ultra-feminist so many believe me to be or hope I am. I

adore the quiet life I have in Calgary. Chris and I have two dogs
that I walk for two hours every day except when it's too
freaking cold. I watch hockey occasionally but rarely watch
anything else other than escapist movies and headline news. It's a
normal life and I would not trade it for the world. That being said,
I still have my rebel tendencies and spend a lot of time blogging
anonymously. The newscasts in Canada are biased based on what
media giant owns the station so I make sure to watch more than
one. Fukushima was broadcast every night for three weeks
because of the severity of the problem and we were drawn to our
TV sets fully comprehending the danger if the fire was not
contained. Then… it disappeared as if everything was back to
normal. General Electric exhaled a big breath of relief and began
preparations for new nuclear power plants. I find that… so sad.
GE wiped their hands and were exonerated of any wrongdoing.
What is even more striking or pitiful or downright distressing is
that we, the people that are being affected, will continue to die for
decades to come from this fallout and we have seemingly
forgotten. It's Chernobyl all over again but twice as bad."

"You know this for sure?"

"Oh Aaron, there's no doubt. Thyroid rates will be over
the top in Japan *and* in California. Cancer rates will soar but the
IAEA will find other reasons for it. For me personally, I feel like I
am reliving to a lesser extent, what I experienced with Chernobyl.
You know, for years the media blamed cancer on the industrial
revolution and chemicals. The corporate world never factored in
nuclear debris or secret isotope emissions but there's no way to
hide it now. That's fine and dandy but our most unsettling
problem is that mainstream media is more concerned with what is
new and fascinating and what their sponsors are interested in.

451

That's why I mentioned Lindsay Lohan. I shake my head when I listen to the radio in the morning and the announcers are jabbering nonstop about celebrities. Give it a fucking rest. You know what I'd like to see? I'd really be impressed to see a celebrity with balls who isn't concerned of being blacklisted. Even if you're a mega handsome movie star, if you look at a picture of a fish washed up on your shoreline with two thousand times the norm of radiation... it must worry the shit out of you. If one-third of your children are being diagnosed with thyroid cancer then maybe it's time to veer off the path of being the lamb and maybe become the tiger instead. But the producers have sponsors and if you want a job in La-La land you have to appease the producers. General Electric is a big sponsor by the way. I think every American should be required to own a Geiger counter and to take a mandatory trip to the Columbia River. For us in Canada, just whip out a Geiger after a rainstorm. That'll scare the crap out of everyone and maybe we'll march en masse with the Yanks afterwards."

"Like the Occupy Movement," I added.

"I actually liked that until self-serving assholes took over. They were right you know… the original protesters I mean. I don't have a full time job so I spend my free hours studying everything I can about the corporate world and corporate injustices. I sometimes wonder if unemployment numbers or unemployment itself is skewed so corporations can continue to screw the peasants. *We need you so I'll bend over. It's okay if you poison my children as long as I can feed them.*"

Mila stopped speaking and closed her eyes for a few seconds. I couldn't help but think that very few people in this world had ever shared quiet introspective moments with this icon and I was now one of them.

"My sister Tania was incredibly beautiful when she was younger. There was purity about her… like a shiny uncut diamond. I stared at her today wondering why she succumbed to cancer while I haven't suffered anything, not even an insignificant lump. The only difference I could think of was that she drank a lot of milk and I wouldn't touch the stuff. Mama would try to force it into me but I wouldn't budge. I hated the taste but didn't know much else about what the rest of my family was drinking. Do you drink a lot of milk Aaron?"

"I wouldn't say a lot but sure."

I would listen to her argument but as always, form my own opinion. Even legends don't have all the correct answers.

"It's kind of hard to ignore the "Got Milk" commercials and not want to make your bones stronger. So let me throw out the following and then you can tell me if you'll continue to drink what I call the white liquid toxin. In 1970, the average cow was good for seven thousand liters a year. Nowadays, with growth hormones, each cow gives us nineteen thousand liters. You realize of course that most of us can't really digest milk properly. I don't mean just those that are lactose intolerant, I mean all of us. The enzymes in animal milk are not compatible with our digestive system. Scientists have known this for years but if we were to suddenly stop consumption then millions would be out of work and thousands of politicians would lose lobbyist kickbacks." Mila chuckled for an odd reason. "Milk is good for your teeth, we're told. You wanna know how to save your teeth? Stop eating sugar you freaking idiots. Then of course, that would be another goldmine down the tubes. And, let's not forget the milk we're drinking has a good chance of being irradiated to a degree. Do you see where I'm going with this, Aaron? If we got rid of what was killing us we would all be unemployed. The government agencies and more importantly the corporations, have us by the short hairs. I like to call it Corporate Communism or the Corporate Collective. I was saved from the remnants of the Soviet era only to be dropped into a different version of collectivism. It goes to show you that more often than not, the grass is never greener on the other side."

"You are not freer in Canada?"

"Oh yes - yada, yada as we now say. We're free until someone doesn't like what we're saying and then the government checks you out or someone else is free to put a bullet in your head. It's all relevant, Aaron. Is our life better in general? Yes, most definitely but for how long? What's totally inane is if I could sit with Valeri Markov again just for five minutes, I would actually listen to his ideas."

"That's... *interesting*," I said with a high level of curiosity.

I wasn't sure how a mass murderer could be someone with promising input.

Mila's eyebrows rose for a moment and she pushed upward on the lounger arms to sit more comfortably.

"About a week ago I had a very vivid dream that I don't think I'll ever forget. You only have a few of these in your lifetime and this was one of them for me. It was Sunday dinner in Pripyat and everyone was there except Lena. *Thank God*. Yuri, Vera, Georgie and my family. I think even Simon was visiting but for some reason or another, I am not certain. They were all chatting and laughing like we always did but I was the quiet one, which I guess you have determined is never the case. *It was a*

454

dream after all. Mama came out of the kitchen with a large silver tray. The lid was polished so the light from the lamp that hung over our kitchen table reflected off it. It was kind of nice. She lifted the lid and there in the center with garnishes surrounding, was a huge black rotted catfish with worms crawling out of it. I gasped but no one noticed, they just continued their discussions. I looked at my father and when he smiled at me his face turned grey and his cheeks began to invert into is face like a sinkhole. The same was happening to everyone else but they kept on talking. I was yelling something, I can't remember what and suddenly my chair lifted off the ground and I was being transported backwards. I called out to my family but no one heard me. The chair swiveled one hundred and eighty degrees and I saw Valeri Markov in the distance with his arms reaching out towards me. He wasn't laughing or grimacing. His face was welcoming as if he was waiting there to save me. I wanted to jump off but there was no ground below. I was trapped.

And then I woke up."

She didn't speak, and I figured she was waiting for me to say anything. "And the hidden meaning was…?"

"It was just a fucking dream?" Mila replied and then chuckled. "Sure, I thought about it but I also know a lot had to do with the painting he sent and the memories that flooded back because of it. Markov believes or at least I think he believes that Russia could be stronger the way it was but with a few tweaks. I would have to agree with him but only because of the great inequalities I see in our capitalist society. Don't get me wrong Aaron, it's nice to be living in a big home with a loving husband who dotes on me… but we are more privileged than many who live only minutes away. From what Pilov explained, Markov went off the deep end when he saw how well we lived in Pripyat. He was always different as per Pilov and a trained psychopath but seeing the wealth with his own eyes was a defining moment. I hear stuff like this Aaron… and I correlate it to the crime and tensions that exist in our communities. How many potential Valeri Markov's do we have next door to us or down the street or teaching our children? I think each of us is one disaster away from crossing a line from sane to temporarily or forever insane. To this day I can't help but wonder what would have become of me if I did not have Tania or Lena to keep my feet grounded."

Mila got up and walked to the refrigerator. She took out a juice box and returned to the lounger.

"Pilov said that Markov spoke often of a woman he met in a Ukrainian village and how she went from nothing to total control of a population only to have it slip away because of her greed and lust for power. She was his example of why a capitalist society promoted the innermost worse in people. As far as he was concerned, Chernobyl was a result of this greed and God showered his anger upon us. As he told Pilov, Chernobyl was the Seven Sins en masse. I think he saw pieces of this woman in me. If I could sit with him now, I would tell him straight out that I understand his viewpoint… but I would tell him we should not be afraid of the government. The government should be afraid of us. That being said, the man is a psychopath who lives in his own tiny world so he probably wouldn't listen to anything I said."

"Do you think Mila that your viewpoints are merely reflections of your experiences in the Soviet Union."

"Well of course they are but let me ask you this. How many people are dead or will die because of Fukushima?"

I shrugged.

456

"You don't know because no one will tell you. The Japanese government is tight lipped and in denial. I would safely say this is the same tactic the Kremlin used with Chernobyl but at least those guys had the audacity to publicly lie. In the west, it's a closely guarded secret for the sake of the almighty dollar. *Screw the health of Japanese and California children…reopen those plants.*

Why is cancer so prevalent in western countries? Do you think it's because of cigarettes? No, not even remotely accurate. As I said earlier, it's chemicals and isotopes. We sued the bejesus out of the tobacco companies but has General Electric been sued for Fukushima? How about all those chemical corporations that continue to blow smoke into our sky… have they been sued? No they haven't. Each one of these companies and western governments are fully aware they are intentionally poisoning us but they keep winning contracts and licenses to build more nuclear plants and pipelines and what not. I wish we would all wake up and fight back and be angry. It's no different for me then it was when I was writing letters to the samizdat. In fact, it is exactly the same. We don't live in a democratic society Aaron, not even close and I apologize in advance if this offends you. We live in a corporate society or even a plutocracy. In so many ways we are too similar to the former Soviet Union."

This wasn't an off-the-cuff comment that Mila grabbed out of a hat. It was obvious she had thought of this long before she had verbalized it but the mere fact she had spent so many hours researching made me think about my own positions in life.

I had none.

I wrote autobiographies for some lovely people and for others who I found to be vain and shallow. Some of these clients had lived interesting lives but nothing in comparison to the

457

Kharmalov sisters or even Lena. I pondered if any of my clients could have survived what Mila and Tania endured and if their views on life itself would be as encompassing as the views shared by my future mother-in-law. Before meeting my girlfriend's family, I never delved into anything outside my safety zone. I was in what we call uncharted waters but by being here in Ukraine, I was unknowingly mapping my own destiny. I couldn't help but consider that hearing so many stories firsthand was leading me on the same path followed by the Kharmalov sisters.

"What's the alternative Mila?" I asked.

Mila slid out of the lounger and kissed me on the forehead. "You're the writer... you tell me."

She returned to the bed I was supposed to be sleeping in. I'm the writer... *so what*? Other people tell me what to write. I had no clue what the alternative was.

Maybe it was on my map.

The Second Midnight Visitor

The nurses at the reception desk were told not to stare at the late night visitor. He was a Ukrainian hero and deserved the highest level of respect. He arrived at midnight wearing sunglasses and a hoodie that covered most of his face. He said his name and the three nurses stood to welcome him as if honored by his presence. He was then led to Tania's room. A wall light was lit above the bed. He didn't recognize her.

Twenty-seven years had passed since the last time they spoke. Tania was worried that Yuri would miss their wedding. He told her not to worry. She could have had a huge ceremony if he had not been so naïve with Asimov. If he had said no to the Colonels request, Yuri would still be alive. Tania didn't know this part of the story. She didn't know the love of her life agreed to dive into the radiated water to protect his best friend.

It was his fault.

Samizdat adored the sisters but the government-owned newspapers wrote horrible articles about them. He plowed their path and never admitted so. Tania disappeared into obscurity, visited only by curious weekend thrill seekers. She has no hair and her skin is yellow.

It was his fault.

Alex pulled a chair next to the bed and touched her hand. She groaned but her eyes remained closed.

"I don't know where to begin. I'm hoping you don't open your eyes to see me speak. To watch the hurt in your eyes would be more painful than the burns on my face. I abandoned you Tania. I abandoned you to hide from life…and to

459

hide from you. My memories of the days before the explosion are what allow me to wake each morning. They are my life force and I owe this to you and Yuri. Without the two of you, I would have been a lonely man with few true friends.

And I still abandoned you. "

"I thought you were dead," Tania whispered.

A startled Alex let go of her hand and almost tumbled off his chair. "I've awoken you," he said between excited breaths.

"If I remember correctly, it's not the first time. Am I dreaming Alex?"

"No my friend," he replied. "It's me next to you."

Tania rubbed her eyes attempting to see her friend better. "Why are you covering your face?"

Alex tugged on the top of his hoodie and lowered his head. He dared not remove his sunglasses fearing he would startle Tania. A patient on the other side of the room exhaled a long painful groan. This was followed by a seemingly chorused shuffling by the other patients. He closed his eyes. Everywhere he visited, there was suffering. It followed him like a shadow. Tania repeated her question.

"The left side of my face including my eye is scarred from radiation. In situations such as this, I am more comfortable not revealing my deformity. Please don't ask me to do so."

"And I look better?" Tania replied with a short snort. "I won't ask you to do what you don't want Alex. You were always a stubborn man anyway." She paused. "I wish you had come see me many years ago but I'm thrilled to have you here."

"I've wanted to sit with you for a long time," Alex responded.

"Then why didn't you?" Tania asked between short breaths. "Why do you choose now when my last breath is so near? Alex, we mourned your death. Your mother was heartbroken. I visited her little hut in the Exclusion Zone and it was a memoriam. Photos of you adorned every inch on every wall. Asimov gave her a medal from the Kremlin in your memory that was front and centre above the main room couch. She picked flowers and left them on your gravesite every day. She cried for years and died alone." Tania inhaled a long breath. "I always wondered why your body was not entombed at Mitino."

A full cup of water lay on the bed table and Alex handed it to his friend. She raised herself and sat upright. The sole light in the room warmed her bumpy, hairless scalp.

"They told me I saved the Soviet Union," Alex whispered. "They told me I saved Europe. I was a hero in so many eyes…" His voice trailed for a few seconds and he continued. "I didn't feel like a hero. The guilt was too heavy to endure. I ruined your life."

"My life was not yours to ruin. You're obviously here to say your peace so take a deep breath and tell me what has encumbered you all these years." Tania stroked his hand with her fingertips. "Don't fear judgment my old friend, it is not mine to deliver."

Alex contemplated removing his sunglasses but did not. He had thought of this moment for more than two decades. The conversation took place hundreds of times while he lay in bed struggling to find sleep. He must stay strong.

"Asimov summoned us when someone from Pripyat mentioned Yuri and I were champion swimmers. I didn't fully understand what the Commander was asking us to do but Yuri

461

did. He didn't chastise me when I eagerly volunteered. He was more concerned about you.

The suits they gave us were flimsy at best. After opening the sluice gates we tried to swim back as fast as we could but our legs were numb. My face stung like I had fallen on a bee hive. Smiles greeted us at the pond edge and pulled us out of the water. Within seconds I vomited, as did Yuri and Breshevski. I lay on my side and Breshevski was staring wide-eyed at me. I smiled, but he did not acknowledge me. His eyes were shining. I couldn't understand how he could stare at me and not blink. Two men lifted him and as he was transported outside he yelled that Yuri and I were still in the water and someone had to save us. He was looking right at us. I learned later that his goggles were defective. By the time he reached the hospital his corneas had melted.

Yuri vomited for a second time in less than three minutes. His arms could not hold him and he slumped into his own regurgitation. I was about to stand when two comrades wrapped my arms around their shoulders and dragged me outside. Yuri was not far behind and was eased onto a stretcher while we waited for another ambulance. I wasn't suffering like Yuri and was strong enough to kneel next to him. I was overcome with emotion when I looked at his bright red face. The skin on his forehead was cracked like a car window. I cried openly, and a photographer snapped a picture. Yuri mumbled that if I continued to cry he would start calling me Alexandra. These were the last words he would ever say to me. I couldn't stop bawling. Asimov was nearby and put his hand on my shoulder. Paramedics lifted Yuri and placed him in the ambulance that had mercifully arrived. I yelled out his name. I told him I was sorry. I was trembling and frozen in place. I didn't hear the cheers from the workers in the background. I didn't hear Asimov whispering in my ear. I could barely move so I sat with my head on bent knees. My best friend may die and it was my fault. Flashing lights blurred my vision. More photographers had gathered to take more photos.

Asimov, with the help of a few men, got me into a jeep and we drove back to the same hotel that Kremlin dignitaries were staying. They gave me a room with a shower that I used until no hot water remained. Aside from the tingling in my face, I was fine. They brought me new clothes. I had dinner with the Colonel and some other man I have long forgotten. They praised my efforts. I asked for updates on Yuri but none were available except that he was being flown to Moscow. I told Asimov that Yuri's fiancée had to be called. The other man made a note and mentioned that Yuri's condition and whereabouts would be posted in every newspaper across the Soviet Union. Asimov found his assistant's comment inappropriate and said he would fly to Moscow himself and I was not to worry.

I did worry. It was all I did for years to come.

I had the strangest dream. It was an evening of sleep I never forgot. I excused myself from dinner early and returned to my room. Within minutes I was sleeping. I remember four white walls, a white floor and a white door. I was yelling for someone to save me but no one came. Every time I reached to open the door it would disappear and reappear on a different wall. A bright light blinded me temporarily, and I realized the door had opened. The same light shone whenever the door opened except once. Yuri walked in through the lights and stood in front of me. He said nothing and shook his head with disapproval before leaving through the wall behind me. You were next Tania, and you did the same as Yuri. Mila followed, as did my mother, Yulia, David and many others. Each paraded by me with contempt in their eyes. The last person to visit was Valeri Markov, a man I knew from the academy. When he entered the room there was no bright light. The door opened and shut. He smiled, tapped me on the shoulder and sat in the far corner. I asked what he was doing and where he thought he was. He said he was sharing a room with me… in hell. I woke up. Firecrackers from May Day celebrations burst in succession. Drunken soldiers and liquidators were singing. My face hurt.

The next morning I told Asimov I would return to my duties. He replied that I was to rest and not to worry about work for the next few days. He handed me two bottles of vodka and a radio. I wanted a newspaper and one was delivered to me along with breakfast and a prostitute. She drank my vodka and ate my breakfast. I read a small blurb about Reactor Four and that all was safe. There was no mention of Yuri or Breshevski. Maybe tomorrow, I thought. The prostitute danced around the room with a bottle of vodka in her hand. She had undressed and wore only her panties. She spent most of the previous evening celebrating May Day with married politburo officials and smelled like liquor and old men. She passed out but not before puking on the curtains.

I was bored and decided to take a stroll. More trucks were arriving from Russia and Belarus. The men looked confused and frightened. I waved, but no one waved back. I thought they would recognize me. It was much hotter than the day before and I should have worn a hat and mask. Yuri would be furious with me if he knew. As I crossed in front of an ice cream parlor, I saw Markov's friend and thought it a good idea to follow him. He was

464

a smallish man who walked with his head down. His face was disfigured, and I felt pity for him.

I stayed a good distance away, which was a tactic my father taught me. He walked the opposite direction of the Reactor, towards the Marina. I heard two horn blasts from a jeep and saw Markov driving. He noticed me immediately. My father would have been disappointed. Markov veered right and drove towards me. He asked how I was feeling and I replied I was fine. I asked him where he was going and he didn't answer. I told him I knew what he was doing, I had heard stories. He stepped out of the jeep and stuck his hand in his pocket. I was sweating profusely. I wasn't nervous to lock horns with Markov but I was suddenly dizzy. It was so hot. He told me to get in the jeep and I told him to fuck off. My knees buckled, and I lost my balance. Markov asked if I was drunk. He pulled his hand half way out of his jacket and I saw a knife. My face hurt. I pointed my finger at the knife before losing consciousness.

I awoke after a fifteen hour slumber in the Pripyat hospital. The first face I saw belonged to Colonel Asimov's assistant. Asimov had departed for Moscow an hour earlier. I told him I was okay, and he left. A nurse wearing gloves and a mask told me I may have to travel to Moscow. Like I told the assistant, I said I was fine. She handed me a mirror, and I saw blisters from my left ear to the bottom of my left eye. Tiny cracks, like those I saw on Yuri, were seeping puss. The bubbles hurt to touch. I was scared and asked the nurse if my face would heal. She answered that neither she nor the other nurses was trained in radiation. I found it odd that a nurse in hospital next to a nuclear reactor was not trained in radiology. She left me with two pills and a plastic cup half full of water. No one visited until dinner time.

My mother wasn't contacted, and I was thankful for that. I
didn't want her to see me lying in a hospital bed. I asked a nurse
to contact Asimov's assistant. He showed up a day later
and would not look at me. I asked him to phone Asimov, and he
did. The mirror was removed from my room and the
bathroom down the hall. The nurse would not discuss the subject.
I found out why two hours before Colonel Asimov visited.

The skin from the side of my nose to my left ear and up to
my eye had either fallen off or shriveled. My cheek was sunken. It
made no sense that I was in little pain. I should have been doped
on morphine at this point. The doctor said the nerves were dead
and the skin could not heal or grow back. He considered skin
grafts but not until the damage was complete. I was near
traumatized and wanted to know what else could happen. The
following week my eye hurt.

I learned that same day that both Yuri and Roman had
passed away. My suffering seemed minimal. I cried and tears fell
from my one working eye. I couldn't see them buried. I was too
ashamed of my face. I was too ashamed of my actions and I was
too cowardly to slit my wrists.

Colonel Asimov promised that Mother Russia would take
care of me and she did. I was given an apartment in a quiet
neighborhood of Kyiv. No one would bother me there. My mother
was told I died in an explosion and my body was never found.

It was better this way.

I felt guilty, but it passed. I slept during the day and
walked for an hour in the early morning hours. For a decade I
rarely saw sunlight and aside from the delivery men bringing
food and clothing, I rarely saw anyone. The world
forgot about me. I imagine they've forgotten about Yuri and

Breshevski too. I watched a documentary on Chernobyl and there was mention of three divers but no names were given. I should have felt cheated, but I was numb to the Russian media.

Again, I told myself it was better this way.

The collection of books in my apartment swelled to over five hundred. I became fascinated in psychology and often wondered if Mila had read the same books. Religion was new to me and I found it fascinating if not utterly confusing. I started praying but wasn't sure if I was doing it right. Asimov arranged for a priest to visit me. I was strongly opposed to the idea until I met the man.

He was old and blind. He told me I was to address him simply as Priest. Every Wednesday at eight p.m. he was dropped off at my apartment and picked up at ten. I looked forward to these meetings and my enthusiasm pleased the old man. He said I reminded him of a pupil he had many years ago when he was the bishop of a church in Lyiv called Dormiton. He asked me if I was an artist and was mildly disappointed when I said no. His visits stopped after two years and I had no explanation of why until Asimov broke the news. He hung himself for no apparent reason. To this day I think Asimov lied to me.

The colonel was retired by 1996 but made a point of visiting. He always worried about you, Mila and me. He made a promise to Yuri and never broke it and for that, I commend him. There was a hospital near my apartment filled with cancer and AIDS patients. I didn't know what AIDS was. Asimov explained and said the patients were awake throughout the days and evenings and I might consider helping out. I thought of my disfigurement and said no. He offered to build me a mask. I found that intriguing but strange. It reminded me of an opera I never saw. I changed my answer to maybe.

I began my volunteer shifts at the hospital in and around the same time Mila moved to Canada and you moved to the Exclusion Zone. I found it a happy coincidence that the three of us helped in hospitals. The difference is that you and Mila ended up in jail. Well, my jail was my home so maybe not that different. No one wrote articles about me; that much I know.

Most, if not all of the patients, were terminal. They were expected to die. A few surprised us but only a few. I learned their names, their parent's names, their children's names, and I learned their lives. I documented everything because I believe they deserved that much. Tania, Chernobyl had much to do with the epidemic of cases this hospital received. I watched children die. No parent should outlive their child. Have you ever heard of the Chernobyl necklace? Silly question, of course you have. When the thyroid is removed it leaves a scar around the neck from one end to the other. These kids wear scarves and turtlenecks every day to blend in. I saw young adults with weak immune systems reduced to skeletons in mere weeks. A nurse told me it was because of their immoral behavior. Another blamed it on western tourists. I didn't believe them. I was wrong. We are a godless country.

I prayed for the patients. They accepted me because of my disfigurement. I told them stories about the Kharmalov sisters before they became famous. Some knew you, some did not. Most were interested in an afterlife. The priest talked extensively about heaven and I relayed this information to the patients. It was a tough sell but I could see in their eyes that they hoped it was true.

I never removed the mask and by five a.m. I was out the door. Parents and relatives inquired about the 'phantom' man who visited their loved one every evening. The morning staff was oblivious but the head practitioner explained I was a volunteer. I received letters of thanks and kept them all. I worried about cameras and some journalist thinking it would be a good idea to write an article. A couple of relatives complained about my religious beliefs and the doctors answered they would put a halt to this as soon as possible. They never have.

The head practitioner is a tough prick with a good heart. He's the person who enlightened me on the legacy that Chernobyl has had on our people. Once a week he cleans my face with an antiseptic and gives me ointment to soften hardened skin. He met you once and said it changed his life. I told him who I was and at first he didn't believe me but in time he did. He has a friend at a museum that confirmed my stories. I asked him to never tell anyone as I was supposed to be dead. It was never an issue after Colonel Asimov paid him a short visit."

"Igor was here yesterday morning," Tania interrupted. "Mila and I met him after his father died. He was just a child at the time."

"Small world," Alex replied.

"Sasha," Tania began. "You've lived a very solitary life as have I. You can't blame yourself for any acts that Yuri decided to take. If anything, he displayed his love for you as a brother."

"Yes… he was my brother."

"You heard about Yulia?" Tania queried.

Alex dropped his head. "Yes… a sad ending. I read about her and Simon. I never believed the explanation behind their deaths. Yulia was erratic at times but even in moments of despair she would never have left Mila's child alone. It wasn't her nature. She was the maternal type."

469

"I agree. She sent Mila letters while we were imprisoned. She wrote that Lena was told stories about Mila and that Yulia would never claim to be Lena's mother. She asked of your whereabouts. Mila had no idea and never replied. Every week a letter would arrive telling Mila of Lena's progress, and every letter asked about you."

His hood inched up his forehead and he pulled it back down. "My life is a series of disconnects like a sputtering engine that never turns over. Yulia is my most haunting memory. I ask myself if the Reactor had never exploded would I have ever married Yulia, and the answer is probably not. Maybe she would have settled for me after other plans fell by the wayside but she would never have been happy." He exhaled a long breath. "I think I've been fated as a footnote in other people's stories. My twenty-four hours of glory was just that…twenty-four hours. And I shared it with a drunken hooker."

Tania was showing signs of fatigue. She slid back under her covers and asked Alex to place her pillow under head.

"Will I see Yuri and my family when I die?"

Alex was surprised by the question. "I believe so… yes."

She smiled and closed her eyes. "Tell me about heaven."

The Letter

Tania died last night.

Igor called at eight in the morning to let us know. Boris whispered that his cousin had been waiting for Mila before she passed so she died happy. After visiting the hospital one last time, we gathered in the living room while Vera, Boris and Mila told stories of Tania and Pripyat. I could not help but feel I was part of a special moment bonding me with everyone in the room. Tania wrote a letter that made Mila cry nonstop for a good half hour. When Boris translated it to me, I understood her heartbreak.

We consoled each other for the day and made arrangements for Tania's funeral. That was the design until five p.m. when TV crews set up shop outside the apartment building. Security guards and police officers refused any entry into the building. By eight o'clock a large crowd had gathered outside, and many were holding lit candles. Flowers were dropped off on the sidewalk. How these people knew Mila Kharmalov was inside was never explained to me and in all honesty, I didn't bother to ask.

Sometimes fame is fleeting and unrewarding. The infamous fifteen minutes before you're gone and forgotten. I can't imagine the emotion rollercoaster Mila was experiencing. She wanted to disappear but at the same time was grateful her sister was being remembered by fellow countrymen. Their contribution so many years ago was not fleeting nor was it forgotten. After much deliberation, she decided to thank those in attendance and walked downstairs with Boris and myself. Vera and Lena watched from the balcony window.

The moment Mila exited the building, the flash from cameras became blinding. People clapped and cheered. Boris and I stopped reporters from rushing the icon while Mila, with her bravado, decided to stand on the hood of a car parked a few feet from the main entrance. A reporter handed her his microphone. She bowed her head and addressed the throng.

Sensing her distress, the crowd was politely hushed.

"Hello my friends," she said before clearing her throat. "At seven this morning, my sister Tania Kharmalov died quietly in her sleep. For those of you that do not know, Tania was diagnosed with advanced cancer six weeks ago. She would have been forty-seven-years old in thirty days. Seeing you here this evening reinforces my love for the Ukrainian people and Tania would say the same. Many years ago she could have returned to Moscow but always claimed her heart was in Ukraine."

A few in the crowd cheered but most clapped respectively.

"I don't have to tell you why Tania contracted this horrible disease, we all know. I don't have to tell you what a lovely person my sister was, we all know. She left me a letter, which I would read to you but I am certain my tears will prevail therefore my cousin, Boris, will read it for you."

Mila stepped off the hood with help from Boris and he then took the microphone from her hand. Mila stood next to me and locked her arm in mine. I'm sure she was using me for support as her body was visibly shaking. Boris, meanwhile, was not even a tiny bit shy or nervous to be standing in front of so many people or the television cameras. He took the letter from his coat pocket and read it with surprising eloquence. Mila kept her head bowed the whole time.

A parent can give no greater gift than a brother or a sister. I was blessed with one of each and to this day have never had better friends than the ones I shared a home and my childhood with. My sister is a friend by birth and a friend by choice. When I laugh she laughs and when I cry she holds me until I cry no more. She knows me like no other and carry's my secrets as protected as she carries her own. She shoulders my burdens as if they are coins in her pocket, saved and later dispensed for something needful. Her presence nourishes me and I am weak without her. I cannot be selfish or vain or troubled or sorrowed when I am loved by her. I am a sister to a sister; I am a friend to a friend.

I am Tania to Mila. We are the sisters Kharmalov.

My Dearest Mila,

I have accepted my body's vindication. Even as cancer devours my cells, I dream of better days and my thoughts are as beautiful as a sunny Pripyat morning.

Not a month passed in the last fifteen years without a package arriving from the city you now call home. I not only welcomed them, I cherished every memento and every new fascinating incident you wrote. My neighbours would gather inside the tiny shack to listen to my voice as I read your letters. All these years later, words from Mila Kharmalov mean so much to so many. I was often asked if I was envious of your new life and I always answered that I am only envious of your husband as he is the lucky one who wakes each morning with the most glorious person I have ever known.

There was much solitude in the Exclusion Zone and I wondered if I was not unlike a Tibetan monk scratching out an existence under the auspicious eyes of a higher being. We had a small corn field that the men harvested with antique equipment. It was a genuine hammer and sickle livelihood. I tended to my garden and read the books delivered by the

473

charitable men and women who were always surprised to see that I was still alive. They brought me teas and sweets and on many occasions snuck in boxes filled with cans of processed meat. I would read them your letters and they would question me on the experiences of the Kharmalov sisters. Even in the most barren and dangerous environment, I was given special treatment. Two decades after our escapades, strangers had to meet me… they needed to meet me as if I was the end of a long religious trek or a voyage to find ones true self. They would leave in tears fearing I would not be there if or when they returned. We once complained of how our popularity was an awful annoyance but in my later years it became satisfying in a quiet, maternal way. It fed my soul as much as it fed my belly.

You were always stronger than me. Your tremendous influence became transparent to me one day as I tended to my vegetables in the front yard garden. Two stray dogs had snuck onto my property to watch my every movement. Their tongues were wagging in desperation as they contemplated their next decision. I stood, walked into my home and opened one of the cans of processed meat which I then flung towards them. They lapped it up in seconds. The smaller dog began to approach me as if his hunger had not been satisfied but the older one bit his companions tail to stop him. They left and never returned. That moment strung together a series of metaphors, which I will allow you to decipher at your convenience.

I always heeded your direction Mila because I knew your decisions were not spontaneous or made in desperation. If not for your guidance I would have been destitute many times over yet even in the harshest surroundings, my base requirements excelled. Could you have ever imagined way back when while we peeled potatoes in mama's kitchen that our family name would signify courage to an entire generation? It goes without saying that both of us would replace this

474

fame if it permitted us to have Yuri and Roman by our side but no matter how tragic their deaths were, it would have been a lifelong travesty if we did not choose the path we tread. I have chosen to forgive the samizdat for their deception and I hope you do the same.

As I lie in this hospital bed I dread saying goodbye but I am altogether excited to be reunited with Yuri and our family. You are thankfully not alone. Lena is exceptional in every way. I look at her in wonderment thinking what an incredible coincidence that she appears to be a perfect combination of both you and me. She has a silent passion Mila that she guards as if it is a treasure. I cannot decide if this is a good or bad character trait but have faith that she will shine in whatever she chooses. Lena is a Kharmalov thus her destiny is preordained.

I love you my sister. My life has always been your life and my love for you has always exceeded the love I have for myself or anyone else. Even in your complexity you bare simplicity. Even in rage you bare softness. If I had one wish for the world it would be that every family had a Mila Kharmalov. There is no other like you and I have been blessed by God himself to be your right hand.

I loved you, I love you, I will forever love you.

Boris thanked the crowd and helped Mila up on the car hood. She had been crying and took a few seconds to wipe her eyes. The crowd clapped very loudly and someone yelled, "We love you Mila".

"Many others have lost loved ones for the same reason I lost my sister today. I have heard your government wishes to build new nuclear plants across this wonderful nation. Don't let them do it. You know me only because of what Tania and I did after a horrible accident. I beg of you, don't let this happen again.

You don't need another Tania and Mila Kharmalov. Thank you so much for treasuring my sister. God bless you all."

I took Mila's hand, and we rushed back into the apartment. Boris stayed outside and answered a few more questions. He was enjoying the attention and as he would later tell me, the chicks love a guy on television. Mila could barely stand when we entered the elevator, and I placed her arm around my shoulder while I wrapped my right arm around her waist.

"I'm so tired," she whispered.

April 25th 2013

The next morning at approximately 10 A.M., the kitchen phone rang, startling Vera, Lena and me. Boris preferred it at its highest volume because he was often passed out in his bedroom. Vera was closest and answered. She said a few words, put the receiver on the kitchen counter and walked to the bathroom. She knocked on the door and told Mila that the call was for her. Vera returned to the phone and asked the caller to wait.

A minute later Mila appeared from the bathroom wearing only a short towel that barely covered her ass. Lena and I were having a coffee in the living room and she watched me staring at her mother long enough to warrant a strong pinch on my arm.

"Give me a break," I said trying to limit my embarrassment." I just happened to be looking in that direction."

"Yah, I've heard that line before," Lena grimaced.

Mila appeared excited, found a pen and started scribbling on a notepad. She hung up the phone, left the kitchen and walked directly in front me towards the balcony window. While she stared out the window, Lena covered my eyes.

"Seriously?" I sighed.

While Mila returned to the bathroom, Lena mentioned that I was checking her out.

Mila turned nonchalantly and glared at me. "Don't check me out Aaron, it's weird."

"I wasn't checking you out… I wasn't checking you out."

Boris exited his bedroom and gawked at Mila. "You're still hot my cousin… God was good to you girl."

Mila chuckled and disappeared into the bathroom.

I glanced at Lena, then Boris and back at Lena. My arms were raised, but I didn't say anything. Boris noticed me blushing and laughed.

"It's okay for me to look. You, on the other hand, should be ashamed. Pervert."

Boris was pouring a cup of coffee when the phone rang again. He cursed in Ukrainian, which was quickly met with admonishment from his mother.

"Grand Central Station," he joked while answering the phone. He shook his head, dropped the receiver and lumbered to the bathroom. "Hey Princess, there's another call for you. Put on some clothes. Aaron's a pervert."

I sighed loudly, took a sip of coffee and put one of my feet on the living room table.

Boris walked into the living room, stopped and looked at me. "This isn't your igloo… feet off the table, it's not a block of ice."

Mila re-appeared wearing her customary black jeans and a white tee shirt. She glanced at me and grinned, trying not to laugh.

"Aaron, would you prefer I face you or would you like to look at my bum?"

"Oh my God," I shrieked, while turning to Lena. "You're my future wife, make this stop."

Lena shrugged and Boris laughed. I stared straight ahead making no eye contact with Mila.

Her phone conversation was very animated at first and caught the attention of Lena and Boris. After ten minutes Mila hung up and sat with us.

"That was a government official. He is going to visit with us at noon. He wants Tania to be remembered at European Square tomorrow at two p.m. I agreed."

No one had any arguments, but we asked why the government wanted Tania to have a dignitaries' send off. Mila didn't answer but said that no matter the reasoning, it was a fitting farewell for Tania. She then mentioned that radio talk shows were alive with the news about Tania's demise and the majority of callers asked for a public memorial. Boris turned on is only radio and we listened. Lena translated as much as she could. We later learned that the newspapers were re-printing the old samizdat articles and detailing how important the Kharmalov sisters had been for Ukraine. It was spine tingling. Judging from the younger voices, a new fan base had been created in less than twenty-four hours.

"I've got to step out at two," Mila said matter of fact. "So the government guy has to be out of here at half past one."

"Where are you going mama?" Lena asked.

She stood and ran a hand down the side of her leg. "I have to speak with an old acquaintance. I'll be back for dinner." She then returned to her bedroom. Boris was watching to see if my eyes followed the tall woman. I forbid the urge and kept my line of vision on the table in front of me.

I was learning quickly that Mila never said more than she had to when the conversation was centered on her. Lena shook her head in wonderment.

"She bought me a pet rock when I was eleven. I wanted a cat, but I got a rock. I think she was preparing me for future conversations with her."

****

At eleven-thirty, Mila told Lena that she'd back in ten minutes. She stepped outside the apartment building and glanced at the grey clouds that were thickening like a potato soup. Across the street, the familiar police car was stationed, waiting for anything to happen. Mila grimaced, thinking how useless the cops were in Kiev. She walked towards the vehicle.

The officer stepped out of his car and greeted Mila. She was taller than he expected and he felt shy about the height difference.

"You're Mila Kharmalov," he gushed.

"Nice to meet you comrade," she replied. "I have something that may skyrocket your career. Would you like to hear about it or would you prefer to remain at your present rank?"

The officer's eyes widened and he asked Mila to tell him.

"Don't get too excited, you have to remain very alert as the man you'll be arresting is a psychopath." Mila handed the police officer a note with the home address of Valeri Markov. "We have no recent photographs. He's approximately one hundred and seventy three centimeters and thin with a black ponytail. Get into the house via force if necessary, apprehend Markov and drive him back to Colonel Drubli."

"Drubli?" the man questioned enthusiastically. "This is very serious."

Mila huffed quietly. "I would bring an extra round of bullets for that gun of yours," the beautiful woman warned. "If I am correct in my assumptions, this man is still scary dangerous."

****

Every morning he walked to the local grocery next to the butcher shop and bought fresh vegetables for his daily soup. He spoke with no one but would tip his hat to say hello if only to reciprocate. The old lady at the food mart had a running bet with her husband that some day she would get the quiet man with the long silvery hair to speak. He knew this because he once caught them in the act. Today was her lucky day.

Wearing a tired dress and head scarf she bid him good morning as soon as he walked through the wood door with the bell attached. He nodded and proceeded to pick out what was needed for a leek soup. The carrots looked good as did the barley. The potatoes were soft, and he decided against picking up his usual three. At the cash table he dropped the required amount of change into the old lady's waiting hand and was about to turn away when she asked if he recalled the name Tania Kharmalov. He stared back at her but did not reply. The old lady told him Tania died yesterday and her sister Mila gave a pre-eulogy to a massive crowd.

A few days later the cashier would describe this moment as entirely terrifying. In front of television cameras and wearing far too much makeup for the occasion, she exclaimed the man's face turned from blank to pure evil. His eyes were filled with a hate she had not witnessed since the Kremlin's soldiers invaded her village fifty years earlier. He said one word and only one word.

"Where?"

He darted out of the grocery and returned home. It would take a couple of hours to drive to Kiev yet he had no plan. The first rule to any new task is to always have a plan. Thoughts raced through his brain causing him to become dizzy and disoriented. He hated this relatively new sensation and lately it was happening often. He blacked out at his kitchen table a few days ago and woke up not knowing where he was. It freaked the hell out of him. The medical book taken from the tall, crazy woman said blackouts could be caused by a bad diet. He was thinking maybe Chernobyl had caught up with him, which made more sense than the food he ate.

There was a girl downstairs; she had been finished off yesterday once the new painting was completed. He was ordered to dismember the body this morning but now he had no time. He was told that she was a total waste of effort and didn't even know who Tania Kharmalov was.

How did he know that? Who told him this?

Fucking younger generation had become western sissies caring only about their lipstick and genitals. This one had an earring attached to her vagina lip. It was disgustingly vulgar. He barely wrote anything about her as he had learned little that would be of any substance to his ever growing manifesto. She would be another footnote on why a Soviet civilization must be reinstated as soon as possible.

First things first: Chop the carrots and let them soak with the barley and leeks. Then go for a long drive and think of what needs to be done. There was a café in a village not too far away with newspapers from Kiev. Maybe he could get clues from one of the articles. He didn't like the waitress at this café. She was nosy and overweight. His car keys were on the kitchen table, which angered him. They should have been on top of the refrigerator where he always kept them. An alarming smell filled his nostrils and after five minutes of sniffing kitchen corners, he realized it was he himself who reeked. When was the last time he did a laundry? After changing his shirt he stepped outside and locked the front door. The Latin sign, which translated meant 'Enter at Your Own Risk', was hanging crooked and he adjusted it so that the four by six inch wooden tablet was properly centered. The tall woman in the crazy village had the same sign on her bedroom door. When he got back from his drive he would read his notes to remember her name. He looked across the street at the large tree and wondered if he had ever seen it before. He had been in this house for twenty-five years and never noticed it. Or did he?

Something is wrong with me.

Tania is dead. My love is dead.

He did not sense any pain but felt it necessary to mourn for a few minutes while sitting in his car. He tried to think of why Mila Kharmalov was to blame for his loss but he could find no reason. He barely remembered the discussion he once had with her and where it took place.

There has to be a reason or I wouldn't be driving to Kiev.

He dreaded turning the key to start the engine. His vision was not as good as it was only six months ago and although he had made an appointment to see the optometrist, he couldn't recall where the doctor's office was or at least at this very moment he wasn't sure. Thankfully, Kiev was easy to get to because it was

483

a single highway followed by one street that led directly to downtown. The village café was a different story altogether. He swore trying to remember the name of the small town. The sun made a brief appearance while he was at the grocery but had now disappeared, replaced by very ominous clouds. Valeri Markov turned off at the first street and headed west. For the next five hours he would drive around in circles only to return home flustered. He never made it to the café nor did he find a newspaper carrying a story about Tania.

Turning onto his street, he was baffled to see a police cruiser outside his home. This was not good. Why were they visiting him after all these years? Did they think he had something to do with Tania dying? The heavy rain had finally dissipated and as he walked cautiously to his back door he saw muddy footprints on the soft grass. The cop was in his house, probably messing up his clean floor. Lying on top of the logs against the fence that he built years ago was an axe he remembered sharpening only last week. For no apparent reason his memory was now intact and the events of the last few days flooded his brain. He had remembered to cover the floorboards that led down to his basement, he was certain of this. What he didn't understand was why his head hurt. He was unfamiliar with headaches. Markov heard screaming inside his home, which he found odd until he peeked through the kitchen window. The cop was bleeding for some strange reason. He wondered if there was a second person in his home. All he could do was wait and pounce. When the backdoor opened he swung his axe as hard as he could and struck the officer in the Adams Apple. The cop fell to the concrete instantly and almost in total silence. Instead of checking for a pulse, Markov's instincts guided his eyes across a flooded kitchen floor.

"*Fucking prick,*" the long-haired murderer swore. "*Do you know how long it's going to take to clean up your mess?*"

Grandfather

The white SUV door opened and a sopping wet Boris stepped inside. The seats had been rearranged to allow Boris to sit facing his grandfather and the newest *Teacher*. A towel had been placed on his seat beforehand and Boris dried his hair and face. His grandfather had aged a lot in the last five years and had deep lines on his forehead and crow's feet next to his eyes. He wore an ostentatious purple shirt, unbuttoned at the neck with white pants. Teacher wore the same colors with a white miniskirt and t-shirt hiding her hormone induced breasts. She was prettier than the last few and it was obvious that his grandfather had spent money on plastic surgery. Her nose was near perfect.

"They've grown since I last saw you," Boris said while pointing at her chest.

Judging from his grandfather's face, the old man was not amused so Boris looked away.

"When did Kharmalov arrive"? He asked.

Boris closed his eyes and sighed. "My *cousin* arrived two days ago. In case you're not aware, Tania died yesterday morning."

"Who in Ukraine is not aware?" He huffed. "It's on every damn channel. Is she going ahead with this public ceremony?"

"It's considered a state funeral at this point," Boris replied. "Mila sees it as the government's way to console Kiev protesters who are worried about the possible Custom Union."

The grandfather shook his head several times. "Fucking fools. They've forgotten who Mila Kharmalov is. She's

Tymoshenko times ten." He covered his mouth and studied Boris. "Are you going to be with her?"

"Yes grandfather."

Teacher crossed her legs and hiked her skirt purposely, distracting Boris momentarily.

She's gonna meet the Samaski Butcher soon if she's not careful.

"I received news today that the Russians are nearing a deal with Kirghizstan to join the Customs Union. It will cut off my distribution of cheap goods from China and that includes cell phones. Medicine will flow through Moscow as of next year. Igor will be paying more as will everyone else. All proceeds going to Mother Russia. They're giving us money but getting it back every time we make a purchase."

Boris thought of what he was just told. This would effectively ruin his grandfather's business and his as well.

"What will you do?"

The old man stared at Boris pleased that his grandson was worried. "I have more money than I will ever need. I'll sell my corporations and properties and then Teacher and I will move to a warm climate. I hate Lugansk winters. You needn't worry about your finances. I'll transfer some properties to you, including one of the clubs, and if you wish to continue your cell phone business, I'll put you in contact with a few people that may be able to keep your prices low. I guess I should be happy that I have lived long enough to enjoy my money. Maybe the fucking Russians have done me a favor."

"Thank-you Grandfather," Boris whispered.

The old man raised his hand and smiled. "I owe you much more… don't think I don't know the horror I've put you through. I hate myself for my past transgressions."

487

"And Mila?"

He exhaled a long breath. "Mila Kharmalov... you're worrying about her? I wonder if she has any idea how many times a bullet was aimed at her head." He chuckled before continuing. "Or how many times her arrest papers were left on a minister's desk. I'm not proud of my actions but her father's death saved her life. I have no doubt of this but nonetheless, I hope she lets loose tomorrow. I pray her spirit is still alive."

"Sir?"

The grandfather shrugged. "I hope she gives the speech of her life and riles up the masses against Russia. If ever there was a time to do it, it's now. I remember when those pieces of shit used to visit Samaski... I wanted to kill them myself but we had people for that. They looked down on us back then and they look down on us now. We mean nothing to them. We're gum on the soles of their shoes. Even within my industry, they expected servitude from me. I hate them with a passion Boris, so I hope very much that Mila Kharmalov goes ape shit on them."

"So you're telling me she's safe?"

"Boris," he grinned, "She took a cab from the airport. If I wanted her dead she would have been dead before she hit the highway. No one is concerned about her. Her daughter and the Canadian are protected. To be clear, I'm doing this for Tania Kharmalov. I adored everything about Tania, she was a magnificent woman." He rubbed his chin and mouth before continuing. "The police called me today. I guess Mila sent someone to investigate an address that she believed belonged to Valeri Markov."

Boris nodded yes.

"Yah well, the cop was almost beheaded and Markov is gone. That means he's probably in the vicinity or waiting for tomorrow's funeral. I would bet on tomorrow. Don't go fretting too much. Last time we checked up on him he was a blithering idiot. He barely remembered who I was. It's the other little prick that worries me more." The grandfather shook his head several times and sighed loudly. "I should have had them eliminated a long time ago but I made a promise. I made a promise with the Devil… another mistake on my part.

Let this be a lesson to you Boris. When you think with your heart or with your memories, you will err. I did it for Iona. I never told you anything about her but Iona was your mom's Aunt. I should have had her killed but didn't have the heart and because of this so many lives have been lost. I once loved Iona like a daughter and she loved me. She was so innocent, and I changed her… I did this. The chaos I caused by building the self-esteem of a broken girl has been devastating for me and so many others. She was my most haunting disappointment."

"There was no way for you to know grandfather," Boris interjected.

"Teacher knew… she knew, and I thought she was jealous of the attention I gave to Iona. My greatest love was murdered because my ego was too large."

Boris glanced at Teacher number Five and saw nothing that resembled jealousy on her face. She didn't seem to care. He felt pity for his grandfather.

"Tell me about Iona," Boris asked.

His grandfather shook his head. "Don't have to. You can read for yourself. There are two large boxes of books and notepads in the trunk filled with notes from both Iona and

Markov. My men found them yesterday when the police alerted us. I have his paintings too. Take the boxes to Mila and let her do as she wishes. You *will* tell her something for me."

"What's that?"

"You tell her thank-you. It took me a long time to realize that bullshit appeals only to the desperate and followers of the desperate. Mila Kharmalov was a flame of hope for this dismal country. I dimmed that flame Boris. It was me... I was no better than a fucking Russian. I have been the bullshit that has quashed a generation. Drugs and prostitution in Odessa... I started this. I am the true enemy of Ukraine. Mila and Tania were heroes. We need more heroes."

Boris opened his mouth to speak but his grandfather stopped him.

"I had a young man sit with me a little while back asking if I would teach him everything I know. Apparently, I was his idol. His face was wide-eyed, and all I wanted do was slay him right there and then. Never idolize bullshit my grandson or anyone for that matter but listen to and remember genuine people. No one else matters. The properties and money I give to you should be used to build and strengthen Ukraine. Be that person Boris, don't be me. Promise me you will be a strong Ukrainian and you will make me a proud grandfather."

"I promise grandfather," Boris replied.

"You tell Mila Kharmalov that an old man respects her and you tell her that Tania will never be forgotten. Certainly not by me."

"It will be the first thing I say when I get back inside," Boris said happily. "I love you, grandfather."

The old man looked at Boris for a few seconds. "I love you too boy." He stopped to clear his throat and a wave of emotion burst out of nowhere. "I'm sorry Boris… I'm so, so sorry."

He grabbed his grandson's hand and held on tight. Boris put his other hand on top.

"I know," he whispered.

The old man was done speaking and dropped his head. Teacher smiled seductively at Boris and rubbed the inside of her thigh invitingly. Boris wanted to spit on her. He stepped out of the van and walked to the back of the SUV. The driver met him and they carried the heavy boxes into his building.

Mila would finally have her answers.

****

Lena warned me ahead of time that when her mother was in the process of something big, she became quiet and secretive. Mila, Lena and Vera had disappeared into Mila's room an hour ago and I was stuck in the living room with a pensive Boris. He was reading one of the notebooks from the two boxes.

"What do you think she's up to?" I asked.

The burly man grunted purposely before looking at me. "Just sit back and enjoy the ride," he replied. "For anyone that shows up tomorrow, they'll learn what they have missed for almost two decades."

My question wasn't answered, but I didn't bother to ask for more details.

"Listen to the first paragraph from Markov's… what does he call it… manifesto. "

The big man had three of the diary-like books on his lap. I told Boris to go ahead.

"You will hate me initially and believe me to be a monster without conscience or moral boundary. The sham practitioners known as psychologists will portray me as inhuman and decipher my writings as narcissistic or delusional. In actuality, I am quite sane and acknowledge my lowly beginnings as a catalyst to my behavior but not as a foundation. If you wish to formulate your own opinion, study my manifesto and then read your daily newspaper for a week. If you are not intrigued by what you have learned, then I have failed you. If the opposite has occurred and you are thus enlightened, then in the name of our God, maim as directed.

The Prince,
Valeri Markov

"I wouldn't call that egotistical. More defensive," I responded. "If anything, it'll make me want to read more."

"Yah maybe," Bruno replied. "It sounds to me like he wants to live forever as a fictional character far from his everyday reach. It's fantasy."

"I'm not following you," I said.

Boris blew a horse sounding wind out of his partially closed lips. "What's so hard to follow? You write biographies for old people wishing to leave behind a legend of some sort. If they had interesting lives they'd be a TV documentary. Get real man, your clients are egomaniacs trying to live forever. Markov is no different."

"My clients don't kill or steal," I answered angrily.

"You don't know that for sure and don't get pissed. I am only stating the obvious. You're going to write about Tania and Mila because the world needs to know what really happened here. They need to know the before and after. Your clients are telling their life story to people who already know it. They're not heroes nor are they extraordinary. All they're doing is preserving their memories so they won't be forgotten when they're worm food."

"I'm not going to argue with you Boris." I sighed. "I'm much too tired. What's in those books?"

Boris shrugged. "I just started, don't know yet." He reached into his back pocket and pulled out a piece of paper. "I forgot about this. Igor wanted me to talk about this when Evgeni wasn't around. He can't do it tomorrow."

"Yah sure... go ahead."

"I told you before about Evgeni," he began. "As far as he's concerned, the evils in our land are caused by Chernobyl. No one with any common sense will fall for that. Igor believes Chernobyl is still a huge problem but Ukraine has numerous unresolved issues. He wants you to understand as many as possible so that you don't try to tie pieces together that don't belong together. Get it?"

I nodded. "I think I do."

"Ok, well I'll speak anyway but only because the sound of my voice is soothing to me. First off, I want you to appreciate the time that Igor has spent with you. He normally works seven days a week from early morning to late in the evening, so taking time off to hang out with you was a small gift. Doctors in Ukraine hold prestige Aaron but they're not well paid. I think the lady who cuts my hair makes more than Igor. Because of this, many of the good doctors and nurses emigrate. The doctors that remain end up working like field horses during September harvest. I'm not saying Igor is not a good doctor because he is excellent but as you have probably deduced, he is obligated at the moment, to stay. Of course, that could change soon."

Boris stood suddenly and walked to the kitchen. As usual he went for a beer. "Do you want one?"

"No," I replied. "I'm all beer-ed out."

He looked at me quizzically. "I don't know what that means. Speak English." He slumped too heavily on his lounger and for a second I thought it would tilt over. "Ukraine is the second largest country in land mass in Europe but the second from the bottom in economy. Our economy is as weak as Nigeria's so if you wanted to, you could call us a Third World nation. We will argue that our schools and education are excellent but what is the value of this if there is no work or if our graduates emigrate. We are dirt poor Aaron and have been for decades. This is not a post-Soviet phenomenon… this is a result of being Soviets. And, of course, instead of distancing ourselves, we have once again fallen into Russia's trap."

"Boris, I empathize with your country's state but what is the relevance of what you're telling me with Mila and Tania or even Reactor Four at Chernobyl?"

Boris nodded a few times and then reached for his cigarette pack. He smoked too much, and I hated the smell.

"Because… people in the west will never give a damn about us until we are distanced from Russia. You need to put some focus on this when you are writing about Tania. We need help to break the chains from Russia and our corrupt politicians. We're broken Aaron. We are tamed animals in a

Russian circus. Mila could never be tamed, but she is not here anymore. Our rebels and our talent have escaped the zoo. The Americans overthrow governments every second Tuesday. Why can't they do that here?"

"Umm, because your neighbor is Russia?" I said matter of fact.

"Iraq's neighbor is Iran. That didn't stop Bush… did it?" Boris replied. "Listen, just make mention of our poverty and do some research on my country's history in the last century. I will be doing what I can from this day on. Let's hope this is not the last time you see me."

"What the hell does that mean?"

Mila and Lena walked out of the bedroom and plopped down on the couch next to me. Both were wearing pink cotton pajamas. Lena held my hand and kissed me on the cheek. I was still staring at Boris who was now avoiding eye contact.

"The two of you will be leaving before us tomorrow afternoon," Mila said. "Lena, Vera and I will drive in the limo. I need the two of you to make sure everything is in place and the microphones work."

"Are you shitting me Mila?" Boris said while chuckling. "I've known you my whole life cousin… what are you up to?"

"Nothing," Mila replied innocently. "We just decided it should be women only walking up to the podium."

Boris wished his mother was there so he could tell if they were lying. That's more than likely why she stayed in the room.

"Uh-huh," he uttered. "Sure… why not. Aaron and I will leave earlier. Tell you what, we'll leave first thing in the morning and go to a club for a couple of hours."

Lena lifted her finger quickly. "He's my fiancé, Boris, don't push your luck. No more clubs."

"Already she starts with that nonsense," Boris shook his head. "You'll never go out again Aaron. Your life is over, you'll grow old fast and die young."

I crossed my arms and grimaced. "Actually, its common knowledge that married men live longer."

Boris burst out laughing. "Yah right and so do indoor cats."

Mila laughed heartily. "When did you get so funny?"

"The day that the substitute Yankee got here," he said pointing at me.

"Let me see that list you wrote," I blurted jokingly.

I jumped on him and he started giggling. Boris screamed at me telling me to not spill his beer.

From the corner of my eye I caught Mila staring at us with a smile of contentment. She looked at her daughter, slid next to her and wrapped an arm around Lena's stomach.

"I love my family," she said.

April 26th 2013

It rained first thing in the morning but cleared by ten a.m. By eleven it was very hot. I didn't grasp the significance of the day until Lena mentioned it over breakfast. I didn't have many clean clothes left but my lady somehow put together an ensemble that was passable for an important funeral. Boris, meanwhile, wore an expensive blue Armani, making me look like a country boy. Evgeni arrived ten minutes before we were scheduled to leave. He wore a suit but nothing near as fancy as Boris.

"The place we're going is not where the protests were happening," Evgeni said in passing. "No worry of being caught in the middle of a riot. I think today will be a day of remembrance anyway."

Nice to know, I thought. Boris summoned us and we left the apartment but not until I kissed Lena several times. The drive to Kiev Square was quiet, and we listened to music instead of talking. Upon arrival at the Square, a parking attendant waved us in to a special spot near the stage that was near finished. A large photograph of Tania and Mila was hanging on the stage as a backdrop against a makeshift wall of painted drywall. It covered most of the wall and looked like a photograph from a newspaper article.

"It's from the samizdat article," Boris said, noticing my confusion. "Twenty-seven years ago minus a couple of months."

While he was speaking, his cell phone rang, and he excused himself.

"Yes, grandfather?"

"He's here," the old man said.

"Who?" Boris questioned.

"Valerie Markov. One of my men has been scouting since noon. He's been circling the square for the last hour."

Boris looked around but could see nothing past the police and the growing crowd. "There are six hundred people here. I can't see a thing."

Boris heard his grandfather speak into another cell phone but his words were muffled. He told Evgeni and I who he was speaking with and mentioned Markov. Thirty seconds later the grandfather returned.

"Walk towards the Convention Centre quickly. Tell me if you see a very tall man with a black beret."

Boris waved for me and Evgeni to follow him. He asked us to search for a man fitting the description his grandfather gave. I saw him right away. The man was putting something in his pocket.

"He's there…" I said before stopping in mid-sentence. He was pushing a man away from the crowd, heading towards the Convention Centre. It was difficult to see from this distance but the man being pushed had a ponytail.

"Is that Valeri Markov?" I was suddenly seized with fear.

Boris saw it too. "Grandfather, I think this man has Markov."

There was silence on the other side for ten seconds. "I guess then that your problem is solved."

Boris repeated to us in English. "What does that mean?" Boris said. Evgeni translated to me.

"The man is Nikolai Drubli. He's a cop… a very vindictive cop with long ties to your cousin Mila."

Boris put his hand over his cell and told us what his grandfather said. Evgeni shrugged, not understanding the correlation.

"I'm not following," Boris said.

"I have sent contracts to your home my boy," the old man said, changing the subject. "Sign them and bring them to city hall tomorrow. You must do this tomorrow. These properties will keep you wealthy for many years to come. I will contact you when I arrive at my new home. If you wish to learn more about Drubli and Mila, then follow him. He won't harm anyone.

Boris… I love you. Come visit when you get a chance. I will call your mother tomorrow."

"Grandfather…"

"Tania was the good sister. She was the angel. I've tried to tell you this and now I'm warning you. Mila changed when her father was shot. Just be careful, she's not the woman you believe her to be. Help save your country Boris before it's too late."

He hung up, leaving Boris with an astonished expression. *Only yesterday he spoke of admiration for Mila.*

I couldn't decipher the message when Boris told us but hoped they were just the rambling of an old man. Of course Mila changed. She was angry because her father was taken away from her. Who wouldn't be angry?

We did the only thing we could do. We followed Drubli to the Convention Centre.

****

There was a thunderous applause when Mila's name was called. Dressed in a tight black skirt with black boots, she looked more like a businessperson than a mourning sister. She stood behind the microphone and began her speech, speaking entirely in Ukrainian.

"I wish first to thank you for joining the Kharmalov family in commemorating my beautiful sister. It's no secret that she loved this nation and called it her home. She was born a Russian but she died a proud Ukrainian.

Many of you are too young to remember Tania so I will describe her in a few words: Loving, sentimental, loyal and shy. Tania preferred to watch from the sidelines as opposed to talking to large audiences and cameras. She had no ambition to be recognized by strangers or to sign her name on scraps of paper but... she was a quiet rebel. Many of the words I have spoken on the streets of Kiev were Tania's words and Tania's thoughts. My sister spent hours in the libraries of this city researching whatever was necessary for me to get a message across to those I spoke to or harassed, depending on who our target audience was."

Mila grinned and lowered her head for a moment.

"I've watched you from my home in Canada. Scanning the crowd I see such lovely girls' and handsome young men. Almost all of you are educated, almost all nationalists... almost all desperate for change. You worry about your future. So did we... it was many years ago, but so did we. The timing is crazy...purely coincidental but crazy. Twenty-seven years ago today, my life was forever changed by an explosion at the Chernobyl nuclear plant. Tania was to be married on this very day. Instead of marriage and children, she lived a solitary, lonely life. Twenty-seven years later, we will bury her.

500

If you believe for a second that someone like me does not understand or can't possibly comprehend the struggles you are presently experiencing, then think again. Tania was often despondent because of despair and hopelessness. Despair is a word my brother shared with me before he passed away."

Mila walked from behind the podium to face the crowd. She carried the microphone as far as she could before it tugged her back.

"How many of you have protested at Maiden or elsewhere? Don't worry about the police. I'll get to them soon."

Many hands were raised and Mila nodded appreciatively.

"I have two empty chairs behind me and would be proud if two protesters joined me on stage."

Mila chose one young brunette woman and one young blond man from the front row and helped them onstage. She led them to their chairs and shook their hands.

"I wonder if the oligarchs that allowed me to speak here today did so to mock me. I am but a woman from a foreign nation, with no citizenship in this country that I still call my homeland. I couldn't figure out why they would want me or even allow me to speak to old and new friends. It wasn't until this morning that I realized their intention. I read the front page article of the Kiev Post. A journalist, whom I have never heard of, described Tania and me as Russians who befriended Ukraine. We were examples of the friendship that could be attained when these two nations worked together. I nearly shit myself."

Several of the younger crowd laughed at Mila's crudeness.

"Tania would have giggled for hours if she read this. For those of you that don't know, we were banned from entering Russia. Today, I would be arrested if I set foot in Moscow. In all honesty, I am the last person who would ever lower to being a political ploy. So, reading the article was good piece of entertainment for me.

If I go off on a rant, will you promise to listen?"

A few people in the crowd clapped as if they recalled previous Mila Kharmalov speeches.

"I'll ask again. Will you allow me to voice my opinion?"

The majority of the crowd clapped and Mila seemed content with the response.

"Good, because many of you will not appreciate my opinion but let me finish.

I remember my days here and they have made me who I am. Please don't think otherwise but at the same time, I'm not going to bullshit you. My life in Canada is like a dream come true. My life is easy… it's what all of you, every single one of you, dream of attaining. It's what you *should* have.

Canada has its own trade agreements. Canada sets its own laws and Canadians do not and will not accept leaders that won't represent them with fierce loyalty.

So I ask you all… why the *fuck* can't you do the same? Hey, don't get mad, I'm not here to disgrace you and it was a rhetorical question anyway. For months you've protested in union but, I have to say, public protests will only get you so much. Hear me out before you groan. Riots, fires and hooligans are not the answer. It worked with the Orange Revolution because it was fresh… it was unexpected and even the cops got involved. It's old news now. It didn't work for the Greeks and it's not going to work for you. Your leaders are always two steps ahead of you. They know you're going to hit the streets and they prepare speeches ahead of time. They'll plant people in the crowd to act as antagonists so that you look like hooligans. This is textbook, my friends… they will do whatever to save face."

Mila stuck her hands in her coat pocket and surveyed the crowd.

"After a government official left our home yesterday, I was on my laptop searching for the proper words in Ukrainian. At the time, I believed my speech would be short and sweet. I pounded on my keyboard and nothing worked. I thought it was broken until a Word document opened and words started appearing. I was being hacked. Whoever it was, knew who I was and where I was. I called my cousin and we were equally worried. I, actually, was scared but the hacker put me at ease quickly. He asked me how much I knew about present day Ukraine and I replied that I knew what I read from newspapers and blogs. He then asked me a question that sent shivers down my arms. He asked how much I thought he knew about me. At that point, I wanted to power off my computer but for some crazy reason I allowed the conversation to continue. This guy knew everything about me. Every website I visited, my income, my address… you name it - he knew it. This was really frightening until he explained his intentions. And this, my friends, is why I inferred that protests may not be the way to go.

In order for our bodies to be healthy, we have to purge the crap that is sickening us from inside our bowels. Oh, and when I'm voicing my opinion I want you to consider that if a woman who lives thousands of miles away knows this shit, then every foreign nation in the world has been following it too and knows hundred times more.

The people of this country have been beaten down by thieves and leaders that willingly oppress you, economically and morally. This is not a secret. I've read about old women that can't afford potatoes while politicians flaunt their diamond studded watches. Criminals live without fear of retribution in mansions the size of a Kiev apartment building. I hear of gas companies that have admittedly robbed your purses and livelihoods. There is corruption in every aspect of your society. This is what sickens you and this is why foreign nations question your worthiness. You have to trust me my friends… western countries don't want anything to do with nations they can't trust. They don't trust Ukraine. They want to… but not now. You *are* the breadbasket of Europe and you're so close to greatness but…you're tainted, and it's time for an exorcism. Until you decontaminate the body of this nation, you are doomed to be the filthy underbelly of Europe. You will be forever known as the Bangkok of Europe."

Mila returned behind the podium and laid her elbows on the smooth and polished wood.

"I don't hate anyone with money. That's the truth. If you've earned it legally, then good for you. What I despise is the rich man who doesn't use his money to help his fellow citizens. Once you have more than you could possibly spend, you must – as a subject of God – share your wealth. When you have the opportunity to save a homeless child from a life of destitution, why would you choose to walk away? But… it happens every day in this country. Contrary to what I just said, at this point in Ukraine's history, I don't care if you've earned your money illegally or on the backs of your countrymen… I ask that you save your people and save your country. Humanity is a warm meal on a cold night. Sit and eat with your countrymen.

Still, I'm not a total naïve fool, so back to my hacker. He – or maybe she – requested that I forward a message from the entire

Ukraine hacking nation. I, at first declined but then he showed me things that sickened me. I was stunned to say the least and said so. I agreed that I would mention the group and within seconds a letter was produced on my screen. I wish to make it clear that I don't condone their actions but at the same time, I realize that every day brings fewer options. I will read it to you now.

At this time, I'd like to speak directly to the politicians and the criminals who have pillaged this nation and turned Ukraine into a moral dead zone. Your greed is paralleled with the greatest dictators and tyrants the world has ever known yet somehow the world knows little about you. Greed is a disease, uniquely human and not shared by any other creature. The psychology of greed is lost on anyone who worships it like they would any false idol. The logic of its effects is very simple. For every possession you don't need, you earn an enemy. For every brother you demoralize, you earn an enemy. For every sister you defile, you earn an enemy. The more you own, the more enemies you have and the less you trust. When all trust escapes you and enemies lurk at every corner, no amount of possessions can return happiness into your life or save you from a soulless death. This, "comrades", is the curse of greed.

But there's hope for you if you want it. There is redemption in benevolence and benevolence is what your countrymen desperately need from you. If you decide to ignore the pleas of your people, then I'm afraid the people you have extorted for generations must return the favor.

Let me explain.

The world has changed and although we have allowed you to hide amongst us, this will no longer be the case. There is nowhere to hide. We can find you no matter where you go and we have no compassion for you or those who benefit from your crimes. Your photos will appear on websites, blogs and International social media, telling the world of your criminal activities. We will staple your photo on telephone poles across the country with the words, Enemy of Ukraine. Local television stations will broadcast your photos whether they agree to or not. Your children and their children will live with the stigma that they are the sons or daughters of traitors to Ukraine. They will become shit in our eyes and you will become shit in theirs.

We will recruit an army of hackers to disrupt your businesses, cell phones and bank accounts. No VPN in the world can shelter you. For every one of our women you sell to foreigners, we will post embarrassing photos of your mothers, daughters, wives and mistresses. For every needle injected into a teenage arm, we will post photos of your employees and their families on billboards. We will send photos of the people you have ruined to your mothers, fathers, uncles, aunts and priests. We call ourselves both patriotic paparazzi and/or Internet vigilantes. Wherever you travel, your reputation will reach that land before you do. But, in time, you won't be able to travel anywhere.

This initiative is already in action. Tomorrow, across this nation, your photos will begin to appear in high traffic areas. The address of a very special website will be distributed in universities, restaurants and metros across Kiev. This speech, by the way, is being streamed live to every corner of the globe to foreign dignitaries and embassies very interested in what we're doing. Two hundred known traitors of Ukraine are listed on our website with photos of them and their family. We have indicated where they live and work, where they eat and where their children go to school and most importantly, the crimes they have committed against Ukraine. This project has been completed in a short period with only a dozen brave compatriots, so you can imagine what the coming months will bring with thousands of volunteer warriors. Many of you may find that a line has been crossed but let me remind you that these men – and women - have made you widows, orphans, addicts, slaves and very poor. They have sold your children and sold your future for their own benefit. We have been very careful to ensure that these criminals are responsible for the claims we posted so have no doubts and feel no pity.

Traitors, welcome to the revolution of payback. The choice is yours. Give back what you have stolen and we will laud you as a hero. That is a promise from our group to you; we'll make you a hero. Do nothing and you... and your family and your security forces will forever be enemies, scorned by an entire country. And one more thing... don't bother looking for us. We know you're coming before you make the call.

Mila stuck the paper in her coat pocket and shrugged. "Maybe the new world doesn't require protests but at the same time, I must admit that I find this approach troubling. I wasn't going to read this because of the danger I felt for my family but then realized I was in a no win situation. I don't know how or if this vigilante group will succeed or if it will cause increased violence. I chose to tell you because of the risk and inevitable retributions. I would prefer we relied on the humanity of those that have stolen from you but obviously, that isn't going to happen. Maybe, these are your Robin Hoods or maybe they are just hoodlums. We'll see what happens. What I can assure you is that the day Ukraine is free from widespread corruption, every western country will come calling. I guarantee it. When you have quietly rebuilt this country without hate and without scorn, your large neighboring bear will look to you as an equal and beg for your attention. There won't be any backroom deals.

My dear friends, this is goodbye for me. I won't be on any more stages. My Tania has left me and without her, I don't possess the strength to be a spokesperson nor do you need me to be. Each one of you can and should be the voice of Ukraine. You're such wonderful people and there is great opportunity for each of you to make a difference. Please be the difference.

Thank-you for loving my sister and God bless you all. Long live the Ukrainian spirit but most of all... long live Ukraine."

Conclusion

The plane refueled at Heathrow for about two hours. Mila spent most of that time outside on a cell phone while smoking cigarettes. I didn't know she smoked. Lena and I had coffee and scones inside one of the cafes. The last ten hours had been a whirlwind and it was now approaching midnight, Kiev time. My body and mind were exhausted but I can't sleep on planes.

After the memoriam, Mila rushed us to the airport. Our luggage was in the back seat of a taxi that had been waiting half an hour before Mila took the stage to speak. She orchestrated our departure with perfect precision. Everything had been planned well in advance.

I didn't get much time to say goodbye to Boris. He hugged me and said he was proud to have me as family. Evgeni and Igor shook my hand and asked me to keep in touch. I said I would but I'm no longer certain I can. Boris spoke with Mila for about thirty seconds after me. His face was expressionless when she turned away from him. He called for her but she didn't answer. Lena grabbed my shirt from inside the cab and pulled me in. It wasn't my business, she told me. I thought Lena had told me everything I needed to know. Obviously, she didn't.

The plane ride home to Toronto was half empty. Lena took the window seat, I slumped into the aisle seat and Mila sat between us. Within twenty minutes of departure, Lena was fast asleep. Mila, now dressed in her usual black jeans and white tee-shirt, was reading Markov's manifesto and circling what she found interesting with a red pen. She dropped her pen and looked sideways at me.

"You missed my speech, Aaron."

I was hoping this discussion would never happen but that was wishful thinking on my part.

"We were a bit occupied."

"But you still heard it from where you were?" She asked. "Why don't you explain to me in detail what you were doing?"

"I'm quite certain Mila that you already know," I whispered.

She grinned momentarily before becoming serious. Her famous eyes were not as entrancing as they were twenty-four hours earlier.

"I'd like you to tell me…in full detail…what happened."

With nowhere to hide, the spider had me in her trap. I searched for an attendant, hoping for another cup of java but none were near. My head was numb with information I wished I had never learned. Coffee wasn't going to help me. I needed three days on my living room couch with an unending supply of Jack Daniels.

She was staring at me. Waiting. Playing me like a cat with its kill.

My name is Byrd.

"Boris received a phone call telling us that Valeri Markov was in the crowd," I began.

"Who called him, Aaron?" She interrupted. "Full details please."

"His grandfather told us that Markov was close and I saw him almost instantly. He was being walked away by a taller man with broad shoulders and dressed entirely in black. The grandfather told us it was a cop named Drubli. He said if we wanted to know more about you and Drubli's link to you then we should follow him and Markov. He assured us that we would not be harmed."

I turned my head quickly to see what Mila was doing and she had turned sideways to watch my every expression. It freaked me out a bit but I kept my cool.

"They headed to the Convention Centre past a line of cops who paid them no heed whatsoever. He wasn't walking too fast and Evgeni mentioned that it seemed as if Drubli knew we were following him. Boris said that assumption was ridiculous but I silently agreed with Evgeni.

When they arrived at the Centre, Drubli ushered Markov to the third floor via the stairs. This level had offices that amazingly were all unlocked. That's when Boris started to take Evgeni's suspicion a bit more seriously. We opened the first two offices cautiously and breathed sighs of relief when we found nothing. When we opened the third door, Drubli was standing cross armed in front of an open window with a view of the Square. Markov was sitting on a chair but we couldn't see him because Drubli had covered him with a white bed sheet. Where the sheet came from was even more cause for concern. This was planned. The office was large but cluttered. The only desk had a laptop and it looked like someone had tossed all its paper contents on the floor next to window.

"Hello gentlemen," he said in English with a big grin. "What took so long?"

Boris had no doubts now.

"Close the door behind you please," Drubli ordered.

His face was badly pock marked. It was hard not to notice yet he was seemingly undaunted by his appearance. When I saw a black beret hanging out of his right pant pocket I remembered Tania's discussion on the samizdat journalist at Hospital Six.

He pointed at me first and spoke in English. "You are Lena Kharmalov's boyfriend?"

"Her last name is Langley," I replied.

Drubli shook his head and smirked. "Don't be foolish my young Canadian. She is a Kharmalov and you can't call a Kharmalov anything but Kharmalov."

"How do you know me?" I asked. He didn't reply.

He motioned towards Evgeni. "The Museum Director ... correct?" Evgeni nodded yes. "You should consider another occupation."

He finally stood in front of Boris and looked him directly in the eye. "Boris Kharmalov, you are a disgrace to the name. You're nothing but the grandson of a Ukrainian enemy."

Boris stayed silent.

"Let me introduce myself gentlemen before we direct our attention to the star of our show. I am Nikolai Drubli, captain of the Ukrainian Guard and proud follower of one of my country's greatest heroes. The name of this leader is not important at the moment but before you leave this room today, I imagine that this will be less of a mystery."

"The Ukrainian Guard? You mean the Berkut? You sound proud to be leading a group of thugs. What are you doing Drubli?" Evgeni questioned while glancing at Markov.

"Oh this," he said while strolling beside his captive.

He removed the sheet and a disoriented Valeri Markov looked at us with curiosity. The man had no idea why he was in the room. His wrist and ankles were bound by handcuffs.

"This piece of shit is the infamous Valeri Markov. Known by few at the moment but by this time tomorrow he will be known throughout the world as Eastern Europe's most disgusting serial killer. It's not the title he dreamed of but his other dream, thankfully, will be read by few. You, Canadian man, may have the opportunity to write about him. Of course, that depends on you."

He looked me up and down. His stern expression told me to make wise decisions. Nothing was making sense.

"Take a look at him. He's riddled with disease and partially blind. How he got here from his home to Kiev would interest you, grandson of an enemy to Ukraine. With any luck, he'll snap out of his brain freeze and give us a few minutes of lucidity."

"Aaron," Evgeni interrupted. "When you get a chance, research Berkut and learn what these *officers* have done to their own people. Yet, he calls us the enemy of the people. Those cops we walked by earlier…they were Berkut, so it's no wonder they paid no attention to us. I'll ask again Drubli ," Evgeni said with brave confidence. "What are you doing?"

"Cut your fucking hair," Drubli cursed, making reference to my friend's ponytail. "You look like a renaissance fag. You look like this dipshit," he said, pointing at Markov's hair. "What do you think I'm doing? I'm prepping to kill the motherfucker. This sheet is his noose. I'm hoping he figures out what's going on and then I'm going to tie a knot, slip it around his neck and hang him like he hung Yulia Danilova. Have you got a problem with that?"

"The guy is a mental case," Boris shouted. "Put him in jail."

Drubli shook his head and chuckled. "And why would I do that, *grandchild of the enemy*? Do you think because I'm a police officer I should swallow my anger and give this animal a chance to defend himself? Do you have any idea how many families have lost their daughters because of this rapist? After fucking them unmercifully, he chopped up their bodies and dropped their limbs in a bucket of acid. I'm not going to let that be his defining moment. The Children of Israel are in the conference room below us. His corpse is going to swing in front of a window full of people he despised for no reason. It's most fitting don't you agree? I want their faces to be the last he sees."

"You wrote the article," I blurted. The words just came out of nowhere but I was glad I said them.

"What's that Canadian man?" he deferred to me. "Speak up so we can all hear."

I don't know why but I wasn't frightened of this guy even though he was what my father once called, evil with a side order of good.

"You wrote the samizdat article about Tania and Mila… it was you."

Boris looked at me with surprise, probably wondering how I deduced something so illogical.

Drubli glanced out the window. "The memoriam is about to begin. Mila will be speaking after the politicians blow some smoke out of their asses."

He turned on a laptop that had been set up on the once cluttered desk. Within seconds he navigated to a Ukrainian server that was streaming the eulogy. Drubli turned down the sound.

"When your friend speaks I'll let you listen," the officer said. "Yes, I was the author of the original article that made Tania and Mila famous."

"You ruined their lives," I retorted.

"I did no such thing. They were dead inside, especially Tania. Mila had her daughter…Tania had no one but her family. If I don't write that article, you would never have met your girlfriend and Mila would still be in Ukraine. Look at the big picture, *kiddo*. I made them celebrities, not for a day but instead a lifetime. There will be a thousand people here today to say goodbye to someone they haven't heard from for twenty-years. How many movie stars become famous after their first film? They do a few bombs before the award winner. I paved their roads to glory with one article and made them icons with one run of my press."

"You're speaking in riddles," I replied. "Say what needs to be said."

"What's your rush…let's discuss Valeri Markov for a bit."

He lifted Markov's chin with one finger and stared into the man's eyes. Drubli said something in Russian and Markov smiled before dropping his head.

"He's accepted his fate. I guess he knew this day would eventually come. We found a nineteen-year old student in his basement. He gutted her throat while she was still alive. Clean cuts; he used an X-Acto knife and carved a circle through the front and back of her neck. How do you feel about that museum director? You would have puked your stomach out of your mouth if you saw what I saw. After she stopped breathing he painted her as he saw her. Can you imagine how ruthless he is? He mutilated this child and then calmly put a brush in his hand. He was careless though because he used the victims face. Usually, he would paint Mila's face on his victim's bodies. Do you know why? He's forgotten what Mila looks like or who she is to him. The man is dead from the neck up. He had been quiet for years and then suddenly decided in the last five months to go on a killing spree. Purely by instinct...it's truly fascinating. I'd love to know what triggered it because I have no previous case to establish reason. I've never heard anything like it. This time tomorrow, Markov will be a household name."

Evgeni grabbed Boris by the arm. "We should leave now. There's no reason for us to be here."

"Actually, I have no need for the two of you," Drubli said dryly. "But the Canadian has to stay." He pulled a gun out of the back of his pants and immediately cocked it. "If we want to be precise, I could shoot the two of you now with no repercussions. You've been deemed expendable."

Evgeni raised his hands slowly. "Not unlike the street kids whose heads you bash in."

Boris slid back a step.

Drubli aimed at Boris and smiled. "Sit in front of the laptop and shut up. Mila will be speaking in ten minutes. If Markov awakes from his dream state, we'll have some fun and maybe you'll learn something... if I don't decide to end your useless lives." He took a glimpse at the crowd and nodded. Boris and Evgeni sat silently and stared at the laptop screen. "There's a lot more than a thousand in attendance. It's a proud moment in Ukrainian history." He slapped Markov on the back of the head. "Wake up prick... this is important."

This whole scenario was inexplicable. Why did he need me in the room with him and why would anyone want me here? I could run out the door and get help but he walked by a line of cops earlier and they let him be as if they knew what was happening. Was I imagining that?

"Don't be stupid, Canadian," Drubli grinned sardonically. He had noticed me eyeing the exit. "Never over-think the obvious. Take a deep breath and think."

Over-think? I could barely think at all until a coherent thought dropped out of my mouth like a well-placed bomb.

"This psycho hated Mila. Maybe it was your article that created a monster."

Drubli nodded his head several times as if impressed with my deduction. "You know, I've considered that theory but his murdering days began long before my article. His obsession with Mila was nothing more than an excuse to substantiate his egotistical manifesto. What better target than a heroine that openly defied the communist machine? He was sexually sadistic... but as I said earlier, you will be given the opportunity to decipher as you please."

"More riddles Drubli," I said while exhaling a deep breath.

Boris looked at me with a frightened expression. He worried more about me than himself. This did not go unnoticed by Drubli and it confused him.

Drubli disregard my remark. He pushed Markov's chair in front of the laptop.

"Maybe this will wake you up dickhead."

In a moment of levity, Drubli shoved his face in front of Markov and repeated Mila's name close to ten times in succession. The prisoner did not respond.

"Say Tania instead," I blurted.

I caught Evgeni looking back at me and Drubli nodded as if it was a good idea.

He needed only to utter Tania's name once and Markov came to life like a toy with new batteries.

517

"Well look at that," Drubli noted. "The zombie awakes."

He said something in Russian and Markov responded.

"I told him you were a writer that came from Canada to interview him. The idiot believes me so give it your best shot, Aaron."

I frowned wondering what Drubli was expecting from me. It took a few seconds to collect my thoughts but I lead with the obvious.

"Why did you kill all those girls... what possessed you to do something so heinous."

Drubli translated but not before asking what heinous meant. Markov nodded but did not look at me.

"It is something I have pondered for the last decade," Markov began. Evgeni and Boris turned to listen as Markov spoke more eloquently than we expected. He took his time when speaking as if he was creating a story. "I had stopped for many years understanding that my evil deeds were not as relative to my writing as I once supposed. There was a period of seven to eight years when I could not be satiated and my insecurities were masked as conquests for the Soviet Union. I chose weak girls with low esteem... with seemingly no hope for a bright future. I tricked myself to believe that they were fallibilities to a strong union of nations. A union I know can still exist. I painted them and then logged what I learned from their demise and how the USSR benefitted. Eventually, it became more and more difficult to reason their murders with my manifesto. You should all read my manifesto... it is your future."

"Stop this," Evgeni shouted. "Listen to him speak, he's not right in the head. His responses are obviously rehearsed. The man has been coached."

518

Drubli slapped Evgeni and then pointed at me to continue.

"What was the turning point?" I asked paying little attention to his request.

Markov glanced at me for a second and actually smiled. "Vlaska changed me. She was the mother of a girl I had murdered only a couple of weeks earlier. I did not expect her to be the woman she was. She was supposed to be what I envisioned from the daughter's diary but…I stopped after Vlaska. After that, I worked for his grandfather." Markov glanced at Boris before turning back to me.

"Do you hate women?" I questioned, thinking he wouldn't respond.

Drubli acknowledged that it was a decent inquiry. Markov had no issues in replying.

"For the most part, I am incapable of deep emotion of any kind. I survived on implied logic, therefore hate is irrelevant. My mother was the leader of the village I grew up in. She was very strict and would often drug us with Valerian root. I was named after this plant. As a young boy I would often awake in the morning with belt marks on my back, not remembering when or why I was punished. My father did nothing so at a young age I theorized that women were the stronger sex. None of the girls in the village would date me, saying I was too small or too thin or too weak. It didn't matter that my mother was the leader… they wanted nothing to do with me. *They* were in charge. The men in the village would flock to a tiny hut at the edge of town, where a woman would accept money for sexual favors. I thought these men were scared of their wives, lending credence to my theory. And when I learned the sex was paid for and not given, it strengthened my conviction. I didn't want anyone to control me, especially not a female. There were times I believed that by killing a young woman, I saved a man future suffering. Again, I was wrong."

"It had nothing to do with Mila Kharmalov?"

Markov thought about the question. He squeezed his eyes shut and then reopened them slowly.

"She is not someone who would work for the collective cause and would be confrontational with me, I am certain of this. She must be the leader at all times."

"You painted her face on almost all your victim paintings," Drubli cut in.

"Yes, I remember now," Markov nodded. "Only because she was the opposite of her sister. Tania was an angel therefore Mila had to be Satan-like. My victims had to be portrayed as negative influences on the Soviet Union. In hindsight, that was an error on my part."

This is not right and Evgeni was right. The man answering these questions was rattling off responses as if he was reading a script.

"How so? I questioned.

Markov squinted as if the question itself was silly. "You are a reporter, how can you not know this? Mila has already commented on my work and praised me for my effort. She is here to save us. If my manifesto could walk and talk, it would be Mila Kharmalov."

Drubli did not translate this but Evgeni did, infuriating the Berkut leader. Drubli slapped Markov and told him to be quiet.

"What the hell does that mean?" I asked, hoping Drubli would respond.

"It means nothing," he answered. "It is nothing but the ramblings of a crazy person. Your friend is about to speak; turn up the volume and listen."

He sat behind Markov and began tying the bed sheet into a workable noose. Minutes after Mila finished speaking, Valeri Markov hung by his neck outside the window of the Sons of Israel while the children of Ukraine danced to "The Nations Rose".

****

"I need details Aaron," Mila said, shaking me from my trance.

"Those are exact details," I replied with an angry tone.

"You said Drubli waved at you. Was there anything else you noticed?"

"He was grinning like an idiot. A murderous idiot."

"Think harder Aaron," she insisted.

What does she want from me?

"When the speeches were over, Drubli instructed us to run out of the building and stand below the office window. We all knew what was going to happen but out of some sick curiosity we did as he asked. Drubli yelled something from the third floor window but we couldn't hear him because the loud speakers were playing the song written about Tania and Mila. It was the first time I heard it and I noticed some of the crowd slow dancing in the Square. We waited for about thirty seconds and then Markov was tossed out of the window. The three of us covered our heads thinking he would crash on top of us but his body stopped and swayed for a few seconds ten feet above us. Drubli poked his head out again and waved goodbye. There's nothing else to say…

And then my memory caught a flash of that last moment.

"He was wearing black gloves," I said, perplexed.

"That's what I mean by detail," Mila responded. "Now, when you first walked into that room, who opened the door?"

I looked sideways for a moment being careful not to get caught in a locked stare. "Boris did," I said in an inquisitive tone.

Mila seemed happy with this response. "Drubli wore gloves when handling the doors and window. If he touched anything else, he would have wiped it clean. The man is a professional."

It took me a few seconds to understand her admiration for a man that was heartless but then the realization of what she was alluding to weighed me to my seat.

She set us up. Oh my God, she's as bad as Drubli. This can't be happening. She's Mila Kharmalov, she's a national treasure and a hero… she's a manipulative bitch.

"You framed your cousin?" I blurted loudly before remembering where I was. "Are you insane?"

"It's one of the reasons the taxi was waiting for us," Mila bragged. "I made sure Boris attended to my sister's burial."

"You framed your cousin… what were you thinking?"

I thought of Boris sitting in his apartment with his mother trying to imagine what tomorrow would bring.

"Well, that's the gist of it, isn't it? I'm always thinking and important people want to know what I'm thinking. In my speech, I mentioned politicians who were always thinking two steps ahead of everyone else. I plan ten steps ahead and every step has a backup step. It's the only way to stay relevant to men who change their minds every time a perfect set of breasts enters a room."

I lowered my head and once again exhaled. "What? What does that mean to me? I thought you were special. It was just a mirage."

"Get a grip Aaron. I am who I've always been. After Chernobyl, I helped one person at a time. I don't have enough days to do this again. Our plan is to heal a nation in one giant swoop and no one is going to stop me. Ukraine will be a leader after we've completed every step."

"You framed your cousin."

I noticed she said stop *me* instead of stop us.

"You're not listening," she said calmly. "Your friend Boris will be fine if he toes the line and does as we say. If he doesn't then a gaggle of cops will gladly testify that Drubli followed the three of you into the Convention Centre. Ten steps ahead Aaron. Stop whining and learn from me."

I rubbed my forehead several times, trying to find a reason why I shouldn't move to another seat. She was telling me stuff I shouldn't be privy to, yet knowing what I know now about her it seemed rather obvious that I was soon to find out my part in all this. I can only imagine her plan was secretive and in motion for some time but why now and why was she telling me?

"Your daughter is my future wife. Why would you put your daughter's fiancé in a traumatic situation? I'm scared to fall asleep."

Mila sighed very loud. "The nightmares will come and go. I needed you to see Markov. To be honest, this piece of the puzzle was entirely last minute because there was no means for me to do it myself. All of his notebooks will be translated and you're going to write his story but... with a different slant."

"Really? I'm not sure why I would agree to work with you Mila considering what I've heard thus far." I paused and once again glanced sideways. "The *last minute* part caught my attention so if you wouldn't mind indulging my curiosity... how could you know ahead of time that Markov would be at the Square?"

Mila shrugged and stared at me for a good ten seconds. "I like Colonel Asimov and appreciate everything he has done for my family but he's getting on in age and can't cover the same ground as an experienced investigator like Drubli. I guess Asimov continued his search to keep active and I understand that. Drubli traced a link between Markov and Boris's grandfather, also known as The Doctor. He gave us Markov's whereabouts and we sent a cop yesterday to pick him up. It didn't work out too well.

"What does that mean?" I asked

Mila shrugged before continuing. "It means the cop was not good at his job. We sent more cops in the afternoon but Markov had disappeared. Drubli called The Doctor and the old man sent a search team.

The grandfather found Markov in a café this morning and drove him in. The Doctor is very astute for an old pervert. I met him yesterday afternoon with Igor. And yes, he brought along his transvestite. Stupid thing thought she could analyze me. In ten minutes, her and her estrogen pills were hiding in the bedroom."

"I know little about the transvestite and don't care. Why did you meet the grandfather and Igor?"

"They are intertwined. I was negotiating Igor's freedom to some extent. As for the grandfather, he is my cousin's lifeline and also the number one villain on the website I spoke of earlier today.

I offered him an opportunity to leave Ukraine before he is hunted and shamed."

"Why would he agree to anything you offer?"

"Aaron," Mila continued. "My project is not just me at home with a computer. It involves men and women with high standing in our country, Germany and France. There are very influential fingers in the pie. I showed "the Doctor" what his options were and how exactly I was about to uproot his legacy. There is very little about him that I don't know and the same applies to the other one hundred and ninety-nine criminals on the website. When you speak to someone face-to-face and show them how their lives will change by doing this or that, they either get angry or they get smart. The Doctor is smart. He will sign over two large properties to one of my partners who in turn will sell them to buy medicine for Igor's hospital."

"He killed your father," I said quietly. "Boris told me the whole story."

"Your three new friends have taken quite the liking to you Aaron, as if you are one of them. It's impressive. Yes, I've been aware of the Doctor's deed for years. My daughter doesn't know so keep it like that. And yes, I know the *whole* story and it was my primary reason to make this man my number one criminal. I arranged to meet with the Doctor before I left Calgary. My partners have persuasion skills I don't possess and the old man agreed. My goal yesterday was to make him leave quietly and to donate some of his wealth to the rebuilding of this country. He agreed willingly and quickly as if he knew his time had come to an end. Drubli was downstairs and gave him Markov's writings to give to Boris. That part was a ruse to give an excuse for the old man to speak with his grandson. He's already on a plane to some

525

island on the Pacific. When the other shitheads find out that one of their own has flown the coop, they'll consider the same."

"Everything seems flawless Mila but why would your partners care about Ukrainian gangsters?"

Mila yawned and for a second I thought she faked it. "You were there on a vacation of sort and were treated to Pierogies and fake smiles. Unless we told you so, you would have no idea of what lies beneath the surface. Who wants to do business in a country where half the business is run through criminals? After our independence the gates opened for them to seize control of trade routes. The police were in disarray and weren't being paid. The gangsters pounced on the opportunity and have run with it since. Students are still getting their heads bashed trying to overturn the Customs Union with Russia. Quite frankly, I believe these poor kids are wasting their time. The European Union didn't make much of an effort to pull Ukraine into their bosom and why would they? Why would they add one more Greece or Spain to their portfolio, especially when Ukraine is crooked? We're going to change that Aaron. Step one is to purge the criminal element and believe me when I tell you, this will happen fast. We installed a lot of cameras when no one was paying attention. We'll hijack TV stations until these guys leave or agree to our demands. We'll let everybody in cities, towns and villages know where the criminal is at any given time. Couch potatoes get pissed off when they can't watch TV." Mila smiled after saying this. "If we can't win that way then we'll put a bounty on their heads. This is not a game Aaron. These traitors are going to play by our rules or they will die."

That last part gave me shivers. "And when or if this step is accomplished successfully, what's next?"

526

Mila fidgeted with a napkin she had kept on her lap for the last half hour. "Then we will make Ukraine the most important country in Europe."

I almost burst out laughing. "They don't have a pot to piss in, you just admitted that yourself. The breadbasket is long gone and from what I'm gathering, there's no infrastructure to enable any growth."

She nodded in agreement. "Yes you are correct but are you suggesting that they are bound to a life of nothing? To a dismal existence? I, for one, will no longer accept this. Our plan will bring Russia to its knees and transform Ukraine into the busiest nation in all of Europe, if not the world."

I stopped an attendant who was making the rounds and asked for more coffee. She nodded listlessly and walked away.

"You have my full attention Mila," I said.

"We're going back to Chernobyl." She said it as if it was matter of fact; as if it was as safe as selling candy apples at the farmer's market.

I shifted my body to face her. "Did I hear you right?"

"We'll be building fifty reactors over the next two decades. Ukraine will power all of Europe and parts of China."

"Are you out of your mind? You've been fighting against nuclear energy for over two decades. Your sister died because of radiation and you even mentioned something to the sort twelve hours after Tania died. I can't believe I'm hearing this from your mouth."

"Spare me the guilt trip. When a country has been ravaged for years, options diminish. Germany and France run clean nuclear operations but their citizens are rebelling against any new plants. They're more than willing to get their energy from one source and have agreed to partially fund the building of new reactors here. It's not like this is new in the economic world. Americans didn't want to work in manufacturing plants so they shipped all their work to China. Who's laughing now? The trickledown theory will ensure new businesses and new opportunities for every Ukrainian. The gas from Russia that flows through the pipes that Ukraine no longer owns will eventually dry up. Europeans won't need dirty energy anymore and that, my future son-in-law, means that Russia will dry up too. Fuck the Custom agreements… they'll be begging us to buy their shitty goods. Ten steps ahead Aaron, always think ten steps ahead."

"And fifty more chances for disaster. You rid Ukraine of gangsters but then you offer the survivors a chance to die of radioactivity."

Mila rolled her eyes. "You know Aaron… *we* Canadians are such sanctimonious hypocrites. The oil sands outside of Fort McMurray are a disaster waiting to happen. Sure, it's better than coal but the danger and the harm to the environment is ever present. Our country sells wheat, gas and uranium. That's who we are. We fuel stomachs, homes and cars. We're known around the world as the nicest people and yet we sell danger. The uranium in these new Ukrainian reactors will come from Canada. The deal's already done. So in effect, if anything goes wrong, we're partially responsible. In frightening terminology, we're the gun in a parent's bedroom."

A tired brunette attendant placed a Styrofoam cup on the tray I had just opened. I poured the milk and stirred. I had no intelligent argument for Mila or maybe I was too tired to continue. It's hard to argue with someone who has an answer to every question. I was trying to figure out if she was doing all this as vengeance against Russia or if she was truly working for the people of Ukraine. The more I thought of it, her plan made sense for a desperate people. Evgeni would flip if he knew.

"How did this all start? I mean, how could a housewife in Calgary arrange something so intricate?"

"Again, Lena will not hear any of this." I nodded and she continued. "I was never a housewife per se Aaron. From the day I stepped off the plane in Calgary, I was introduced to higher up's interested in my story. Chris and I were invited to dinners with corporate and political leaders. I met them all, they insisted on it. I quickly learned that the story of Mila and Tania Kharmalov crossed many borders. Many of these new acquaintances followed me on blogs and made correct assumptions. They shared the same fire I felt.

About two years ago a German businessman called with a proposal for nuclear reactors. In all honesty, I didn't even bat an eye because the thought had been kicked around by others in our network. For me, I saw it as a chance to end dreary lives. The employment opportunities would solve poverty across Ukraine. My part of the puzzle was miniscule yet I insisted my name never be mentioned. I was asked to create an environment that would make criminals disappear. That, in a nutshell, was my primary purpose in the project. Many of the contacts I had made over the decade, including Drubli, were more than happy to help me. A lot of this was covert, which I will admit was exciting and we had a few tense moments. Interpol was very helpful and without them, we would have hit a lot of dead ends. I'm happy to say that there will be many arrests in Toronto, New York and London this week. You should know that Drubli has been a big part of my success. Aside from his contempt for the mob, he has a deep hate of

Russia. I guess he also has some guilt for pushing me in a direction I had no desire – at the time – to follow. Anyway, he installed a thousand cameras over the last eighteen months."

I sneered openly. "He's a sick bastard and don't try to make me think he's something different. So, you were going to travel to Kiev anyway?"

Mila shook her head. "God no… I only came for Tania. Don't even consider thinking otherwise. My sister was my heart and soul and aside from Lena, was the most important person in my life. Politically, Ukraine is the worst place possible for me at the moment. I figured, while I was here, I would take care of business but I didn't expect to do it so fast. I wish I had had one more day with Tania."

I took a moment before asking my last question, giving Mila a moment to think of her sister. "What did you say to Boris before we left?"

She shrugged. "I told him I understood that he was only twelve when he led my father to slaughter. Then I told him if he fucked up, he would see his face on the website."

"It's not his nature," I responded in a hushed tone.

"Oh my God, you haven't learned a thing Aaron. You've been told an incredible story and you've seen the end result yet you make presumptions based on your sheltered life. Boris is not you…do you understand me? He is not you. None of the people you've met are you. Boris doesn't have his grandfather's protection anymore and every crooked cop in Kiev has my cousin's scent. When you put a scared cat in a cage, it's gonna do whatever it can to get out. I love my cousin, don't misinterpret everything. I am daring him to step up. We'll see what happens in the next year."

"Igor and Evgeni will watch him closely."

"Your optimism is endearing and I can see why my daughter loves you. Just don't be surprised if the personal news from Ukraine is disappointing."

"Just don't be surprised if it's not," I retorted.

Mila smiled and ran a finger over her left eyebrow. "I sincerely hope it's not. I've made enough mistakes, Aaron and I can't bear to make any more. Do you want to hear what I learned while we waited in London? It'll, umm…surprise you."

I wasn't sure what to say so I nodded yes. Mila suddenly looked troubled and it was a good thirty seconds before she continued.

"Valeri Markov had an IQ of one hundred and sixty. I didn't bat an eye when I heard this because truth be told, I found him to be very articulate. What I didn't know was that he had superior recall abilities which helped his love for acting. The freak show we know as Valeri Markov was well known in local theatres up until a year before the reactor accident.

Colonel Asimov grew restless with police inactivity and decided to do his own investigating. I felt bad when he called me earlier because as I just told you, I have been communicating with Drubli and basically leaving Asimov out of the loop. That was my mistake because the colonel learned more in the last thirty hours than both Drubli and I did in two years. He received a call from a connection about the cop killing in Dubovi Makharyntsi and promptly drove there from Kiev. While officers were collecting whatever info they could from Markov's home, Asimov chose to visit the local mayor. From this meeting he worked backward."

"What could the mayor possible know?" I asked.

Mila circled her neck as if to release tension. "That's what I asked too but Asimov can be a Pitbull when he gets an idea in his head.

Every new home purchase goes through the mayor's office and the purchaser must meet with the mayor. Valeri Markov met with the mayor -Andrei Malkin - twenty plus years ago. When Asimov showed him the photo of Markov, the mayor shook his head and said nyet. Asimov pointed at the photograph and told Malkin that this was Valeri Markov. The mayor again shook his head. He said the photo was the resident of the home but not Markov. Markov, he said, had a long scar on his left cheek. The person in the house was Stani Pilov, an actor from Kiev. He said that Pilov was very smart but crazy as a loon."

"What?" I questioned while pursing my lips.

"Again," Mila nodded," That's what I said too. Malkin pulled out the original paperwork for the house which also contained Markov's birth address. Two hours later, Asimov was in the village of Kopachi."

I grunted. "Back to Kopachi."

"Yes, back to that stupid town," Mila said. "Asimov brought several bottles of vodka otherwise no one would speak to him. The first dozen homes claimed ignorance of the name Markov but a woman who said she was his second cousin agreed to sit with the Colonel. She said that she was engaged to Markov's brother but his mother disapproved and the union was called off."

"Yah, that and three of his fingers," I added.

Mila was curious as to how I knew that until I pointed towards one of the manifest diaries.

"Asimov showed the woman a photo of Markov, or who we thought Markov was. As expected, she shook her head and said *nyet*. The colonel then described a shorter man with a long scar and the woman said yes but the injury happened after he left Kopachi. Aaron, there was now no doubt that Markov and Pilov changed names. Asimov then inquired about Valeri or what the woman thought of him. She lowered her eyes and said that as a boy and young man, Markov was wicked. She sighed several times recalling memories of beatings and animal abuse. His mother was also a terrible woman but Markov was pure evil. If he changed his name it was only to hide from the eventual revenge of Kopachi villagers."

"You were duped by a genius," I said while drawing a long breath. "Everyone was."

"Yes but it still doesn't explain the person we knew as Valeri Markov... the vain man with a ponytail. What was his story?"

"I'm going to guess that Asimov put those pieces together too," I countered.

"And you would guess correctly. No one placed any emphasis on Pilov, which in hindsight was beyond stupid. Even in the role we believed he played, the guy was an accomplice."

"An accomplice to crimes you could never prove," I added. "And crimes that no one was investigating until recently."

"Yah, doesn't make me feel better. Anyway, fake Markov grew up in Lyiv, a few blocks from the Dormiton Church. Asimov found the address of the theatre where Pilov occasionally worked and met someone very interesting."

Mila paused before I asked her to continue.

"Lyiv is a good eight hours from Kopachi so Asimov arrived only minutes before the theatre doors were locked. The only person inside was an older lady in her fifties, mopping an aisle. She shouted that the theatre was closed but Asimov waved a badge as if he was a police officer. She laid her mop against a chair and approached the Colonel.

Even in the dim lighting, the ex-army officer noticed that the woman had a distinct limp.

"How can I help you," she questioned, now standing in front of Asimov.

"Have you worked in this establishment for a long time?"

"I am the owner of this theatre," she replied rapidly. "Why do you ask?"

"I am Colonel Andrei Asimov, thank-you for your time." He extended his hand and the woman shook it gently. He imagined that twenty years ago she was very attractive. "I am searching for information on a man who I believe acted on your stage."

"Many of my performers had pseudonyms so if you have a photograph, I should be able to help you."

Asimov had nothing and shook his head. "I have only a name comrade. Stani Pilov, do you know him?"

"It's *Stanislav* Pilov and why are you asking about my brother?"

The Colonel stepped back, unbelieving of his good fortune.

"My apologies if the following shocks you, but I believe your brother is an accomplice to a mass murderer."

The woman turned away from Asimov for a moment and bowed her head.

"My name is Yana Pilov. My brother's choices have come back to haunt him. This supposed murderer… is it Valeri Markov?"

The Colonels first impression was that the woman was not surprised after he nodded his response of yes. Instead, she appeared disappointed.

"Stanislav was a brilliant boy," she spoke with a hushed voice. "His writing skills were advanced, so much so that teachers expected him to be a literary giant in the Soviet Union. My parents lauded over him and barely gave me the time of day. I was jealous of the attention he received but in hindsight I believe I had every right to this emotion.

Valeri Markov entered our lives when he joined a church that my family attended. My brother and Markov were altar boys and thus began a friendship, albeit a strange alliance.

I didn't like Markov. He was short, slimy and always staring at my breasts. The things he'd tell my brother about me were pure fantasy and slanderous. I wished him dead a1nd once, in my school, he tried to force himself on me. My father gave me a pocketknife for my tenth birthday and I had it with me at all times. When Markov became too aggressive and I feared for my life, I pulled the knife out of my sweater and slashed his face."

The Colonel nodded. "The long scar on his left cheek."

"I never regretted my actions," Yana whispered. "Stanislav adored Markov and absorbed every word the crazy man spoke. He mimicked Markov's mannerisms and slowly began to lose his own persona. Markov would recount a story and my brother would write it in his notebook being careful not to miss any important detail. He would read these stories over and over until he believed they were his own. It was disturbing to watch Stanislav's transformation from a quiet boy to a man with a severe personality disorder."

"Are you saying that your brother became Markov?"

Yana shrugged. "He was acting on stage at the age of eight and staying in character for weeks at a time. He was a method actor before it became popular and he took it to the extreme, so becoming Markov – his hero – was a natural progression. When Stanislav learned that Markov dabbled in paints, he made art his passion. Markov was a staunch communist so my brother researched and became the same. I have no doubt that Markov knew what was happening and manipulated Stanislav. He was plotting future endeavors."

"Well, he certainly had us fooled," Asimov cut in. "We believed he was Valeri Markov."

Yana sat on one of the theatres blue seats and stretched her legs.

"Yes, his obsession with Markov is the definition of sociopath but I think we can say the same for the real Markov. My brother, being the actor he was, may have been nothing more than a psycho-in-training.

He hated the name Stanislav and asked anyone who would listen to call him by his second name, Adana. I think the name gave him an opportunity to start over or at least be the person he really was. Father quashed the name within our home but I know for a fact that my brother considered his life as "Adana", to be his real identity and his real orientation."

What does that mean?" The Colonel inquired.

Yana shrugged. "To this day, I have no idea if my brother has ever had any sexual relation. Judging from his secret writings, I believe his interests were with the same sex. He hid this from everyone, including my father but imagined scenarios in which his true identity became known. That being revealed, I also believe he was in love with Markov and would do anything for him."

"Speculation?" Asimov asked.

"No," she replied. "I am certain. He sponged Markov's persona to become normal or at least his version of normal. I haven't seen my brother in a year and a half and that was the first time in decades. He visited me here and we sat in this exact spot. When I asked him what he had been doing for the last twenty years he replied that he cleaned a lot... his exact words were that he cleaned dirty whore blood. It was a strange conversation as you may well imagine. I called him Adana and he smiled briefly before losing himself in Markov's persona. It was too hard for me to bear so I asked him to leave and he did graciously."

Asimov sat next to Yana and sighed loudly. "Six months ago, we had him in our grasp."

"Markov?"

The Colonel nodded. "He had us believing that your brother was responsible for everything. He was pathologically perfect. I pride myself on my ability to read people and Markov had me bewitched." The older man had to catch his breath before speaking again. "How many girls will never return to their families because I allowed this monster to walk free?"

"I cut open his face," Yana responded. "I should have cut open his heart."

The woman stood and walked Asimov to the exit. They shook hands and he left quietly. The Colonel was the first of many that would seek her knowledge of Stanislav Pilov and Valeri Markov.

Mila was having difficulty keeping her eyes open. She stuffed Pilov's writing into a carry-on bag and pushed her chair back.

"I say successful loosely, but every successful serial killer continued their involvement in their local communities before, during and after each murder. How many times have we heard the words, 'he was a quiet man', after police start asking questions? The secret is to blend in and stay quiet. Pilov, excuse me, Markov did just that." I nodded yes and she continued. "You have a big job ahead of you, Aaron. There are many different stories meshed into one. Still, I'm not sure how you'll be able to connect all the dots. If you read the first page of Pilov's manifesto - and unless Pilov was taking instruction from Markov – you'd swear that Pilov was completely lucid and very proud of his motives. *I encourage you to follow your feelings and maim as directed.* How far was this guy unattached from his true self?"

Before closing her eyes, Mila told me that she was lucky to have me in her family and that I was to consider the entire picture before judging her motives. I didn't say the same to her because I wasn't sure what to think anymore. I wasn't sure if she was being honest with me or being calculating. Maybe she already knew how to push my buttons…I don't know. Boris once told me that Mila knew everything she needed to know about someone by the way he or she approached her. I wasn't sure what to think but then something crazy and totally unexpected happened. My thoughts suddenly began to connect like on-ramps to a super highway. One after another, memories of the past week joined together drawing a clear picture.

Khalil Gibral once wrote, '*Out of suffering have emerged the strongest souls. The most massive characters are seared with scars.*' No matter how jaw dropping beautiful this woman is, Mila Kharmalov is seared with scars yet she pretends or assumes she is like anyone else. Tania wrote that even in Mila's complexities she bared simplicity and even in rage she bared softness. I saw this now.

Maybe she isn't as *nice* as her sister but Mila was a livewire. Ukraine will remember Tania as a soft soul but they will always remember Mila as their rose. So lovely to gaze upon but it will cut you if you grab it. She is a gift of love, a gift to brag about and a gift to cherish.

She's not evil. Vindictive maybe, but not evil.

I thought she was for the last few hours but she's not. She cares more than most. She's more passionate and courageous than anyone I'll ever meet in this lifetime. I could never do what this woman has done or attempting to do. I'd like to think I could but…I can't. Very few can or ever will. If not for the samizdat she would have done everything anonymously. It's not about her and never has been.

It's about Ukraine.

It's always been about her family and Ukraine.

She opened one eye and caught me staring at her.

"Do you know what Markov called his manifesto?" Mila whispered.

"No clue," I answered, forgetting she had already read it.

"Twenty-Three Minutes Past One A.M. Son of a bitch eh? What time is it now?"

I glanced at my watch and grinned sarcastically. "Nice timing," I said. "*Coincidentally...* it's twenty-three minutes past one a.m."

Mila Kharmalov reached out blindly and held my hand tight. "Good night Aaron," she said. "I will love you like a son."

At that precise moment we heard a loud explosion and the plane dropped from the sky.

THE END

Additional Notes

The book you have just read contains fictional characters in a factual historical setting. I would be negligent not to mention the real names of the three divers from the pool of death that saved thousands of lives.

- Valeri Bezpalov
- Alexie Ananenko
- Boris Baranov

These men willingly shortened their lives to lengthen ours. If I was to ask the average person who David Beckham was, most would reply quickly. If I asked you who Valeri Bezpalov was, chances are good that you wouldn't have a clue. That seems very unfair to me but I understand. Very few people know the details behind the Chernobyl accident and even for those that do; no one wants to remember horror.

Nuclear accidents never go away. Don't believe otherwise. We cannot escape the radiation that continuously seeps into our oceans, lakes and food supplies. We breathe radiation. We bathe in radiation and we digest radiation. Understand the following: No amount of radiation is good for you. Don't believe politicians who raise the acceptable levels of radiation like they were betting in a poker game. If you're living on the west coast of the United States or Canada, your health is already in danger.

On March 11, 2011, Reactors One through Four of the Fukushima Daiichi Nuclear Plant suffered severe damage and in turn, released unbelievable amounts of cesium into the ocean and atmosphere. That being said, it is now near impossible to get any information out of Japan because that government has imposed strict regulations against journalists reporting anything negative on Fukushima; threatening prison terms of ten years or more.

There are websites that argue the benefits of nuclear technology and debunk the *conspiracy theorists* that spread Fukushima fear, gloom and doom. The articles are well-written and seemingly accurate. The obvious question is where are they getting their information? The Japanese government has banned any and all negative Fukushima (nuclear) articles therefore anything released is based on scientific articles approved by the Japanese government.

These pro-nuclear websites consistently argue "acceptable" levels of radiation and base articles on the lack of proof or the lack of deaths thus far. I respectively ask them to study Chernobyl and to also consider that no level of radiation is acceptable.

If the threat of disease was not prevalent, why would the Japanese government put aside millions of dollars to care for the TEPCO employees (and their families) working at Fukushima?

If nuclear energy was safe, explain why Germany, France, Switzerland and Italy have begun a phase out or have given up entirely on nuclear power.

Cesium-137 has been detected off the shores of British Columbia. True, they are low values but they weren't there a year ago. It takes time for the ocean pockets of radiation to arrive from Japan. They'll be on North American shores soon. Japanese scientists estimate this event will occur in 2016.

The true extent of the Fukushima disaster will not be apparent for years and given the government censorship, we may never learn. I encourage everyone to do their own research to derive an unbiased opinion.

What we do know about Fukushima as of April 2014 is:

- 300 tons of radioactive waste is dumped into the Pacific Ocean every day. Many argue that much more than 300 tons is leaked/dumped.
- 150 U.S. Marines assert to have caught radiation sickness because of their close proximity to Fukushima. This is in court and there are many arguments against the sailor's claims.
- Experts believe that it will take close to forty years to clean up the Daiichi plant.
- The area immediately around Fukushima is permanently uninhabitable.
- Cesium-137 has been found in fish as far away as California.
- Four years later, Japan and IAEA have not come remotely close to containing this disaster.

The only groups that back nuclear power are those that benefit monetarily from nuclear power. As always, it's all about money and all about "me". What moral person would willingly promote anything nuclear unless they were directly involved or benefitting from that industry? Does it not terrify you that China is in the process of constructing one hundred new nuclear plants? The same country that knowingly puts lead in your children's toys, will be building a hundred nuclear plants.

Understanding that alternative energies are safe and becoming cheaper by the day, why - in this progressive age - is the nuclear industry even discussed? Small communities can build their own grids and be self-sufficient within a couple of months. Solar and wind energy can power vertical farms for pennies. The benefits are infinite.

But it won't happen.

It won't happen because too many of us are desperate, greedy pigs. Greedy pigs who need a Lexus or a BMW and a home much too big for three families, let alone one. We refuse to accept responsibility for the destruction of our world based on our desire to flaunt our line of credit or spark up our oversized barbeques. We're as sick as our planet.

That being said, there is a small yet growing community that embraces the need for change in environment controls and a change in humanity. I look forward to the phone call or email that invites me to help build the community of the future.

There were thousands of villages in Ukraine during the 60's, 70's and 80's. Many of them were collectives, working for the Soviet regime but many were safe havens for countless numbers of Ukrainians, hiding from oppression, persecution and possible prison terms. They were villages that had their own rules and rarely if ever saw the faces of their oppressors.

In the late eighties and early nineties, many if these rebel villages were raided by police officers and thousands of village inhabitants were sent to Siberian villages, camps and/or prisons to live out their remaining years.

Thank-you for reading *23 Minutes Past 1 A.M.*

23 Minutes Past 1 AM

Tania loves Yuri and Yuri loves her
Tomorrow they'd wed under the giant Fir
He kissed her lips and stroked her face
He had to go to work he had to make haste
At the Plant in town
Their beautiful town

Mama loved Alex he was her only boy
He made her so happy he was her pride and joy
He set off to work it was his very first day
Start a new life, gonna bring home some pay
At the Plant in town
His beautiful town

And Niko lived content in his own little bliss
He was a party leader and a good communist
He studied his plans for the annual march
Praising the party line down to Lenin's Arch
Through the middle of town
This beautiful town

It was hailed by leaders to be the Year Of Peace
No more fighting, all wars would cease
In the blink of an eye, lives were crushed
Ashes to ashes, dust to dust
No one foresaw the danger or the mayhem
23 minutes past one a.m.

They were testing to ensure the turbines would spin
When the power came back it blew a cap off the bin
When the wind rushed in the graphite caught fire
Like grease on oil, flames grew higher and higher
Then the walls came down
So close to the town

The firemen were called but were never told
The gamma rays fried them and they never went home
It took pilots nine days to extinguish the flame
The government jailed those they chose to blame
Bodies piled up…
Outside of town

From rooftops they watched this sight so brilliant
Admiring the shiny cloud above the nuclear plant
The name of the city means the end of the world
Children still played while the deadly winds swirled
Throughout out the town
And for miles around

It was hailed by leaders to be the Year Of Peace
No more fighting, all wars would cease
In the blink of an eye lives were crushed
Ashes to ashes, dust to dust
No one foresaw the danger or the mayhem
23 minutes past one a.m.

For days the reactor glowed an awesome bright crimson
Thousands of men were sent by the Kremlin

One day later they were told to pack
Never realizing they would not be back
To their dying town
Their once beautiful town

They were sent on buses to cities down south
And waited for news via word of mouth
Strangers in their own land, from Kiev to the Dnieper
The locals kept their distance and called them lepers
They shouted **go back home**…
To your filthy town

Those that stayed had to suppress their anger
Learned new words like meltdown and Geiger
They ate from cans wrapped in plastic and silk
Babies fed on breasts filled with nuclear milk
And they died one by one
In their hometown

It was hailed by leaders to be the Year Of Peace
No more fighting, all wars would cease
In the blink of an eye lives were crushed
Ashes to ashes, dust to dust
No one foresaw the danger or the mayhem
23 minutes past one a.m.

Elena drives her bike through the ruins of this land
Taking photos with a Geiger safe at hand
She talks to villagers who show her trust
She drives alone so not to breathe the dust

From the dangerous town
The radioactive town

Tania loves Yuri but Yuri's long gone
Twenty years later she's lonely, withdrawn
Mama loves Alex but Alex is dead
Never found his body, got a medal instead
She leaves flowers at his grave
On the edge of town
The memories are fresh; they summon them at will
Ferris Wheel weekends and parties on the Hill
They dream of returning, forever and until
Living in the middle of a nuclear spill
At the end of the world…Chernobyl

Books by Robert J Dornan

Jack City

Gwydion

23 Minutes Past 1 A.M.

Coming Soon:

Jack City 2: The Watchers

Sins of the Samurai

The 99